1

Eden Lake

Author's Note: The characters and events in this book are fictional. While some names of places are real and some of the events are historically accurate, the story is a product of the author's imagination.

Scripture quotations are taken from the New American Standard Bible copyright: Creation House, Inc., 1960, 1962, 1963, 1971, 1972, 1973

"Cover design by Renee Barratt, thecovercounts.com"

Special Thanks

To my husband, whose love and support strengthens me daily

To my family and friends who are my cheerleaders

To Ann Marie Amstad and Ken Funk, Director of the Sandy Historical Society

Praise For Eden Lake

A second historical novel by Donna Hues. The continued story of Max, Maggie and Nellie, now back from their adventures in Scotland and in the United States. Max's cabin on Eden Lake is the perfect paradise, but is it? Max has mysterious neighbors, a woman he is drawn to and a mountain man he finds repelling. But which is truly the most deadly? Maggie and Nellie arrive to visit Max and the three friends are once again embroiled in mystery and romance. Don't miss this enjoyable read by a talented new author. ---Lorna Woods, author of Southeast Alaska series

Hues's well-written story follows the adventures of four friends dealing with their struggles with health and romantic problems among other issues. The tale includes a beautiful devil-filled woman and a strange man who leaves dead animals on a porch. The discovery of why is a cool surprise. — Geni J. I. White, author of Figleaf, Anders Village and Ho, Ho, Ha, Merry Heart Medicine.

Other Books by Donna Hues

Without A Doubt: Accident or Murder
MNM Mystery Series Book One

Contact Donna at: https://donnahues.com/
or: donnahues@hotmail.com

Eden Lake

Not Quite Paradise

MNM Mystery Series

Book 2

Donna Hues

*"There are far better things ahead than anything
we left behind."*

— *C.S. Lewis* —

Chapter 1

"Saying good-bye to relatives too?" asked a young man who gripped a small Scotland flag. He couldn't be more than sixteen years old. Peach fuzz blossomed on his cheeks, anticipation of adventures that beaconed him on distant shores sparkled in his eyes. Their heads are so full of romance. Young men can't see the obstacles before them. Max scrunched his eyelids together. The gravity of his previous two weeks in Rolen weighed heavy on his shoulders. How he wished the outcome had been different.

"Not really. I've been solving a mystery with a friend. Time to go home." Max knew the lad would not be interested in the daring trio who waded into the dangerous world of a murderer. He said no more.

The ocean liner's whistle screeched and sent a cloud of steam into the air. With his two companions, Nellie Cox and Maggie Richards directed to their room, Max had secured an empty spot by the rail. The workers heaved the heavy ropes off the dock and released the majestic ship from her moorage. The wide blue expanse of sea awaited.

Passengers bunched at the railing. The cacophony of voices sounded like a gaggle of geese. Max wrapped his overcoat's collar around his ears to muffle the din. Young men and women leaned over the guard rail and threw paper streamers toward their family and friends far below. How many of these passengers would ever see their loved ones again? Many Scotsmen left their homeland in search of a better life. For Max, however, his 'better life' could only be with Maggie.

He fiddled with his watch fob. The Sullivan family crest had been embossed on one side and gave him a sense of pride. He longed to make Maggie a member of his family. His parents would have loved her. Their whirlwind courtship encompassed the length of the ocean voyage from Scotland. His mother and father married in a dingy courthouse a week after they had arrived in New York.

Rolling waves gently rocked the ocean liner from side to side. Scotland's shores would soon be a distant memory. A two-week voyage lay ahead before the Statue of Liberty's burning torch guided the liner safely into the harbor and Ellis Island would welcome a new flood of immigrants.

Max's heart ached. When they docked he feared he would be separated from his dear Maggie and board a train to Oregon. Construction on a new immigrant processing building was underway when they had left New York. The original Georgia Pine structure had burnt to the ground. Max looked forward to whatever progress they'd made to the new building. But for now he was consumed with the prospect of leaving Maggie. Maybe forever.

He paced the deck. Past images of lunch with her in Portland's Meier & Frank Department Store flooded his memory. He had known her longer than his parents' pre-marital relationship. And after the harrowing experience in Scotland, his feelings had solidified. He loved her. Heartbeats raced, speech stammered and voices "timid and shy" caused the words "I love you," to stick in his craw. An experienced mystery writer, Max could always find the words to draw his readers into a story. His characters were heroes of the highest caliber. Yet, he failed miserably around Maggie.

Max closed his eyes and waited for sleep to engulf him. The ship's motion lingered even though he lay in his own bed. Eden Lake relaxed his body, but not his mind.

He reminisced about one glorious day on the ocean liner when Maggie's essence had filled his entire being. Her calming lavender scent wafted on the breeze.

The sun had warmed the deck and the waves were unusually calm. An occasional seagull squawked overhead. He had reclined in a deck chair, closed his eyes and rehearsed his proposal.

"Maggie, my dear, our experience in Scotland tore at my heart. I was gripped with a sense of emptiness at the thought of losing you to MacLaren, or worse, death, by his hand. His marriage proposal crushed my heart with fear that you might accept. In that instant my hopes were gone. I can't bear to lose you. Maggie, I love you. I believe I've known for some time, but never how deeply until a few weeks ago."

Max imagined her soft hands nestled in his. His eyes riveted to hers. "Maggie Richards, will you do me the honor of becoming my wife?"

A distant noise startled him. Reality sunk in that he no longer enjoyed the comfort of a deck chair on the ocean liner. His head reeled from the annoying noise that jolted him awake. Bang. Bang. His ears rang. Wait. He can't wake up and interrupt this dream. He needed to know Maggie's answer.

"Whoever's there, please go away," his voice thundered over the noise. Max fluffed the pillow, rearranged the blankets and snuggled deeper under the covers. Dream world, come back.

"Mr. Sullivan, Mr. Sullivan," someone yelled from the porch. Max plopped the pillow over his head and squeezed his eyes closed. The pounding continued.

"Mr. Sullivan. Mr. Sullivan."

"I ask that you kindly go away and leave me in peace." Max yelled louder.

"But Mr. Sullivan, I have a telegram for you. The postmistress, Miss Greene, said it's urgent I come right away." Silence followed, then more pounding.

Max gave in. Sleep would never return. He opened one eye as Jed licked his face, hind legs on the floor, front legs across Max's chest. Slobber covered his cheek.

"Yes, yes, Jed. Good morning to you, and yes, I know someone's here."

He threw the blankets aside, slid his feet into his slippers and straightened his nightshirt. With his faithful dog beside him, he trudged toward the door. The front door rattled from another bang.

"Mr. Sullivan, are you coming? I got to be getting back, but need your signature on this paper. Mr. Sullivan?"

"Yes, yes, I'm coming. Keep your boots on." Max bumped into a chair then strained to force his eyes open. He grabbed the latch and flung the door wide. A fist stopped midair short of his forehead. Jed rushed to sniff their uninvited visitor.

"Oh, Mr. Sullivan, I'm sorry. I almost hit you." The lad bent down to rub the hound's ears. "Hi there, Jed." The hound dog wagged his tail then skedaddled off the porch into the crisp morning air. He made a bee-line through the snow and into the trees.

"Mr. Sullivan, I didn't hear any movement inside and I need to get back. Miss Greene doesn't take lightly to what she calls lollygagging." Joel lowered his head in a sheepish manner.

Max knew Joel, a tall, gangly teenager, felt blessed to have a job. These were hard times for a young man who had been called "slow" as a little boy. Max hated it when people put labels on children. Those words stuck like pitch to a person's soul.

With one leg noticeably shorter than the other, Joel moved with an awkward gait which made him an easy target for ridicule. Max grieved for the young man. In a way, the two were kindred spirits. "Timid and shy" clung to Max still as an adult. How he wished he could take his Bowie knife and scrape the label off as easy as scaling a fish.

Max placed a hand on Joel's shoulder, "No, it's I who am sorry, Joel. Still having those dreams I'm on the ocean liner and rocking with the waves." He scratched his head and rubbed his eyes open. "Now, what did you need?"

"Here's a telegram for you from Scotland. I need your signature on this line."

Stunned, Max examined the telegram as he turned the envelope over in his hand. A telegram. From Scotland. Who would be sending a telegram? And why?

Joel grunted. "Mr. Sullivan. Please?"

Max wrote his name where Joel pointed and apologized for his discourteousness.

"I forgive you, Mr. Sullivan. Someday I'd like to hear about Scotland. I dream of traveling, but it's hard to save money these days. Well, gotta get back. Have a nice day."

Joel replaced his hat and tugged the ear flaps. He chose his footing carefully on the icy steps as he descended and mounted his horse.

"Fresh layer of snow last night, Mr. Sullivan." Joel saluted Max then prodded his mount toward town.

Max exhaled into the cool air. A fog cloud formed in front of his face and drifted upward. He inspected the envelope and ripped the sealed flap open. The only time he'd ever received a telegram it proclaimed dire news. To Max they seemed to bring tidings of a calamity.

He held the paper tight in his moist hands, closed his eyes and prayed, "Oh, Lord, let this be good news."

His chest rose with the crisp morning air. He unfolded the telegram and focused on the message: "Holiday your place - STOP - June - STOP - Respond please - STOP - Ernest"

Ernest McIntyre? My fishing pal from Scotland? Coming to Eden Lake? Max's eyes were now fully opened. The lake shone like a freshly washed mirror reflecting Mt. Hood and a small run-down cabin on the opposite side. The majestic trees, veiled in snow, towered toward the blue sky. The mountain reached over eleven-thousand feet. One of the tallest semi-dormant volcanoes in the Cascade Range, white, glistening snow gave it a magical appearance. By June only a fraction of the snow would remain.

His teeth chattered. Goosebumps tingled on his arms and legs. The realization he stood outside clothed in a nightshirt and floppy slippers while icicles dangled from the eaves, drove him inside in an instant. He stoked up the leftover embers in the potbelly stove and added kindling. Almost as cold indoors as out, Max grabbed his robe. He checked the fire in the cook stove. No life remained.

While crumpling paper, he thought of Maggie again. Why had he been so stupid? He had plenty of opportunities on the ocean trip. After all, two weeks is fourteen days and he only needed to get a few sentences out of his mouth. She slipped out of his life one more time as she boarded the train for Chicago while his locomotive followed the tracks to Oregon. He dumped the dregs from last night's coffee, added fresh water and placed the pot on the stove to heat. Max checked the tin can then added "coffee" to his shopping list.

He flopped on the couch and re-read the telegram while the wood crackled and spit. Already the cabin seemed warmer. With a two-week ocean crossing, then a week or so on the train and another day by coach from Portland, Max understood why Ernest would send a telegram in March. A long trip awaited.

June. That would be a good month. The fish would be biting. The days were longer and warmer. Excitement set in as Max anticipated fishing with Ernest. The boiling water and growling stomach brought him back to the urgency to cook breakfast, chop wood, finish a shopping list, make his bed and, oh yes, get dressed. His mind far outreached his actions. Time to slow down and calculate the best use of today.

Max flipped a page on his calendar and browsed for any commitments. Jolted to a halt, he had forgotten a doctor's appointment next week. Why could he not erase this notation from the page as easily as he dismissed it from his mind? He had an aversion to doctors, especially ones that seemed to know all the answers. And the long trip to Portland didn't help matters. Too much time to think. A scratch and moan from the porch reminded Max that Jed waited outside.

"Sorry, boy." Max opened the door and rubbed the black dog's cold ears. Jed nestled in the old blankets that created a bed by the fire. Max filled Jed's water dish.

"This is a special day for me, so how about a treat?" Jed wagged his tail extra hard, let his tongue dangle, and trotted to Max's side.

Bacon and eggs ready, Max ladled his breakfast to a plate, then covered Jed's dry food with the bacon grease. "Wait now, boy. Don't want to be burning yourself." Jed lay down in front of his dish setting his snout on the edge. His nose twitched with the smell of run-off grease. He kept an eye on Max and waited for the "go ahead" signal.

Max gobbled his food and charted his activities for the day. One day at a time, the doctor said. After all, no one is promised more than one day. With the premature death of his parents, Max knew all too well, no one is even promised a full day.

He revisited his morning dream. Maggie. Her vision floated through his mind. Red hair, petite body, winsome smile and adventurous spirit. How he wished she were here, in his kitchen, sharing his cabin, perhaps the mother of his children. But that may never be. What did Maggie say when they were in Scotland? "Wishing and hoping and thinking and even praying, didn't make it so." How he longed to be back among the heather and thistle. He regretted so many missed opportunities to express his love.

Voices from the past replayed in his mind, "You're so timid and shy. You'll never amount to anything." He had tried hard to rip those labels off, but succumbed and returned to his shell. He recognized the need to reverse that image, yet he lacked the power. So, once again, he foolishly let those prime moments slip through his fingers, lost forever.

Lost forever. Would she be? He knew the time had arrived for him to test the waters of his new found faith. Time to get serious with God. He remembered Ernest's comment in Scotland, "We're fishing, and yet, I'm casting my faith line out to you in the hopes you will latch on to the bait and follow Jesus." Max definitely needed to cast his faith line to the Lord and catch strength and guidance for what lay ahead. A moan interrupted his thoughts.

"Oh, Jed, I'm so sorry. That grease should be cool enough now. Go ahead."

Chapter 2

A perfect morning for fishing, Max rowed to his favorite spot on the far side of the lake. Old tree trunks were wedged together about twenty feet from shore. The timber formed an ideal feeding ground for trout. The final owl hoots echoed across the lake. As the night prowlers prepared for slumberland, rustling in the brush announced woodland critters foraged for breakfast. Max loved dawn as the sun poured it's rosy light upon majestic Mt. Hood.

Jed reserved the bow of the twelve foot row boat for himself. As he faced the wind, his ears flapped and nostrils quivered with the early morning smells. Max's chuckle skimmed across the lake, then faded in the distance. Jed's tail looked like a whisk broom as it swept the bottom of the boat. Jed loved the lake as much as Max.

"Hey there, boy. Settle down. You'll scare the fish." Max dug into his can of dirt, his fingers ably distinguishing between clods of mud and worms. The slimy earthworm squirmed in his hand. He held the hook between two fingers and positioned the fish bait to slide on the barb.

A light from the run-down cabin across the lake diverted his attention. During his time in Scotland, someone had moved into the abandoned shelter. "And a mite pretty one too, Mr. Sullivan. You'd do well to get to know her." Miss Greene had mentioned something about the young lady when Max had gathered his mail.

"A mite pretty one" indeed. No one could top Maggie. Miss Greene will need to control her matchmaker instincts.

"Ouch!" Jed bolted off the seat and inched toward Max. "Oh, Jed, thanks for the comfort. I need to pay attention to what I'm doing. Got my finger on the hook along with the bait. Can't stop thinking about Maggie. You go on back now. I'm fine." The cool lake water soothed his bleeding finger. After applying a strip of cloth on the puncture wound, he cast the line off the boat's stern.

A faint humming sound carried across the lake. He gazed in the direction of the forlorn cabin. A young lady appeared on the porch. The light behind her from the open door highlighted her shapely figure. With long strokes, she brushed hair that reached below her waist. She waved both arms in the air and ran toward her dock. *Does she really think I'm going to stop fishing, row over there and say, "Good morning" and "How do you do?"* Max waved back, then held up his pole. She waved again and danced up the dock back to her cabin. An elfin-image crossed Max's mind. Light on her feet, tiny of stature, wavy, flowing hair and voice like a songbird.

A tug on the line brought Max back to the task at hand. In short order, he landed three nice sized trout, reeled in his line and maneuvered the boat back to his dock.

"Come on, Jed, you move back now so I can tie the rope to the pier."

The hair on Jed's neck bristled. A low growl emanated from deep in his throat.

"Jed, what's the matter, boy?" He followed the dog's gaze to the dock. The she-elf had positioned herself square in the middle of the platform. A grin on her face, one hand on her hip, she reached the other hand toward Max.

"Good morning, neighbor, I'm Emeline. Emeline Toliver."

Max gaped at her. His eyes bulged and once again, words wouldn't come. Beautiful wavy blond hair blew around her waist. Most unthinkable for women of this day and age. Emeline loosened the knot that held a scarf to her waist, gathered her hair behind her head and tied it off. Her blue eyes were brighter than any forget-me-not he had ever seen and pierced through to his heart. And that body. As his chums in school would say, "She's well-endowed."

"I'm the girl across the lake." She pointed to the cabin. "You know? You saw me brushing my hair. We waved to each other. I've been waiting for you to get back from Scotland." Emeline placed both hands on her waist. Another elfin quirk. "Miss Greene said it might be late-fall. Then I had to make a trip south and got home last week. Been waiting for you to come out of that cabin for a spell so we could get to know each other. I'm mighty lonely all by myself."

Max, get a grip. "I'm — sorry," he gulped. "How did you get here so quickly?"

"I'm light on my feet and fly like the wind," she said. "But it helps to have a fast horse." She moved aside revealing a magnificent black steed waiting in the road. He pawed the ground. A clump of snow and dirt were tossed in the air.

"His name isn't Fireball, is it?"

"Fireball? What a strange name. No, I named him Beelzebub. But Fireball would probably suit him. He's a spitfire of a horse. Three-quarter Arabian which sometimes gets him in trouble." She extended her hand toward Max. "Can I help you with your fishing gear? Did you catch anything?"

Max handed her his pole, set his tackle box and creel on the dock, then accepted her hand. With her assistance out of the boat, he now faced this beauty. Strikingly gorgeous. Her skin, as smooth as silk. And those eyes. Max thought an azure color at first, but now face-to-face, they were like a cool refreshing pond on a sweltering summer's day. They beckoned him to dive in. He forced his eyes closed and prayed that when he opened them, she would be gone. *Didn't work.*

"Thanks for your help. I'm Max Sullivan. That's Jed sniffing your boots. And yes, we caught three nice sized trout. Would you like to take one home?" He thought about asking her to stay for a lunch of fresh cooked fish, but with his pulse racing, keeping his distance would be safer.

"That's very neighborly of you, but I don't eat fish. If you have some coffee, I'll have a cup."

Jed cautiously led the way toward Beelzebub. Then changed his mind and cowered behind Max and Emeline.

"Well, you're a fine hound dog, letting a horse get the best of you." Max patted Jed's back. "I don't blame you though. He's definitely intimidating. Do you have a dog too, or is Beelzebub your protector?"

"I thought about a dog, living all alone in that cabin, but Bub usually snorts and makes enough of a commotion to alert me to danger. I keep a rifle by the front door, another in the lean-to and a handgun in my bedroom. Like to have options available wherever I am. Do you have a horse?"

"I have two horses in that stable over there." Max nodded toward the side of his cabin. "They're both great riding horses and pull my wagon with ease."

When they reached the porch, Emeline looped Beelzebub's reins over the railing. Max placed his tackle box and creel on the porch bench, then opened the front door.

"Make yourself at home. I'll start the coffee."

"I'll soak in the view from the porch while you do that. This is magnificent. With my cabin at the base of the mountain, I don't have any postcard shots. You're lucky to enjoy this scenery every day." Emeline paused. "Oops, I see a glimmer of light in the window. Probably forgot to blow out the lantern. Think I better take a rain check on that coffee and get back in case something happens. This is my first time living so isolated and I'm probably overly cautious about burning flames, even if they are contained. Perhaps another time?"

"Sure. Nice to meet you and thanks for carrying my fishing pole."

"Totally my pleasure. To be honest, I'd asked Miss Greene about you. She said I would probably fall in love with you the first time we met." Emeline's eyes sparkled. "She may be right."

She scampered down the steps and flew onto Beelzebub's back. With a kick of her heels, her horse pranced down the road, gone from sight before Max could wave good-bye.

"What was that, Jed? A real girl, or an apparition? Whichever, she's definitely mesmerizing."

Jed hunched over and scratched his side. Max grabbed the creel and glanced down the road one last time. He shook his head. "Lunch will be ready in a jiff." Jed lapped water from his dish, then curled up beside the cook stove.

Max slathered a cast iron fry pan with bacon grease and gently laid the cleaned trout in the sizzling fat. Some coffee remained in the pot, so he moved it to a warmer spot on the stove top. No need to start a fresh brew since he had no company for lunch.

While enjoying fresh tasty trout and warmed coffee, Max reached for Ernest's telegram. He held the paper as a prized possession and pulled his calendar closer to him. He found a pad of paper and pencil for a shopping list and jotted a few notes.

"Let's see, Jed. This is April 26. Only two more months before you meet Ernest. You'll like him, Jed, and I know he'll like you. We'll go hiking and fishing every day. What do you say to that?"

No sound came from the direction of the cook stove. Jed slept like a worn out puppy, his legs twitched. Must be in dreamland. But what do dogs dream about anyway? Hiking, fishing, chasing rabbits and squirrels?

Time to let Emeline blend into the forest and refocus on something more foundational: not a skittish lady. Max placed his dishes in the sink. He poured the last drops of coffee in his mug and picked up his Bible. A comfy chair by a side window had become his devotion spot.

"Lord, please lead me into what you have for me today. Emeline haunts my mind. I need you to refocus my thoughts on what's really important. Thank you."

Chapter 3

One last swig of coffee then Max leafed through his Bible to the New Testament book of Matthew. He reasoned that since he was a new Christian, he should start reading the first book of the New Testament. He had read the account of Jesus' birth a few days ago and stopped at chapter three.

"Hey, Jed, listen to this." Max glanced at Jed to be sure he had his dog's attention. "'The voice of one crying in the wilderness, make ready the way of the Lord, make His paths straight.' Sounds like someone would come to Judea to tell people to get ready for the Lord. Wonder what the people thought when they heard that? Do you think they cleaned their houses, baked bread, mended fences?" Jed sat by Max's feet, tail wagged, head cocked to one side, he listened intently to his master's voice.

"I think it must have a deeper meaning. Like 'get your heart ready to hear what the Lord has to say' kind of thing." Max read on a few more verses, then laughed. He leaned his head on the back of his chair, eyes closed.

"Jed, I'm trying to imagine this John the Baptist guy. These words paint quite an interesting picture. Are you ready?" Jed barked a sweet little yelp and laid his head on Max's lap.

"This John had been living in the wilderness, surviving off the land and eating locust and honey. He's wearing a garment of camel's hair with a leather belt around his waist. Can you form an image, Jed? Where do you take a bath in the wilderness? And gathering wild honey could be a formidable task. Wonder if he had any black bears to compete with like we do."

Max closed his eyes once more and smiled. "I got it." He straightened his back. "John must have been an eloquent speaker for people to take notice since his appearance wouldn't gather any fair maidens. Not to mention his smell. So I envision him as about 6' 4", maybe on the thin side, not knowing the caloric value of locust and honey. His hair, long, greasy and matted. His beard scraggly with scruffs of grass and dried moss that grew in the moist areas. The camel hair garment probably needed a good brushing too. What do you think? If he walked into Eden Lake proclaiming the Lord was coming he may be arrested and hauled off to the hospital in Salem. Yet, these people listened to him. Must have said something important."

Jed wandered back to his cozy bed. He slurped some water, then laid down.

"Wait, Jed, here's the best part. These people came from all over to be baptized by John in the Jordan River. They confessed their sins and sought clean hearts. Isn't that amazing?" Max stopped at verse eleven.

He closed the Bible, laid his hand on the cover and prayed. "Lord, I want my heart to be cleansed and my mind only filled with you. John said you would come to baptize with the Holy Spirit and fire. I desire that for my life. Too many distractions and desires that pull me where I dare not go. Help me to follow you. Amen."

Max carried his coffee mug to the sink, careful not to disturb Jed's nap, and conjured up an image of John the Baptist. *What a rough mountain man he would have made. If I had seen him face-to-face, I wonder what I would have done?*

Heavy footsteps on the porch jolted Jed from his slumber. The hound bounded to the door and barked. "Jed, it's okay. Maybe Joel again, although his footsteps wouldn't be so loud."

Max picked up his rifle and chambered a load. He leaned it against the wall and lifted the door latch.

"Jed, heel," Max commanded the hound. He opened the door and couldn't believe his eyes. There stood John the Baptist; a mountain man with dirty dungarees, torn shirt, hole in one shoe, and body odor that could challenge a skunk. His unkept beard and long hair were matted with grass and twigs. A stained worn felt hat leaned to one side of his head. Max estimated he stood at least 6' 5" and weighed about 260 lb.. *Not living on locusts and wild honey.*

Tied to a tree across the path, a vicious coon dog barked with teeth bared. He strained on the rope. Max reached to restrain Jed, but found him cowering. Jed's head pushed between Max's legs, his body stiffened. Both the man and his beast created an intimidating presence.

"Good afternoon. My name's Frank Molech. I've been hunting and killed more than I can eat. Thought you might like these here possums." Molech raised his arm. Two carcasses dangled by their tails. Max's eyes darted from the possums to Molech's teeth. The few he did have were blackened by tobacco juice that dripped out the corner of his mouth.

"Hi, Frank. I'm Max Sullivan. Thank you for thinking of me, but I had lake trout for lunch and couldn't eat another bite." Max pulled his partially open door closed. No need to fill the cabin with Molech's fragrance.

"Well, I'll leave them here on the porch for later."

Frank faced his dog, "Shut up," he yelled. A dirty rag hung from his back pocket. Max shut his eyes. John the Baptist couldn't have been this bad. Max removed his handkerchief from his front pocket. He feigned the need to blow his nose.

"I can skin 'em if you like. Won't take but a few minutes. Then you and I can get to know each other." Molech pulled a ten inch Bowie knife from its sheath. Just as dirty as the man.

"That's very kind of you, but I'm getting ready to leave for town. Maybe another time. Do you live around here? I don't remember seeing you before."

Molech laid the possums on a bench by the door and put his knife away.

"I live wherever I can find a vacant spot. Survive off the land. I don't rely on anyone and no one needs to take care of me. Just me and old Bear, my dog. We get along fine." Molech glanced down at Jed. "You sure got a scrawny mutt. Is he good for anything?"

"Jed's a cast off hound dog. I rescued him from an abandoned shed the other side of town. His owners vacated their home unexpectedly and left him behind. Guess you could say I redeemed him. Gave him a new chance at life."

"Well, if he's going to compete with Bear in any cougar treeing contest you best feed him more than what it looks like he's getting." Molech smeared his nose on his shirt sleeve. "I might have some badger meat left. I'm told its high in fat. I'll drop some off next time I'm down this way."

"Thank you again for the possums. No need to bring any badger meat. And we don't hunt cougars. Jed and I think every animal helps to balance nature and should be left alone." Max rubbed Jed's ears. "There's no sheep farmers for miles, so I don't believe mountain lions are a threat."

Max closed his door to a crack. "I'll see you later, Frank. Have a nice day."

"Yeah, same to you. Oh, I'd rather you call me Molech than Frank. Thanks." His heavy footsteps clambered down the steps.

With Bear loosed from the tree, he bolted down the path from side to side while Molech followed him into the forest.

Max practiced shallow breathing. Once dog and man left the premises, a cool breeze arrived. Almost as if the Lord knew the porch needed a cleansing. Max inhaled fresh air to his lungs full capacity. "Thank you, Lord. A deep breath felt good. And thanks that Molech didn't spit on my porch. Several blessings already and the day's barely begun."

Chapter 4

The usual activity outside Greene's Mercantile-Post Office-Cafe greeted Max and Jed. With the wagon left on a side street, they meandered to the store. Inside, the shelves were stocked near to the ceiling with dry goods and staples. During the winter, Miss Greene ordered special requests. An ice crate in the back of the store kept the fresh produce. Most residents grew their own vegetables in the summer as well as raised chickens, pigs and a milk cow or two. Root cellars were dug in every yard and an ice house sat at the edge of town.

Max liked Eden Lake. Immigrants from Sweden and Germany settled here. This community was perfect if you liked living in town, but Max preferred the forest, closer to nature.

"Good afternoon, Max. I can almost set my clock by your arrival. Same time, same day of the week. Back in a flash." Miss Greene weighed sugar for a customer, tied the bag with twine and replaced the sugar tin on a shelf.

Max retrieved his grocery list from his pocket. He scanned the counters and shelves. Miss Greene listed fresh produce on her slate board: oranges - 50 cents a dozen.

A water dish sat by the front door for thirsty dogs. Jed slurped a few gulps, then curled up by the potbelly stove for a nap.

"Now, Max, what can I get you? Besides your mail that is." Miss Greene laughed. She always laughed when she talked. "Here, have one of my oatmeal raisin cookies. I'll get your mail."

Cookies and Miss Greene. A perfect match. Probably too many oatmeal cookies had contributed to her ample size. Her jovial personality and easy smile gave the appearance that she hid a secret. Then again, perhaps the result of too much sugar.

Max handed the list to Miss Greene and picked up an empty box from a pile at the end of the counter. As she placed items in the box, she drew a line through each listed item.

"How about a treat for old Jed?"

At the sound of his name, Jed lifted his head and wagged his tail.

"Looks like he approves," Max said. "Thanks."

Jed sat tall, opened his mouth and allowed the treat to sail in. Miss Greene checked the list one last time. "Think I've got everything in your box. Now, how about telling me what you've been up to the past week."

"Oh, not much. The usual hiking and fishing. Caught three nice sized trout this morning across the lake by a cluster of downed trees."

"Did you say 'across the lake'? Did you catch anything besides fish? Like maybe a glimpse of your new neighbor?"

"As a matter of fact, yes, I did meet her. She saw me fishing. By the time I rowed back to my dock she waited with a helping hand."

Miss Greene's eye twinkled.

"Beautiful, isn't she?"

"Now, Miss Greene, you take off that matchmaker hat. And don't be putting ideas in her head either."

Max slid the grocery box off the counter and placed it on a table near the door.

"I had another visitor this morning I hoped you might know. A Frank Molech."

"Frank Molech." Miss Greene glanced at the ceiling as she did when some heavy thinking was necessary. "Frank Molech." She scratched her head. "That name isn't familiar. Can you describe him?" She reached her hand in the cookie jar, "Here, have another. You need more meat on your bones."

Max wrapped the treat in brown paper. "I'll enjoy this more after dinner tonight. Thanks." He leaned on the counter.

"He's a very dirty man. Stands about 6' 5" and weighs maybe 260lb. Scruffy beard and matted hair. Patched dungarees, hole worn in the toe of one shoe, chews tobacco and smells like his body hasn't touched soap and water for months."

Miss Greene's rosy complexion vanished. A wrinkled brow replaced her smile. She leaned close to Max.

"Did he have a dog?"

"Yes. A vicious animal he kept tied to a tree."

"What was the dog's name?"

"Bear"

"And did he give you anything?"

"He did. Two dead possums. Offered to skin them for me. Left them on the porch."

Miss Greene's complexion turned ashen. Max gasped as she teetered, then ran around the counter. He grabbed a chair and slid it under her as her knees buckled. He poured a glass of water and encouraged her to drink. Once Miss Greene held the glass, he found a scrap of cardboard and fanned her collapsed body. Sweat trickled down her temples. She undid the top button of her dress, dipped a hanky in the water and wiped her neck. She dipped again and drew the cool water across her brow.

"Max, close the door will you? Lock it and pull down the shade."

Mystified why this dirty vagrant had such a profound effect on Miss Greene, Max hurried to follow her instructions.

"Find another chair and come sit beside me." Miss Greene fought to regain her composure.

"What did you do with the possums?"

"I dug a hole and buried them about twenty feet behind my cabin. Afraid some varmint might dig them up, I piled several heavy rocks on top."

"Did you discover how they were killed before you buried them?"

"You know, that's the strangest thing. Molech said he 'killed' them, but I found no gunshot wounds or evidence they were caught in a trap. And while he showed me his Bowie knife, there were no signs of fresh blood. Come to think of it, there were no knife wounds on the possums either. I don't know how they were killed, unless he strangled them."

"He's back." Miss Greene clutched her chest and stared at Max. Her wide eyes and clammy skin signaled this may be a situation fraught with peril. "Max, I fear for you with all my heart. That was no mere man you met today." Miss Greene gulped down the remaining water in the glass and motioned to Max for a refill. "You pour yourself a glass, too. Although something a mite stronger may be more beneficial."

"What do you mean? 'No mere man'? He had all the markings of a man, albeit extremely rough and dirty. But I don't believe in aliens if that's what you're getting at."

"Not an alien, Max, but definitely not of this world. Did you detect a sulphur smell?"

Max thought long and hard. His senses had been so assaulted it would be difficult to distinguish one smell from another. Certainly all smells that were sweet, comforting, homey, good memory-making, could be eliminated. Rancid, sour, stale, putrid, malodorous and rotten came to mind. Sulphur? Max inhaled deeply trying to recapture all the smells that hovered on his porch.

"You know, I do recall a faint sulphur smell. Don't know where that could have come from. There's nothing in the mountains that gives off that odor."

"It's not from the mountains, Max. It's him. Himself." Miss Greene wiped the last traces of sweat from her forehead, leaned toward Max and rested a hand on his leg.

"Like I said, I fear for you and must emphasize that he is not of this world. Do you remember the Anderson's? Good people. Good, God-fearing people. They're the ones who had Jed." Miss Greene leaned against the back of her chair. "Poor scared dog. How did he react to your visitor?"

"Scared stiff. Tried to hide between my legs. In fact, he didn't even bark when I opened the door. Just trembled as if he had a past history with this guy."

"Probably from his experience watching the Anderson's being tormented. Frightened them enough to cause them to leave Eden Lake. All this happened while you were in Scotland. Now there's a mystery waiting to be solved. Everyone assumes they left. No one knows for sure." Miss Greene reached for another cookie. "They didn't say anything about plans to leave. Just disappeared one day and left old Jed behind. I think they disappeared mysteriously, if you get my drift, and Jed hid in the shed for his own protection — protection from Molech."

"You said you didn't know Frank Molech. Yet when I described him, you obviously knew him and his acquaintance with the Anderson's. I don't understand."

Miss Greene straightened in her chair and sighed. "I'm sure this all sounds very strange to you. When this beast started visiting the Anderson's, he brought them two possums the first visit. The next time he brought three foxes. The next time, four raccoons. Mrs. Anderson came to see me scared to death. I suggested she talk to the parson when he came to town and to Mr. Olson in the meantime. When anyone needs spiritual advice, Mr. Olson's the one to see if the parson's not available."

"Did you ever see Molech?"

"No, I only have Mrs. Anderson's word. But I have no reason to believe she would lie. She was an honest, spirit-filled Christian who loved the Lord with all her heart. She'd only been a believer for a few months, but definitely on fire for the Lord. They shared the Lord with everyone and there are many new converts in Eden Lake because of them." Miss Greene squinted her eyes sternly at Max. "No, sir. She wouldn't lie."

"What advice did she receive?"

"I can't tell you. It had been over a week since she'd been in my store and their mail piled up, so I told Joel to take the bundle out to them. Maybe they were sick and there was something we could do. Joel came back white as a sheet, sweat dripping down his face. He collapsed in a chair and all he could say was, "They're gone. Both of them, gone." Poor boy. He was in shock. But he thought it strange that all their belongings were still there. Even the horse. Now, what do you make of that? As a mystery writer, wouldn't this be right up your alley?"

Max closed his eyes and tried to make sense of the jumbled information swirling around in his head.

"Well," Miss Greene said, "your visitor, Molech, and the man that visited the Anderson must be one and the same. Couldn't possibly be two creatures that look alike and both kill possums. But my spirit tells me they are one and the same. If he shows up again with foxes or raccoons, then I'd hustle over to the pastor, if he's in town, or Mr. Olson, if he's not. They'll both give you good advice based on God's word. In the meantime, I'll be saying lots of prayer for your protection." Miss Greene tenderly held Max's hands and prayed for him.

"Now, go lift the shade, unlock and open the door. The good people of Eden Lake have been patient long enough. Time for business."

"Thank you for your information, advice and prayer, Miss Greene. I'll meditate on everything you've said and seek the Lord's guidance."

"That's the best way, Max." Miss Greene's smile returned. "Maybe a new mystery story in the making. Yes?" She placed her water glass on the back counter. "Oh, how'd you like that telegram from Scotland? Got a friend coming?"

"The best news of the day. You and Ernest will be good friends. I know it."

Max heaved up his box of groceries, called to Jed and headed into the sunshine and fresh air. He placed the box in the back of his wagon as Jed jumped up to the seat. Max lifted a leg to hoist himself up, then remembered his mail. He climbed down and scooped out the bundle from the grocery box. Max riffled through the envelopes. The handwriting on one envelope stopped him cold.

He glanced at the return address: Chicago, Illinois. Could it be? Max ripped open the envelope, tore the paper out, unfolded it and read.

Dear Max,

Nellie is traveling to Portland at the request of the Metropolitan Police and would like me to accompany her on the train. Her fame has spread beyond Chicago. I wondered if I might stop and visit you for a while. I'd love to see Eden Lake, and I miss you. She hasn't finalized her plans, but thinks it would be sometime in June. Would you let me know if you are open to a visit?

Fondly,
Maggie

Chapter 5

Max fairly danced into the wagon where Jed waited.

"Jed, Jed, she's coming, Maggie's coming. I can hardly believe it." He scratched Jed behind his ears, under his chin, then patted his shoulders like an old school buddy. Jed lost his balance. One paw slipped off the seat. Max grabbed his dog and gave him a big hug.

"Sorry, fella. I'm so excited. This letter from Maggie certainly tops what I heard from Miss Greene. You know, about Molech. Some of her story seemed true. Especially about your reaction to him. But the rest? I don't know. If she's right, Eden Lake may have a madman on the loose. We'll need eyes like an eagle and ears like an owl." Max read Maggie's letter again, neatly folded the paper and carefully slipped it back into the envelope. He tucked it into his shirt pocket and gave it a pat. Close to his heart.

"Well, can't let spook stories spoil a great day. Let's go home."

Max drove the team back to his cabin dreaming of Maggie. The slight drizzle reminded him of their days in Scotland. Such sweet days mixed with unnerving times. The warmth he had felt holding her close engulfed his emotions. *Wouldn't it be wonderful if she were waiting at the cabin? Waving as the wagon came into sight, then running to meet me? The cabin filled with the sweet smells of freshly baked brownies.*

He wrapped his arm around Jed and drew him close. *Not the same.* But maybe someday. Maybe things would work out and coming home would be just like that.

"Well, Jed, what would you like to do after we put the team and groceries away? How about a nice hike? Always a good day for a walk even if the drizzle doesn't let up."

The team clomped down the road and around the final bend before the cabin came into view. Max raised his head and glanced at the lake and Mt. Hood. How beautiful was this part of God's creation. And how blessed he felt to call a little portion of it home.

He turned toward the cabin and blinked several times. Someone stood on the porch, waving to him. She sprang from the porch and ran toward the wagon. *Maggie?*

"Hi, Max, welcome home. I've been sitting on the porch absorbing the beauty of the Cascades."

"Emeline? Hi, yourself." Max shoulders tightened.

She grabbed the horses' bridles and led them toward the stable.

"Here, let me help with your groceries."

"No need to. One box is all this trip."

Jed leapt off the wagon, then high-tailed it into the trees. Max picked up the box of groceries and headed for the cabin.

"I'll unhitch the team after I put these groceries away. Would you like that cup of coffee now?"

"No, thanks. I need to be getting back, but I brought you something. How about I meet you at the front door?" Emeline dashed from the stable.

Max entered through the side door, set the box of groceries on the kitchen counter then unlatched the front door. When he pulled the door open, Emeline stood on the threshold. She held a box in her outstretched hands, an impish grin covered her face.

"This is for you, Max." As she raised the box closer to him, Max reached to accept the gift. When his hands grasped the box, Emeline placed her hands on his. Shivers ran up his back. *What now?* Stammer time.

"Thank…you. You…you don't need to…to bring me anything."

"I know that, but I wanted to. Sort of a welcome home and it's nice-to-meet-you gift." She swayed from side to side. Max became entranced with her beauty. Her long hair swirled around her body like tall grass in a breeze. Hypnotizing.

"I hope you weren't waiting long."

"Oh, I lost track of time enjoying the beauty of nature. And, hope you don't mind, peeked in your windows to get sense of who you are. Besides, I didn't want to leave this box on the porch. Too many four-legged beasties that might steal your treat."

Max gestured to a wooden box mounted beside the front door. A red scarf hung from a hook next to the box and a bent nail looped through a latch kept the lid tight.

"This is my mail box. Now I know we don't have mail delivery up here, but if Joel needs to bring a parcel and I'm not home, he puts it inside along with the red scarf. When I get home, if the red scarf is gone, I know there's something inside. I've had friends who borrowed books do the same thing. But what am I saying? You didn't know. I'm sorry."

"No need to be. Truly delightful relaxing on your porch, waiting for you. But that's good information should I bring something again. And very clever of you, I might add." Emeline leaned her face closer to Max. "Aren't you going to remove the box lid?"

Max motioned for her to join him on the porch bench. He slid the lid up. The aroma was delightful.

"Brownies. How did you know these are my favorite?"

"A logical guess, I'm sure. Most men adore brownies. I make mine extra moist so they stay together longer when dipped in a cup of tea. That's my favorite way to eat them."

Her smile melted his heart. And those eyes. Max felt he could have sat there all day just staring into the blue depths. A sweet lavender smell wafted on the gentle breeze that blew across the porch. His mind transported him to his boat. He envisioned Emeline. As she reclined in the bow he would row to a sunny picnic spot. A warmth came to his leg. Her hand rested on his knee. Then another weight on his other leg. Max turned to his right. Jed panted, tongue hung low with a begging tilt of his head.

"Emeline, I'm sorry. I promised Jed we would go for a hike this afternoon. I've learned that Jed won't let me forget promises." Max replaced the box lid and accompanied Emeline to the porch steps.

"I don't see Beelzebub. Did you walk around the lake?"

"Yes. It's a lovely walk and a pleasant day. There is a light drizzle, but most of the snow has melted. Besides, this old body needs the exercise."

Max chuckled. "You seem just right to me." *Did I really say that?*

"Why, thank you, Max. I'm flattered you noticed." She ran her hands down her svelte body accentuating her perfect hour-glass figure. Moisture formed on the back of Max's neck.

"I better go. Want to get back before dusk." Emeline skipped down the steps to the road.

"Are you carrying a gun? There are lots of black bears around the lake."

"I have a pea-shooter. I know it won't stop a bear. I've found when I sing my way home and brush the vegetation with a stick, no bear comes near. Thanks for your concern, but I'll be fine. In fact, if you like, I'll light the porch lantern when I get back."

"I'd like that, Emeline. Jed and I will wait here on the porch until I see your lantern light. And thanks again for the brownies. Each one will be savored."

Off she pranced. Max wondered if she had springs in her legs, so light on her feet and so graceful.

He entered the cabin and placed the box on his kitchen table. Max hurried to the stable to unhitch the team and rub down the horses. Extra feed and fresh water, a pat on the horses' rumps and back to his cabin.

"Hang on, Jed. Need to put the groceries away, then we're off."

As he reached in the box to remove the can of coffee, his hand brushed the mail. He patted his shirt pocket and removed Maggie's letter. How could he forget her in such a short time? Maggie is coming in two months. He glanced out his cabin window to Emeline's across the lake. Conflicting emotions filled Max. The box of brownies called him. He knew he would have to sort things out very quickly. He loved Maggie. This she-elf neighbor had become a disturbance.

"Come on, Jed. We better get going before the drizzle turns to a downpour. Although that might be exactly what this old brain of mine needs: a cleansing from Emeline's beguiling power."

Jed bounced down the road like a puppy fresh out of a kennel. He darted from side to side sniffing bushes and marking trees. He leapt at early spring butterflies, yet gently nuzzled trilliums barely opened. Couldn't be a better day for the hound. Free-roaming in the wild Cascades with his best buddy dawdling behind.

Max strolled at a much slower pace captured in his thoughts of Maggie. He forced Emeline out and allowed his one love to saturate every fiber.

Plans were needed regarding the sleeping arrangements in his two bedroom cabin. He hoped Ernest wouldn't mind sleeping on the porch. He'd slept there many times in the summer and with his camping gear, it would be cozy for the two men. Max would write Maggie to ask if Nellie could stop as well. The women could have the bedrooms. That would work just fine.

With Ernest visiting at the same time, it would be a reunion and sharing Scotland memories. How he looked forward to his friend's arrival. Perhaps Ernest would have good news about Ramsay MacLaren. Ramsay had looked so forlorn when they'd left Scotland for America.

Up ahead a loud commotion diverted his attention. Jed see-sawed his way between the path and the bushes. He must have cornered some wild animal. Max ran in the direction of spraying mud afraid Jed had met with a skunk. He yelled to get Jed's attention in the hopes of sparing both dog and man the result of an indiscretion. He prayed Jed would hear his command and obey.

As Max cleared the last bush in his line of vision, he stopped dead in his tracks. A black animal to be sure, with a small white spot under its chin. But no skunk. Oh, why couldn't it be a skunk? Instead Jed played "catch-me-if-you-can" with a young bear cub. The two black animals chased each other in circles. The cub may not be weaned yet, which meant mama could be in eyesight. With each quick turn, the bear tripped over its legs and tumbled to the ground. Jed, much more agile, out-maneuvered the youngster.

Max, hands on his waist, leaned back and laughed. What a sight. The two black critters romped in the forest and emitted little grunts from time to time.

Then reality took hold. *Where was Mama?* Max slapped his hand to his holstered gun, but met with nothing but jeans. In his haste to leave the cabin, he had forgotten to fasten his gun belt. *Emeline's fault with her bewitching ways.*

Totally unarmed, Max frantically searched the woods for any sign of Mom. They were not far from a stream that dumped trout into Eden Lake. He focused his attention in that direction assuming she could be fishing for dinner. Huckleberries weren't ripe yet, so fish would be a stable of their diet after hibernation. Max knew if her belly wasn't full their meeting would not be amiable.

"Jed. Jed. Here boy. Leave that bear alone and come here. Now!" Jed took one last pounce at his playmate and ran to Max. Too late. The breaking branches and flurry of snow residue on bushes announced Mama's coming. Baby heard her too and ran to greet her. Mama displayed body language that said she was not in the mood for a sit down chat. Her back hunched, shoulder hair straight up and eyes on fire signaled to Max evasive action was critical.

Max cast a frantic eye for a nearby tree. Those beside him were not good climbers. He found a great tree a few feet away, but knew black bears can run as fast as a horse and mama would beat him there. Black bears are expert climbers and he hadn't shinned a tree since a kid. She'd win. Besides, dogs can't climb and he couldn't leave Jed behind.

Rocks, sticks, anything he could throw her way might bide them some time. A layer of snow covered the rocks beside him. No time to brush it off in search of the ideal stone.

He decided to stand his ground. He raised his arms in the air. Appearing larger should help. Yet Max knew even in this position he was no match for an almost 400lb., baby-protective mother bear.

He talked to the bear in soothing tones and moved backwards. Not wanting her to think he was challenging her, he avoided direct eye contact.

"Jed, stay with me. Here, boy. We're going to move very slowly backwards. The cabin's quite a distance yet, but I hope her baby will take her attention from us and they'll move back to the stream."

One cautious step followed another as the distance grew between man and beast. Max's heart raced. He realized it wasn't Emeline's fault, but his own that he left without his sidearm. *Lord, if you get me through this, I'll never make that mistake again.*

Mama emitted blowing noises and swatted the ground with her forepaws. Then raised on her hind legs to her full body height, slammed her front paws on the ground and moved toward Max. In an instant, Jed darted straight for her.

"Jed. Jed. Come back. You're no match for her. Jed." Max was panic-stricken. He had heard black bears rarely attack humans, but what about dogs?

"You've got your baby. Now go catch more fish." His tone no longer soothing as he watched Jed close the gap.

Mama's eyes were riveted to this scrawny black hound dog who made a valiant effort to save his master. Her pace increased. Within feet of her sweeping paw, Jed pivoted at a right angle and headed up the hill into the forest. Mama, up to the challenge, followed at full bore.

Max also pivoted and ran to the cabin faster than a humming-bird to a nectar laden flower. Crashing through the front door, he grabbed his Winchester 1894 rifle, chambered a load and high-tailed it back down the path.

He hadn't gone very far when he stopped short and saw mama and baby's hind ends as they clambered their way to the lake.

Once they were out of sight he called for Jed. Silence. He listened for any rustling in the bushes. He called again, this time forming a funnel around his mouth with his hands. Still nothing. Fearing the worst, he hurried back to the cabin for cloth bandages.

With heavy heart and panting like old Jed, he bent over and rested his hands on his knees. He waited to catch his breath before he climbed the steps. Ready to gather whatever may be left of his beloved dog, Max lifted his head and put one foot on a riser. There, blocking the front door, lay Jed. His chest heaved, tail wagged, and saliva dripped from his dangling tongue. Jed pulled himself up to all fours and met Max.

Max sat his rifle down and examined his faithful protector.

Except for twigs caught in his tail, mud on his belly and very wet ears, Max couldn't find a mark on him.

"Oh, Jed, you crazy hound. I guess this makes us even. I rescued you from the Anderson's shed and you rescued me from that maternal bear. Thank you." Max hugged Jed and promised him an extra helping of bacon for dinner. Minus the grease.

Max held the door for Jed, then turned toward Emeline's cabin. Her porch lantern glowed.

Chapter 6

The long trip back to Eden Lake from Portland afforded Max time to think; perhaps too much. As he watched the passing panorama, he realized his life flitted away as quickly. June would be upon him in a few weeks. His dear friends' visit must take precedence over everything else.

"The field of medicine is making strides toward cancer treatment." Dr. Thompson's words echoed in Max's mind. "Paul Ehrlich developed what he called a 'magic bullet' in '97, but we're not sure how this treatment works. Or even if it does work in every case. Surgery for breast cancer has been successful since 1880. Thankfully Roentgen's discovery of the x-ray technology in '96 led to radiation cancer treatment in '99. But we have no data if radiation would be the best for your diagnosis. I suggest the first step would be exploratory surgery on that lump and find out what we're dealing with."

My diagnosis. Why does he make it sound like I'm special?

"We could subject you to a few radiation treatments. Then monitor your progress. You would have to stay in Portland. Perhaps one month. I don't think we should take chances and wait too long."

Not willing to take chances? What chance had he at longevity without any treatment? Then again the mortality rates were discouraging at this point.

"We could schedule the surgery for June or July. I wouldn't go longer if I were you."

June or July? His friends would be here. What kind of a host skips out on his company? What would Ernest think if he arrived to find a note nailed to the cabin door: "Gone to Portland — Be back in August — Make yourself at home." No. He would delay the surgery. Jesus healed when He was on earth. Max believed the Lord was the same yesterday, today and forever, as he read in the Bible. He would trust and believe God.

The seriousness of his situation weighed heavy on his mind. Both his parents died of cancer. His mother before her fortieth birthday and his father barely fifty years old. He felt destined to follow in their footsteps. Thirty-four now, he was dangerously close to his mother's death age. Yes, he would have to trust and believe God for a miracle. Max closed his eyes for a rest. The constant rhythm of the horses clip-clops and the warm stuffy atmosphere of the coach lulled Max to sleep.

"Welcome home, Mr. Sullivan. How's the vacation in Portland? Take in any plays?" Max stretched his arm to grab Joel's hand. He felt sorry for this teenager who longed for adventure.

"Thanks for the greeting, Joel," Max paused. "Let me breathe the clear mountain air. Six hours, crammed in a stage coach with five other passengers makes for stuffed quarters. We did a thirty minute lay-over in Gresham and another ten minutes in Sandy. My legs thanked me for the stretch." Max inhaled deeply and slowly exhaled, then glanced at his beloved Mt. Hood.

"You should see our mountain from the city. Looks much smaller from there. I walked around mostly. Beautiful town, built right by the Willamette River. Makes it easy for ships to come and go with their cargo. Walk with me to the Mercantile and I'll buy you a soda." Max grabbed his satchel. "How's old Jed?"

"Ah, he's a great dog, Mr. Sullivan." Joel limped beside Max. "You can leave him with me any time you want. Maybe one day my folks will let me have a dog. If they do, I hope he's just like Jed. I left him with Miss Greene."

They climbed the steps and entered the Merc., the nickname the town folk called the store-post office-cafe.

"Max, you're home." Miss Greene scooted around the counter. Max held his ground as her portly figure barreled toward him with open arms. "I missed you." Her hug brought back memories of that mama bear he almost tangled with. A true bear hug.

"Here," reaching her hand in the jar of cookies. "You lost weight again. Have two." She thrust two large molasses cookies his way. "Sorry about the hug. I couldn't resist."

"Miss Greene, I was going to say you haven't changed in the two weeks I've been gone. But I'd be wrong. You've got to stop eating so many cookies." Her quick smile and hearty laughter reminded Max how good it felt to be home.

"Now if I did that, I'd be as skinny as you. Then no one would recognize me. That'd be no fun at all."

Max shook his head and couldn't help but chuckle with her.

"Seriously though, I read a scripture on the stage coach and have been considering how to apply it to my life. 'Do you not know that your body is a temple of the Holy Spirit who is in you, whom you now have from God, and that you are not your own? Miss Greene, I'm concerned about your health. I want you around for a long time. How about we make a commitment to each other to take better care of these bodies?"

Miss Greene scrunched her eyes and tilted her head back. "Max, I'll consider your words. The Holy Spirit has a lot more room in my body for roaming than He does yours. Ask me again next time you're in. Now, what can I get you?"

"Joel and I will have one of your delicious ice cream sodas. And Joel will have a cookie as well."

Max heard a whimper from the back room. Miss Greene scurried to the storeroom and in a flash Jed bounded into the store, tail wagging so hard he lost his balance and toppled at Max's feet.

"Good to see you too, boy." Max knelt beside Jed and scrubbed him down from head to out-of-control tail.

With treats in hand, the two friends found an empty bench in the shade. "How's this, Joel?"

Max had forgotten about teenagers' hollow legs. Joel's soda seemed to vanish in seconds. He handed a cookie to the youth who devoured the morsel in an instant.

"Now Joel, to answer your question. No plays, but I spent time exploring Portland; a day at the zoo, another day at the Art Association and the parks. They built a fine City Hall and Union Station for train travel in '96. Some days I passed the time on a bench in the train station and watched passengers. I would have liked to ask a few of the travelers where they were from and where they were going. An interesting mix of people." Max finished his soda.

"I marveled at what they call horse-drawn streetcars. They've switched to electric cars now as well as electric street lamps. Wonder if Eden Lake will ever get power from water up here. Did you get the postcard I sent?"

"I did, Mr. Sullivan. Thanks for thinking of me. Great to see where you were staying. Anything else? How about the night life?" Joel's curiosity grew.

"Oh, a few baseball games and some evenings at the public

house. Great fun to hear the local gossip and get a taste of the big city life. Every night the piano player plunked out the same tune. I hear a great success back east. When the chanteuse sang, all the ladies cried. "A Bird in a Gilded Cage" was the title of the ditty. Someone mentioned this ballad had sold more than two million copies. I agree, a mighty pretty tune, but I felt sorry for the ladies. They couldn't stop crying. Called it a tear-jerker. Anyway, it's good to be home." Max grasped Joel's empty soda glass and headed back to the Merc.

"Delish, as ever, Miss Greene. Now if I could get my mail. Joel's got my wagon ready and Jed's perched in the seat. I'm tired from that trip."

"I've got it right here." Miss Greene produced a bundle secured with twine. "It won't be long now before your friend from Scotland arrives and your sweet thing from Chicago, too. Is her friend gonna stay also?"

"Just three more weeks and Ernest will be here. Maggie comes the week after and her friend, Nellie, will arrive a few days later. This will be a grand time. It may be a bit crowded in my cabin, but Ernest and I will bunk down on the porch. I'm praying for no rain."

"We've had lovely weather while you were gone. I'm going to plant some vegetables in the next few days. I'll ask the Lord for the gift of forecasting. T'would be nice to predict the weather," chuckled Miss Greene.

"Did you know the people in Portland use our Mt. Hood to predict the weather? They say if the mountaintop is covered with a cloud, or a hood, it will rain. If the clouds form a collar around her, we can expect fair weather. To me it doesn't matter. I love Eden Lake any day."

Max tipped his hat good-bye to Miss Greene and Joel, then climbed in the wagon. Jed panted and wagged his tail. "Good to be going home, huh boy?"

During a quiet ride to his cabin, Max continued to rehearse Dr. Thompson's words. He weighed the pros and cons of telling his friends about his illness. But in the end, he decided not to. No need to worry them and it would definitely spoil their vacations. He anticipated a joyous time and hoped that nothing would sabotage their days together.

Max unhitched the horses and led them into the stable. Then filled their feed troughs and water buckets, grabbed his satchel and approached the porch steps. A haze above a heap on the bench drew his attention. Hard to see clearly as the sun dipped farther behind the Cascades. Max caught a whiff of a foul odor that grew stronger as he climbed the steps. A horde of flies buzzed around the lump. He reached for his red mail scarf to tie over his nose, but the hook was empty. His dusty neckerchief would have to do.

Max withdrew a match from his coat pocket and lit the porch lantern. The glowing light shone on the object of disgust. Three young red foxes in assorted stages of decomposition. The maggot colonies told Max they had been dead at least four days. And from the gouges in the foxes' sides, hawks must have partaken a few meals. Max struggled to stifle a gag reflex.

"Jed, no boy. Stay back." Max pointed to the other side of the porch. "Go lay down." Jed cowered, then laid down with his front paws over his nose.

Max hurried to the stable, found an old gunny sack and some rags. He grabbed a shovel and returned to the rotting flesh. Sliding the shovel under the heap proved a difficult task. One or more of the carcasses flopped on the porch leaving a trail of maggots. Max's maneuvering with the shovel improved as he gathered one fox at a time and plunged each into the sack. Max then used the rags to corral wayward larva and tossed them in the sack as well. The flies continued to enwrap his head demanding their just-desserts.

With a firm grip on the gunny sack, Max hurried off the porch. One hand held the bag and shovel, the other grabbed his lantern. He ventured deep into the woods. Jed trudged close be-hind. He found a good spot with soft dirt and dug a deep hole. Then dropped the sack in and covered the remains. He pushed a small trunk of a dead tree on top and hustled back to the cabin.

"I'll clean the shovel, bench, and porch off in the morning, Jed. Right now, I need some sleep. Miss Greene and her Mr. Mole-ch will have to wait until tomorrow. Let's check the mailbox and then be off to slumberland."

Max replaced the porch lantern. He unlatched and raised the mailbox lid. As he reached inside for the red scarf to hang it back on its hook, he felt a small box.

Max read the writing on the lid. "I thought you could use a pick-me-up after your trip. Emeline." He glanced across the lake. A lamp burned in her cabin window. He unlatched the front door, put his satchel inside and lit another lantern. As he blew out the porch lantern, the light went out in Emeline's cabin.

"Come on in, Jed. First thing is to scrub my hands until possi-

bly I wash some skin off as well as the foul odor and contamina-
tion from those poor foxes. Then we'll see what Emeline brought."

Disinfecting complete, Max opened Emeline's box to discover
four popovers. A small folded paper rested on them. "Waited until
I knew you'd be home. Baked today. Enjoy."

What should he make of her? Was she being friendly? A good
neighbor? Or did she have an ulterior motive? And how could she
get these into the mailbox with such a foul smell from the foxes?
She didn't even mention them.

"Oh, well. Jed, I say we call it a night. No more thinking.
Quaker biscuits for breakfast. For now, only sweet dreams of Maggie. Won't be long, boy." He rubbed Jed's ears one more time, blew
out the lantern and collapsed into bed.

Chapter 7

A good night's rest was exactly what the doctor ordered. Max awoke refreshed. Mentally he listed his activities for the day; two mouth-watering biscuits and coffee, mail would come next, then cleaning that disgusting mess from his porch. Who did Molech think he was leaving more dead animals? The time had come to use his mystery solving talents. This could be his next published story — "Find Molech."

"Good morning, Jed. Here, go out the side door. The smell won't be quite as bad. Bark when you return." Max opened the door and Jed scampered into the woods. The hound seemed to exert extra effort to mark his territory, probably due to the morbid invasion on the porch last night.

Max allowed his Bible to flop open on the table. Reading the first passage that caught his attention had become part of his morning ritual. As he leaned on the table he read, "Humble yourselves, therefore, under the mighty hand of God, that He may exalt you at the proper time, casting all your anxiety upon Him, because He cares for you. Be of sober spirit, be on the alert. Your adversary, the devil, prowls about like a roaring lion, seeking someone to devour. I Peter 5:6-8."

Humble, he understood. Alcohol rarely crossed his lips. But that part about the devil prowling like a roaring lion searching for his next meal worried Max. Lions are sneaky. Cagey. Crafty. Not like a mama bear who simply charges ahead creating a thunderous noise in her wake. He'd seen cougars stock their prey. With no face-to-face experience with the devil, Max determined to heed God's Word and keep vigilant — on the alert.

After a bite of Emeline's delicious biscuits and slurp of coffee, Max riffled through his mail. The bills were set aside. A reminder about his doctor's appointment. *Late with that one.* A letter from his publisher. Max hoped they hadn't rejected his Scotland story. He needed money for this friends visit.

Dear Mr. Sullivan,

Loved your story about the murderer in Scotland. Hard to fathom a son would kill his step-mother, ship his father off to an insane asylum and plan to kill again out of greed for the family manor. We assumed most of the story was fabricated only loosely based on a real scenario. The edition will be out next week. We will send you your usual complementary issue. Please find remuneration enclosed.

We're collecting stories based on things that go bump in the night. You know, ghouls, goblins, and the like. Some items have come across our desk referring to a Bigfoot that's supposed to live in your area. Make up something wild and send our way.

Sincerely.

Blackwood Publishers, Blackwood Magazine

Something wild? Absolutely. But only if he discovered hard evidence about this Molech character. Without proof, his publisher would assume the story wasn't true. While they accepted out-of-the-ordinary tales, they required a nougat of truth. Scotland's escapade was complete truth. Just hard to believe. This time he'd write a sensational story about dead animals, missing residents, a man and his dog bigger than life.

A scratch at the door distracted Max. Time to let Jed in.

"Jed, how about you and I do some sleuthing today? I'm going to clean the porch, then we'll search for clues about this Molech fella. Maybe interview him for my next story. Sound all right?" Jed whimpered and lay down on his bed by the cookstove. His actions told Max he wanted nothing to do with cleaning the porch. "Yeah, I'll wake you when I'm done."

Cleaning and disinfecting the porch and bench filled the morning. Max fed the horses then he and Jed were ready for their adventure. He glanced at Emeline's. No light shone through the windows. No sign of Beelzebub. And no sign of any movement outside. Maybe his binoculars would help. Emotions tugged on his heart as he turned his face skyward. "Lord, you've got to help me here. Keep me focused on Maggie. Please?"

Max checked his sidearm, slid a box of cartridges in his jacket pocket and grabbed his trusty '84 Winchester rifle. As he closed his cabin door he inhaled deeply. "The odor is gone, Jed. Only clean mountain air for our lungs."

The first time Molech had visited, he left by walking southward. He may have gone the same way after depositing those poor foxes on his porch. Max and Jed moved carefully examining the ground for any signs of activity.

"Look, there, Jed. Large boot prints along with a big dog's paw marks. Your turn to prove your worth as a hound dog. Sniff away, boy. Get the scent and let's do some tracking."

Jed lowered his head to the oversized boot impressions and paw prints. His sniffer worked overtime as he captured a scent. Sprinting four or five prints ahead and then back to Max, he emitted a yap, wagged his tail and led the way. He had the scent.

"Stay close, boy. If we encounter Molech and his dog I want you near enough in case that beast attacks."

They followed the tracks for a half mile, then the scent veered off the road and into the woods. This would be tough for old Jed. A heavy covering of salal bushes and bracken ferns made tracking difficult. They followed a narrow path. Finding deer scat, Max assumed the four legged beauties were responsible for such a skinny walk-way. Jed's nose remained low to the ground. No hesitation on his part, so Max felt confident Molech used the same path.

Max pivoted to get his bearings. With the road home now a slit of brown, he knew the deeper they went into the woods the more likely they could lose their way. A trail of the pathfinder plant lay beside the broken ground cover. Anyone hiking uncharted forests searched for the heart shaped green leaf that hid a silver underside. "Thank you, Lord for Your incredible creation." He used his foot to turn over a leaf every few feet exposing the silver heart. "These will guide us out, Jed."

The woods became denser, and Max, venturing into a part of the Cascades he didn't frequent, felt uneasy. Jed seemed to loose the scent. He jutted from side to side, scurried into the forest, then returned to Max, head down.

"That's all right Jed. I'm not familiar with this area either. Maybe we should head back." Max tilted his head skyward. "It can't be more than three o'clock yet the sky is darkening."

Jed froze, his hair bristled as he pointed toward the darkest section of the woods and growled. Max swung his rifle into ready position, chambered a load and took aim. Stomach tied in knots, heart pounded, his neck hair matched Jed's.

Something's out there. A crack of breaking branches on his left then on his right. Max faced each sound with rifle poised. An ominous atmosphere filled the dense forest as a sudden wind blew tree branches and sword ferns. Fog entered the woods. The darkness became a shroud that covered everything visible to Max. Definitely time to leave.

Petrified, afraid to turn his back on whatever possessed the woods, the letter from his publisher flashed through his mind. Bigfoot. Was there really such a creature? If so, he should stand his ground, aim well and put the myth to rest.

The wind increased and thrust a sulfur smell into Max's nostrils. Molech. The darkness and fog overwhelmed Max. He had to escape now. Anything out there could be on top of him before he had a chance to fire. He hated running from a battle, but this was one he wanted to live through. He had little chance if he remained.

"Come on, Jed. We're leaving." He took a few steps backward. That would never do. Too much to trip over. He turned and hunted for the pathfinder's silver leaves. Securing his rifle to his chest he traveled at a fast clip down the path. Another loud snap captured his attention. He halted, swung around and aimed his rifle. Nothing there.

Jed pushed hard against the back of Max's legs and barked. Max turned and tried to take a step, but Jed prevented him.

"Jed, what are you doing? We need to get out of here. Stop blocking the path. Move, boy."

The hound would not budge and pushed even harder on Max's legs. Immobilized, Max was infuriated. He aimed his foot to kick Jed, but knew from experience this was the dog's way of protecting him.

Fingers of fog reached out to Max and the rustling bushes magnified.

"Show me what's wrong, Jed. We can't stand still." Jed moved slowly to the side of the path away from Max. Nose pointed down and eyes focused on Max, he whined and whimpered. Max squatted to the ground and noticed something under the crushed blades of grass. He carefully moved them out of the way and saw the object of Jed's concern. A Victor coil spring animal trap sat square in the middle of the path, loaded for the kill. Max plunged a downed branch into the base striking the distinctive "V". The jaws of the trap snapped shut breaking the limb in two.

He hugged Jed. "I don't remember that being here before. We would have seen it. Yet the silver pathfinder leaves indicate we're going the right way. I'll give you a proper thank you when we get home. For now, let's high-tail it out of here."

Max picked up the trap then he and Jed sped down the path. When they reached the road Max scanned the woods for any movement. The sun brightened the forest. Max felt he had left a foreign world. No wind. No noise. As calm and serene as when they started their journey.

"Let's go home, boy. I feel the need to read this morning's verse again and cast my anxiety upon the Lord. I felt as nervous as a fledgling plummeting to the ground."

Jed led the way back to the cabin. Max tucked his rifle under his arm, removed his hat and scratched his head. He glanced into the woods. The weight of the animal trap in his left hand was a grim reminder of what could have been. Part of the branch still clutched securely in the jaws.

"Something's not right here. I know what we saw and the scent you picked up from those prints was real. And this trap. I sure didn't see it on our way in. One of us would have stepped in it. Jed, we may have an honest-to-goodness mystery in our quaint town of Eden Lake. Time to jot more notes for my next mystery story. Bacon, eggs and biscuits for dinner sound good?" Jed barked and the two buddies meandered back home. Max continued to turn around every few steps in case Mama bear, Bigfoot or Molech appeared.

So good to see the cabin. Still quiet behind them, Max relaxed his grip on his rifle. A cup of hot coffee and a sit on the porch waited. Time to drink in the beauty of Eden Lake and fill his lungs with the scent of wild flowers, not sulphur.

"Hi there. Welcome home." Emeline sprung off the porch bench, flew over the steps and sashayed beside Max before he could swallow. "I've been waiting for you. Wanted to know if you liked my Quaker biscuits. If you do, I'll make more."

"Yes, I did. Thank you. And yes, they were delicious. And no, you don't need to make me any more. That was thoughtful of you and made a wonderful breakfast this morning."

"Where are you coming from? A hike with your dog there? And why are you carrying an old rusty trap? With a stick in it? Do you collect old things?" She paused long enough to scan Max's body. "You lost weight in Portland. No good restaurants, huh? And why are you shaking?"

"Emeline, do you ever slow down? You're like a woodpecker. A person starts to respond to the first blast and another is right on it's heels."

"Here, let me carry the trap for you and then I'll be quiet."

Max handed her the corroded torturous device. When they reached the porch, he unlatched the door.

"Want to come in?"

"No, thank you. I'll wait right here. Where do you want me to put this thing?" Emeline wrinkled her nose and scrunched her eyes as she raised the trap in the air.

"Over in the corner would be fine. I'll put my gun away, wash up and be right out. Would you like some coffee?"

"No thanks. A glass of water would be nice though."

What to do? While Max scrubbed his hands he imagined washing this young elf out of his life. She showed up so unexpectedly and always threw him off-kilter. She seemed to dominate every conversation. Maybe from a need to control. And a controlling female did not fit into his life, now or ever.

"Here's your water." He handed a glass to her then purposely stood across from the bench and leaned against the railing.

"Don't you want to sit here beside me? Might help your shaking."

"No, this is fine."

Emeline jumped up. "Then I'll stand beside you."

"Please Emeline. It's easier to talk to you facing each other."

Disgruntled, Emeline returned to the bench.

"Sorry. I didn't mean any harm. You've been gone two weeks and I missed having someone to talk to. Well, all right, I missed you." The sparkling light left her eyes. A heavy frown furrowed her brow.

Max drank his coffee, sighed, and mustered a no timid-and-shy attitude.

"Emeline, I'm sorry. I didn't mean to make you sad. It's been a difficult two weeks. Today has not been easier. Do you mind if I ask you some questions?"

She perked up. "Anything at all. Ask away."

"I had a visitor after I got back from Scotland. A mountain man and his vicious dog. He said his name was Frank Molech. Do you know him, or maybe know of him?"

"Molech, huh. And a mountain man, you say." She drank some water then continued. "No, I haven't seen anyone around here. I thought you and I were the only ones with cabins up this way. Most evenings I sit on the porch. The only smoke I've seen comes from your cabin. Even on my walks around the lake and exploring into the woods, I've seen no signs of another human being."

No need to describe Molech if she hadn't seen anyone. Next question.

"From your note, you must have left the biscuits in my box yesterday. Did you see anything on the porch?"

"Not a thing. Oh, some small branches and leaves. We had a

terrific wind storm a week ago. I picked them off for you. Wanted your homecoming to be a pleasant one. Didn't want you thinking about a mess on the porch to clean up first thing back."

"Nothing on the bench?"

"No, other than some leaves that I brushed off. These are curious questions. Why are you asking?"

"I've had some strange experiences lately. Jed and I tracked the sulphur smelling mountain man into the woods today and almost stepped in that trap. There's something strange deep in the forest. Scared us so much I believe even my ears were shaking. I'm better now though."

"Okay, you've explained about Molech. Now tell me why the concern about your porch."

"The first time he came he brought two dead possums. When I got home last night, there were three decomposing foxes on that bench."

Emeline leaped to her feet and studied the bench.

"No, you won't find anything. I cleaned and disinfected this morning."

She joined him by the railing. "Clean or not, I'm not sitting where some dead animals were."

Max faced Mt. Hood. "I love it here, Emeline. I'm glad you're in the cabin across from me. Kind of comforting knowing another human being lives up here. But I'm also concerned about your well-being with this crazed man living in the Cascades. Maybe if he hasn't visited you yet, he won't. Keep your rifle loaded and handy in case the need arises."

"I'll do that. You know, Max, you do look thinner than when you went to Portland. Maybe you should see a doctor. Possibly you're sick and hallucinating."

Max knew this conversation had come to an end. If she had no experience with strange occurrences, she wouldn't be able to understand or empathize with him.

"Thanks for the advice, Emeline. If you don't mind, I'd like to lay down for a bit. Are you walking home again?"

"No, I left Beelzebub behind your stable. Hope you don't mind. I found some nice green grass for him to munch. You get some rest. I'll see you another day."

Emeline handed her glass to Max, then skipped off the porch to the stable. In a few minutes she and Beelzebub passed Max, waved and disappeared down the road.

Max found a pad of paper on his kitchen table. He jotted

down thoughts about Molech, his dog, the dead animals and their tracking experience. A whopper of a story. Made to order for Blackwood Publishers.

Chapter 8

First stop, the Feed and Seed store. Bess and Kate's oats and alfalfa were mighty low. These two horses had served Max well these past five years. Perhaps some apples and carrots from the Merc for a special treat. All of God's creation needs loving care like a shepherd tends his flock. The love Max felt from his Savior overwhelmed him. Struggling with his own self-esteem issues, the long road to confidence shortened as he continued his daily devotion practice.

"Good morning, Fred. A hundred pounds each of oats and alfalfa. While you're loading the wagon, I'm off to the Merc. Move the wagon out of your way if you need to. See you later."

"Sure thing, Max. Don't eat too many of that lady's cookies." The owner of the Feed and Seed, tipped his hat.

The Merc seemed unusually busy. Residents waited to pay their bill as they balanced arm loads of food. Miss Greene stood behind the counter. She frantically jotted prices on a notepad. *Poor Miss Greene, still not accustomed to using her cash register.* The technology of the 1890s remained a challenge for her.

"Hold on now. I'm working these fingers to the bone keeping you folks happy. There's only one of me. Have some patience."

"Miss Greene, you've had that cash register for a year. We thought you'd know how to use it by now." A woman placed her food basket on the floor while her two young children clutched her skirt. "Things would go much faster if you did."

Max sensed frustration from this customer as well as several others. Some tapped a foot, others used short terse sentences with their fidgety children. Obviously something besides food was on their minds. Miss Greene's sluggishness added to the tense atmosphere. Max slid behind the counter next to Miss Greene.

"Can I help?"

"Can you? My, oh my, you're a sight for sore eyes. That contraption," she motioned toward the cash register, "has too many buttons. I don't know which to push first. I've got change in the drawer, but forget how the stupid thing opens."

They worked as a team and had the customers out the door in record time. Miss Greene poured a glass of water for Max and herself, then plopped down in a chair.

"Don't know what I would have done without you. With one or two customers I'm fine, but give me a line up like this morning and its like riding a carousel in my mind. Sure miss the barter system. So much simpler back then." She raised her glass high. "A toast to my knight in shining armor. Well, okay, plaid shirt, jeans and leather boots. But close enough for me."

"You're very welcome." Max clinked her glass. "One of my jobs in Portland was soda jerking. My boss purchased one of the first National Cash Registers. Then he gave me the responsibility to master the contraption and teach the other employees. I enjoy mechanical devices, so I mastered what you see as a beast in no time. I'd be glad to give you a few lessons."

"Thanks, Max. That monster has been on the counter a good long time. One of these days I'll take out the owner's manual and practice when no one's around." Max chuckled, but Miss Greene did not join him.

"How about a stick of jerky as your reward?" She reached into the former cookie jar and retrieved a dried piece of venison.

"Miss Greene, you took my challenge seriously. No more cookies?"

"You, my young man, were the kick I needed to change very bad habits. I see all these happy families come and go from the Merc. I long for a family of my own. My age would prevent having children, but a husband would be nice. After you left that day, I looked in the mirror and realized I had gotten out of control with my eating. So, jerky now, instead of cookies. I buy it from old man Glover. He's always short on cash and has been curing venison each year for jerky. So we made a bargain. Jerky for staples. Bartering has been the backbone of civilization for hundreds of years. Don't see why we have to throw it out the window just 'cause technology wants to move in." She slapped the side of the cash register.

"I'm proud of you, Miss Greene. Great way to get back your girlish figure, snag a husband and help a needy man at the same time." Max ripped of piece of jerky off. "This is delicious."

"To be honest, I doubt my girlish figure will ever return. You see, I never had one. Always on the plump side. My mom called it 'good old Norwegian genes.' I called it 'fat.' But I haven't given up sweets yet. Too many little big-eyed kids traipse in here asking for a cookie. Can't disappoint them."

A quick scan around the shop revealed no cookie jar.

"Where do you keep them?"

"They're in the back room, on a high shelf that I can barely reach. I planned that so I would have to walk some extra steps and then stretch to reach them. Exercise before sugar. It might work. You know the 'out-of-sight, out-of-mind.' I debate with myself about how badly I really want a cookie. If I give in to temptation, at least some exercise comes first." Miss Greene ran her hands down the sides of her body. "That thin girl is in there somewhere." Her jolly laugh delighted Max.

"Why were so many people here at one time? Is there something happening I don't know about?"

"We got word there's talk in Sandy about building a Lutheran church. Only St. Michael's Catholic is there now. A meeting's being planned for all interested folk from the surrounding towns. Over half Eden Lake residents are Lutheran, so they're heading that way this afternoon. The meeting's tonight, but most plan to make it a mini-vacation. You know, a few days in the big city. If you call ninety-six people a big city." Miss Greene shrugged. "With the surrounding small lumber towns, the population swells a bit more. Always does a body good to have a change of scenery anyway."

"How can they do that? The mill runs twelve hour days, seven days a week?"

"When the owner and foreman are both Lutherans, they can close it for a few days. Now, what can I do for you?"

"Wondered if you had some apples and carrots for Bess and Kate. They deserve a treat. Then my mail and if you have some free time, questions."

Miss Greene vanished into the storeroom and returned with a basket of apples and bucket of carrots. Max relieved her of the heavy load and placed them by the front door. Gone in a flash she reappeared with his mail and a small package.

"Did your sweetie send you something? I see the package is from Chicago."

"Miss Greene, you're like a sponge, soaking up information about everyone and everything in Eden Lake. No, it's not from Maggie. I ordered the newest George Hill publication. This will be my evening read. "The Wizard of Oz" by L. Frank Baum. When

I'm done, I'll loan it to you if you like."

"A story about wizards? Why would I want to read something like that?"

"I read a great review of the book while in Portland and with another visit from Molech, we may have a wizard in our midst."

"Another visit, you say? How do you know?"

"There were three rather ripe fox carcasses on my porch when I arrived home from Portland. From the condition of the poor things they must have been there for some time."

"Max, he's out to get you, just like the Anderson's. I don't understand why though." Miss Greene refilled their water glasses. "Are you going after him?"

"I'd like to confront him. At least to discover where he lives. Jed and I tried to follow his trail into the woods, but lost it. I won't go into details. Let's just say we found no evidence of a cabin or camp. Only some pretty strange noises that frightened us enough to scramble back to the cabin in short order.

"I did some research in Portland and discovered that in 1847 a Paul Kane reported stories he had heard from native people. They believed there was a race of cannibalistic wild men living on the peak of Mount St. Helens across the Columbia River in Washington. They called them skoocooms and considered them to be supernatural. Wondered if they might have traveled down the Cascades and Molech is a remnant. That would explain the Anderson's sudden disappearance."

"Oh, Max, how disgusting." Miss Greene winched her face. "To think that could be true sets my skin to quivering." Miss Greene's ample size shook like soft-set gelatin.

"There's more. In 1840, a Protestant missionary named Elkanah Walter found stories of giants among the Native Americans living around Spokane. According to the stories, these giants lived on and around the peaks of mountains and stole salmon from fishermen's nets. We're a ways from the Columbia River, but a portion of these giants could have wandered to Mt. Hood. Then there's stories of other creatures about five feet tall that resemble apes. I'd like to confront Molech with this information. His reaction may give me a clue about who he is. Right now, it's all a mystery."

Miss Greene refreshed the water in Jed's bowl. He eagerly lapped the cool liquid, then laid down, nose on his front paws.

"Can we change the subject, Max. My goose-bumps have goose-bumps. I'm going to have nightmares if I don't fill my mind with something more spiritually positive. You mentioned you wanted to ask some questions. As long as they're not about Molech. He gives me the willies."

Max gulped some water then continued. "Emeline greeted me with her usual frivolity following our search for Molech. Our conversation centered on her knowledge of this strange man, dead foxes and a rusty animal trap. She denied even a twinge of understanding. It's hard for me to believe she didn't see, or smell, the corpses on my porch. Something's very amiss here. Now for my questions." Max pulled a stool up to the counter. "What do you know about Miss Toliver? Where is she from? Does she have any family? How about mail? When did she buy the cabin? Anything at all would be helpful."

Miss Greene scratched her head, then glanced at the ceiling in her usual 'let-me-think' pose.

"Well, I don't know where she's from. Don't know if she has any family. Never receives mail. Nor sends any that I'm aware of. Don't know if, or when, she bought that abandoned cabin. My goodness, Max, when I think hard about Emeline I realize I don't know much at all. But I do believe she loves you. There's a sparkle in her eye whenever she asks about you. She may be another mystery for you to unravel."

"I can't figure her, Miss Greene. There are times when I think she doesn't have a brain in that pretty little head of hers. Yet, she must have a keen sense of her surroundings. She displays no apprehension when she walks home from my cabin. With protective mama bears, cougars, bobcats and that itinerant wild man in the area, she seems to have no fear. She tells me she packs a gun, but I've never seen it or heard any target practice from the other side of the lake."

"Max, you're right." A twinkle in her eye. Her excitement increased. "I am like a sponge, soaking up bits of conversations. How about if I become your cohort? Whenever that sweet lady comes in I'll work the conversation around to her. Women love to talk about themselves. I'll store the juicy details up here," she tapped her head, "and report to you."

Max felt a rub on his leg. "Hi, Jed. Yes, I know. It is time to get our wagon and head home." He moseyed toward the door and stooped to pick up the treats for his horses.

"Max, didn't you hear me?" Miss Greene rounded the counter and drew close to Max as a customer entered. Then she whispered, "I want to help. Let me be, oh, what are they called? Yes, a private eye. I'll be careful. She won't suspect a thing."

"Thank you, Miss Greene for the offer. I didn't mean to be rude and not answer. I was thinking if your suggestion was a good idea. At times I wonder if Emeline is putting on a show, trying to convince me she's dense. Yet when we make eye contact it seems like she's working things out. Problem solving while already knowing the correct answer. You know, stringing me along. If you hear something worth passing on that would be fine. But please don't intentionally pry. I fear there's more to that woman than we can see."

Miss Greene squeezed his arm. "And you, dear boy, watch out for that Molech guy. He scares me."

"I will. Thanks again for the apples and carrots. Put it on my tab."

Max called Jed and the two buddies headed for the wagon and home.

Chapter 9

A dust cloud rose high above the trees signaling the coach's impending arrival. With clear blue skies, warm, but not hot, a beautiful afternoon in June welcomed Max's visitor. Elderly ladies tended to become nervous with a dog underfoot, so Max left Jed at the Merc.

Max noticed a young boy holding a sign, "Welcome Home, Dad." The boy's mother stood beside him switching weight from one foot to the other. Max smiled as he studied the young wife. With make-up a little over-done to his liking, she reminded him of a mannequin in the store windows in Portland; lots of rouge, powder and lipstick to accentuate facial features, and modeling the latest frock, with a perfect background scene. Advertising of the day whet the customers' appetites and imaginations. Max had recognized a longing look in the faces of the window shoppers. Yet he knew their pockets would be empty after purchasing necessities. Luxuries did not fit their lifestyle.

"Whoa, there." The driver yelled to his team, as he strained to pull the reins. "Whoa, now ladies. We're in Eden Lake and the trip's over." The horses halted right on their mark with the coach steps perfectly positioned above the wooden platform.

Joel scooted over to the door. He grabbed the handle and flung it open. The warm air from the cramped quarters blew on the teen's face. A smartly dressed gentlemen stepped out then held a hand to assist an elderly lady.

"Dad," the boy squealed. He dropped the homemade sign and ran with open arms. His mother picked up the fallen placard and tried to compose herself while father and son were reunited. Max noticed her gloved hands shake while she fussed with her hair one last time. Her husband raised his head from the top of the boy's head. The young couples' eyes met. The young man stood tall and released himself from his son's embrace. After a moment of hesitation, the two lovers hurried together. Their son plucked the sign from his mother's hand. Then the couples' arms enwrapped each other. Cognizant they were in public, the embrace was short lived. A tender scene indeed.

Max's imagination replaced the couple with himself and Maggie. How he longed to hold her tight and kiss her tender lips. Maybe she would be receptive to his forthrightness and his love reciprocated. For now, he lived vicariously through this young couple.

"Ah, hum. I say there Laddie, where's my greeting?"

The loud Scottish accent bellowed above the noise of the crowd.

"Ernest!"

"I'll take a hug and handshake. No kissy-kissy stuff," the robust Scotsman said.

Once greetings were exchanged, the two men, at arms' length, surveyed each other.

"Ernest, I dare say you've put on some weight. Not hiking much?"

"You're right, Max. My foot slipped from the stirrup dismounting one day. I fell on hard ground and broke my leg. Still have a bit of a limp. Mabel insisted I bunk with them in town while she played nurse. You remember her cooking?" Ernest slapped his hands on his belly. "Well, good food and little exercise equals a growing girth."

Ernest backed several steps. Max feared what would come next.

"Max. What happened to you? Where did you put the other half of yourself?"

"Have to eat my own cooking. No Mabel in Eden Lake." Max hoped that answer would suffice. "Let's get your bags, toss them in the wagon and, if you're not too tired, I'll buy you a treat at the Merc."

Max lifted the satchels into his wagon then led Ernest toward Miss Greene's. The two friends shared their lives on the way. They climbed the steps and waited for a customer, arms filled with parcels, to exit.

"Miss Greene, I want you to meet one of the dearest men you could ever know. This is Ernest McIntyre. Ernest, meet Miss Greene."

Was Max imagining sparks flying between these two? Is this love at first sight? As Ernest drew close to Miss Greene, she seemed to revert back to a school girl. Her face flushed. She timidly held out her hand. Gone was the forthrightness that usually exuded from this lady.

And Ernest. Max had never seen him so nervous. Ernest removed his tam o'shanter and crumpled the wool cap in his hands. Then he dabbed the sweat across his brow with his thistle embroidered handkerchief he kept in his jacket pocket.

The sound of Max's voice brought Jed from the back room. Wagging his tail, Jed stopped abruptly.

"Jed, meet Ernest. Ernest, meet my faithful dog, Jed." Jed sniffed Ernest's pant legs and boots.

"Ernest, this is my dog, Jed." Miss Greene's presence captivated Ernest's attention. "Ernest, this is Jed, my dog," Max shouted.

Miss Greene and Ernest were strangers no longer. They couldn't take their eyes off each other. *What's going on here?* Max cleared his throat.

"Ah, hum. Might there be a Scotsman in our midst? Might he have a friend named Max?" Time to break up this interlude. He drew close to Miss Greene. "May we have a glass of water, Miss Greene?"

"What? Water? Oh, yes, where's my manners. I'll be right back." Miss Greene said although she didn't move.

"Ernest, this amazing coon dog has saved me from danger more than once."

Ernest glared at Max, then bent down to pet Jed. "Sorry, old fella. Guess the trip was too much."

"Miss Greene, two chocolate fudge sundaes and water, if you please."

Miss Greene's eyes were glazed over. "Miss Greene, may we have two chocolate fudge sundaes?" Max repeated with emphasis.

Miss Greene blinked. "I'm sorry, what did you want? Oh, yes, two chocolate fudge sundaes. Coming right up." Her eyes glued to Ernest with that silly puppy-love grin spread across her face. Miss Greene stepped backwards and bumped into the counter.

"Ops, better watch where I'm going." She covered her mouth and chuckled. Max hoped she would remember to put ice cream in the dish.

"Well, Ernest," Max nudged Ernest with his elbow. "I'm surprised at you. A grown man, yet you acted like a school boy. You just met her. You don't know anything about Miss Greene."

Max led the way outdoors and found a bench.

"That's where you're wrong, Laddie. I know she has dark brown eyes like quicksand that held me fast. I know her sweet smile melted this Scots' heart like butter on Mabel's fresh-from-the-oven cinnamon rolls. I know she is gentle beyond measure like a sleeping bairn. And the most important of all: she's not married." Max felt an elbow nudge his side. He joined Ernest in a jovial laugh.

"Ernest, it's so good to have you here. Not only for your friendship, but for your wise counsel." Max allowed a bite of ice cream to melt in his mouth. "I've met a couple of people who live in the woods close to my cabin. Well, one lives in my area. The others' locale has been elusive. If you're willing to join me on an adventure, I would be most grateful."

"We made a good team in Scotland, why not here as well? Tell me about these two puzzles on the way to your cabin. Can't wait to see Eden Lake."

By the time they reached the cabin, Max had filled Ernest in on his encounters with Emeline and Molech.

"Why, Max, you didn't tell me what a beautiful lake you lived by. And yes, I do see the similarities to Loch Morlich back home. Can we fish tomorrow?"

"Absolutely. For now, you can unpack and freshen up before dinner. A quiet sit on the porch after our meal."

Ernest breathed in the crisp mountain air. "Smells like sweet cedar."

"Why don't you walk down to the lake while I take care of the horses," Max suggested.

With the wagon unloaded, Max dumped a few apples and carrots in the troughs for the horses to munch on. He closed the stable door and joined Ernest by the lake.

"Incredible view, isn't it. I often stand here for what seems like hours and thank the Lord for the eyes to see His beautiful creation. I never thought I would live in such a magnificent part of the Northwest."

"Max," Ernest pointed. "Is that Emeline's cabin across the lake? Looks empty to me. Has she gone somewhere?"

"Yes, that's her cabin. She never tells me what she's doing only that she waits for me to come home." Max picked up a rock and skipped it across the lake. "She's spooky, Ernest. I hope you'll have some insights."

"Well, I have one insight from the little you've told me. I believe she may have come here to escape something or someone. Or perhaps she has another purpose and you may be her target, for whatever reason, I don't know. And now a straight question for you and I demand a straight answer."

Max gazed at Ernest. He had never seen his friend so serious. "Do you love her?"

Max lost his footing and tripped over Jed. The dog's yelp echoed across the lake.

"Love her? How could I possibly love her? You know I love Maggie. This Emeline. I wish she would move back to wherever she came from."

"Max, I sense something about her nature unnerves you. Confrontation is difficult for all of us, but I believe you need to confront her. Find out why she's wooing you, if you think that's what it is. You stood up to MacLaren in Scotland. You can stand up to Emeline. Let's have some prayer time after dinner and seek the Lord's guidance and strength in this matter."

Max put his arm around Ernest's shoulders as they walked to the cabin. Jed pranced ahead, then stopped at the bottom of the steps and growled.

"What's the matter, boy? More visitors?"

As Max drew near he saw a mound of several pelts heaped on the top step. Then the stench filled his nostrils. Raccoons. The third animal Molech had left the Anderson's.

"Poor things. From the foul smell, they must have been placed here after I left for town. Well, Ernest. Welcome to my bizarre cabin in the woods. This Eden is not quite paradise. I'll get a shovel and gloves to carry them to their final resting spot."

Ernest carried the shovel while Max slipped on his gloves and picked up the raccoons by their tails.

"One, two, three, four little furry buddies. No signs of violence on their bodies. Well, Ernest, you are now involved in the mystery of Eden Lake, or "Where's Molech?" I wish one time he would come while I'm here."

Breaking a trail deep into the woods, Ernest dug a large hole for the critters final resting place. Max carefully placed them at the bottom and Ernest covered the carcasses with sod. They returned to the cabin in silence. Max placed the shovel and gloves by the bottom step.

"Ernest let's go inside to talk. I feel that someone constantly watches me. Listening to my conversations, even with Jed."

Max's hand reached for the latch, then noticed the red flag was missing. Opening his mailbox, he found a small parcel. A handwritten note on the lid read: "Thought you and your friend from Scotland might enjoy some brownies. Emeline."

Shooting a glare toward her cabin, he wished she was here on the porch. How he longed to have an in-depth conversation and find out her intentions. The superficial, meaningless dribble that passed between the two of them always ended as if in a dark alley with no end in sight.

"Well," said Ernest, "I hope you didn't make dessert."

Max gathered the satchels from the side porch and showed Ernest to his room. Then he pulled out a pot of stew he'd cooked earlier that day. Rousting the remaining coals in the cook stove, he added some kindling. The smell of bubbling stew filled the cabin. Max positioned two bowls opposite each other on the table, then added a basket of bakery rolls.

"Something smells delicious, Max." Ernest entered the living area. "Your cabin has a man's special touch. Did you build it yourself?"

"The main section of the cabin was here when I purchased it. I added the room on the side for an entrance to the stable. Use it mostly to change from muddy boots. Also helps to keep drafts out. Then I built the two bedrooms. This was an old trapper's shack, so he didn't need much space. I suppose gone too much to check his trap lines to care. Lastly, I added the sitting porch. There were only a few steps to the front door and I wanted a place to relax and enjoy the lake."

"I understand why you love it so much. I could live here too."

The two friends assumed their places and bowed their heads.

"Father," Max prayed, "thank you for bringing my dear friend, Ernest to Eden Lake. I pray you will give him insight into the strange happenings. Also please protect us from any danger. Bless this food to strengthen our bodies for your service. Amen."

The patter of Jed's front paw nails on the wood floor distracted Max. "Waiting for scraps, huh boy?"

"That was excellent stew, Max. Do you eat like this all the time?"

"I try to fix a hearty meal several times a week. With an abundance of fish and game, I do pretty well. Usually there's extra in case a friend stops by unexpectedly. Glad you liked it."

Ernest pushed his chair back from the table. "If that is true, then tell me why are you so thin? I suspect you weren't telling me everything in town. No one else here and we're good enough friends to share secrets. What is it, Max?"

Max rose and carried the dishes to the sink. "How about some coffee? Won't take long to brew a pot. Or would you prefer, tea?"

"I would prefer you sit yourself right back down and tell me what's going on." Ernest raised his voice. "Coffee and tea can keep but my concern grows by the minute. What's wrong, Max?"

Max added water to Jed's bowl, gave him a pat, then trudged to the table. He had difficulty facing his friend and kept his head bowed.

"I haven't told anyone what I'm about to tell you." Max gulped. "You must promise to never divulge this information to anyone. The right to share is mine and mine alone. Do you understand?"

"Yes, Max. I promise to keep your words to myself." Ernest paused. "Except for talking to the Lord, that is."

"I hadn't been feeling well for quite some time. A doctor comes to town every two weeks, so I stopped by his office. He gave me some medicine to take and I saw him again when he returned. Since I didn't feel any better after the two weeks, he set up an appointment with a specialist in Portland." Max refilled his water glass and drank slowly and deeply.

"A nice man who knows his stuff. He examined me and did some tests, then gave me more medicine. That was in February. I noticed a lump in my abdomen and returned in March feeling worse. Apparently the medicine had no effect. During my two week stay in Portland, the doctor did exploratory surgery removing some tissue from the lump. I explored the city for a week, then back to his office for the results. Ernest, I have cancer." Max swallowed more water. He glanced at Ernest for the first time since their conversation began. His friend's face was ashen, his brow furrowed.

"Did he give you more medicine? When do you see him again? Is there another doctor with more experience?" Ernest leaned on the table closer to Max.

"Yes. He gave me more medicine, but I think it's more like snake-oil. Just to keep me thinking it might do some good when I know it's a bunch of bunk. The pain lessens though when I take it, so maybe that's the good."

"Max, there must be something they can do. I can go with you to Portland and we can stay there until a solution is found."

"That's very thoughtful, Ernest and I do appreciate your offer. The doctor said they could open me up and remove the lump. Cancer treatment now includes radiation and surgery, but there would be no assurance they could get it all. Nor could he promise the radiation treatments would have a positive outcome. And I would have to spend several weeks, maybe a month or more in Portland. I told him I'd let him know if I changed my mind, but at that point I wasn't interested. I prefer to live out whatever days the Lord gives right here in my cabin by the lake."

"Max, you must do something. It sounds like you're giving up." Ernest's concern intensified.

"I am doing something, Ernest. I'm living in paradise; fishing, hiking, enjoying Jed and my friends, writing short stories and magazine articles. I'm content doing the things I love and, I believe, the Lord created me for this purpose. My life. Just as it is." Max rubbed his chin. "If He determines something else is better for me, then I'm in His hands. No radiation, no knife, no experiments. And, please, no pity. I need strong people around me. People, like you, who love the Lord and thrill in living each day for Him."

Silence filled the cabin. A few crackles from dying embers in the cook stove and Jed's dog-sleep groans were all that remained. Ernest pulled his chair beside Max, laid his hand on a shoulder and prayed for his dear friend.

"Thanks, Ernest. I've looked forward to your visit since we met back in Scotland. Let's agree to make wonderful memories. Now, if you don't mind, I'm worn out. Fish will be biting early tomorrow and I'm sure you're tired." Max pushed his chair back, checked the cook stove embers, then dragged himself to his bedroom.

"Good-night, Ernest."

"Good-night, Max."

Chapter 10

Max spotted Ernest on the porch, a mug of coffee in his hand and Jed by his feet.

"Sorry, Ernest, I don't usually sleep this late. Must have been extra tired from the excitement of your arrival. I'll get some coffee and join you."

Max filled his mug and grabbed the box of apple muffins he'd set aside for this morning.

"This is truly a beautiful lake, Max. I understand the Eden Lake name. It's a piece of paradise. I came out early this morning for some quiet time with the Lord." Max offered Ernest a muffin. "Thanks. They look delicious."

"I often have my morning devotions here on the porch," Max said as he decided which muffin to choose. "It's quiet with only the forest creatures to stir things up." Max finished a bite and blew in his mug of steaming coffee. "Thought we could read some scripture out in the boat while we wait for the fish to bite."

"Sounds fine." Ernest sipped from his cup, then placed it on a side table. "I'm concerned for you, Max. I've talked to the Lord about your illness and it just doesn't sit well with me that you're not going to do anything. If your doctor thinks you have a chance, why not take it? You're still young. Lots of time ahead. You need to ask Maggie to marry you and share this bit of paradise together."

The seriousness of Ernest's face read like a book cover. His friends' eyes were riveted on Max. Ernest's frown and crumpled brow spoke volumes.

"Ernest, I really appreciate your concern. I would love to marry Maggie." Max stopped abruptly.

"Maggie." His voice raised and an echo traveled back from the lake. "Maggie. Ernest, in my excitement yesterday, I completely forgot to tell you. Maggie is coming — coming to Eden Lake. In fact, she'll be here next week." He missed the table with his coffee cup and spilt the hot liquid on the porch. "Oh yes, Nellie also. The girls are staying in Portland for two days while Nellie has a job interview. Maggie mentioned she wanted to discover how the city had changed since she'd left. What do you think of that? We'll all be together again."

Max wrapped one arm around Ernest's shoulders and pulled his friend to him. Ernest's downcast demeanor changed as his eyes sparkled and a large grin brightened his face.

"That's wonderful, Max. You seem to have a knack of changing a serious discussion in a snap. We're going to have to work on your evasive nature. I'm old enough to be your father and I love you like a son, so don't be surprised if I chastise you when needed. You and Maggie belong together, but we have some bigger fish to fry before she and Nellie arrive." He motioned toward Emeline's cabin.

"Speaking of fish, if we don't get going their stomachs will be full of bugs and won't be much interested in our measly worms." Max gulped his remaining coffee.

He retrieved the fishing gear and handed Ernest the poles. Then Max whistled for Jed and in a flash the mutt scampered down to the lake and bounded in the boat.

Max baited the hooks while Ernest rowed.

"Jed, you hang over much farther you're gonna fall in. Get back, boy." Max wiped his hands on a towel. "He likes to try and catch fish in his mouth. He's been successful several times, but ended with a mouthful of water more often than a fish. He lets them go again, but sometimes he's actually fallen in. I keep this old towel to dry him off just in case."

Max stopped baiting the hooks when he noticed Ernest had the boat half way across the lake. No good fishing here.

"Wait, Ernest, we need to go back. Didn't realize you had rowed this far. The best fishing spot is over toward the bank." Max pointed.

"I'm curious, Max. Let's explore that cove by Emeline's cabin. We can cast our line and then read the Bible once we get there. I want to get as close as possible. Any young lassie in her right mind would still be in bed this time of morning. I hope to catch a glimpse when she comes out."

"Ernest, you're up to the challenge the very first day. All right then, I'm with you. Perhaps we shouldn't talk for a while if you want to sneak in close. You know how voices carry on a lake."

The two men continued in silence. With Ernest's back to the cabin, Max used hand motions to direct his rowing. The boat glided noiselessly across the smooth water. Even the oars were silent.

"Jed, lay still, boy." Max whispered. He could feel his heartbeat as they paddled nearer the bank. He motioned to Ernest to turn the boat parallel to shore. After the oars rested inside the craft, Max handed a pole to Ernest and the two, nonchalantly tossed their lines into the water.

Both men stared at the cabin. Max scanned the grounds around the run-down shack, but saw no sign of Beelzebub. No light from inside either. He craned his neck toward Emeline's dock. Her boat was gone.

"Good morning, you two. I don't think you'll have much luck catching anything here. You're too close."

Max jerked in his seat. "Emeline, where did you come from? We didn't see your boat on the lake."

"Oh, I have my ways. You know the saying 'quiet as the grave'? Well, I like to think I'm as quiet as the dead. One can hear things they're not supposed to hear and sidle close to people totally unawares. I consider this a gift." Her smile set Max on edge. That twinkle in her eye announced loud and clear mischief resided in her head.

"This must be your visitor from Scotland. Ernest, I believe. Welcome to Eden Lake. I'm Emeline Toliver. I'd hold out my hand to you, but afraid the boat might tip and I never did learn to swim."

"It's my pleasure to meet you, Miss Toliver." Ernest tipped his hat.

"Please, Emeline. Miss Toliver sounds so formal."

Max, still confused, demanded an answer.

"Emeline, gift or no gift, I want to know how you got along side so quickly. We would have heard you rowing toward us. Noise on lakes carry. Any little sound would reverberate this early in the morning."

Max felt strength in his being for the first time. Perhaps it was Ernest's presence that gave him the courage he lacked around Emeline. Or maybe because Maggie would arrive in a few days, Max wanted to push this young lady to confession time. The sun glared off his Bible. Max shut his eyes from the blinding light. *Thank You, Lord for reminding me of the strength in Your word.*

"Well, Emeline? I'm waiting for your explanation."

"My, my, aren't we demanding this morning? Did you get your coffee yet, Max? Maybe you ate too many sweets for breakfast and the sugar is irritating your disposition. Whatever the problem, I'm sure your buddy here can be of assistance." Max saw that gleam in her eye as she gazed at Ernest. He prayed that Ernest wouldn't get wrapped up in her delusion. He believed this man of faith could see through her veneer of womanly virtues.

"Thank you for your confidence in me, Emeline. I plan to assist Max whenever and however I can. And since I don't know how long I'll be staying at Eden Lake, I hope we can forego trivialities and delve to the heart of the matter. I, for one, will honor you with direct answers to any questions you may have of me, and I will expect the same from you. Now, will you answer Max's question? I'm also curious. How did you get here without us hearing you?"

Max noticed Emeline fidget with her skirt. Her mouth seemed to clench shut like an oyster protecting a beautiful pearl.

With her hand shading her eyes, she glanced upward. "Oh, my, I didn't realize how late the time. I tethered Beelzebub in the meadow over the hill. I must retrieve him and ride to town for an appointment this morning. Nice to meet you, Ernest."

Max grabbed for her boat. Out of reach. Her oars hit the water and the boat skimmed back to the dock.

"Emeline," Max called, "you haven't answered my question. Emeline." He cupped his hands around his mouth and yelled one last time. "Emeline."

The two men sat in silence as she rowed skillfully to the dock, threw a rope over a piling, climbed out and ran to the cabin.

"Well, Ernest, you've met Emeline. One of the mysteries of Eden Lake." Max shook his head. "I can't make her out. Not one iota. She seems sweet one minute and becomes a different woman the next. Any insights to share?"

"Max," Ernest removed his hat and scratched his head, "I have never, in all my years reporting for the newspaper, met a woman like her. Here I thought you changed the subject to meet your needs—but that lass. Why she doesn't even entertain the subject. She's one flighty lady, and I use the term loosely. My first impression is that she's no lady at all."

"What do you mean, no lady at all?" Max squinted his eyes as the sun crested the tree tops.

"I sense something deep inside her soul. Something either in her spirit or perhaps controlling her spirit. During one of my visits with Ramsay at Stuart Hall back home, we talked about his stay at the asylum. He described some of the patients he tried to befriend. Their mannerisms were not unlike Emeline's."

"In what way?"

"They could carry on a seemingly normal conversation and

then, totally out of the blue, their eyes appeared vacant and the sentences made no sense. Ramsay said this vacant state, as he called it, remained from a few seconds to several minutes. I noticed Emeline's eyes as you pressed her for the truth and again while she faced me and I demanded she answer your question. Her eyes glazed over and the color seemed to disappear. Remember her explanation of appearing so quickly without us noticing? A gift of being as quiet as the dead? Well, I've seen enough dead people in my line of work and I can tell you the color seems to leave their eyes when they die. It just disappears. Like Emeline's."

Max shivered and pulled his coat tight. He grabbed his leather canteen and gulped half the water inside. He wiped his mouth on his coat sleeve and stared at the cabin. By now, he expected to see Emeline riding Beelzebub. Or, at least, a cloud of brown dust. Only one road went from her cabin to town. The forest would be too difficult to navigate. Yet, there was no sign of her, her horse, or a light shining through her cabin window.

"Ernest, do you think she's mentally ill? Eden Lake's doctor comes again this week. Should we consult with him?"

"No, Max. I don't believe we are dealing with an earthly illness. I can't explain it yet. We need to commit her and our search for answers to the Lord. Let's row back to your cabin. I don't feel much like fishing anymore."

"I agree completely. How about I put on another pot of coffee, fry some bacon and eggs? After breakfast we can pray and search God's word. I know the Holy Spirit will teach us what we need to learn."

Max and Ernest reeled in their lines. Max started to remove the bait from the hooks, but none was left. He patted the hooks dry and repacked the tackle box while Ernest rowed to the dock.

As Max reached the porch, he leaned the poles against the cabin. Ernest placed the tackle box on the bench. The red scarf still hung from the mail box and no greeting by any dead animals.

"You stay here, Ernest while I get a fire started and the coffee going. Won't take long for the bacon and eggs to cook."

Max joined Ernest who leaned on the porch railing. "Are you still waiting for Beelzebub or Emeline to show? Can't imagine what's taking so long. Have you seen them, Ernest?"

"No, I haven't," Ernest inhaled deeply then faced Max. "Max, do you know the name Beelzebub in the Bible refers to Satan? Could be significant or just a coincidence. My concern for you rests on two levels now: physical and spiritual."

Max scanned the distant cabin and the road one last time. Still no sign of life.

Chapter 11

The next few days were uneventful as far as treats or visits from Emeline were concerned. Max and Ernest disciplined themselves to start and end each day with Bible study. They focused their search for wisdom and the Holy Spirits' guidance.

"Ernest, if you are up for a hike, I'd like to take you to the path Jed and I followed. The one we thought would lead to Molech. I'm sure I have a pair of hiking boots that will fit."

"I've been waiting for you to ask. Since Miss Toliver hasn't shown her face for a while, I believe it's time to track down your mystery man." Ernest closed the Bible. "You okay? You seem keyed up."

"The thought I may have to confront him frightens me. He reminds me of a man-grizzly bear. Big, dirty and lots of hair. And that dog. I worry for Jed should they get in a fight." Max placed his hat on his head. "We'll take the canteens, my Bowie knife and sidearms. I meant to get more ammo for my Winchester, but we can take what I have and pray we don't need the rifle. This is the start of huckleberry season, so the bears will be out in full force. We'll need to keep alert."

Max gave a sidearm to Ernest, who tucked it in his belt. They filled the canteens, stuffed extra cartridges in their pockets and headed south down the road.

"Ernest, remember to talk loud enough to not surprise the bears, yet not too loud. Don't want Molech to hide at the sound of our voices. The path should be right around here." Max kept a sharp eye on the edge of the road.

"Jed, find his scent. You remember. Molech, boy. Let's get him." Max's chest swelled with pride as he watched his faithful dog, nose to the ground while his tail wagged in the air.

"I told you how Jed saved me from the mama bear and found the trap on the path." Max removed his hat to swipe at a fly. "But I haven't recounted the miracle in which old Jed played a key role.

We made a hike to the high country late last fall, scouting for game: about the 3,000 foot level, on the south side of Mt. Hood. Most of the snow had melted, but there were a few patches here and there. The skies were beautiful when out of nowhere a dense fog rolled in." Max halted and scanned the woods. "We must be close now, Jed. Anything yet?" The black hound ignored Max and sniffed and snorted to expel debris from his nostrils. Jed veered off the road and disappeared into the brush.

"He's found it, Ernest. Come on."

The two men hurried to the spot where the forest camouflaged Jed. The dog vanished.

"Jed, where are you?" Max called as quietly as he could, yet still be heard. "Jed?"

Frantic, Max rushed headlong down the path, eyes darted from left to right. Then he stopped cold and listened.

Max held up a hand to signal Ernest to stop. With a hand cupped behind one ear he slowly revolved and listened for any sound of crashing dog feet in the brush. Nothing.

He traveled a few more feet, then stopped again and repeated the search. Still nothing.

"Max, should we separate? I see an adjoining path. You could follow that and I'll stay on this one. Signal with one gun shot when either of us find him," Ernest said.

Relieved Ernest used the word "when" and not "if," Max agreed to the plan. Littered with downed branches and burrowed holes, Max hurried as quickly as was feasibly possible. He scoured the forest from side to side and called to Jed. The top priority was to find his beloved companion. He cared not about bruins or Molech and his dog, Bear.

A gunshot rang through the trees. Max jolted to a halt, reversed direction and retraced his steps. He hurdled the branches and dashed back to where the paths converged. Ernest waved his arms in the air. Max raced toward him.

"Ernest, where is he? Is he all right?" Panting heavily, Max felt desperate to know about Jed.

"Slow down there, Max. Take some deep breaths. Your chest is pulsating. I don't want to lose you. Jed's okay. Here," handing Max a canteen, "sip some water, then I'll take you to him."

The calmness of Ernest's words comforted Max to comply with his directions. The cool water quenched his dry mouth and his heart slowed to a regular pace.

"I'm calm now," Max said as he wiped a trail of water on his sleeve. "Where is he? I don't see him anywhere." Max tried not to let his emotions escalate again. A hand on his shoulder quieted his nerves.

"Come, follow me."

Compelled to stay close, Max nearly stepped on his friend's heels. They walked a few feet then turned onto a smaller path. Riddled with larger branches and fallen rotted trees, Max lifted his legs to navigate the now vanished path. Crushed ferns, Oregon grape and salal engulfed them. A breeze circulated around the tree trunks. Max breathed a hint of sulphur.

"I didn't find Jed, Max. He found me. He almost knocked me over, then grabbed my coat sleeve and pulled. Jed finally released me when we got here."

Ernest backed out of Max's way. There sat Jed. He romped over to Max, waged his tail and flopped by his boots.

"You crazy dog. You frightened me." Max knelt down and rubbed Jed. Max accepted a slobbery tongue in return.

"Now, let's see what you found."

The crumpled grass reminded Max of a place where deer might bed down. The brush had been cleared and the undergrowth flattened. A ragged blanket, torn and shredded in places, a pile of small branches, an old tobacco tin, and rusted metal bowl were in disarray on the flattened ground. Tufts of animal fur clung to the branch pile.

"Jed must have picked up Molech's scent somewhere on the path and followed it here." Max scrutinized the area.

"What do you make of this, Max?" Ernest lifted the blanket with a stick.

"That blanket, whew, the sulphur's almost overpowering. We're in the right place. The branches could be used for a campfire, yet there's no evidence. No charcoal or ashes anywhere. Maybe they're used to scrap animal flesh off the hide. Look, Ernest. Possum, fox and rabbit fur. Molech might use the metal bowl as a dog food dish or for water." Max picked up the tobacco tin and grasped the lid.

"I see no clues, Max. It appears to be more rag than blanket. Can't provide much warmth for man or beast." Ernest let the covering fall back to the ground.

Something stirred in the forest. Jed growled and Max saw the hair on the nape of his neck straighten. He dropped the unopened tin on the crumpled leaves.

"What is it, boy?" Max hurried to Jed's side and stroked his fur. "It's all right Jed. We're here and ready."

Both Max and Ernest aimed their guns into the forest and cocked the triggers. Brush moved and branches cracked. Their attention riveted in one direction. Something stirred and continued on a direct path to where they stood. Like frozen statues, the threesome held their breath. Max tried to mentally calm his pounding heart, but it was useless, as Molech, Bear or a brown bear could be drawing closer. Or all three.

His imagination went wild. He envisioned Molech on the back of a brown bear, as his dog lumbered beside them. Five dead animals would dangle from his hands, maybe skunks this time. Always one more than the previous count. His dog would devour Jed. Then he would rub the skunk smell all over Ernest and finally reveal that he was a descendent of the skoocooms and invite Max for dinner. *Pull yourself together. Lord, we need Your help right now.*

Whatever caused the noise and movement stopped short. Max noticed Ernest's hand shook. He scooted beside his friend.

"Ernest, I'm right beside you. We need to trust that the Lord is beside us also."

"Thanks, Max." Ernest inhaled deeply than exhaled slowly. "I'm ready now."

Silence prevailed as the men and dog waited patiently for their predator to appear. More crunching and brush movement and finally the object of their trepidation revealed itself. A young buck with four inch nubbins pushed through the last bush and walked a few more steps. Then he stopped, raised his head, starred at the intruders and bolted into the dense foliage.

Max turned to Ernest. The two men held each other's gaze for a moment then broke out in laughter.

"Are you kidding me? We're scared of a young buck?" Max lowered his arms, replaced his gun and grabbed his stomach as he bent over and released a loud guffaw. His face came within inches of Jed who gave Max a good lick.

"Laughter is good medicine, declares the Lord." Ernest said. "What a great reliever of stress."

Max watched his friend grab his ribs as he joined in the moment.

Once tears of joy were wiped from his eyes, Max patted Ernest on his back.

"Good track job, Jed." Max sighed. "Now Ernest, I suggest that we remove ourselves from this spot. I don't know about you, but I sure don't relish the thought that my imaginative vision could become reality."

Sighs of relief with pats on each others' backs, Max fairly leaped in the air when they reached the road back to his cabin. He laughed again as he watched Jed snap at a butterfly.

"Oh, Jed," Max said with a chuckle. "You're relieved too." He watched Jed leap in the air. The joy expressed by his best companion overflowed to the men.

"Well, Ernest, you may not have met Molech, but you got a taste, or should I say smell, of this mountain man. I could tell you were as scared as I."

"Max, I've been thinking. Remember the scripture we read this morning from Isaiah, "Trust in the Lord forever, for in God the Lord, we have an everlasting Rock." We sure let that good word slip right through our brains. One more reminder that we need to not only read His word, but put it into practice. Need to work on that one." Ernest stopped and untied a boot.

"Got something in there. Had it for a long time, but didn't want to stop to get it out." He dumped a twig with one small leaf onto the road.

Max supported his friend while he retied the laces.

"I know what you mean that scripture floats right on through. Maybe we could stuff a piece of cloth in one ear." Max chuckled. "The scripture that came to me after little buck bounced away was when Paul admonished the Corinthians. You know. To take every thought captive? I sure let my thoughts run amok."

A breeze rustled the tree tops and a cloud darkened the sun. Max knew the unpredictability of Oregon's weather.

"Doesn't look like rain, but you can never tell. We best pick up our pace to the cabin."

The two men walked briskly while Jed snapped at bugs.

"Wait a minute." Max felt a hand on his arm. Ernest halted. "You didn't finish your story about this here miracle dog. Not one more step, rain or no rain, until you tell me the rest."

"Story?" Max scratched his head. "Oh, yeah. I didn't finish did I? Well, let's see, where were we?"

"At the 3,000 foot level, some unmelted snow and a fog set in."

Max removed his hat. "Oh, yes. Now I remember. Well, we were trailing large deer tracks in the snow. Didn't pay much attention to the surroundings. My eyes were glued to the ground. Jed, a few feet in front sniffed like crazy. This fog came out of the blue and became denser by the minute. I stopped and searched for Jed. He disappeared in the white haze. By now I couldn't even see my out-stretched hand. I've never been in fog that thick." Max wiped sweat that dripped down his face.

"Well, I figured I had to move and yelled for Jed. My foot instinctively advanced, but before I could put it down, Jed barked, leaped and grabbed the bottom of my jacket. He pulled me to the ground like I was his prey. I banged my elbow, hit my head on a rock and my rifle sailed through the air. When I came to my senses, after a few choice words for that hound, I rose slowly and got my bearings. The fog lifted and exposed the reason for Jed's actions. I had become disoriented and instead of staying on the path, I had swerved off course. Jed caught me before I walked off the edge and into a deep ravine. In fact, it reminded me of the ravine at Stuart Hall back in Scotland."

Max replaced the hat on his head.

"Here, Jed." Jed sprinted back to his beloved master. Max knelt down to greet him.

"This is the best old hound dog in the world, Ernest. I have never regretted the day I carried him out of the Anderson's shed and gave him a home." Max scrunched Jed on the top of his head. "Come on, we better get home." Max said. "Those dark clouds are filled with rain and we may be the target."

Chapter 12

The two men picked up their pace back to the cabin eager to put more distance between themselves and Molech's camp. The vegetation was bone dry from a lack of rain. Max was thankful he found no evidence Molech had started a fire.

"So, Ernest. What do you think awaits us? Molech's animal remains? Emeline? Her treats, or perhaps all of those? One more bend then a short distance to the cabin." Max paused then added, "I'll bet there'll be nothing to greet us." Max waited his friend's response.

"How can you be so sure?" Ernest picked up a branch off the road and tossed it into the woods. "We haven't seen Emeline in several days. I bet she's been cooking up a storm and not only a dessert, but a full-scale meal. Maybe even piping hot." Ernest rubbed his stomach.

"Nope, I believe one or both constantly watch me. I am never out of their sight. And since it appears we may have found Molech's sleeping spot, I don't believe he'd show himself, at least, not today." Max tipped his head backwards, stared at the sky and called, "Am I right, Lord?"

They met the final bend with determination. No sulphur smell, no breeze, no fog and no sweet baking aroma to tantalize their senses. A good sign all would be well.

"Jed, where ya going?" Jed bolted ahead. Something had caught his eye. Could be a jackrabbit in the road that challenged Jed to a chase.

"Come on, Ernest. This'll be great fun. Jed won't give up if he's got a rabbit in his sights." Max rushed ahead with Ernest close behind. Jed barked as he raced down the road on a straight line to the cabin. No rabbit chase ensued. Max froze when he saw the object of Jed's sprint.

"Ernest, I hate to say it, but you were right. Emeline's on the cabin porch."

"Ah, I can taste it now: roast beef, cut thin, layered on thick slices of home-made bread, brown gravy oozes down the mound. Fresh shucked corn-on-the-cob covered in melted butter. And mashed tatties. A Scot's meal is never complete without tatties. Then for dessert…"

"Stop it, Ernest," Max interrupted, "you're making me hungry." He squinted his eyes. "Jed knows something's not right with her. Look how he keeps his distance. She's never pet him. Don't think she likes dogs. Just big horses."

"Do you think I'm right about the meal though? I'm famished." Ernest undid his vest and removed his hat. "Kinda warm, don't you think?"

Max shook his head. "Your stomach is never satisfied. Right, Ernest?" Max removed a cloth from his pocket and wiped the sweat from his hands. "No, I don't believe she cooked a meal for us. She could easily get in the cabin if she wanted to. I've invited her in several times, but she always has an excuse. She hasn't set foot inside yet."

How graceful, this she-elf, and what an enchantress. Max tried to keep his emotions in check as she flowed down the steps to meet him.

"Good afternoon, Max, Ernest. Been out hunting? Find any big game?"

There's that twinkle in her eye again. *What did she mean "big game"? She knows it's not hunting season. Does she mean Molech?*

"Hi, Emeline. I wanted Ernest to compare our forest with his in Scotland. We hiked deep in the woods, almost to Lost Lake. Always pack my guns, never know what surprises you may find. Been waiting long?" Max leaned his rifle against the porch steps and tossed his hat on the bench.

"Oh, a while, I guess. I remembered you have guests coming, but forgot the exact date. Thought I'd welcome them with some of my cookies. Wondered when they would arrive and what you think I might bake. From back east somewhere, is that right?"

"If you'll excuse me," Ernest said, "I need a drink." He entered the cabin, then called back. "I'll bring out water for us all."

"Thanks, Ernest," Max said. "I need to sit, Emeline. Let's go up on the porch."

Max undid the top button on his shirt. "Long trek heats up a body."

To avoid any intimate thoughts Emeline may be entertaining, Max collapsed in his lone chair. Emeline plunked herself close to him on the bench.

"Now, to answer your questions. First of all, that's very thoughtful to make cookies for my guests. You certainly don't need to. But if I know you at all, you won't resist the opportunity to welcome them. My two guests, Maggie Richards and Nellie Cox, will be here tomorrow afternoon. They're both from Chicago and like anything chocolate."

That light in her eyes again. Does it ever go out?

"Chocolate? I love chocolate. I have an incredible recipe for chocolate fudge. I'll leave the nuts out as so many people are allergic to squirrel food. Maggie and Nellie, huh? Which one are you partial to, Max? There's no use denying it because I hear fondness in your voice. Especially for Maggie. Am I right? Is she your sweetie?"

"Here you are. Water for all." Ernest said as he offered a glass to each from a dinner plate. "Sorry, Max. Couldn't find a tray and we men usually don't care much for, what's it called? Oh, yes, etiquette."

Relieved for the interruption, Max guzzled the full glass of water.

"Ah, much better." He returned his glass to the plate.

"Emeline said she would make chocolate fudge for when the girls arrive tomorrow. I insisted that she really didn't need to…."

"Well, I, for one, insist that she does." Ernest interrupted, then faced Emeline. "You create the most delicious desserts. That is except for Mabel's cinnamon rolls. She and her husband own the cafe in my little hamlet of Rolen, Lassie. Please don't pay Max any mind. You bake to your hearts' content. Miss Richards and Miss Cox will truly appreciate your gesture of welcome."

"Ernest, you've made me one happy lady. I will make an extra chocolate portion for you. Now if you gentlemen will excuse me, I must return home, find the recipe and prepare a sweet welcome for your two lovelies."

Max and Ernest accompanied Emeline to the bottom of the steps.

"Where's your horse?" Max asked.

"I rowed across the lake today. My arms are a bit flabby." She lifted her arm into a bicep curl and grabbed a pinch of skin. "Got to keep this body in top form. Never know when the right man will come along."

She winked at Max. His cheeks blushed and a queasy stomach demanded attention.

"Ernest, would you walk her to the dock? I'll go in and start lunch." Max needed to get away from Emeline. This could be a good time for Ernest to put his discernment skills to work.

Ernest's chance came to interrogate Emeline, at least that was his plan. He mentally arranged his questions. The short distance to the dock afforded him little time.

"Emeline, I'd like to know more about you. Do you mind if I ask some questions?" Ernest said. He preferred to dive right to the heart of the matter and with her evasiveness earlier he didn't want to lose a moment.

"Where did you live before coming to Eden Lake?"

"Oh, here, there, and just about everywhere. I don't stay in one place very long. Gets monotonous. Like to keep on the move. Makes things more interesting."

"Why did you move to Eden Lake?"

"Never lived in the Pacific Northwest. I had heard about the nice people and the beauty of the seasons."

"But your cabin is very remote and from what I understand you're rarely in town. You seem to isolate yourself. Can't meet people that way."

"Ernest, I didn't say I wanted to meet the people, just that I'd heard they were nice." Emeline paused. "I feel like I'm being cross-examined. What do you care where I came from and why I'm here?"

Her demeanor changed. Her once animated walk became stiff. Her words no longer flowed. He may have touched a nerve.

"Max is a good friend and you seem to take special interest in him. Homemade goodies, an extra large smile and an obvious desire to be close to him. I also noticed you winked when you described the need to keep your body in top form should 'the right man come along.' I believe those were your exact words. Are you interested in Max, for, let's say, a husband?"

Emeline skipped part way down the path, and if she responded, Ernest didn't hear anything.

"I asked if you were interested in Max." Ernest spoke louder, but Emeline continued to ignore him. He hurried closer and grabbed her arm.

"I asked you if you're interested in Max and demand an answer."

Ernest felt an electric jolt travel up his arm. His heart skipped, his pulse raced and sweat dripped down his face. His fingers were like cement around her arm. He couldn't release his hand as she faced him. Her pupils dilated. The strong grip of her hand squeezed his wrist, then jerked his arm to his side. Her strength frightened Ernest. He grew dizzy. He stepped back, but caught himself before an inevitable fall into the lake.

"My business is my business and you would do well to remember that. I seek those who are vulnerable and timid. If you get in my way, you'll regret it."

His mind numbed. Words froze. She leapt into the boat and rowed away with eyes fixed on Ernest.

Frozen on the dock, he replayed their conversation. He imagined he had spoken with two different people: the sweet, flitting young lass and, dare he think it, a demon-possessed wench. Another thought entered his mind: she might be a demon straight from the pit of hell.

Her boat and image grew smaller. Ernest's eyes burned from her gaze that seemed to travel deep into his soul. His hands moistened, his pulse increased and a disquieted spirit aroused within. He forcefully shut his eyes, then purposefully pulled his thoughts back to the Lord and prayed for this demented woman. When he opened his eyes, she had vanished. Her and the row boat.

He must warn Max, but would he believe Emeline was not what she pretended to be. And possibly not of this world? Would Max have the spiritual maturity to confront the truth of scripture: we live in an unseen world of powers, principalities and angels of darkness. He prayed for Max as he hurried back to the cabin. *Give me the right words and insights to prepare Max for whatever battle may lie ahead, Lord. And help me keep vigilant against the powers of the evil one. You are victorious.*

"You seem unusually quiet, Ernest. Did Emeline throw you off-kilter, or maybe the lunch didn't settle?" Ernest's silence hadn't escaped Max's notice. Hardly a word was said during the meal. How unlike this Scot who always spoke his mind. "How about another glass of water?"

Max's eyes followed Ernest while his friend rose from the table and filled his water glass. Ernest returned and plopped down in his chair.

"Max, I don't know how to tell you. I've been rehearsing my lines carefully, but think it best to just blurt them out. I pray I don't offend you and you truly hear the truth of my words."

Max's stomach churned. "I trust you, Ernest, to always tell me the truth. This must concern Emeline. Am I right?"

"Yes, my friend." Ernest cleared his throat. "I believe you understand that as surely as there are powers of good in our world, so are there powers of evil. The Bible tells us we are struggling not against flesh and blood, but rather spiritual forces of wickedness. You know that just as God desires to lavish us with His goodness, so Satan attempts to invade every dimension of our lives with his wickedness. God wants the best for us. Satan wants to destroy us."

Max leaned forward, elbows on the table, intent to hear every word.

"My conversation with Emeline leads me to believe she is from the devil. Her persona changed in front of my eyes and I felt my spirit grieved beyond words. Almost as if she tried to suck the very life out of me. Her plan is not to win you for a husband, but to win you back into the kingdom of darkness. Young Christians remain vulnerable to Satan's attacks because they are still babes in the faith. She recognizes that you are a young Christian and will do all she can to thwart your efforts to grow up. I represent a threat to her scheme, so I must be on my guard at all times and bathe my day in prayer."

Max swallowed hard, then reclined in his chair. "I can't believe that, Ernest. She's always been sweet without a serious thought in her head. I know Satan is conniving and he attacks at will, but, Emeline? Maybe you pressed too hard with your questions and she became defensive. She can't be demon possessed. I'm sure I would have sensed that."

Max observed his friend's eyes intensify as Ernest glared straight into his own. Ernest leaned forward, the muscles on his neck bulged as he slammed a fist on the table.

"You're not hearing me, Max. Still filtering my words through a friendship with what you call a 'she-elf.' I didn't say she may be possessed. I said she may be a demon. She's not human, Max. I pray the Holy Spirit will show you her true form. Too many young Christians rely on God to speak to them; to show Himself in supernatural ways. But, Max, He has spoken to us, in the Holy Bible. That is His word."

Max noticed Ernest calm down, his voice softer, yet just as forceful. "I remember a pastor teaching the Greek word for power is the same as our word for dynamite. And by the power of His word we can be victorious. I, for one, will intensify my prayer life. We need to concentrate on scriptures focused on how to combat Satan. We'll start by putting on the armor of God through prayer, mediation and study. Only with God's word and in His strength can we blast her back where she came from." Ernest paused, leaned against the back of his chair. "I'm sorry I fired off at you. I fear her bewitching ways may cloud your spiritual eyes."

The cabin became silent. No wind disturbed the woods, no birds chattered, even Jed slept without his usual dreamland woofs.

"The further the soul advances, the greater are the adversaries against which it must contend."

— *Evagrius of Pontus* —

Chapter 13

The morning sun streamed through the window. Max pulled his covers up to block its rays. Yesterday's conversation with Ernest swirled in his head like lake water on a stormy day. Waves beat against the bank, crash over rocks and throw debris helter-skelter. He tried to take control and stop the steady ranting of Ernest's forceful words against Emeline.

They hardly spoke the rest of that day. Max had spent his time in the stable. He had curried the horses, mucked out their stalls, and cleaned their hooves. Then a long walk in the woods to clear his head. Finally, some quiet time in his boat on Eden Lake. He'd even left Jed on the bank which displeased his dog to no end. As he stared at the small cabin on the other side, he noticed there were no signs of life. No movement outside. No large black stallion. No light inside. No smoke from the chimney.

And his friend? How did he spend the day? Max's stomach tied in knots. When he left the cabin he noticed Ernest at the table, his Bible opened and a note pad beside him. Max felt barred from the activity, yet he could only blame himself. Uncertain Ernest was right about Emeline, Max felt some power pull at him to resist God's word. A dagger of conviction pierced him when he had invited Ernest for dinner.

"Thanks anyway, Max. But I'm fasting and praying for answers and direction."

Fasting and praying? Had it really come to that?

Max pushed the covers off, dangled his legs over the edge of the bed and scratched his head. A new day awaited, perhaps with new beginnings. He picked up his Bible from the nightstand and allowed it to open at will. The story of Mary and Martha reached his eyes. As he read the tale of these sisters, he was impressed how much he and Ernest were like them. He had busied himself with tasks while Ernest stayed immersed in God's word. The final verse pricked his spirit; "...but only a few things are necessary, really only one, for Mary has chosen the good part, which shall not be taken away from her." Max substituted his name for Martha and Ernest for Mary, then re-read the scriptures. Convicted of his spiritual jealousy, he repented, entered the living room and found Ernest immersed in God's word.

"Ernest, I must ask your forgiveness as I asked for the Lord's. My foolishness and stubborn attitude toward your evaluation of Emeline tainted my thoughts and actions yesterday. Will you forgive me and disciple me in my walk with the Lord?"

His friend reached Max's side instantly. Ernest's big arms of love and forgiveness enveloped Max. The wall Max had erected crumbled.

"I forgive you, Max, and this hug is also from the Lord. Welcome back to the journey of faith."

Tears welled in Max's eyes. Ernest was a true friend and a brother in Christ. Definitely time to grow up and learn more about this walk with the Lord.

A rub on Max's leg unbalanced him. He glanced down. Jed waited eagerly. His tail wagged and his tongue flopped dangling a few drops of saliva. Max realized he had not only turned his back on Ernest, but neglected his faithful companion.

"I now realize that it is time to get back on the right path to positive relations with a most gracious God, my good friend, and faithful dog. Ernest, will you help me?"

Max's hand connected with Ernest's. Reconciliation happened in that tiny cabin between two friends now on a journey into spiritual warfare.

"You know, Max, we view our circumstances by what we see in the physical world. God, however, views our circumstances by what He wants to teach us." Ernest returned to his chair. Max pulled another chair beside his friend, elbows on the table.

"We notice the surface," Ernest continued. "God sees the depths. We walk in the physical world, God wants us to walk in the spiritual world. When the Holy Spirit removes the blinders from our eyes, only then can we truly see the spiritual realm all around us. God knows it is time for you to grow deeper in your walk with Him. You're in a battle and haven't seen that truth. I believe the Lord brought me here at this time for just this purpose: to disciple you."

"And I'm so glad He did," said Max. "Now, how about I start breakfast. I'm famished. Then we need to clean the cabin and prepare for our special guests this afternoon. While I can hardly wait to see Maggie, at the same time, I'm overcome with jitters. No coffee for me, this morning. Eggs, bacon and toast sound okay? And Jed some slabs of bacon for you as well."

"No, Max. You have a higher agenda this morning. I'll cook breakfast while you study my notes and read the scriptures listed on the note pad. Ask the Lord to give you one nugget of truth from each verse."

Max followed Ernest's directions and dug into the scriptures focused on combating Satan. Ernest had starred several, so Max concentrated on those first. He discovered that God warned believers to be ready to wage war against the devil. Put on God's armor to "...stand firm against the schemes of the devil." God's armor. Max pondered what that really meant. He remembered stories about knights of old whose armor was so heavy they could hardly move. Spiritual armor weighed nothing, yet protected believers against the greatest force combating Christians.

"Ernest, will you explain this whole armor of God to me?"

"Sure, Max," Ernest laid another slab of bacon in the cast-iron skillet. "If you look carefully you will see the armor; loins girded with truth, breastplate of righteousness, feet shod with the gospel of peace, shield of faith and the helmet of salvation are all defensive tools. All that is except the sword of the Spirit which is the word of God. It's our only offensive tool and we must be immersed in His word if we are to keep our sword sharp. The Lord admonishes us to be strong in Him, and in His strength to stand solid against Satan's devices. We must pray at all times to bring growth and wisdom in our quest to liberate you from Emeline's clutches."

Max gazed out his window toward the neglected cabin. Still hard for him to believe she may be a demon, but ready to take Ernest at his word and prepare for whatever lay ahead. He agreed with Ernest. Still a young child in the faith. Boys become men in battle, so Max anticipated that he would take a giant leap into manhood with the battle that lay before him.

A good conversation during breakfast set the tone for the rest of the day. The two men now had a plan and agreed to hold each other accountable for their faith-walk.

"Not too late. How about we do some fishing before we head to town? Maybe catch a couple of trout for a welcome dinner for the girls. While you clean up from breakfast, I'll prepare their rooms, sweep and clean off the porch." Max carried their dishes to the sink, then grabbed a broom, dust pan and rag. "I think I'll

sition, almost capsizing the small craft, raised the oars and splashed them in the water.

"Wait a minute, Max. I'm not going back before I land this fish. You wanted the girls to have fresh trout for dinner. Don't row yet. Grab the net and scoop him up when he comes close to the side."

"Ernest, you're on your own. I'm rowing and that fish will have to follow us to the dock. I'm not missing Molech this time."

Max held the oars firmly in his hands and used all his strength to turn the boat toward home and his unwelcome visitors. With Ernest in full view, Max realized his friend strained as he continued to reel in the line. The pole arched dramatically. He instinctively knew the right thing to do. Max placed the oars inside the boat and retrieved the net.

"Okay, Ernest, I'm ready when you are."

A silver gleam flashed. The fish's tail flung water into the boat and on Max's shirt as he leaned over the side.

"One more good pull and I should be able to reach him. Pull, Ernest."

This granddaddy trout gave one last twist of his body. Both the fish and Ernest were vying for victory. Only one would win in the end. In this case, the stronger of the two. Max thought how alike his spiritual battle. Only one would be victorious, and in the end, that's the Lord.

"Now, Max. There he is. Get the net under before he dives again."

Max held the net with both hands and snatched up the trout. Still twisting and flaying, the fish fought for his life. Max lay the fish laden net in the bottom of the boat and tossed a rag to Ernest. Sweat dripped down his friend's brow.

"You finish the job, Ernest. I'm back on duty."

Max threw the oars over the boat's side and pulled them through the water. His muscles ached as he watched Emeline's cabin diminish. *Please, Lord, let Molech still be there when we reach the dock.*

Rather than tie up, Max maneuvered the boat passed the dock and into the bank. He jumped out, Jed on his heels, and raced for the cabin. Max halted in the middle of the road and glanced both directions. No sign of Molech. He'd been too late and missed him again. Five dead rabbits reposed on the steps.

Heavy footsteps behind Max sent chills down his back. *Had Molech returned?* He twirled around. Only Ernest as he trudged back to the cabin, all the fishing paraphernalia in his hands. Max met his friend to relieve part of the load.

"I'm sorry, Ernest. I became so distracted by Molech, I completely forgot our fishing gear."

"That's okay, Max." Ernest handed Max the poles and tackle box. "Did you catch a glimpse of him?"

"Unfortunately, nothing. A slight sulphur smell lingers, but that's all."

Max led the way up the steps and leaned the poles against the cabin wall.

"After I clean up, I'll hitch the team to the wagon. We can get some lunch in Eden Lake before the girls' coach arrives," Max opened the door.

"Sounds good. Once your Ol' Moses is filleted out, I'll wash up and meet you outside." Ernest glanced at the porch. "And the rabbits? They look pretty scrawny for rabbit stew. Their pelts show signs of a tick infestation. When we get back, I'll bury them deep in the woods. For now they belong behind the stable. This would be a dismal welcome to Eden Lake for two city lassies."

"Thank you, Ernest. I'll meet you at the wagon." Max slapped his leg. "Come on, Jed. You're going to meet a real lady."

Chapter 14

Max tied his horses to a railing at the coach station, then he and Ernest walked to the Merc. Another glorious day in Eden Lake to welcome Maggie and Nellie.

"Good afternoon, Miss Greene. Ernest and I wondered if you might have any sandwich fixings?"

Miss Greene's eyes lit up. She didn't scurry around the counter for her usual hug time.

"Good morning to you, Ernest," she paused. "And you also, Max. I've been wondering how you two bachelors were getting along in the wilderness." Max watched her sashay across the floor. Her skirt swayed as she walked with a noticeable exaggerated movement. She reminded him of a young girl on the prowl for a husband.

"We've managed fine," Ernest responded as he held out a hand in greeting. "Miss your tasty morsels though."

Miss Greene's cheeks redden, eye-lashes fluttered, (*they seemed longer than usual*) and a cock of her head instantly removed twenty years. She obviously flirted with Ernest, and in Max's mind, Ernest reciprocated. These two. Don't they realize the adult years should demonstrate mature behavior?

"So, Miss Greene, any lunch fixings? We're hungry, but can go to the cafe if need be."

"Oh, no you don't, Max Sullivan. You two have a seat on the porch and I'll bring something out in a jiffy." She gazed at Ernest. "And an extra sweet for you."

"How about I help Miss Greene and bring our lunch out? Max, you go ahead and find a spot in the shade."

Max received the hint loud and clear. Ernest courted Miss Greene. He certainly wasted no time. But then, at their age, why not?

How about Maggie? With eight years difference, would she think he was too old for her? She could have her pick of several young men. Why would she want to marry an old man of thirty-four?

The questions slammed him like a woodpecker who pounded a tree for ants. His heart raced as he pictured her exiting the coach. He checked his pocket watch. Another two hours.

"Well, Max Sullivan," Max bumped into Mr. Olson the patriarch of Eden Lake. "Haven't seen you for quite some time. Hear you have a guest from Scotland and two more coming from Chicago. Am I right?"

Max found Mr. Olson to be a likable fellow. Considered the grandfather of the entire community, his gray thick mustache, bushy eyebrows and well-worn hands from hard lumber work created the appearance of wisdom. Still as lean as a twenty year old, he stood erect rather than stooped over, the usual posture for some older men.

"I'm sorry, Mr. Olson." Max apologized. "Didn't mean to jostle you. My mind has taken to wandering lately." Max repositioned his hat. "My friend Ernest from Scotland, has been with me a couple of weeks or so. He's inside the Merc helping Miss Greene make lunch. I'm afraid he may be smitten with her and she with him. Don't understand why he doesn't realize long distance relationships seldom work. He in Scotland, she in Eden Lake." Max shook his head. "I just don't get it."

"Really, Max? From the conversations around town, I thought you were enamored with one of the young ladies coming from Chicago. I believe Maggie is her name, and if I'm not mistaken, she arrives this afternoon. Don't you agree you're in a long distance relationship as well? That is unless you're planning to marry her."

"News sure travels fast in this small community." Max scratched his head. "Mr. Olson, do you have a moment? I'd like to talk with you about something serious."

"Sure, Max. Let's go to the bench under that pine tree." Max followed Mr. Olson and scanned the area for anyone who may hear their conversation.

"I understand you counsel people when the minister is not in town. I need your advice." Max bowed his head and inhaled deeply. "You may have noticed my weight loss. This must be kept in strictest confidence. I'm very sick, Mr. Olson, and my days are numbered."

"Max, all of our days are numbered. Some of us are given the privilege to know our time is close. To see Jesus face-to-face in glory is the ultimate healing. But I don't believe you seek answers about the hereafter."

"No, Jesus is my Lord and Savior and I trust Him to take me home whenever He's ready. My question involves the pros and cons of whether I should marry. Maggie will be here in a couple of hours. I want to ask her to be my wife. Do you think I'm being selfish? We may not have much time together. She's in her twenties, so she could certainly marry again after I'm gone. I'm so mixed up. She's not even here yet and I'm already concerned she may leave before I propose. That is, if I should propose." Max lowered his head, held the brim of his hat and rotated it with his fingers.

"You're in quite a quandary, Max. If you're sure she loves you as the Lord loves, unconditionally, she would want to spend as much time with you as she could. The amount of time would not matter. Moments would. I assume you will tell her of your illness. She needs to know the circumstances and the impending outcome."

Max watched Mr. Olson reach into his coat pocket. He removed a tiny book.

"I carry this with me. The print is small, but the Lord has granted me good eye-sight thus far." Max had never seen a Bible so compact. He watched Mr. Olson flip through to find a verse.

"This verse speaks to court proceedings, to stand up to the truth when put on trial. Your situation is not of the persecution kind, but you are anxious nonetheless. Mark 13:11 says, 'And when they arrest you and deliver you up, do not be anxious beforehand about what you are to say, but say whatever is given you in that hour; for it is not you who speak, but it is the Holy Spirit.'" Mr. Olson slipped the book back into his pocket.

"Max, I believe whenever dilemmas face us, the Holy Spirit gives the words to speak and they will be words of truth. There's always hope when a door is open. If Maggie shuts the door, metaphorically speaking, then your muddle has ended. I will pray for you and ask the Lord's guidance in this matter."

"Thank you. As a young child, people branded me timid and shy. I believe, with the Lord's help, I continue to rise above those labels. And now, with my life disappearing at a swift pace, I need to be more forthright and allow what other's think or say about me to run off my back like water on goose feathers. You have been a great help. I will trust the Holy Spirit to lead and should He prompt me at an opportune time, I will ask Maggie."

Max wiped his moist hands on his pants, glanced toward the Merc and cleared his throat.

"I sense there is something else on your mind, Max. How can I help you?" Mr. Olson asked.

"Don't know where to start. I assume you know about the mountain man named Molech."

"Yes. I've never seen him, but recollect his name, and the Anderson's disappearance being connected. Miss Greene doesn't hold him in high regard as do many of the townspeople. Has he been bothering you?"

"Oh, not really bothering. I've only had one opportunity to talk with him. Ernest and I are pretty sure we found his campsite, but his habit is to leave dead animals on my porch. Then there's this sulphur smell that follows him." Max rubbed his knees and straightened his back. "I just don't know what to do. I'd like to talk to him again and find out who he really is and why the dead animals, but he's so elusive. And he frightens me. Any suggestions?"

"I believe the name Molech is mentioned at least three times in the Bible; in Leviticus, Isaiah and 1 Kings. Each time God's people are warned to stay away from him. Children were being sacrificed, precious oil and perfume were offered to him, and in 1 Kings he is called the abomination of the Ammonites. Clearly a god people of the Lord should avoid." Mr. Olson stood and faced Max.

"I don't believe this Molech is a god, but he consistently leaves a bad taste in the mouths of all he contacts. My advice is to steer clear of him, carry your sidearm at all times and take a defensive posture. And the dead animals, well bury them. If he's watching you and noticing you're not exhibiting signs of fear or annoyance, maybe he'll go away. One more prayer request on my list."

Max raised his head and noticed Ernest as he closed the gap from the Merc. He carried a tray of food.

"Ernest, this is Mr. Olson. Mr. Olson, my good friend, Ernest McIntyre." Max clutched the tray and rested it on the bench while the two men shook hands.

"I best be off and let you two eat your lunch. Nice meeting you, Ernest. May the Lord bless your day." Max grasped Mr. Olson's hand and thanked him once more.

"Well, Ernest, these sandwiches better be fit for a king. You and Miss Greene had enough time to fix a ham dinner." Max elbowed Ernest. His friend chuckled and smiled.

"Max, I haven't known that lady long, and I've been in love only once in my life. If butterflies in the stomach are any indication, then Max, I think I'm in love," Ernest said as he picked up a sandwich.

"In love? Are you kidding? You've spent all of, maybe, thirty minutes with her."

"Let's call it love-at-first-sight."

"Oh, Ernest, do you really believe in that? I mean, you see someone from across the room, you glide closer together, bells sound, everyone else in the room disappears, butterflies party in your stomach and you call it love." Max shook his head and picked up a half of sandwich. "You need to know a person in depth. All you know about Miss Greene is that she likes to cook."

"No, that's not true. I know she loves the Lord. She's never been married. She doesn't want to get to the end of her life alone. She loves Eden Lake, but is willing to travel. She's jovial, sweet, considerate, and is deeply concerned for you, Max. And on top of that, I think she loves me."

Max checked his watch. One hour to go. One hour before his love walked back into his life. One hour to convince Ernest there is no such thing as love-at-first-sight. He bit into his sandwich. Ham, cheese, tomato and lettuce with a light layer of butter on home-made sour-dough bread. "This is delicious," Max said.

The Merc's screen door slammed and drew his attention. Jed trotted toward the bench with an immense ham shank wedged between his jaws. Max slapped his leg and Jed settled down beside him. The dog secured the bone with his front paws and ripped the meaty portions off.

"I bet you don't even know her first name," Max challenged Ernest.

"It's Heather. Isn't that just about perfect as can be, for a Scotsman to marry a Heather?"

"So if you're thinking about marriage is she willing to move to Scotland? Her whole life has been spent in Eden Lake." Max wiped his mouth on a napkin. "What would we do without her?"

"Max, I do believe you're jealous. I may have found the love of my life. Wouldn't even blink an eye in hesitation to leave my Scottish life and friends behind and settle here with sweet Heather. Perhaps we could make it a double wedding, if you're ready to ask Maggie. Think of it. We could go fishing all the time. Now that's a great benefit. What do you say?"

Max downed the water that remained in his glass and cleared his throat.

"Ernest, I'm sorry. Here you are overjoyed with Miss Greene and the prospect of marrying her and all I can think of is it should be me first." Max slapped Ernest on the back, grabbed his hand, stood up and pulled Ernest to his feet.

"I congratulate you from the bottom of my heart. She's a wonderful woman and you're a wonderful man. I wish you a long and happy marriage. You're the perfect match for her." Max wrapped his arms around Ernest's shoulders and squeezed bear-hug style.

"Am I interrupting something?" Miss Greene asked.

"Not at all. I was congratulating Ernest on a fine lunch. I'm sure you coached him all the way," Max said. He hoped she hadn't overheard their conversation.

"Only a little. I laid the fixings out and he put the layers to-gether. I may have to add this lunch item to my slate board. Think I'll call it the Ernest Special."

A twinkle in her eye informed Max she not only wanted Ernest's name on her wall, but ultimately wanted her name to be the same as his.

"That's sweet of you, Heather. I would be honored to have a sandwich named after me."

Max smiled as Ernest grinned with delight. This would, indeed, be a wonderful match. And the thought of Ernest moving to Eden Lake, no words could express the joy he felt.

"Haven't you forgot something, Max?" Miss Greene asked. "The coach arrives in ten minutes. You should be at the station."

Panic filled Max's body. His feet didn't know which way to turn.

"Ernest, help me out here. Do I have any crumbs on my face? Does my hair need combing? Look at these boots. They're covered with dust." Max bent to brush them off, then spun around, arms outstretched for Ernest to give the once-over. "Well?"

"Goodness, gracious, Max. I would expect this 'looky-me' from a woman, but not a mountain man like you," Miss Greene kidded.

"I'm so nervous, Miss Greene." Max stretched his arm in front of him and tried to hold his hand still. "See how I shake? Haven't seen Maggie for several months now. Oh, yes, and Nellie. I want them to love Eden Lake as much as I do."

"Are you sure it's just Eden Lake you want them to love? Or, at least, you want Maggie to love?" Miss Greene winked.

"Don't worry, I'll be by your side and hold your hand if need be." Ernest patted Max on the back.

"Thanks again for lunch, Miss Greene. Add it to my bill."

"No need to, Max. Ernest paid for it already." Miss Greene placed her hands on the men's backs and gave a slight push. "Off you two go now. Bring them to the Merc before you leave. I want to inspect this ravishing beauty."

Max hesitated, then with Ernest's assistance, placed one foot forward, surprised how the other foot followed suit.

"Don't worry about Jed. He can stay with me. Too focused on that bone to pay you any mind," Miss Greene called to them.

Chapter 15

"Nellie, you would be perfect for the detective job. You've complained about the political system and the syndicate activity in Chicago." Maggie expressed her excitement that her dear friend may possibly move to the Pacific Northwest. Even though it meant leaving her behind, she desired the best for her friend.

"Absolutely right, my dear. Yet, it is only a consulting position at this point. If I do well, there's a chance I will be hired on the police force as a permanent employee." Nellie sighed. "A change of scenery would be perfect. Mt. Hood close by, the Willamette River divides the city into east and west. The chief mentioned the Pacific Ocean was only a day trip away. He asked me to read through a booklet outlining some of the unsolved cases. And I'll still have time to write. All of these factors entice me to accept the position."

Deep inside Maggie felt a twinge of jealousy. She grew up in this city and inwardly longed to leave Chicago and settle back on the West coast. Maybe live a few miles out of town, surrounded by trees, perhaps a babbling brook or small lake. Atmosphere is conducive to creativity and she felt drained in the big city. A change would do her good. Fresh faces, new challenges, could be just what the doctor ordered. A depression slump didn't suit her one bit.

"Why don't you scour the city for design studios? You may find one or two who create playbills and magazine covers that need your kind of imagination. If not here, Seattle isn't too far and we could still visit each other." Nellie said.

Maggie appreciated Nellie's thoughtfulness. They had been friends so long, it would be difficult to part ways.

The coach from Portland to Sandy left right on time. The conductor loaded their luggage in the boot. Both ladies carried a small handbag inside the coach. Maggie was thankful only two other passengers joined them for this leg of the journey to Gresham. Cramped quarters in hot weather sometimes caused irritability.

"That man who picked up our luggage said he would put our cases in the boot, Nellie. I've always wondered who came up with that word. Why don't they call it a luggage holder?"

"Maybe boot sounded more western. He has conductor embroidered on his suit. Only conductor I know of stands in front of an orchestra. We city dwellers would probably call it a luggage rack, or some such term. Whatever it is, we're on our way to Eden Lake," Nellie said.

Before the horses eased into a smooth pace, Maggie removed her bonnet and stuck her hat pin securely in the brim. She brushed a few wayward hairs off her face, then realized they may need to lower the windows if the compartment grew uncomfortably warm. What use would a few hair pins do then?

The countryside was beautiful. They passed through farmlands and uncultivated areas filled with Douglas fir. Maggie had forgotten how tall they grew. The denseness reminded her of parts of Scotland around Rolen. Here, they were much closer together, yet the sunlight still managed to squeeze through the branches. The warmth and sway of the coach lulled the other two passengers to sleep. Maggie glanced at Nellie who focused on a booklet compiled of unsolved cases.

Maggie became lost in her thoughts. Would Max be glad to see her? Would he feel the same about her as he had demonstrated in Scotland? Would she feel the same about Max? Would it be possible for them to have a life together? In Chicago? In Eden Lake? Maybe in Portland?

"Nellie, we're slowing down. Do you think we're in Eden Lake?" Maggie wiped her bare hands on her skirt, opened her gloves and prepared to slide her hands inside.

"No, this must be Gresham. We can stretch for twenty minutes, then off to Sandy. That's the last stop before Eden Lake. So still a ways to go, my dear." She patted Maggie's leg.

Maggie felt the butterflies in her stomach flit for a few seconds then quiet down again. She refolded her gloves, placed them inside her hat and waited for the coach to come to a complete stop.

"Let's go for a walk, Maggie and stretch these lazy legs. Need to soak in some sunshine, too."

After pinning her hat in place, Maggie slipped her gloves inside her handbag and followed Nellie onto the platform. A drugstore across the street caught her eye.

"Nellie, the sign reads root beer floats, five cents and sundaes for ten. My treat for either one."

"That's a hard decision, as I love both, but my waistline has taken a turn for the worst. I prefer the coffee for ten cents and a piece of cake for a nickel." Nellie massaged her sides. "No, skip the cake. Just a cup of coffee. Too much seating and eating lately."

Maggie secured a place in line while Nellie found a small bench under a large oak tree. The soda jerk quickly scooped ice cream and covered the mounds with hot fudge.

"Here you are, one cup of hot coffee. Can't quite understand drinking something hot on a hot day. Maybe two hots make a cold." Maggie chuckled as she thought about any two hot things making something cold. "I'm sorry. The heat must have frazzled my brain. This ice cream will cool it down."

Maggie slid close to Nellie and still hung over the edge on the bench. She nudged Nellie.

"Do you have any more room on the other end? I'm almost on the ground."

"Sure. I'll move a bit, than you squeeze in tighter. We'll make it work. I'll set my purse on my lap in case you set off my personal protector." Nellie moved her purse from the bench beside Maggie, then sipped her coffee.

"Your what?" Maggie raised her voice in surprise only to receive a shush sign from Nellie.

"My personal protector." Nellie leaned close to Maggie's ear. "The Chicago Chief of Police suggested I carry a palm pistol when he heard I was coming out west. Small enough to hold in the palm of your hand. Designed in France, the Chicago Firearms manufactured over 12,000 in '92." Nellie blew her coffee. "Great little gun. It has a 7-round revolving magazine, yet so small you hold it in your fist with the barrel protruding between two fingers and then squeeze the trigger with your palm to fire the gun. I have the safety on. Don't want to take any chances. I'll show you when we're by ourselves."

"So you're carrying a concealed weapon? Why not keep it in your suitcase?" Maggie's brow wrinkled with concern. She had never seen a real gun, let alone known someone who carried a firearm.

"Some of the cases I worked in Chicago may have a trail that leads to Oregon. Don't think I'm too popular with some of the syndicates. No way to check the identity of those traveling on the coach with us, so felt safer keeping it close. I do have a derringer in my suitcase, but with only one shot possible, I felt safer with the palm pistol. Hope this doesn't scare you."

Maggie inhaled deeply, squinted her eyes as if trying to push this new image of her dear friend out of her mind. Nellie, a gun-toting undercover detective. Why would any woman want to take on this dangerous job? Always apprehensive, glancing over her shoulder at every turn and probably jumping at every unfamiliar sound. No thank you. She preferred a quiet day at the drawing board, a walk in the cool of the evening, a good book and cozy fire before bed. No cops and robbers for her. No dead bodies. No sleuthing around abandoned houses to locate clues.

"Sorry I didn't tell you sooner, but I was afraid you may become anxious. Besides, I don't have a human protector. You do, sweet Maggie."

"What do you mean, a human protector?"

"Has the obvious escaped you? Time and time again, Max donned his 'knight-in-shining-armor' persona and came to your rescue in Scotland. His eyes sparkled when you were by his side and grew dim if you were not. I wouldn't be surprised if this would be your one-and-only trip to Eden Lake, with no exit foretold."

There's those pesky butterflies again. Cheeks on fire, Maggie rubbed her arms with her hands one more time and hoped all would calm down. The journey wasn't over. One more stop, another short coach ride, then she would be in Eden Lake, face-to-face with Max.

"I haven't stopped thinking about how often Max rescued me from that murderer. He was always there at just the right time." Maggie scooped another portion of ice cream and chocolate fudge on her spoon. Lost in her thoughts, this bite made its way in slow motion to her mouth.

"You're right, Nellie. Max won my heart when we met in Portland. Don't know if I ever told you, but we both worked at Meier & Frank Department Store downtown. He soda jerked and I had a position as a salesgirl. The store owners installed a big clock that hung over the middle of the main floor. We often met under the clock for lunch break. I wanted to put my art skills to work, so played the demure, 'marriage? — not-me-girl.' But deep inside I truly loved him."

"You better hurry with that ice cream sundae. Almost time to board for Sandy." Nellie finished her coffee, then placed a hand on Maggie's knee. "Don't worry, Maggie. I've had safety classes and shooting range practice. Think of me as a personal bodyguard. I'll always be there to protect you. And I have a feeling, Max will too."

Maggie knew she could count on Nellie in any situation. She had proven her loyalty time and again, especially during their investigation in Scotland. She'd have to get used to this new development. And who knows, maybe in the untamed wilderness around Mt. Hood, she would do well to carry a pistol. She'd ask Max for his advice.

The ladies returned the sundae bowl and coffee cup to the drug store. Maggie purchased a sack of peppermint drops and slipped them into her leather handbag.

"Listen, Nellie, they're playing "Hello Ma Baby" sung by Arthur Collins. What a catchy tune."

Maggie hurried to the coin-operated arcade machine. Fascinated how the spinning cylinder of the graphophone could generate music. She searched her purse for a coin to plunk in for one more play.

"We don't have time for another song, Maggie. Time to go. The passengers are boarding the coach." Nellie clutched Maggie's hand and escorted her to the boarding platform.

"I wonder if they have a graphophone in Eden Lake. I'd love to listen again."

"It's not the end of the world. I'm sure Eden Lake has all the modern conveniences."

"I'm not so sure. From Max's description of the town, it sounded rather remote."

"I understand the song is about a relationship carried on over the telephone. Not like you and Max. I've got an idea, Maggie. When you disembark from the coach at Eden Lake, why not sing that song to Max. I can hear it now. You, crooning 'Hello, ma baby, hello, ma honey, hello, ma mountain man.' Have to change the words a bit."

"Oh, Nellie," Maggie poked her friend. "You and your imagination."

Maggie's face blushed.

"And for your information, Max is not 'ma baby.'" Maggie noticed the other passengers had boarded the coach. "At least, not yet."

The two girls giggled all the way to the platform. Laughter is good medicine, says the Bible, and Maggie sure needed a dose of it's calming power.

Chapter 16

A crowd gathered at the coach platform. Some waited for the arrivals to Eden Lake. Others waited to leave and suppressed their emotional good-byes until the last minute. Max noticed a mother who clung to her son. Her husband wrapped his arm around her for support. This young adult man might be leaving Eden Lake to find work outside the logging industry. The need to find gainful employment without the risks. Hadn't Max chosen the same path? He longed to be a writer, not a logger. The young man left his mother's side to greet Max.

"Mr. Sullivan, I want to thank you for your advice a year ago. Your words haunted me until I finally made the decision to leave Eden Lake. Logging's not for me. Too dangerous. I love to write, like you, so I'm off to Portland. Saved up enough money for a year. Then I'll reevaluate."

Max shook his hand. "Adventure awaits, Sam. Your mom appears heartbroken, but Portland's not that far and you can return for the holidays."

"A friend of mine got me a job. He has an apartment big enough for the both of us." Sam grabbed Max's hand one more time. "Thanks again, Mr. Sullivan."

"I have encouraged you," said Max, "now time for you to encourage your mother. Good luck, Sam and God's blessings on your studies."

Had it really been eight years since Max did the same thing; left Eden Lake, moved to her town, Portland, and met Maggie? He felt they had come full circle. Soon Maggie would be in his town. His heart skipped a beat and his pulse increased. Got to keep these nerves under control.

"Are you counting down the minutes, Max?"

Startled, Max jumped. "Ernest, you're so quiet. I didn't hear you approach."

"Helped Heather wash our lunch dishes and lost track of time.

Afraid I'd be late, but the sign reads "Coach from Sandy - delayed." So, I'm early."

"You and Miss Greene have a good time washing dishes?" Max asked.

"I always have a good time with Heather. Max, she's everything I want in a woman. Where can I buy an engagement ring? I'm ready to propose."

The only other time Max had seen his friend so excited was in Scotland fishing for Ol' Moses. And maybe on Eden Lake with granddaddy hooked on his line.

"Sandy has two general merchandise stores. Both are larger than our Merc and one has a ballroom and saloon. I'm not sure if either have wedding rings. Possibly a small selection, but reasonably priced."

"Hang the price, Laddie. This is one time this Scot's not going to be thrifty. You yanks say we're stingy, but not true. We know the value of our money and use it wisely. Never proposed before, so I'm making a memory to last a lifetime." Ernest's smile covered his face.

"When can we go to Sandy? My money's burning a hole in my pouch and I want to spend days, and nights, with my gal."

"Whoa there, boy. A few days' time won't hurt. Besides, it's close to July fourth. A big day for us yanks and Sandy puts on a great celebration. We could go a day early while the stores are still open. Everything shuts down for the Fourth. Maggie and Nellie would enjoy the festivities also."

"Okay, July third we go. Yes?"

"Yes, Ernest, July third we go. Now you better wipe that lip rouge off your cheek before the girls arrive. You should be able to see yourself in the station window. You want to surprise them, I'm sure, but not on their first day in Eden Lake."

"Coach should be here any minute now, folks. Please stay back from the edge of the platform," the station master announced.

"Any minute now." Those words bounced around in Max's head like an echo in a ravine. Any minute now, Maggie and Nellie would step off the coach. What would Maggie do when she saw him? Would she run with open arms? Slowly reach his side? Or would she faint as she saw his gaunt face and small frame? *Pull yourself together.*

"I'm back, Max, and still in time. There's a cloud of brown dust rising above the trees. Won't be long now. You ready?" Ernest asked.

"As ready as I'll ever be." Max checked for dust on his boots, hand brushed his pants and ran his fingers through his tousled hair. He tucked in his shirt and inhaled deeply. "Flowers. We should have flowers to welcome the girls."

From behind Ernest's back came two lovely bouquets of wild-flowers. One in each hand.

"Miss Heather brought them. Sweetest lady in the whole world," Ernest said.

"Bless her heart." Max held one bouquet and Ernest the other as the coach came into view.

"Ernest, not a word about Emeline or Molech, I don't want to scare the girls. They'll find out soon enough. Promise?"

"Yes, Max, I promise. Not a word until needed. I pray for Maggie and Nellie's protection and hope they never meet either one of the evil demons."

"Nellie, can you see anything? Can you see Max? Are we almost there?"

"I declare, Maggie, you sound like a smitten school girl. You should have sat on this side of the coach from Sandy. Hold my hat and I'll stick my head outside."

Maggie clutched Nellie's hat. Nellie received the full force of the blowing wind and immediately pulled back inside.

"I'm not doing that again. Look at my hair now and I bet my face is brown from the flying dust. You'll have to wait."

Maggie retrieved her hankie and removed the specs of dust that dotted Nellie's face. She reapplied rouge to Nellie's lips and brushed her disheveled tresses under her hair combs.

"There, all better. Here's my mirror. Can I fix anything else?" Maggie asked.

"Yes, my disposition." Nellie glanced in the mirror then returned it to Maggie.

"I'm sorry, Maggie. I certainly don't mean to be an old bear. This body likes to be on the move and all we've done today is sit. My brain craves stimulation. When one end goes to sleep, so does the other." Nellie raised off the seat and rubbed her backside.

"I totally understand." Maggie repositioned herself. "Maybe we can go for a walk this afternoon. Breathe some refreshing mountain air instead of the coach's stale substitute."

The two other passengers awoke and fidgeted with their ties and satchels.

"Have you two ladies been to Eden Lake before?" The older gentleman asked.

"No, this is our first time." Nellie said. "Have you?"

"No, neither one of us. We're salesmen down from Seattle and don't mind telling you how scared we are."

"Of the people?" Maggie asked.

"No, not of the people, but of the four legged predators. We'd like to hike the forest, but not without an experienced guide and lots of firearms. Never seen a bear or mountain lion up close and don't plan to. But would like to see some deer," the younger man said as he pulled out a small handgun from his satchel. "Came prepared. You know, wild west and all."

"I doubt that pea-shooter will protect you from man or beast," Nellie said. "From what I know, Eden Lake is pretty tame, mostly loggers. And as for wild animals, my thought is they have their own territory and we need to respect them and leave them alone. You know, live and let live," Nellie said.

He returned the gun to the satchel. Both men ended eye contact with Nellie and stared outside.

"Houses, Maggie. We must be getting close," Nellie said.

While Nellie held the mirror, Maggie applied a fresh layer of lip rouge and repositioned some loose hairs. After a pinch on each cheek for color, she fastened her hat in place. The time had come.

As the stagecoach came into view, Max's heart matched the hoofbeat of the mules. The two brown mules were trained to stop next to the platform. And stop they did. Max admired these strong creatures. God created the perfect animal for heavy work. Eden Lake loggers used mules to pull the logs down the mountains to the mill. Max considered purchasing mules, but couldn't pass up a great offer on Bess and Kate.

Joel waited until the coach came to a complete stop. He motioned the people on the platform to remain back so the passengers could disembark. Then he opened the stage door.

"Max, you okay?" Ernest brushed off the back of Max's jacket.

Max swayed with eyes closed, almost like a drunken man. He slowly opened his eyes and turned toward Ernest. "I'm fine, Ernest. That is other than my heart preparing to explode, numb lips, wobbly knees, and the feeling of bladder urgency. Yes, I'm fine. Oh, did I mention some of the petals have flown off the flowers in this bouquet due to my shaking hands?"

Max felt Ernest's strong hand wrap around him, grip his arm and pull him close. Then Ernest whispered, "I'm here, Max, and so is the Lord. I pray for calm to overtake your body this very instant."

Max's heart and body calmed at the same moment Nellie stepped out of the coach.

"Ernest, pray the petals jump back on the flowers. Hurry." Max said.

Nellie appeared a bit disheveled to Max. Her hat sat cattywampus with strands of hair tangled in all directions. The scarf at her neck had one loop remaining while her jacket buttons and loops weren't matched.

"Me first," Ernest said. "You wait for Maggie." Ernest opened his arms, held the bouquet of flowers toward Nellie and waited.

"Ernest. Is that you or an American double?" Nellie said while she pushed her hat back in place.

"No, sweet Nellie, it's me in the flesh, Lassie. Come, give old Ernest a hug now."

Joy overflowed in Max as these two friends greeted each other. Nellie wrapped her arms around Ernest and the two briefly embraced.

"I can't believe it. What are you doing in Eden Lake?" Nellie gasped.

"Visiting my dear friend Max and waiting for the two finest lassies I've ever known. Welcome to Eden Lake." Ernest presented Nellie the cluster of flowers.

"And, Max. Where's Max?"

"I'm here, Nellie." Max waited for a spontaneous hug also, but Nellie hesitated.

"Max? Why, of course you are. Don't know where my mind was. Too long a stage time I imagine."

Max instinctively knew from the look in Nellie's eyes that his altered appearance disturbed her. *What about Maggie?*

An awkward hug from Nellie ended as quickly as it started. Now to find Maggie.

Max scanned the platform. Most of the people were gone as the coach had loaded passengers for the return trip to Sandy. A young lady handed the conductor some change, bent over two bags, then faced Max.

Her face was ashen and her hesitancy cautioned Max against over-exuberance. With slow strides, Max ambled toward her. She appeared to take a step, then stopped. Max's emotional turmoil increased. He forced his feet into automatic motion. The less distance between them, the more his legs felt like rubber. Would they hold him up when he faced her?

Only two feet separated them. Max extended the bouquet to Maggie.

"Welcome to Eden Lake, Maggie. These are for you."

What a lame thing to say. The long anticipated wait for Maggie was over and that's all he could think of to greet her?

Maggie's gloved hand grasped the flowers. "Thank you, Max. They're lovely."

If staring was a sign of love, affection, miss you, glad you're here, then these two said it all. Max longed to embrace her. To lift her off her feet in joyous celebration of their reunion. To caress her face and gently bring her lips to his. He had replayed this encounter countless times since her letter last March. Yet, now, face-to-face, all he could do was thrust flowers and welcome her to his town. *What are you waiting for?*

"Maggie." Before Max could utter another word, he clasped her in his arms, smashing the bouquet between their chests. He had imagined this feeling for years, but finally it was a reality. Her body compressed into his. Max held her close, her head resting on his shoulder. He felt her heartbeat and sensed her quivering body.

Max relaxed his arms, place his hands on her shoulders and gazed into her eyes. Filled with tears, she blinked and the moisture cascaded down her cheeks.

"Oh, Max. I'm sorry. It's just that I've waited so long in the hopes you would greet me exactly as you did. This was the perfect welcome. And I love the flowers, squashed or not." Maggie reached for a hankie in her purse.

Max wiped Maggie's tears with his neck scarf. "I will never wash this scarf again, my sweet."

"Well, I must say, you two are off to a good start." Nellie interrupted. "Maggie, if you can tear yourself away from Max, there's someone else waiting to greet you."

Max removed himself from Maggie's view of Ernest.

"Ernest? Is that you?" Maggie exclaimed.

"Must be an echo in this town. That's the same thing Nellie said." Ernest chuckled. "You are even more beautiful than I remember, Lassie. How about a hug for old Ernest?"

Max envied Ernest for his easy way with words. How right this was that all four were together again.

"I came over a few weeks ago to spend time with Max. I was over-joyed to hear both you lassies planned a visit before I return to Scotland." Ernest leaned toward Max. "That is, if I return to Scotland," he whispered with a wink.

While Maggie hugged Ernest, Max retrieved the girls' bags and placed them in his wagon. Ernest strode between the girls as he escorted them toward the Merc, each lassie holding one arm.

"There's someone I want you to meet." Max heard Ernest say when he caught up to the threesome.

Inside the Merc, the corner table was set with four sandwiches, pieces of pie, glasses of water and a vase of wild flowers. A customer finished her transaction, then left the Merc. Miss Greene glanced up from the cash register, grinned and rushed around the counter to Ernest's side.

"Max, I'm so glad you came back." She turned to the ladies. "I'm Miss Greene, owner of the Merc. I've heard so much about you, I feel we're already good friends." She extended a hand toward Nellie, "You must be Miss Cox. Ernest mentioned you were a detective. I'm so glad you're here. We need a good detective." Then to Maggie, "And you must be Miss Richards. I'm also the telegraph lady and have been waiting since March to meet you. Welcome ladies to Eden Lake."

"Thank you so much, Miss Greene. We're honored to meet you as well." Nellie said.

"Miss Greene? Did you set that table for us?" Max asked.

Jed raced from the back room when he heard Max's voice. His tail wagged so hard, he almost lost his balance. With front paws stretched to reach Max's knees, Jed demanded attention.

"Sorry, fella. I almost forgot you in the commotion of welcoming the ladies." Max stroked Jed's fur, then flattened his hand parallel to the floor. Jed sat on his hunches as he obeyed Max's command.

"Maggie, Nellie, this is my wonderful dog, Jed. Jed, meet Nellie and Maggie."

Jed waged his way to each lady. Max directed the girls to open their hands, palms up. Jed gently laid his paw in each open hand to greet them.

"Now, that introductions are over, I knew the ladies would be hungry." Miss Greene said. "And you and Ernest never refuse a meal. Even though you ate such a short time ago, I figured you could always have more. Didn't know what you had planned for dinner, but I wanted satisfied stomachs before they left for your cabin." Miss Greene chuckled as she pulled the chairs out from the table for the ladies.

Conversation filled the air as the friends shared their lives since they left Scotland. Max waited for Ernest to share his news about Miss Greene. With July third only a few days away, perhaps Ernest would wait until he had a ring for the announcement. Max would need to remind himself to keep the joyous news quiet as well.

"If everyone is finished, I'd like to start for the cabin," Max said. "We'll travel the scenic backroads for the girls to view more than the main road home. So it will take a bit longer. Any objections?"

"None at all," they each answered and agreed a journey home, in an open wagon, would be a nice change from the stuffy coach.

Chapter 17

Maggie breathed in the rich smell of pine. How skillfully Max guided his team of horses through the forest over the meandering trail. Steep at times, the path required Bess and Kate to walk slowly as they dug their hoofs into the ground. Jostled, Maggie hung onto the side of the bench. If only Max could brace her in his arms, but with his hands full of reins, this would be impossible.

"How's the ride back there, Nellie?" Maggie asked.

"Not too bad. The boys cushioned the ride with quilts over the feed. I don't even mind the alfalfa smell. Although it does compete with the pine trees," Nellie said. "Jed seems to love it. He darts from side to side staring into the forest. Must spot a squirrel or rabbit. His tail has wagged non-stop since we entered the woods."

The road leveled out. Max make a clicking sound and the horses picked up their pace. A light breeze cooled Maggie's face.

"That breeze feels wonderful. Do we have much farther to go?" Maggie asked.

"Less than a quarter mile. We'll soon meet up with the main road. I own twenty acres and seldom come this way. My purpose was two-fold; for you to see the forest around my place and to check for any fallen trees whether from wind storms or old age."

"What about wild animals? Are we likely to meet any bear or cougar?" Nellie asked.

"That's always possible out here," Max said. "But not to worry, ladies. Ernest has my 30-30 Winchester 94 rifle. It can be ready to fire in a few seconds. My Colt '45 is under our seat, Maggie. So we're well covered. If we were in any eminent danger, Jed's back hair would stand up, followed by a growl, then barking. We'd have plenty of warning."

Maggie breathed a sigh of relief. She could relax and enjoy the beauty of the moss covered trees and fallen trunks which sprouted new growth. Every shadow conjured a bear or cougar image, but since Jed remained quiet, she felt safe.

"Look, Maggie, Nellie. There's Eden Lake. We're almost home." Max's voice filled with excitement. He sounded like a little boy, peeking at the Christmas tree before anyone else arose, eager to check the gifts for his name. She wrapped her arm around his. His muscles bulged against her arm as he pulled on the reins to slow the wagon.

The horses stopped. Max sprang from the wagon with the agility of a much younger man. He raised his arms to help Maggie down. His hands on her waist sent shivers through her body. Their faces, so close together, their lips inches apart.

Ernest cleared his throat as he assisted Nellie to the road, successfully diverting Max's attention.

"This is one of my favorite views of Eden Lake. The other is from my front porch. Thought, you ladies would like to stretch a bit," Max said.

"How close are we now to your cabin, Max?" Maggie stretched her arms behind her back.

"Oh, probably one-eighth of a mile. You can see the bend a ways farther ahead. That's where it meets up with the main road. Once we go around the bend, you'll be able to see the cabin."

Maggie glanced at Nellie. "Maggie, I can read your mind," Nellie said. "We talked about a walk this afternoon, fellas. This seems like the perfect time."

Maggie faced Max. "Do you mind if we walk the rest of the way? You and Ernest could go on ahead and unload the wagon. Sound all right?"

"Sounds fine to me," Max said. "Ernest, any misgivings?"

"Not if they take the rifle. We could give them a shooting lesson right here."

"No need, Ernest," Nellie clutched the rifle and braced the butt against her shoulder. "I've been trained on rifles as well as hand guns. You see, living in Chicago and working with the police, I received training in shooting and safety from the best. I would appreciate it if you left Jed as well. He can be our scout and guide us home."

Maggie rubbed Jed's back. His fur felt silky under her hand. Max gave the command for Jed to stay with the girls. Ernest checked the chamber, handed extra cartridges to Nellie and climbed up next to Max.

"See you at the cabin, girls." Max clicked and the horses pulled the wagon toward home.

Maggie gazed at the back of the wagon as it disappeared into the distance around the bend. She loved to ride beside Max and to feel the warmth of his body next to hers. Jed gently pulled on her skirt. Time to go. She wiped her clammy hands on her hankie and prayed Jed would be their great protector.

"Well, Annie Oakley, you ready to blaze our way through this forest to Max's cabin?" Maggie asked Nellie, a quiver in her voice.

"Maggie, dear, we have Jed, an excellent rifle already loaded, and we're not blazing a trail. We'll follow the road, stroll around the bend and be at his cabin in no time. You relax and enjoy the beautiful scenery." Nellie tucked the rifle butt under her arm and rested the barrel in her hand. "Oh, yes, I also have my palm pistol, but won't be much use unless the cougar stands perfectly still at our feet."

Maggie loved her friend's laughter, but this didn't seem to be the most advantageous time. She inhaled deeply and raised her eyes skyward, "Lord, You've gotten us this far from Chicago, please guide us safely to Max's cabin. Thank you."

Maggie firmly gripped Nellie's free hand. The girls and Jed ventured toward the lake.

"How long will it take the girls to walk to your cabin?" Ernest asked.

"Not too long, depends on whether they dawdle. If you will bury the rabbits, I'll care for the horses and unload the feed."

Max, knees shaking, surveyed the porch for any signs of Emeline or Molech. The red scarf remained suspended from the nail and the porch, except for a few leaves, remained vacant of Molech's offerings.

"Big paw prints back there." Ernest rounded the corner of the stable. "A hungry cougar must have disposed of the rabbits. Only a little fur left."

"Good, one less thing to take care of." Max brushed the leaves off the porch. "Nothing here either. Let's open the cabin windows for some fresh air."

Max and Ernest entered the cabin and opened the shutters. Warm invigorating air streamed through the dwelling. The sun filled the room. Max scrutinized every nook and cranny. It had to be perfect for Maggie.

"Ernest, do you see anything out of place? I want Maggie to love my cabin at first sight."

Max scurried from side to side, corner to corner, checked under chairs and tables and wiped off a speck of dust from the kitchen counter.

"Did I miss anything?" Max asked. "I know — Ernest, go outside and come in as if it were the first time you've been here. Then tell me what needs to be fixed. Hurry. They should be here any moment."

"Max, I will do as you ask, but mainly to humor you." Ernest strolled outside, then re-entered and closed the door behind him. "Everything is in its proper place, Laddie, and your cabin is extremely welcoming."

He patted Max on the back, "I think we need to buy two engagement rings on the third."

"Possibly you're right." Max pumped fresh water into the coffee pot, added some grounds and placed it on the cook stove. "Thought the girls might enjoy a cup of coffee when they get here."

"Hot coffee? You sure, Laddie? I would think something cool and thirst quenching after their stage trip and hike. Ice tea if you have any ice in your root cellar. Otherwise, I would suggest a tall glass of your delicious mountain water. But, coffee? I think not." Ernest wrinkled his brow.

"Now you tell me. I've already dumped the coffee grounds in. Well, we can wait to have coffee this evening." Max stared into the percolator and replaced the lid. He set the tin of Hills Bros. coffee back on a shelf.

"A bit testy, are we?" Ernest said, desperate to lighten the atmosphere.

"Sorry, Ernest. I'm so blamed nervous. I've rehearsed this moment time and again since last fall when we docked in New York and parted ways. I love that girl, Ernest, and if her hug is any indication, I believe she loves me. Why can't we skip these silly preliminaries and pretend she's been here for a week? Perhaps then I could relax and simply enjoy her company."

A comforting hand rested on his shoulder.

"Lord, be with my brother, Max. Calm his spirit, relax his soul and rest his mind. All the circumstances of his life are in Your loving hands. Confirm in him that reality. Amen."

The two men's eyes met in brotherly love. Max sighed heavily and placed his hand on Ernest's shoulder. "Ernest, you truly were sent here for a time as this. Definitely not Esther, but used mightily of the Lord just the same. Thank you."

"You're very welcome and, indeed, it is truly my pleasure. After-dinner coffee sounds great."

Max heard footsteps on the porch. His heart pounded.

Would Maggie approve of my home?

Chapter 18

"Maggie and Nellie. They're here." Max spun toward the door.

"I doubt it, Laddie." Ernest said. "They couldn't walk that fast."

"But I heard footsteps on the porch." Max ran fingers through his unruly hair.

"Maybe you did and maybe you didn't," Ernest said. "No sound of Jed though."

A sharp rap on the door startled Max.

"Maggie's here. Am I ready?"

"Go, Laddie. Let the wee lassie in."

Max inhaled deeply, swallowed hard, gazed at Ernest, who nodded his approval. His hand reached for the latch, slid it aside and slowly pulled the door open.

"Emeline!" Max faltered.

"Max. You seem surprised. Were you expecting someone else?"

"Yes, as a matter of fact. Maggie and Nellie decided to walk a distance to the cabin. I thought you were them."

"From the look on your face, you're greatly disappointed. Only me, your neighborhood welcome committee." Emeline smiled with a twinkle in her eye.

"I'm sorry, Max." She held out a box. "I promised a treat of chocolate fudge for the ladies. I'll leave this box on the porch table. Don't want to bring any dirt or loose leaves into your clean cabin. Then I'll leave you three alone."

"Three? I have three guests, Emeline. There's four of us and you're welcome to stay and meet them."

"Oh, yes, I forgot. There's Ernest. I told him I would bake an extra portion for him. I wrapped it separately. Extra chocolate to sweeten his day. Please be sure he gets it."

Emeline walked to the porch table. "And no, I don't believe I'll stay. I have things to do. If you will excuse me, I'll meet them another time."

Max's eyes followed Emeline as she glided down the steps. *What a graceful woman. How could Ernest judge her demon possessed? This seemed outlandish.* He never saw a hint of demonic activity in any of his conversations with her. He prayed for spiritual discernment and confirmation that Ernest spoke the truth. While he believed his friend, a sliver of doubt remained.

"Hi, there." Nellie's voice broke the silence.

Max stepped back in surprise. "Nellie, you startled me. I didn't see you coming."

He scrambled off the porch toward the girls and relieved Nellie of the rifle. Jed lowered his head, flattened his ears and slinked up the porch steps.

"Nellie, Maggie, I'd like you to meet Emeline Toliver. Emeline, this is Nellie Cox and Maggie Richards from Chicago."

Nellie and Emeline eyed each other like two teenage girls in competition for some reason.

"Miss Toliver," Nellie said with a stilted, yet polite shake of Emeline's hand.

"Miss Cox," Emeline responded. "And Miss Richards." Emeline enfolded Maggie's hand with her own hands in a warm greeting. "I'm so glad to make your acquaintance. I do hope you plan a long stay. I feel we're going to become best friends."

"I noticed you carried Max's rifle on your walk. Is there something you're afraid of, Miss Cox?" Emeline asked.

"Only the unexpected, Miss Toliver. I presume it is 'Miss.'" Nellie said.

"Yes, Miss Cox. I haven't found anyone who compares to Max here, but I believe he's married to his books and the fanciful stories he writes. I'd like to seduce him to write me in as a beautiful heroine in one of his tales. At least then I'd be able to cuddle with him at night."

Heat surged through Max's body as Emeline rubbed her hand on his arm.

"Maybe someday. Yes, Max?" She winked. "But as to your remark about only being afraid of the unexpected, I will caution you. A person can always meet the unexpected at Eden Lake. So be on your guard, Miss Cox."

"I plan to, Miss Toliver."

"Must be off now." Emeline grabbed Beelzebub's reins. "Beel hasn't had a good run for days. We're off to Lost Lake and home before dark. So nice to meet you both. I trust you will have a pleasant, yet eventful stay."

A small cloud of dust rose from the road as Emeline and Beelzebub rode north. Max checked the position of the sun.

"Close to four o'clock now. She's going to have to ride hard if she plans to make Lost Lake and home before nightfall." Max said.

"Who was that?" Nellie asked. "I mean, she's very beautiful, but something about her irks me. Certainly has her eyes on you, Max. Her black steed is magnificent. Amazing how a spritely young woman can manage a horse that size. Well, Max, who is she?"

"A neighbor," Ernest reclined in a porch chair where he had gone unnoticed. "She lives on the other side of Eden Lake. Comes over from time to time."

"Maggie, what did you think?" Ernest asked.

"I found her to be an extremely interesting young woman," Maggie said. "Her spunky personality grew on me as she talked. However, she also impressed me as being a natterer. Those kind of people wear me out."

"And you, Nellie, Miss Investigator, what is your first impression, besides that she "irks" you?" asked Ernest.

"She gives me the heebie-jeebies, Ernest. And Max, I trust you are not interested in Miss Watch-Me-Leap-To-My-Trusty-Stead-In-A-Single-Bound neighbor across the lake. Please say no," Nellie said.

"Nellie, she's a neighbor, that's all."

"Max, let's walk the girls to the lake. The view of Mt. Hood is incredible. Only the reflection of Emeline's shack sullies the beauty."

Max waited for Ernest to join them. His friend then whispered in Max's ear, "I wish she also was no more than a speck. Maybe we could blow her away like dandelion seeds."

Max held Maggie's hand as they strolled toward the dock. Ernest and Nellie followed while Jed scampered ahead of them.

"Oh, Max, this is indeed beautiful. Your description in Scotland didn't do it justice," Maggie said. "I can understand why you prefer to live nestled in the forest. Majestic Mt. Hood to greet you each day and no street noise. If possible, I would trade places with you instantly."

"Would you, Maggie? I assumed you made Chicago your home. Why would you want to leave?" Max asked.

"Oh, lots of reasons. The city is growing which increases industry and employment opportunities, but with growth comes a larger population creating extra noise. I don't know. Guess I miss Portland and the Pacific Northwest."

"Portland's no small town either, Lassie."

"I know, Ernest. I couldn't believe how much it grew since I lived there. But still smaller than Chicago's almost two million. Besides, Nellie's been offered a job with the Portland Metropolitan Police as a consulting investigator. If she moved, I wouldn't have my good friend to chum with. I would miss her."

"Maggie, I would miss you too," said Nellie. "Let's pray that one of the agencies you applied to in Portland will offer you employment. Perhaps when we get home, a letter will be waiting."

Max gazed at Maggie. "If you lived in Portland, you could visit Jed and me anytime. We would love your company."

The four reunited friends soaked in the peacefulness of Eden Lake. The sweet fragrance from the lupin and Jacob's ladder blooms refreshed Max's spirit. Next to him, his sweetheart, her best friend and his best friend close by, what could be more perfect? For Max nothing could upset him, not Emeline's friskiness or even Molech's grotesque behavior.

"Nellie, how about you and I start dinner?" Ernest's voice interrupted the calm. "I caught Eden Lake's Ol' Moses this morning. You can assist me in preparing him and baked tatties. What do you say?"

"I would love to assist you, Ernest. Give me a chance to wash a layer of trail dust off my face." Nellie brushed her skirt with her hands. "Maggie, see you and Max later."

"That's Emeline's cabin across the lake." Max pointed. "If you like, you can use my binoculars for a better glimpse. Actually, it is a shack, as Ernest mentioned. While Ernest fished this morning, I tried to find any sign of life around her place. It seemed so dead. Couldn't even find where she stabled Beelzebub."

"Beelzebub? That's a reference to Satan in the Bible. Why on earth would someone name their horse Beelzebub? Maybe he acts like a demon. He certainly frightens me." Maggie said. "What do you know about her?"

"Not much really. She brings baked goods for me from time to time. Always friendly, but standoffish. Did you notice Jed's behavior, when you arrived at the cabin and Emeline greeted you? He keeps his distance from her. I believe animals have a keen sense of safety and danger. I think Emeline frightens him. Perhaps Nellie can practice her detective skills. We're hungry for information." Max shook his head. "But enough about Emeline. Let me help you into my boat. I'll row you out from shore so you can see the entire lake."

Proud of his lake and mountain, Max enjoyed showcasing the beauty of God's creation. Each day he praised God for allowing him to live in the Pacific Northwest. A distance from shore, he pivoted the boat so Maggie would have a complete view of his cabin.

"Oh, Max. I truly am envious now. A picture postcard to be sure. What a view. I love your place and can't wait to see the inside of your cabin."

"Well, won't be long now. There's Ernest on the porch waving my red scarf. Must be dinner time."

Max absorbed Maggie's beauty as he rowed to shore. He rebelled at the thought that she might leave Eden Lake. This boat, his cabin, even a wagon ride would not be the same if she left. Yet, whenever he forced an honest evaluation of himself and his situation, Max mentally kicked his backside for being so self-centered. A flourishing job as a graphic artist fulfilled her artistic passion, why would she want to be saddled with a sickie, someone who had limited time left on earth. Why, indeed?

"Ernest, I must ask you something before Max and Maggie return."

"Sure, Nellie, what is it?"

"Something's wrong with Max. Am I right? I noticed when we arrived his poor color and weight loss. He doesn't look much like the Max I knew in Scotland. What can you tell me?"

Ernest cleared his throat. He placed napkins and dinner utensils on the table. As he reached for glasses to fill with water, Nellie repeated her question.

"Nellie, I canna say anything about my dear friend. I have sworn confidentiality in this matter and leave the telling to Max. I request that you say nothing. Allow him to share. All I can do is agree with you that Max has lost weight. Let's leave it there."

Ernest's eyes pleaded with Nellie. She did not want to overstep her bounds.

"I will say nothing more. But just so you know, Maggie's heart, and mine, are heavy with concern for Max. If anything can be done we would like to pursue the options."

"You're a bonnie lassie. Pray, Nellie. You and Maggie can pray."

Ernest said."I hear their voices outside. We need to change the subject, Lassie."

"Satan is so much more in earnest than we are —
he buys up the opportunity while we are wondering how
much it will cost."　　　*—Amy Carmichael—*

Chapter 19

Maggie rose early from a refreshing night's slumber. A flood of sunlight touched the tip of Mt. Hood as she leaned against the porch railing and sang a song of praise to God. The mountain's reflection was obscured with a layer of fog covering the water. Fully in love with Eden Lake and Max's cozy cabin, Maggie pondered what a glorious place this would be to live and work. Concern about Max's illness hovered over her like a darkened storm cloud ready to burst.

The lake beckoned. Chilled on the dock, she wrapped her arms around her body. A day on the lake with Max conjured images of picnic baskets, sweet scents from a cluster of wild flowers and a quiet shady spot to cuddle. Some time away from Nellie and Ernest would be wonderful.

"Good morning, Miss Richards."

Maggie jerked to the sound of Emeline's voice.

"Good morning, to you, Miss Toliver," Maggie responded. "So enthralled with the beauty of Eden Lake, I didn't see or hear you."

"In this fog I'm not surprised. People say I'm light on my feet and seldom heard, even in my rowboat." Emeline maneuvered close to Maggie.

"How about an early morning excursion? I'll have you back in time for breakfast. Would love to show you my favorite spot. The view is magnificent."

Maggie considered her offer then glanced at the cabin. She couldn't see any movement on the porch nor smoke rising from the chimney.

"Maybe I should tell Nellie, or leave a note."

"No need to. We won't be long. It's not far and we'll stay in view of the cabin. This fog should lift soon."

Maggie climbed in as Emeline held the dock securely.

"This will be a good chance for us to get acquainted." Emeline shoved off.

"I know you are an artist, live in Chicago, met Max in Portland and vacationed with him and Nellie in Scotland, where you met Ernest. So all the hum-drum stuff can be skipped."

"Well, you certainly know more about me than I of you." Maggie's brow wrinkled.

"What? Max hasn't told you anything about me? He's such a private guy. I love that about him," Emeline winked. "He's my kind of man, Maggie. Rugged, caring, courteous and places the needs of others before his own. Don't find many men like Max, especially in Eden Lake. Maybe one day you'll find someone like him for your own."

The fog thickened and Maggie no longer saw the dock nor the cabin. Even Emeline seemed to fade.

"Emeline, you must be under some misconception. Max hasn't said anything about a relationship with you. I suggest this 'more-than-friendship' is a figment of your imagination. When we return I'll speak to Max and listen to his side of the story." Maggie's voice trembled. "For now, I request you row back to the dock. I'm cold and the fog seems to be getting thicker."

"Miss Richards, you are the one with delusions." Emeline pulled harder on the oars. "Your relationship with Max hasn't been kindled for months. Mine is fresh and new. Only one of us will live in Max's cabin and share his bed. Only one of us will remain in Eden Lake. And, Miss City Gal, it won't be you. You have no idea how to live in the wilderness. Your life is filled with city noises. A minuscule crunch or shadow in the woods terrorizes you." Emeline pulled harder on the oars. The boat reached the middle of the lake.

"No, Miss Richards, you will not be staying. I suggest you pack your bags and board the next stage out of here. Don't worry about Max. If he's broken hearted, I can mend it. Guaranteed."

"I'm not leaving, Miss Toliver." Heat filled Maggie's cheeks. Her heart raced. "No matter how you plan to come between Max and me, you won't win. I've loved him for years. I left him for Chicago and I left him after Scotland. I will NOT leave him again."

The echo bounced across the lake and back again. She had finally announced to the world she loved him. Now to tell Max.

The fog shrouded Emeline's face. Only two coal black sphere's for eyes encircled by a fire-like halo remained. Maggie's body burned from the inside out. Sweat dampened her brow. She wiped the moisture from her hands.

"I demand you row me back to shore. Now." Again her voice

amplified.

A faint, "Maggie?" came from the distant shore.

Max called to her. She cupped her hands around her mouth to answer. The boat rocked violently from side to side.

The heavy jostling heaved young Maggie into the cold water. Her skirt swooshed passed her arms and around her head. She shoved her arms forcefully to her sides and kicked her legs. Propelled to the surface, Maggie gasped for breath. She tread water and searched for Emeline and her boat. No sight of either in the gray haze.

"Miss Toliver? Are you there? Are you all right?" No answer. "Lord, please help me."

The cold water permeated her body. She intensified her kicks and arm strokes, but had no idea which direction to swim. Besides Emeline, the fog had become her enemy. Did each stroke move her toward Max? Or toward Emeline? That evil woman may be an arm's length away. Even if Emeline offered to pull her in the boat, Maggie would resolutely refuse.

"Maggie, Maggie, where are you?" Max's faint voice carried over the water.

Maggie faced the sound of his voice. Her skirt and undergarments weighed her down. Memories of a near fatal drowning as a child in the Columbia River replayed in her head. Not going to happen today either. Maggie reached around her waist and unbuttoned her skirt. She loosened the band. The skirt and petticoats slide off into the lake's depths. With her legs unencumbered she kicked harder and made headway. Still not sure she traveled in the right direction, she maintained her position and listened.

"Maggie, it's me, Max. Where are you?" Panic filled his tone.

"I'm here, Max. Keep talking. I'll follow your voice."

The dense fog thinned and she spotted Max in his boat.

"Here, Max." Maggie raised one arm and waved. "I'm here."

Max pulled her inside. She collapsed into a heap, her body trembled uncontrollably.

"I'll have you to the cabin in no time, Maggie. Hang on, my love."

The boat surged forward. Maggie listened to the water splash the outside of the boat. The cool breeze chilled her body. She prayed the sun would be kind and share some warmth.

"Ernest. Nellie. I've found Maggie." Max yelled to his friends. "Bring a warm quilt to the dock. Hurry."

The boat hit something. A floating log? Emeline's boat? Voices filled the air.

"Ernest, help me lift Maggie. Nellie, you wrap her in that quilt then I'll carry her to the cabin." Max and Ernest worked as a team. Their strong arms lifted Maggie from the boat. The realization her clothes consisted of a blouse and knickers, didn't even disturb her. A change of clothes, warm cabin and dear friends to care for her were all that mattered.

The scrape of wood on wood and an overstuffed chair waited for her next to the wood stove. Feet scampered around the cabin. The clank of metal on metal meant someone put on the coffee pot. The wood stove door creaked as more kindling entered the firebox.

"Men, you turn away," Nellie said by Maggie's side. "Here, my friend, I'll get you out of those wet clothes. Max brought his bathrobe. It'll warm you and absorb the dampness from your body."

Maggie's limp arms gave little assistance as Nellie removed her wet clothes. The nickers would have to stay for now. Another chair dragged beside her.

"Here, Maggie. Some hot coffee to warm you." Max held the cup to Maggie's lips. She forced her eyelids open and glared. *Max, the betrayer. Max, the lover of whoever he was with. Max, the liar.* She tried to move her lips, but they were numb.

"Get me a spoon, Ernest. Maybe I can get a few sips in her mouth. Got to change the blue lips back to normal."

The spoon clicked as it touched the cup. Max raised the coffee filled spoon to Maggie's mouth. "Maggie, try to open your mouth enough for the spoon. We need to get something warm inside you."

With effort, Maggie opened her quivering mouth. The coffee burned against her cold lips.

The wood crackled in the firebox and the heat penetrated the bathrobe. She had the sensation someone rubbed her feet. Maggie glanced down. Max knelt on the hard wood floor and massaged each foot. Warmth moved up her legs as she scrunched her toes.

The quivering of her body slowed. She realized in her shocked state she had harbored a grudge against Max. She had accused, tried and convicted him on baseless charges. Maggie resolved to ask Max for his side of the story before she jumped to conclusions. How could she think such terrible things about the man who assumed the role of a servant and lovingly brought her feet back to life?

"Oh, Max, I'm so sorry. Can you forgive me?" Maggie asked.

"Forgive you, my darling? For what?"

"For being so stupid and believing there was something between you and Emeline."

Max's eyes grew moist. "That's a fool notion. Whoever gave you that idea doesn't know me." He gazed at Maggie. "Maggie, there will never be anyone, but you."

The love which shone from Max's eyes did more good than the coffee to warm her.

"How can I ever thank each of you, my dearest friends?"

"Well, I for one, would like to know why you went for an early morning swim wearing your clothes instead of a bathing suit? And why you didn't invite me?" Nellie asked.

Maggie repositioned herself in the chair and recalled the morning's events for the threesome.

"The dense fog made it impossible to see Emeline. Other than those glaring eyes. Her voice became raspy. Her sweet syrupy words spoken earlier now chaffed like sandpaper on my spirit." Maggie grabbed Max's hand. "Oh, Max, she scares me. Something's not right with that woman."

Another drink of coffee and warmth returned to her body.

"If you were in her boat, how did you get in the water? And where did she go?" Nellie asked.

"In the dense fog I saw nothing. But suddenly the boat tipped from side to side and lake water splashed on my face. I had raised my hands to call to you, Max, so without a grip I was flung into the water. The weight from the heavy skirt and layers of petticoats pulled me down. I had some difficulty unfastening them. When my attention returned to Emeline, I couldn't see her or her boat. I called, but there was no answer. She seemed to vanish."

"I'm so glad you're safe. We could all use a hearty breakfast. I'll cook this morning," Ernest said.

"Thank you, Nellie, for removing my wet clothes."

"That reminds me, your wet garments need hanging to dry. I'll be right back." Nellie grabbed the pile of wet things and headed outside.

"This robe is comfy cozy." Maggie nestled her face in Max's robe. She inhaled his scent. The woodsy fragrance of the man she loved. "Where did you buy this, Max?" Maggie wrapped the robe tighter.

"A gift from Ernest. It's made from flannel, developed in the Highlands of Scotland. You may wear it as long as you wish."

Maggie slipped to the edge of her chair. She rubbed her hands together. With a deep breath she prepared to share with Max, Nellie and Ernest exactly what happened in Emeline's boat.

Chapter 20

Maggie raised her cup for a coffee refill.

"Max, Nellie, Ernest, I'm scared." Her hands trembled spilling her coffee.

"Ouch! That's hotter than I expected." She flinched. "Oh, Max, I'm so sorry. I slopped coffee on your robe."

"Not to worry, Maggie. Flannel does a great job at soaking up liquids. We'll wash it later." Max said.

Maggie inhaled. "Emeline wants me to leave Eden Lake. No, I'll rephrase that. Emeline commands I leave Eden Lake, 'on the next stage' if you please."

"What do you mean, she 'commands' you to leave?" Nellie grabbed a chair and moved it close to Maggie.

"She said only one of us would remain in Eden Lake and it wouldn't be me." Maggie sipped her coffee. "Max, her claws hunger to dig into your flesh. That probably sounds dramatic, but that's the way I feel. She's a designing woman and I'm intruding on her plans."

"How did you respond, Lassie?" Ernest left the stove and joined the group.

"I said I had no intention of leaving. That's when the fog thickened. All I could see were her glaring eyes surrounded by what appeared to be a ring of fire. I felt my heart would explode. The next thing I knew, I was in the lake battling for air." She placed her hand over the top of her mug for warmth. "Must have been a freak wind that blew without warning. Strong enough to hurl me over the side and maybe Emeline too. I called to her, but heard no response. Do you think she's all right? Can she swim? What if she drowned?"

"I'm sure she's fine, Maggie." Max placed his hand on her knee.

"Max, do you have a lake monster like our Nessie?" asked Ernest.

"Nessie? Who, or what is that?" Maggie asked.

"Lassie, the story, or myth whichever you believe, began back in the sixth century with a tale about an Irish monk, Saint Columba. He came across a group of Picts burying a man by the River Ness. They related that as the man swam in the river a water-monster attacked him and drug him under. Unable to rescue their friend, they fished out his corpse." The bacon sizzled. Ernest returned to the cook stove.

"Ernest, don't stop now." Nellie said.

"Well, Columba wanted to put an end to this monster, so he sent one of his followers across the river. When the beast came after his man, Columba made the sign of the cross and commanded the monster to leave the man alone. The creature stopped and fled. Columba and the Picts praised God."

"Oh, Ernest, do Scots truly believe that story?" Maggie asked.

"They probably wouldn't if there hadn't been a sighting in the 1870s. By now the monster had moved into Loch Ness from the river. The eyewitness, a Dr. Mackenzie, described the object as a log or upturned boat "wriggling and churning up the water." He recalled the object moved slowly, then sped up and disappeared."

"Well, Max. Does Eden Lake have a monster lurking in its depths?" Nellie asked.

"No, Nellie. No monster lives here. I'm sure I would have seen something with all the fishing I do."

"Then a wind must have come from nowhere. I certainly didn't feel any strong gusts before, or after, my mishap. Don't know how else to explain it," Maggie said.

Ernest rejoined the group and glanced at Max.

"No, Maggie," Max said. "No wind at all. The lake has remained glass smooth all morning. And the fog? It lifted shortly after sunrise. Only a dense cloud in the distance, north of the dock."

"Then what's your explanation, if you have one. I couldn't have been thrown out of the boat by Emeline. I would have felt her hands on me," said Maggie.

Ernest and Max seemed unusually quiet.

"What's going on, you two?" Nellie asked. "What do you know you're not telling us?"

"Ernest, you share your suspicion with the girls," Max said. He reached for Maggie's trembling hands and held them tight.

"As we travel this journey of faith, Lassies, obstacles block our way. Everything we believe in the sunshine, we need to practice in the valley of darkness. You three are teenagers in the faith. Lots more growing to do. The Bible admonishes us to grow into Christ's likeness. I believe you have started well, but because you're young in the Lord, Satan will do all he can to snatch you back into the kingdom of darkness."

"Ernest, you're not making any sense. What does this have to do with my unexpected swim? If there was no wind, no fog, no monster and no Emeline's hands on me, how did I get into the water?" Maggie glared at him.

Ernest gulped, heaved a heavy sigh and continued.

"Let me preface my next statement with a scripture from I Peter; "...be watchful: your adversary the devil, prowls around like a roaring lion, seeking whom he may devour..." Nellie, Maggie, I believe Emeline is demon possessed."

A sizzle and crackle of bacon then a swishing sound were all that was heard in the room. Everyone seemed to hold their breathe. Maggie caught a glimpse of Jed by the cook stove. His tail swept the floor. A protruding tongue dangled as he anxiously waited for a tasty morsel or pan drippings.

"Hang on, Jed, boy. You'll get a treat soon enough." Ernest pat Jed's head.

"Max, are you and Ernest suggesting that Emeline rocked the boat hard enough to cast me out?" Maggie asked.

"Yes, we are, Maggie," Max said. "I had a hard time believing Ernest's judgement of her at first. However, after more conversations with Emeline, I now agree with his suspicions."

Silence again filled the cabin. No one spoke. No one made eye contact.

"I want to say, 'you can't be serious,' Ernest." Nellie paused. "But within my spirit, I believe you."

"You sensed danger when you first met her, Nellie." Ernest flipped the strips of bacon. "The Holy Spirit prompted you to be on guard. Both of you need to be alert at all times. She's sneaky. Never know where, or when, she'll show up."

"Incredible. She seemed so sweet when I first met her." Maggie pulled her feet inside the robe. "Yet, she was an entirely different person in the boat. Guess we shouldn't judge people by first appearances."

Max released Maggie's hands from his. "Sweet. I forgot. She made chocolate fudge to welcome you girls. I left it on the porch table yesterday." Max rose from Maggie's side.

"I'll get it," Nellie said. "Not that I'm going to eat any, but I'll have the pleasure of throwing it away. Everyone agree?"

With no dissent, Nellie headed for the porch.

"Breakfast is ready. Let's forget Emeline and enjoy our day." Ernest forked the bacon onto a plate and placed the eggs on another.

Maggie wrapped the cozy robe tighter around her now thawed body and cinched the belt. Her tummy waited to be filled with hot, comfort food. Max helped Ernest dish up the pancakes and brought the plates to the table.

The door flew open as Nellie burst into the cabin. "You've got to come with me. I found the torn open box of fudge on the table. But come, quickly." She held the door as the others hurried outside. She led them to the side of the porch.

"Look. Look over the railing, on the ground." Nellie said, her speech rapid. "Do you see them? And what's that next to the squirrels?" Nellie pointed.

Maggie gasped and stepped back. "Those poor things. How could that happen?"

Max and Ernest left the porch to examine the crime scene. Max used a stick to slide a piece of paper aside.

"Chocolate fudge, Ernest. Wrapped in paper." Max flashed concern at Ernest. "She meant this piece for you."

"What happened, Max?" Maggie asked.

"Ernest and Emeline had an altercation a couple of days ago. Emeline threatened Ernest to stay out of her way. When she brought the fudge, she insisted I make sure Ernest ate the extra portion."

"But why are the squirrels dead?" Nellie asked.

"Because, Lassie, squirrels can eat chocolate, but not if it's poisoned." Ernest's eyes closed. "Thank you, Lord, for protecting me."

Max joined Maggie and Nellie on the porch and gathered the remaining fudge.

"Any other animal would have died from eating chocolate. This chunk hasn't been touched. The squirrels must have grabbed the extra portion. I pray their death was quick and painless." Max plopped on a chair, tears streamed down his face.

"Ernest, what have I gotten you involved in?" Max sobbed, bent over, his body swayed.

Maggie cuddled close to him and rested her arm around his shoulder. Ernest rushed to his side.

"Max, you didn't know," Ernest said. "Don't blame yourself, Laddie. We will all need to be on our guard and pray fervently for the Lord's wisdom and protection."

"But Ernest, I could have lost you. I don't know what I would have done. You're my best friend." Max wept.

"And you, mine." Ernest knelt beside him and held Max's hand. Then quietly he said, "I know you are emotionally drained dealing with life decisions right now. But I want you to know that friendships are special indeed. We have one who stays closer than a brother. His name is Jesus. Time we turn this matter, and all matters, over to His capable hands." Ernest sighed.

Max squeezed Ernest's hand. "I'll try, with your help."

"Ernest, what can we do?" Maggie asked.

Ernest scratched his head and leaned against the railing. "Joshua comes to mind, Lassie. Faced with a difficulty, he encouraged the people to do four things: stay in the Word, pray, identify completely with God, and be strong and courageous." He glanced toward Emeline's cabin. "Courage is not the absence of fear, but the moving forward in spite of fear." Ernest shifted his weight. "We must be strong and courageous whenever confronted by Emeline. Remember, the Lord fights for us, with us and through us."

Ernest pulled Max from the chair and hugged him. "I love you, Max, and am thankful the Lord brought us together."

"I smell something burning." Nellie said.

Ernest inhaled a deep breath. "The bacon. I forgot I left a few pieces sizzling in the pan."

"Unless panting Jed has beaten us to it." Nellie said.

Ernest sniffed again. "If Jed has scarfed down our meal, I suggest we hitch up the team and drive to the Merc for breakfast with Miss Greene."

Ernest winked.

Chapter 21

"Well, Laddie." Ernest stacked the breakfast plates in the sink. "What say you and I hitch up Bess and Kate. July third is closing in and I need to invite Miss Greene for our trip to Sandy."

Maggie connected the two: Ernest's earlier wink and Miss Greene.

"Ernest, are you interested in Miss Greene?" Maggie's brow furrowed. "And when are we going to Sandy?"

His face lit up like a boy with his first bicycle.

"You might say that, Lassie. In fact, if you promise to keep mum, I'll tell you." Ernest paused, inhaled deeply then continued. "I'm planning to purchase an engagement ring and ask the sweet lassie to be my wife." His rosy cheeks glowed.

Squeals filled the cabin as the girls flew to Ernest. He leaned against a wall and braced for impact.

"Oh, Ernest, I'm so happy for you," Nellie said. "I liked her instantly. You've been alone long enough. She'll be a great companion, that is if she likes bagpipes and haggis."

"Me too, Ernest." Maggie said. "From the little time we've spent with Miss Greene, I knew you were the perfect match."

Maggie found her hankie and rubbed lip rouge from his cheek.

"Don't want her thinking you have more than one best girl," she said.

Maggie clasped Ernest's hands and pulled him to a chair.

"You have a seat and tell us how this romance blossomed. When did you know you loved her? Do you know if she loves you? When's the wedding? I hope we're still here. Is she willing to move to Scotland?" Maggie's thoughts ran amuck as her questions piled one on top of the other.

"Now, ladies. Give Ernest some breathing room." Max pulled on his boots and straightened his pant legs. "This romance, as you call it, didn't blossom one petal at a time, it burst forth while making sandwiches. And to answer your question, Maggie, we're going to Sandy July third. I wanted Ernest to experience our Fourth of July celebration. He may be surprised by the similarity to his Highland Games we attended in Rolen."

Maggie faced Max. "Are we spending the night?"

"Yes, we are. There are two hotels in Sandy, so we should be able to get two rooms." Max reached for his jacket. "That is, if you ladies don't mind sharing. If Miss Greene joins us, we'll ask for a room with two beds."

"Which one is the nicest, Max? Can't have my intended staying in a shack," Ernest asked.

"The Sandy Hotel. It was built after the Revenue. A bit fancier, and because of its popularity, the owner recently added on more rooms. The Revenue faces Mt. Hood and close to the Barlow trail, one of the most heavily traveled roads by Oregon settlers. Not a shack by any means. Just well used. We'll try the Sandy first."

Max buttoned his jacket. "Ernest, you coming to town with me, or not? I'd like to make it a quick trip so we can show the girls around Eden Lake."

"Max, you know I'm going with you. Wouldn't miss another opportunity to be with my sweetie." Ernest gazed at Max. "And as for your questions, Maggie, I'm not going to ask Heather to move to Scotland. Neither of us have any family, but we do have close friends." Ernest motioned to Max. "We both consider Max a dear friend and once she knows you two lassies, we'll be a great fivesome. I'd rather move here than ask her to give up the Merc and move to Scotland." Ernest grabbed his coat off the hook. "And thank you, lassies for agreeing with me that Miss Heather Greene is the one."

Max unlatched the side door to the stable, then hesitated. "You girls be all right while we're gone?"

"Don't need to worry about us," Maggie said. "After this morning's escapade, I'm donning some comfy clothes and choosing a book from your collection. Then I'll brew a cup of tea and cozy up to the fire for the entire afternoon."

"Nellie, what about you?" Ernest asked.

"After so much sitting on the coach yesterday, think I may go for a hike. I have a notebook of unsolved cases from the Portland Police Chief waiting when I get back."

Max's eyes squinted. "I'd rather you wait until Ernest or I can go with you, but I believe you're one strong-willed lady who won't take my advice. Best carry my Colt '45 and extra cartridges to be on the safe side. There's more in these woods than Emeline. It's in the top drawer of the sideboard. Practice out back first to get the feel of her."

"Thank you, Max. I have my derringer and palm pistol, but they don't provide the best protection except up close. I feel safer already. What about you?"

"I have another '45 in the stable. I keep my Winchester under the wagon seat, so we'll be well protected." Max signaled for Jed's attention. "Jed, you stay here with the girls."

Ernest stomped his boot in place and joined Max. "I'm ready. See you lassies later. Pray she says, "yes" to coming with us to Sandy."

Maggie cinched the robe sash tighter and waited on the porch for one last good-bye wave.

Bess and Kate munched on forest ground cover while Max and Ernest hitched them to the wagon. Max displayed a strength beyond his frail appearance. He climbed in the wagon and clicked to Bess and Kate.

"You be safe, Maggie. If Nellie leaves the cabin, you keep her derringer close beside you." Max yelled and raised an arm.

"I will, Max." Maggie waved back, a lump in her throat. She longed to yell back, "And you be safe too, my love." A tear dripped down her cheek. His thin frame dwarfed next to sturdy Ernest. *What's wrong with him, Lord? Please take care of the man I love.*

A glance across the lake to Emeline's caused anger to resurface. *No. I won't let you quench my joy.*

Maggie latched the door.

"Nellie, are you really going for a walk?"

"Just a short one, dear. I'll be back by the time you're dressed, do something with your matted hair and are curled up with a good book. Jed, want to come?"

Jed leapt to his feet, wagged his tail and trotted to the door.

"Oh, Maggie, you'll hear a couple of shots behind the cabin. Not to worry though. It will be me practicing."

Maggie latched the door behind Nellie and Jed, then double-checked the lock for security. Her eyes followed them through the window until they rounded the side of the cabin. She had forgotten all about her tangled tresses. Time to brush her hair, then dress and relax. She wanted to be beautiful when Max returned, not a mess of snarls.

Once dressed, a pile of dirty breakfast dishes waited and the table needed to be wiped. She gathered her almost-drowned frocks, cleaned off the dried lake grass and blotted any smudges that remained.

The book shelves overflowed. On one end corner she found a stack of Blackwood magazines. Maggie clutched several, cozied herself in the chair by the wood stove and perused the table of contents. Her search stopped abruptly with a story titled "Scottish Murder" by Max Sullivan.

Moisture filled Maggie's palms. Those same pesky butterflies in her stomach that annoyed her in Scotland returned. With two paragraphs read, Maggie knew Max had written their story, their investigation, their discoveries and her near death experience with MacLaren. Condensed for sure and names changed, but still her story, her mother, her fear. She relived the entire experience. Not something she ever wanted to repeat. She thought all memories of this season in her life were erased, yet his words rekindled emotions she felt as Laurence forced her closer to the edge of the cliff.

Maggie jumped at the sound of pounding on the front door. Her heart raced. Emeline! Did she return to finish what she started on the lake? No one here to protect her. Nellie's derringer. Now, where did she keep it?

Nellie's empty satchel rested under the bed. Not there. Maggie scanned the room and tried to remember where Nellie said it would be if she ever needed to arm herself. Arm herself? She'd never shot a gun in her life. Probably shoot her foot off before she halted an attacker.

Another knock and a muffled voice. Maggie stiffened. *Get ahold of yourself. Use your head.* She knew Emeline could break a window and climb into the cabin. She needed to open the door, but not without protection. There, by the sink, her weapon of choice, a newly washed cast iron frypan.

She raised the frypan over her head and placed a hand on the latch. Another knock.

"Who's there?" Maggie stammered, her ear pressed against the heavy wooden door.

"It's me, Nellie, and Jed. Open the door, please."

Maggie released her breath and unlocked the latch.

"Oh, Nellie, am I glad to see you. And you too, Jed." Maggie bent over to pet him.

"What on earth are you doing with a frypan? Is it time for lunch already?" Nellie asked.

"Nellie, I'm sorry. My mind played tricks on me. I was reading Max's story of our time in Scotland and found myself experiencing those same emotions. When you knocked, I thought sure Emeline had come back to finish what she started this morning." Maggie placed the frypan on the counter.

"Didn't even think it might be you and Jed." Maggie wiped her hands on her skirt.

"I can understand, Maggie," Nellie said as she removed her coat. "The entire time I walked down the road, I was sure every noise, every shadow, belonged to Emeline. So thankful for Jed. I studied his back hair at regular intervals. Praise God for giving dogs a keen sense of danger."

Maggie returned to her comfy chair to finish Max's story.

"How about a fresh cup of coffee? Pretty brisk outside in the shade of the trees. I need warming." Nellie tossed her sweater on the bed.

"No, you go ahead. A couple of paragraphs left, then I'm getting some fresh air. I need to clear my head of the day's events. The peacefulness might help me to focus on the Lord and pray for Max." Maggie's eyes moistened. "I'm concerned, Nellie. He's so thin and pale. I wish he would confide in me. Men can be so private."

Maggie finished the story and gathered a sweater for over her blouse. If Nellie felt chilled, she would probably freeze. She always felt colder than anyone else.

"I have three gun choices for you to carry. Any preference?" Nellie asked.

"Yes, I do have a preference. No gun at all, thank you."

"Maggie…"

"No, Nellie. I'm not going far. I'll keep the cabin in sight and call you if I need protection. Only a short venture among the pines, then back. Jed's asleep by the wood stove. You must have worn him out. He can stay here also." Maggie grasped a small bucket by the door. "In case I find something interesting to bring back. Maybe fresh wildflowers for the table."

The brisk air reminded Maggie that she was not in the warm Chicago summer heat. With an elevation over three-thousand feet, the cool mountain air would take getting used to.

Maggie soaked up every ounce of beauty in the majestic forest. She'd gladly trade the towering buildings for the magnificent Douglas fir, spruce and cedar trees. The noisy streets were now replaced with bird songs. She inhaled deeply and reveled in the smell of fresh clean mountain air. A pleasant change from the horse dung and garbage smells of the city. Leave Chicago? In a heart-beat.

A stroll down the road relaxed any lingering tense muscles. Movement in the bushes caught her attention. Some small animal scurried through the underbrush. She decided to follow the moving path hoping to discover the identity of the varmint. The movement stopped, then a high pitched squeal and a flash of brown ascended a tree. Maggie grinned with pleasure as she watch a small squirrel adeptly scurry around the tree trunk as it played hide-and-seek.

"You silly squirrel. You have no idea how much joy you brought to this weary soul. The Bible says laughter is good medicine and I sure needed some laughter today. Thank you."

Her new friend scrambled farther up the tree then jumped to an adjacent branch of another tree and out of sight.

A small red dot of color on the ground not far away caught Maggie's eye. She decided to investigate. Carefully stepping over vines, ferns and branches, she reached the ruby berry. Maggie bent down for a closer look. A cluster of small leaves cupped the tiny strawberry. Trails of vines shot in all directions from this one plant, each encased another small delicacy.

Not enough for a pie, but perhaps ample for four strawberry tarts. She picked those within her reach then tracked the vines and plucked the fruit. The fruit quickly covered the bottom of the pail. The sun warmed her back. She removed her sweater and tied it around her waist. The yield in the small bucket grew deeper as Maggie continued to follow the vines, pick the fruit and add more wild berries to her pail.

A rustling in the brush captured her attention. Perhaps a squirrel, or the same one, followed her and played tag. She marveled at God's gift of animals to lighten a heavy heart.

The rustling advanced toward where Maggie now stood, stiff and quiet. Couldn't be a squirrel. The leaves swished from the bottom of the plant to the top. She estimated whatever drew closer must be three to four feet tall.

Quickly Maggie checked her distance from the cabin. The cabin — where had it gone? She saw nothing but dense forest in every direction. So focused on the strawberries, she neglected to keep track Max's home. Sure that Nellie wouldn't hear her, even with full volume, and scared the animal might attack at the sound of her voice, Maggie remained silent and motionless. A gentle breeze caressed her face. The animal would not detect her scent.

What had Max said? "There's more in these woods than Emeline." Maggie strained to recall what she knew about the Cascades. When she and her parents picnicked on Larch Mountain, her father admonished her not to hike alone and carry a big stick. "Bear would be the largest predator you may encounter. Cougar the fastest," he had said. Now deep in the woods, she had neither a companion nor a stick. What was she thinking?

She quietly hiked up her skirt to prevent the fabric catching on anything. A retreat backwards would be dangerous in all the underbrush, but she could focus on the activity in front of her. If she turned around and withdrew, an attack could come unexpectedly. Why hadn't she taken Nellie's advice and packed Max's '45? Even if she shot herself in the foot, the blast might scare the animal.

The bushes thinned and Maggie glimpsed a large animal covered with black fur. Not being able to see a head, she assumed a bent-over bear ate the strawberries she hadn't reached. So far, oblivious to her presence, she gingerly stepped backwards. Then another step, and another. The activity stopped. Then a shaking in the brush and a blow sound from the nostrils. She wondered if animals were susceptible to hay fever as she was, but this was not the time to ask.

One more step backwards. Crack. Several small branches broke under her foot. The sound nabbed the animal's attention. Run, entered her mind, but both bear and cougar could out-run her. Find a tree to climb. No good either with a long skirt on. Lay down, play dead and pray for the Lord's protection. Nothing else to do.

Chapter 22

Panic engulfed Maggie. She found a bed of twigs, wrapped her skirt around her legs and fell to the ground. Downed fir boughs were within reach. She hurriedly used the branches as a blanket, then curled into a fetal position and waited. The cold ground penetrated her clothes and to her body. Her heart pounded. Never imagined she would die at the paws and jaws of a bear.

Maggie prayed for a miracle from the Lord and repented of her stupidity that she left the cabin without any protection. No, that she left the cabin at all. She should have waited for Max. She should have stayed on the porch. She should have kept the cabin in sight. She should have watched the squirrel from a distance. She should have not picked the strawberries — the strawberries. She still held the handle in her clinched fist. All her 'should have's' melted. The bear would sniff out the berries and then sniff out her. *Oh, Lord, I've been very stupid. Please forgive me. If by some miracle I live through this, help me become more sensitive to the leading of the Holy Spirit, not my own. Thank you.*

Twigs cracked. She squeezed her eyes closed. No desire for eye to eye contact with the black beast. She sensed a warm body. The pail moved. She tried to release her hand but her fingers froze. Large paws scratched at the branches and pulled several aside exposing her shoulder and part of her face. A wet nose touched her cheek as the animal inhaled her scent. She inhaled his at the same time. A gamey, filthy, sweat odor filled her nostrils. She practiced shallow breathing. The animal nudged her shoulder. He pushed harder. Maggie resisted being shoved on her back. The animal encircled her, sniffing with each step. Maggie felt the hot air from it's nostrils. *This is it. He's checking for the easiest entry point. I relinquish my life. I'm yours, Lord. Take care of Max.*

The inspection stopped abruptly. Maggie held her breath and listened. The sound of the animal's paws grew faint, then halted. He came close again. He pawed at the branches. The beast exposed

Maggie to the elements. A wet tongue wiped her face. *Was this a taste test? Too much salt? Not enough?* Maybe she wasn't as delectable as the animal hoped. The heavy paws distanced themselves from Maggie one more time. She peeked with one eye. Nothing there. She clamped her eyes tightly closed and waited. *What's happening, Lord? Is he gathering his buddies?*

He hovered over her now cold body, placed one paw on her hip and howled. Startled, Maggie jerked knocking the paw to the ground. Another howl convinced her this was not a brown or black bear.

"Bear? Bear, where are you?"

A man's voice both scared and comforted Maggie. Whether friend or foe, she was relieved a bear did not stand sentry duty.

Another loud mournful sound pierced the silence.

Then a man's voice, "Bear, where are you?"

The voice grew closer. Maggie peeked in the hopes of sighting the man or animal.

"There you are, Bear. What have you got?"

With Maggie's ear to the ground she heard the impact of two heavy boots. She squinted to catch a glimpse of the origin of the voice. The worn out toes of black leather boots came to rest only a few inches from her face.

"Well, Bear, what's this? A young lady, out in the middle of the forest. Is she alive, or dead? I'll give her a kick and find out."

Maggie bolted to an upright position spilling the pail of straw-berries.

"Oh, please, sir, don't kick me. I am very much alive." Maggie's voice quivered.

"Bear, come see what you caught."

Maggie gasped as a huge dog rounded her and stood by the stranger. No bear, yet his back reached above the man's knees.

"Here," the man said as he offered a hand. "Let me help you up."

Maggie brushed off her skirt and surveyed this mountain man. His clothes were thread bare, tattered and torn. The shoes appeared to be held together with pitch. And his smell. It reminded her of a science experiment she'd performed in sixth grade. In order to get a peeled, hard-boiled egg into a milk bottle, she'd placed a piece of paper inside the bottle with a corner over the edge of the rim. The paper was lit and pushed inside. The peeled egg then balanced on top preventing oxygen from entering and, poof, the egg now rested inside on the bottom of the bottle. But it was the smell that filled the classroom. Strong sulphur odor that could not be forgotten.

This man's clothes reeked of sulphur, or maybe his entire body. Maggie couldn't tell.

"I'm sorry if old Bear scared you, Miss. He has that effect on folks. You don't appear hurt." He glanced at the scattered strawberries. "Let me pick these berries up for you."

"Thank you." Maggie said as she untied her sweater and shook off blades of dried grass. "He did scare me. You see, I thought he was a bear hunting for sweet strawberries and that I'd be next." She brushed dirt off her face.

"I forgot to take my friend's advice and carry a gun, so I felt defenseless. I asked the Lord for help and you're the answer to that prayer." Maggie prayed this man would indeed be friend, not foe.

"No, Miss, I'm no answer to anybody's prayer. Least not that I know of. My name's Frank Molech and this is my dog, Bear. We've been hunting 'coon or bobcat, whichever showed up first."

"I'm very glad to meet you, Frank. My name is Maggie Richards and I'm visiting a friend. I came out for a short hike and lost my way. Too focused chasing silly squirrels and gathering strawberries to pay attention."

"A friend, you say. Who is this friend? Maybe I can get you back where you belong. The woods ain't no place for a city gal to be wandering by herself and without protection." Molech handed the pail of strawberries to Maggie.

"My friend is Max Sullivan. How did you know I lived in a city?"

"You city folk are easy to figure. You stand out by your talk and dress. No mountain gal would be traipsing through the woods with clothes like yours. Too fancy. Too many fancies." Molech snapped around to a distant sound. He hoisted his gun to his shoulder. "Bear, did you hear that?"

The fur on Bear's back stood erect. He bared his teeth and growled.

Maggie stiffened as she absorbed the full force of this giant dog. She stepped back. Her breaths increased.

"No need to worry, Miss. Bear won't attack unless I say so." He lowered the rifle. "Let 'er go, Bear. Could 'a been the wind." He patted the mongrel.

"Max Sullivan, you say. Well, I know where Max lives. If you're okay, I'll take you to his cabin."

"I would be extremely grateful to you."

"See, there you go with that citified language. Always gives you people away." Molech broke several face-high branches for Maggie and blazed a trail with Bear in the rear.

"Maggie, Nellie, we're home," Max called out as he opened the side door.

Nellie rushed from her bedroom into the kitchen. "Thank heavens you boys are back. I've been frantic with worry."

"Worry? For us, Lassie?" Ernest asked. "You don't need to worry about us. We've got each other and Max's fine shooting irons. We're as safe as a new-born wee barin nestled in his mother's arms."

"Not for you. For Maggie."

Max dumped the box of groceries in a chair. His heart pounded as he hurried to Nellie's side.

"What do you mean, Maggie? She said she would stay here in the cabin, all afternoon." Max's forehead creased and eyes squinted. "You didn't let her go outside, did you?"

"Max, I didn't 'let her'," Nellie's voice squeaked. "You can't blame me. She insisted on some fresh air and said she would stay close to the cabin. Promised to call me if needed." Nellie plopped in a chair. "I went outside and called her several times, but no answer. Even asked Jed to sniff out her trail, but he seemed lost too." Her head in her hands, she sobbed. "I'll never forgive myself if something happened to her."

"You're not the only one," Max retorted. "Don't you remember what I told you. 'There's more in these woods than Emeline'? You two are courting danger." Max caught his breath. "I should have stayed, or taken you girls with us." He clenched his fist. "Did she take a gun?"

"I asked her to, but she insisted she didn't need one and promised to stay close. I feel awful." Nellie wiped the tears from her cheeks.

"Attacking each other is not going to help." Ernest tried to diffuse the situation.

Max nudged Jed awake with his foot.

"How long ago did she leave?"

"Seems it's been about an hour, Max."

"Did you use the '45?" Max asked.

"Just two practice shots. Its back in the sideboard."

Max yanked the drawer open spilling cartridges on the floor. He filled the gun's empty chambers and dumped more ammo in his pocket. *If anything's happened to Maggie, Emeline will have to answer to me.*

"Nellie, did you see which direction she headed?" Ernest asked.

"I didn't. She took the small pail by the door. Thought she may find wildflowers." Nellie pushed herself up by the chair arms. "I'm going with you."

"No." Max said. "You stay right here. If she comes back, fire a shot from your derringer. While you wait, I would suggest you pray."

Max stuffed the '45 under his belt and grabbed his Winchester.

"Jed, come on." Max flung open the front door and stomped down the porch steps.

"Max, wait up. I'm right behind you." Ernest called as he changed his walk to a jog.

Max stopped on the road and deliberated which direction would be best.

"I'm not as young as I used to be, Laddie, and this body is letting me know," Ernest said. "Don't blame Nellie. We're all too good a friends to let a riff come between us. I know you are concerned for Maggie. So am I. But remember she's a grown woman. When they get some fool idea in their head, there's no stopping them — especially Scots."

"I don't know which way to go, Ernest. And the longer I hesitate the more I feel Maggie slipping out of my arms." Max wiped his brow. "North would be my first choice. Emeline seems to always come from that direction."

Max faced north and rushed up the road. His sack of burdens weighed on his mind. His stomach knotted with concern for Maggie. *Maggie, Maggie, my darling, where are you?*

"Max," Ernest said, "Nellie mentioned Maggie wanted to find wildflowers. Do you know of any growing by the road?"

Max halted. His eyes bulged. "Wildflowers? Ernest, they're scattered everywhere. Even berries are in full bloom." Max yelled in frustration. "We'll never find her if we scour for patches of wildflowers. Ernest, I can't even think straight."

Max jerked as Ernest grabbed his arm. "We may be going in the wrong direction, Max. Jed hasn't picked up her scent yet. Time to seek the Lord's guidance before we waste another step."

Max glanced at Ernest. "You're right. I'm like a bear with his nose in a bee hive. Full of stings, but without the sense God gave him to pull it out. I'm full of emotional stings, Ernest, and the poison keeps me from thinking straight."

Ernest laid a hand on his shoulder. His friend's touch reassured Max.

"Lord, you know how much we love Maggie, but you love her more. Please help us find this bonnie lass. Amen."

Tears dripped from Max's eyes. He wiped them off with his sleeve, inhaled deeply and thanked Ernest.

A streak of brown caught Max's eye as Jed bolted up the road.

"Ernest, Jed's got something. Hurry."

The crunch of Ernest's boots matched Max's own stride. The throbbing in his head kept pace with his heart beat. Ahead of Max, Jed stopped, faced the woods and bounded into the brush.

"Come on, Ernest. We can't lose him." Max stood motionless by Jed's entry point and searched the woods. "I don't see him, Ernest. Have we lost Jed too?"

"Wait a minute." Ernest said. "He's probably sniffing for her scent. We need to use our ears as well as our eyes."

The two men listened for any sound and scanned the woods in several directions. Nothing indicated Jed's whereabouts.

"I'm going in, Ernest. I can't stand here and do nothing while my love may be in danger."

Ernest grabbed Max's sleeve. "Look, over there." Ernest pointed. "Must be Jed."

Max rushed headlong into the brush and plummeted to the ground.

"What happened? You all right?" Ernest asked.

"Stupid blackberry vines. Caught my boot toe under them." Max handed the Winchester to Ernest as he untangled the vine from his pant leg. "Where's Jed? Do you see him?"

Ernest searched for Jed's movement. "I think he's coming back." Ernest raised the rifle in the air. "Here, boy. We're over here."

Max clasped Ernest's hand for welcomed assistance out of the stickers.

"What's the matter, boy?" Max bent down and clutched Jed. His faithful dog panted and whined.

"You scared, boy? Did you find her? Where's Maggie, Jed?" Jed's back hair raised, then the dog cowered behind Max. The woods remained quiet.

"Max, something spooked Jed. I don't see anything out there.

Do you think you can get him to retrace his steps?" Ernest asked.

A breeze rustled the bushes and tree branches. Max focused on the movement. Another, stronger wind swooshed through the flora.

"I don't know. He seems mighty scared." Max patted Jed's head. "We'll go with you, boy. Come on."

Jed bit into Max's pant leg, pulled him back and growled.

"Don't think he's too excited about returning," Max said. "You hold Jed and I'll explore. I'll fire a shot when I find something."

Max removed the '45 from under his belt. His hands trembled as he cocked the hammer.

"Wait, Max. Did you get a whiff of that smell with the last breeze?" Ernest asked.

Max inhaled as a gust of wind brushed his face.

"Sulphur."

Chapter 23

A stout breeze bowed the tall grass and rustled the leaves. Max faced into the wind. The scent of sulphur sent chills down his back.

He jumped into a shooter's stance and leveled the heavy revolver into the wind. The '45 quavered as he sighted down the barrel. He added his other hand to steady the gun. Over his shoulder he asked, "Ernest, do you see him? Do you see Molech?"

The wind howled as the trees swayed and jerked from the velocity. Max strained to scan the forest as the sulphur smell grew stronger.

Max stood his ground as Ernest came beside him and hoisted the Winchester.

"I don't, Max. Only the wind and heavy sulphur smell. He must be getting closer," Ernest said.

Max's keen eyes and ears were now on full alert. This mountain man would not escape. Either he had Maggie, or knew where she was.

"We must confront him. If he's hurt Maggie, he will answer to me." Sweat dripped down Max's face. His gun slipped in his two-handed grip. He dried his hands on his trousers, one at a time.

The movement in the forest became centralized. Max checked a chamber. Can't afford any mistakes. His '45, now loaded and ready.

"I've got you, Molech. Show yourself. And if that brut of a dog is with you, you best keep him under control. I'll blow his head off if he so much as bares his teeth." Max's heart pounded harder. His head throbbed and cheeks burned. "Ernest, you aim at that dog of his. I'll target Molech."

"Deep breathes, Max. No jumping to conclusions before we talk with him," Ernest said.

Molech's head came into view above the distant brush. He wasn't alone. Max lowered the gun, blinked his eyes and focused on the forms moving closer. Could it be?

His eyes blurred from the puddles of built-up tears. He scrunched his lids together and forced the liquid down his face. Still out-of-focus, the second figure remained indistinguishable.

"Ernest, I can't see the other figure. Is it Emeline? Is it Maggie?"

"Don't think it's Emeline. They're almost to the clearing." Ernest said, squinting for a better focus. "Max, I believe it's Maggie." He lowered the Winchester. "Yes, Max, it is Maggie."

Max pulled back on the trigger to release the hammer. In his haste to reach Maggie, his thumb slipped and sent the discharged bullet into the ground. The shot rang through the woods. Max perceived Molech shove Maggie down and shield her with his body. Bear positioned himself in front of the downed couple. His bark became ear-shattering.

Despite Max's illness, he ran to Maggie as if she were caught in a house ablaze and he, the only one to save her.

"Maggie, I'm coming. The gun went off accidentally. Molech, call off your dog." Max yelled as he narrowed the gap.

Max came to a halt and waited for Molech to control Bear. With Bear to one side, Max bolted to Maggie and lifted her off the ground.

"Oh, Maggie. Are you all right? I've been so frightened something awful had happened."

He wrapped his arms around his sweetheart. The two bodies melted into one. Max gazed into his beloved's eyes, brushed grass from her face. Tears streamed down Maggie's cheeks and mixed with surface dirt. Max removed a handkerchief from his back pocket and tenderly wiped her face.

"I'm fine, Max. Really, I am. I lost my way picking strawberries and this nice man offered to guide me back to your cabin," Maggie smiled at Molech.

"Nice man"? Max would never use that adjective to describe Molech. Dirty. Disgusting. Stinking, mountain vagabond, but never "nice". He realized Maggie appreciated Molech as her rescuer and had no knowledge of the "gifts" he'd left Max.

"Molech, thank you for assisting Miss Richards. If I can repay your kindness somehow, please let me know." Max calmed himself and extended a hand.

"Thanks, Max. My hands are rough and dirty, so a verbal thank you is enough. Don't want to share the filth." Molech said. "Who's that packin' a rifle and your '45?"

"This is Ernest McIntyre, a dear friend from Scotland." Max

placed his arm around Ernest's shoulders. "Ernest, this is Frank Molech. And his dog, Bear."

Ernest extended his hand. "Nice to meet you, Mr. Molech. And thank you for protecting our Miss Richards."

"No hand shaking, if you don't mind. And no Mr. Molech either. Just plain Molech will do."

"Jed? Where's Jed?" Maggie asked.

Max twirled around. "Jed? Where are you, boy? Come, say "Hi" to Maggie."

"There he is. Crawling on his belly from under that bush," Ernest pointed.

"Come on, boy. Nothing to be scared of here. Say hello to Molech and Bear." Max patted his leg coaxing Jed to come.

Jed rose from the ground and slinked to Max.

"Like I said before, he ain't much of a dog." Molech shook his head. "Now that you and Miss Richards are together, I best be going. Gonna be dark in another couple of hours and haven't bagged Bear's and my dinner for tonight. If I get extra, I'll bring 'em by your place."

"No need to, Molech. We have fresh fish for supper. In fact, we have more than we can eat. How about you stop by and I'll give you some in thanks for taking care of Maggie?" Max said.

"Well now, that's real neighborly of you. I just might do that if we don't have any luck." Molech glanced down. "Oh, look, Miss, you spilled your strawberries. I'll pick them up."

Max and Ernest bent down to help Molech retrieve the scattered red fruit.

"Here's your pail, Miss. I hope to see you again."

"Thank you, Molech. And I you," Maggie said.

"Before you go, may I ask you a question?" Max asked.

"Sure. Fire away. I'll answer if I can."

"Where are you from and where do you live?"

"Now, Max, I learned to count to ten and you asked two questions, not one. So I'll answer one." Molech said. "I live close to Eden Lake."

Molech tipped his hat to Maggie, slapped his leg for Bear's attention and wandered back into the woods.

Nellie loaded her derringer and waited on the porch for any sign of her friends. How she wished Max had two dogs. A gun provided protection, but only if you had a visual on your assailant. Fore-warning from a canine gave more comfort.

The lake glistened in the afternoon sun. Max's boat, rocked by the gentle waves, seemed to call for somebody to take a ride. Whether for fishing or not, a boat's purpose is not fulfilled tied up. Nellie didn't belong tied up either. She loved the adventure of her job and while this vacation with her dear friends relaxed her, she was eager to return to Portland.

The excitement of the "hunt" of detective work ignited her emotions like a bolt of lightning on a lightning rod. Max and Maggie, Ernest and Heather, how wonderful for these special people. Marriage wasn't for her. Her time would be divvied up between a man and her passion, between cook books and detective books, between writing letters to his relatives and writing thrillers for the George M. Hill Corp.. At twenty-nine years of age, she'd escaped infatuations and moved on to adulthood.

"Give me something I can sink my teeth into, Lord. And I don't mean a man or T-bone steak."

Nellie descended the porch steps and glanced up and down the road. Still no sign of her friends. She ventured to the dock in the hopes her nerves would mellow. Emeline's cabin nestled dark and dreary in the woods. What a sad life. Desperate, antagonistic, self-centered, vengeful, all inhabited that beautiful facade. Nellie was not acquainted with demon-possessed persons. She trusted Ernest's spiritual maturity. Time to search the scriptures for herself.

As she paced, her hands trembled. She tightened her fists, then stretched her fingers as if she reached for Emeline right through her cabin door. Perhaps diverting her attention from Maggie's rescue would be the balm she needed to calm her racing heart.

She retrieved the notebook of Portland cases from her room. As she filled a glass with water she heard footsteps on the porch. Nellie held her breath. They're back. *Oh, Lord, please let Maggie be all right.* With the notebook and water glass on the counter, Nellie rushed to open the door.

A forceful knock stopped Nellie. Max and Ernest wouldn't knock unless they carried Maggie. Surely a yell to her would be more effective. Her respirations sped up. Nellie held her breath. She'd left her derringer on the porch table.

The door latch moved.

"Who's there?" Nellie asked.

"It's me, Emeline. Can we talk?"

Perspiration rolled down Nellie's neck and dampened her blouse.

"Max and Ernest will be back shortly. Can you wait on the porch for them?"

"I want to talk to you, Nellie. And in private. That's why I waited until they were out of sight."

She'd watched Max and Ernest leave the cabin? Has she got Maggie tied up somewhere? Killed her? Why me? It's Max she wants.

"Just for a minute, Emeline."

Nellie's palm pistol remained loaded, but it may not be enough. Could bullets damage a demon? She placed the gun in her skirt pocket.

"I'm coming." Nellie used her foot as a wedge and cracked open the door.

That flawless porcelain face, piercing blue eyes and flowing blonde hair could captivate any man. A thing of beauty on the outside, yet rotten on the inside.

"What do you want to talk about?"

"Would you mind coming out on the porch? Talking through a door crack is not very personal." Emeline backed up for Nellie to leave the safety of the cabin.

"Okay, I'm here. What is it?" Nellie's perspiration had spread to her underarms and moistened the back of her blouse.

"Look how wet you are. Must be awfully hot in Max's cabin," Emeline said. "I prefer to open all my windows and let the fresh mountain air in." She smiled. "But that's just me. Men tend to leave things as is, including windows."

Nellie glimpsed her derringer. She nonchalantly headed toward it.

"Someone left their gun on that table."

"It's mine, Emeline. I left it there when I went in for a glass of water." Her plan foiled.

"Good for you. Never know what may come out of these woods," Emeline smiled. "And you, being a city gal, a raccoon would probably give you a fright." A twinkle in her eye sent chills down Nellie's back.

"Why don't we sit down," Emeline said. "Always more congenial conversation than standing."

"I prefer to stand, if you don't mind." Nellie leaned against the porch railing and waited for this "private" conversation to begin.

"What's on your mind that couldn't be said in front of Max,

Ernest or Maggie?" Nellie tightened her fists, but resisted the urge to slug Emeline.

"I need to apologize to you and explain what happened this morning on the lake," Emeline said. "Oh, I know you, and the rest, believe I caused Maggie's early morning swim. I didn't. The fog thickened unexpectedly and the wind howled like a banshee. I hung on to the boat and requested Maggie do the same. Either she didn't hear me, or thought she had more experience in lake storms than I. Whatever the reason, the wind tipped the boat on its side and out she fell." Emeline's eyes closed, her mouth frowned.

"Before I knew it, another strong gust of wind forced the boat higher in the air. Over the edge I went. I called to Maggie when I surfaced, but no answer. Then Max's voice in the distance reassured me she would be all right. I climbed back in the boat and rowed to my dock. When I reached shore, I watched the three of you assist Maggie to the cabin." Emeline sighed.

"Do you honestly expect me to believe that?" Nellie's face tightened.

"I don't know you, but I've known Maggie for six years. She has never fabricated a story. She would have no reason to lie. You deliberately caused the boat to rock, or shoved her in. However it happened, we all hold you responsible." Nellie's heart pounded. She reached for her derringer. No playing cat and mouse games with this wench.

"Do you feel safer with that gun in your hand? With the weight in your skirt pocket, I believe that's two. Why do I frighten you? I want to be friends." Emeline held a hand toward Nellie. Nellie backed away.

"Maggie said you planned to get her out of Eden Lake, one way or another. Where's Maggie, Emeline? What did you do with her?"

"Me? Oh, my dear, Nellie. Don't you remember? She went for a walk, and now Max, Ernest, and that good-for-nothing dog, are scouring the woods to find her. You don't need to be afraid of me. There's more danger in Eden Lake than this fair maiden. A mountain man roams the forest. Max may have neglected to tell you. He and his beast of a dog, work as a team. The dog tracks animals down, corners them, then his deranged companion wrings their necks with his bare hands." Emeline twisted her clinched fists in a grinding motion to illustrate.

"No, Nellie dear. My schemes are tame compared to his. I'm sure Max neglected to tell you he often finds fresh, or rotting, kill on his porch. I bring homemade biscuits and cookies." Emeline paused. "Oh, yes, I'm sorry about those squirrels. They probably gorged themselves to death on the fudge. At least, they died happy."

Nellie's cheeks flushed. She wiped her brow on the edge of her sleeve.

"I've heard enough. I believe you have evil intentions toward Maggie. Possibly myself and Ernest also. Max and Maggie love each other and nothing you could do or say will change that. I suggest you go back to your hole across the lake and never step foot here again."

Nellie firmly gripped her derringer. Emeline drew closer.

"I believe in the power of God and his ability to protect me and my friends from fiends like you. None of us want to see your face again." Nellie raised the gun waist high.

"God? What god? The god of the trees, the water, the animals? The god of the wind, lightning and storms?"

"No. The God who created all those things through the power of his son, Jesus Christ."

Nellie faltered as Emeline lifted her arms to shoulder height. Her grotesque fingers spread toward Nellie's face. In an instant, Emeline's face became old and haggard. Her once azure blue eyes lost all color. The jet black pupils cut to Nellie's soul.

A mighty wind swirled leaves across the porch. The sound became deafening. Nellie's hair tousled. She grabbed her derringer with both hands and pointed it at Emeline's face. A hideous screech rose above the wind. Thuds down the steps, another screech, then all was still.

Nellie captured her disheveled hair with one hand. Now with a clear view, she lowered the derringer. Emeline had vanished.

151

Chapter 24

Nellie leapt off the porch. The road lay empty in both directions. Emeline resembled a swift-footed gazelle. One minute threatening Nellie — the next completely gone. Unnerved by her experience with the demon-possessed woman, Nellie's entire body quaked. The derringer hung from her limp hand.

A shot in the far off woods startled Nellie. She lost her balance and staggered. Her derringer, still cocked, miraculously hadn't fired. Nellie carefully released the hammer and regained her composure. Her feet moved forward, but her heart convicted her to stay near the cabin. The shot might have been from Max or Ernest. Did they encounter Emeline? Did she attack them also? Or another danger found Maggie?

The wind and the forest now tranquil gave no hint of life. Nellie held her breath and listened. She considered her options. Stay here and re-cock her derringer, or return to the cabin. Emeline wouldn't return so soon. Perhaps this mountain man Emeline spoke of. If so, she may be in more danger. In the distance, around the bend, soft voices pierced the quiet. Nellie tried to recognize them. *Oh, Lord, let it be Max and Ernest. And I pray Maggie is with them.*

A puff of dust rose from the ground. Nellie glanced in the tree above for falling branches. Nothing appeared to dangle. Another cloud of dust caught her attention. Jed loped into view, retrieved a stick and ran back around the bend. The voices became more distinct. She recognized Max and Ernest's tones. Then Maggie's soft-spoken voice warmed her heart. Nellie sprinted to her dear friend.

With arms wide open, Nellie embraced Maggie. Maggie returned the love she received. Nellie opened her arms to include Max and Ernest. The foursome huddled together while Jed poked his nose between their legs searching for an entrance into the circle.

"Oh, Maggie, I've been so worried. Then the shot frightened me beyond belief," Nellie said.

"I'm so sorry, Nellie. I wandered too far. I should have listened to you and stayed close to the cabin. A silly squirrel distracted me and you know how random my mind works." Maggie hugged Nellie.

"But I did find strawberries." Maggie raised her pail. "And met a mountain man who guided me to Max."

"But the shot. What was that?" Nellie faced Max.

"My fault, Nellie. The gun was cocked and went off accidentally," Max said.

Maggie's comment penetrated Nellie's thoughts. "You met a mountain man? Did he have a large dog?"

"Yes, how did you know?" Maggie asked.

"I had a visitor. Emeline." Nellie quivered. "She told me about him and how dangerous he could be."

"Well, he treated me with kindness. Even though his outside appearance was disgusting. You always told me, never judge the inside of a person from the outside. He's kind-hearted, Nellie. I hope you meet him."

"You're trembling, Nellie." Ernest clasped her arm. "Is it because we're back and safe?" He paused. "Or from Emeline's visit?"

"I need to sit down and have a cup of coffee. Can we finish this conversation in the cabin?" Nellie asked.

"Before we do that, Nellie, I need to apologize. I let my emotions get the best of me and accused you of not caring for Maggie as much as I do. Please forgive me for my outburst." Max faced Nellie.

"I understand, Max. Yes, I forgive you and ask that you forgive me also for not heeding your advice. You know these woods much better than I. Had I followed your wishes all this would have been avoided."

"I forgive you also, Nellie."

The stroll back to the cabin continued in silence. Nellie held Maggie's hand. Maggie held Max's hand and dear Ernest kept Jed busy chasing a stick.

With coffee poured, strawberries washed and Jed's water dish filled, the friends positioned themselves around the dining table. Nellie summarized her confrontation with Emeline. Maggie reached for her hand.

"Ernest, I understand demon-possession now. But it wasn't until I said Jesus' name that Emeline transformed. Can you explain that?" Nellie asked.

"I can try, Nellie." Ernest sipped coffee from his cup. "James, in his New Testament book, congratulates his audience that they believe God is one and commends them. Then he adds, '...the demons also believe, and shudder.' When you invoked Jesus' name you struck Emeline at the very core of her being and the demon within struck out with vengeance. You threatened her demon with the victory we have in the Lord. He knows he's doomed to eternal damnation and strives to take everyone down with him."

Nellie's hand, cupped in Maggie's, grew moist.

"Now that you know the truth about Emeline, Satan will attack you harder. While his attempts will be furious, you must set your resolve to conquer." Ernest laid his hand on the Bible. "Only when we invoke Jesus' name and claim the power of His shed blood will Satan and his demons be sent back to the abyss."

"What about the rest of us, Ernest?" Maggie asked. "Emeline threatened me this morning. Do you think she will attack me also?"

"More than likely," Ernest said. "It's you she wants out of Eden Lake. I believe she hoped Nellie would support her, become allies. Nellie's strength unhinged her. The true obstacle is you. Her sights, humanly speaking, are set on Max." Ernest pointed to Maggie. "You're in her way."

Nellie refilled her mug and scooped a spoonful of washed strawberries from the bowl in the center of the table.

"I'm glad you suggested we munch on these strawberries now. Couldn't wait to enjoy their sweetness for dessert." Nellie drew the shaking spoon to her dish.

"Now, Lassies, Max, I suggest we begin each day in prayer asking the Lord for a strong wall of protection. We need to be on guard at all times. Remember to proclaim Jesus' victory and quote scripture whenever confronted by Emeline," Ernest said.

"I, for one, will pray for Emeline," Max said. "I will pray she comes to know the love of God and repents before it's too late."

"Never thought of her." Maggie scrunched her face. "We all need the Lord, including Emeline."

"I need to tell each of you how blessed I am to watch the transforming growth in your lives of faith," Ernest said. "I had my doubts in Scotland, but the Holy Spirit has worked, and is still working a miracle in each of your lives."

Max and Ernest cooked dinner while Nellie helped Maggie clean her dirty clothes and brush her matted hair.

"Maggie, I'm fearful for you. Until Emeline is vanquished, we must be on guard," Nellie said. "You need to carry a gun at all times. Please talk to Max about purchasing a firearm when we go to Sandy. Then shooting lessons when we return."

"I will, Nellie. I realize how important it is for me to be comfortable toting a gun in this wilderness. Definitely not Chicago. Nor Portland for that matter. There's a different kind of danger here and I need to be able to protect myself and the ones I love."

"Dinner's ready," Max called.

Nellie carried plates to the dining table. When Maggie entered the kitchen Max's eyes lit up. Nellie's heart warmed. He would protect Maggie. He would love her dear friend with an unconditional love. This assurance gave Nellie confidence that all would be well when she returned to Portland. Her heart now ached. She had always been close to Maggie. Separation would be difficult. Time for a new season of life. Maggie would be in good hands.

"Wait a minute. Before we dig into this delicious dinner, I've got a question for Ernest. We've been so wrapped up in the day's events, I forgot to ask about Miss Greene." Nellie said. "Is she coming with us to Sandy tomorrow?"

Ernest beamed. "Yes."

"Hallelujah." Nellie and Maggie shouted.

"Joel's going to watch the Merc tomorrow. Then close on the Fourth." Ernest cheeks reddened. "I have a favor to ask you lassies. I want my proposal to be memorable. So I would appreciate any suggestions you have, being lassies and all."

Maggie's face blushed. Nellie's eyes connected with hers. Surely Maggie wondered how Max would propose? Or, would he? He missed his opportunity in Scotland and again before they docked in New York. What held him back? They needed each other, now more than ever. Max fulfilled Maggie's 'knight in shining armor' image and Maggie longed to care for Max, whatever illness afflicted him.

The atmosphere grew tense. Max rose from the table, filled the water pitcher and opened the door for Jed.

"We'll think on that one and get back to you, Ernest." Nellie said. "I've never been in that situation, so this will be an imagining exercise."

"I've had one proposal, Ernest," Maggie said. "But it wasn't very creative. If I'm ever asked again, I want to be swept off my feet. I long to be the center of his life, after the Lord that is." Maggie paused. "Let me think for a while."

Max returned to the table, but avoided eye contact. Nellie's mouth filled with words, but wisdom prevailed. She did not want to stir up a conversation best left with him and Maggie. Her promise to Ernest about not mentioning his illness would be honored, as difficult as it was. The old proverb replayed in her head; "We get too soon olde, and too late smart." Max had a thirty-four year old mind, yet he couldn't recognize the gem that sat across from him.

"What time will we leave in the morning?" Nellie asked.

"As soon as possible," Ernest replied. "The sooner we get to Sandy, the sooner I can find an engagement ring. And the sooner I buy the ring, the sooner I can propose. And the sooner..."

"We get the idea, Ernest." Max interrupted. "Maybe we should contact the pastor in Sandy first. Be sure he's available for an evening wedding."

"Now, Laddie, as anxious as I am to make Heather, Mrs. Ernest McIntyre, I want her to have the wedding she deserves. I'll leave that event in her capable hands." Ernest pushed his chair away from the table. "But that day can't come soon enough."

Chapter 25

The mule-drawn coach arrived in Sandy mid-morning. Red, white, blue flags and streamers hung from shop awnings. A cloth banner above the road set the festive mood, "The Fourth of July" in hand calligraphed red letters. Then below, in smaller blue letters, "Festivities and Picnic Meinig Park." Flower pots overflowed with red, white and blue carnations. They burst from the pots like exploded fireworks on the narrow wooden sidewalks, beside doors and braced under windows. A red, white and blue ribbon covered apple crate, filled with hand-held flags, rested on a bench outside a mercantile. Each cost two cents. The clerk refilled the gaps as soon as the flags disappeared.

"So many people and a day before the celebration," Ernest said. "This does remind me of our Highland Games in Rolen, Max. As soon as we get off the coach, I'm heading for that store. Got to purchase an American Flag. I'll buy one for each of us."

Ernest, true to his word, assisted Miss Greene from the coach then maneuvered his way down the crowded walk. Max offered a hand to Maggie and Nellie as they climbed from the coach.

"Whoa there, boy," Max said to a youngster as he zig-zagged between Max and the ladies. "You almost knocked us over."

"Sorry, sir, I'm really sorry," the boy called back.

With their luggage beside his feet, Max waited for Ernest's return.

"My, it feels good to stretch my legs." Miss Greene raised her heels behind her. "Haven't been to Sandy for quite some time. Forgot how a long sit can lull various body parts to sleep." She rubbed her backside.

Maggie and Nellie chuckled and mimicked Miss Greene.

"I couldn't agree more." Nellie massaged her derrière.

Max lifted two suitcases while Ernest managed the rest. The Sandy Hotel's sign was easy to spot. A well-kept white two-story building with a wrap-around porch invited guests to chat in the afternoon sun. Max greeted the clerk and secured accommodations.

"They have an extra-large room with two double beds, ladies. It's upstairs if you don't mind the climb." Max held out a key to Maggie. "I hope that will be adequate."

"We'll make it work, Max," Maggie said. "This will be like an old-time sleep-over as little girls. We'll probably talk all night, tell silly tales…"

"And wake up in the morning with bags under our eyes," Miss Greene interrupted.

The ladies giggled and nodded in agreement. Max loved Maggie's laugh. Distinctive above all others, it suited her. Everything about this sweet lady suited her. She couldn't leave Eden Lake. What would he do without her?

"Miss Greene, I've got to tell you, you're exactly what I need right now. Things have been tense lately, but you're the medicine to lighten this heart of mine. I thank you for coming with us." Maggie gave Miss Greene a warm hug.

"Well, then, my sweet girl, if our relationship has come to that, I request you stop calling me Miss Greene. I prefer, Heather. And with your permission, you will be Maggie and Nellie." Miss Greene faced Max. "While we're at it, you've known me long enough, young man. And in all the time I've called you Max, you've never addressed me as anything but Miss Greene. Enough of that, okay?"

"Absolutely, Miss Greene. I mean, Heather." Max smiled. "But that's because I never knew your first name. From this moment on, it will be Heather." He bowed to her.

Max and Ernest carried the luggage to their upstairs rooms. The ladies larger room, in the far back corner, had a nice view of Mt. Hood. Max and Ernest's room, on the other side of the hotel, overlooked an alley-way.

"Any plans this afternoon, ladies?" Max asked when they gathered again in the lobby.

"If there is a clothing store, I, for one, would like a new hat." Maggie said.

"This hair of mine needs something done with it." Heather patted her wind-blown unkempt coif. "I hope Mrs. Moseley still lives here. She cuts hair and sells hats in her back parlor. We'll check there first."

"Not too short, I trust." Ernest's frown dominated his face.

Max placed the room key in his pocket. "Why don't we plan to meet here early evening? I'll give Ernest a tour of the town and we'll find some information about tomorrow's events. Sound all right?"

"Sounds perfect," Heather said. "Come on ladies. Time to explore this grand little town."

The ladies swayed out the front door. Max chuckled at the sight. They moved in unison like the pendulum that undulated in the Ithaca tall clock in the hotel's lobby.

"Ernest, we'll try the Revenue Store first. Its at the far end of town and faces Barlow Road," Max said.

"Barlow Road?" Ernest asked. "Is that the same as the Barlow trail you mentioned earlier?"

"Yes, one and the same. A man named Sam Barlow guided his wagon train from Missouri to The Dalles, up the river to the east of Sandy in 1845. When faced with the treacherous Columbia River and its gorge, he knew there would be a great loss of belongings, not to mention the pioneers lives. Rafting would be too dangerous."

Max pointed at Mt. Hood. "He scouted for an old Indian trail around the south of Mt. Hood. By taking his time he discovered an alternate route. This eighty mile or so stretch of difficult terrain became known as the Barlow Road."

"Did others follow his leading?"

"Just a year later more pioneers drove their wagons on his route. Thousands of hopeful homesteaders, prospectors and miners followed his course." Max parted from Ernest's side to allow room for passersby. "When the train came through to Oregon in the '80s, the wagon train traffic diminished."

Max nodded. "That's the Revenue Hotel. First one in Sandy. Housed a lot of the pioneers in its time. Up the road a bit, John Revenue built his store. Our first stop in the search for the perfect ring. Be warned though that you won't find anything here from Tiffany's."

"That's fine, Max. If I had known I might need a wedding ring out here, I would have stopped in Tiffany's when I had the lay over in New York. I understand he has some beautiful jewels in his store."

Max's heavy boots kicked up some dust as he led the way to the Revenue. The small town bustled with activity. He had never seen the streets so congested. Several alley-ways hosted children's games of marbles. In the vacant lot across from the Revenue, young boys were on their knees. One had his mouth obscured in the dirt.

159

"What are those laddies playing, Max?" Ernest motioned toward the dirt lot.

"It's called mumblety-peg. Young boys compete for dexterity with a knife. The one who succeeds first through all the levels has the honor of pounding a small peg into the ground. He gets three strikes to drive the stake as far as possible. The losers must dig the peg out of the ground with their teeth. Don't know if it's a right-of-passage to have dirt in your mouth or not."

"Did you play that as a lad?"

"No, I stuck with marbles. Still have a leather pouch with my favorite marbles and my winning shooter." Max sighed. "Always hoped I would have a son one day to pass my marbles to."

The Revenue overflowed with customers purchasing flags and yards of ribbon. Little children raided the candy jars while their mothers gossiped in a corner.

"Here, Ernest, if they have wedding rings, they'd be in the case at the back." Max wove his way to the far end of the store.

A glass covered case besides the cash register held expensive knives, pocket watches, with and without fobs, and a few sparkly necklaces. Ernest careened into the case jostling the contents.

"May I help you?" An older gentleman dropped his armload of yard goods at the sound. With scowled face, he glared at Ernest.

"Sorry, I didn't mean to bump the case so hard," Ernest apologized.

"My friend would like to purchase a wedding ring," Max said. "Wonder if you may have some. Perhaps in your storeroom?"

The clerk's face softened. "Yes, in the back room. I don't keep them out front. Never know the intent of the customers." He entered the back room through a heavy curtain that closed behind him.

"Thanks, Max. These old Scottish emotions will get the better of me one day. Sure glad you're here."

"You're fine, Ernest." Max picked up the yard goods and stacked them on a counter. "I imagine I'd be the same if I were in your shoes."

The clerk returned and unlocked three wooden rectangular boxes for Ernest to examine. Two boxes contained several rings set with diamonds or gemstones. The third held plain bands.

"These are beautiful." Ernest's fingers surveyed the beauties. "What do you think, Max?"

"No, Ernest, this decision is completely on your shoulders. You and Heather have a special relationship and I think the ring you choose should be as special."

Max scanned the rings. He chose one for a closer look. The light from a side window glistened off the band. It reminded him of the twinkle in Maggie's eye when she arrived in Eden Lake. A perfect ring for her delicate hand, he twisted it between his fingers. He imagined this golden band resting on Maggie's left hand. A completion to all he felt for her.

"What about this one, Max?" Ernest asked. "There are two small amethysts in the setting. One symbolizing the heather covered hills back home and the one for Heather who adds her fragrance to my life with love."

Max's heart warmed as he listened to Ernest proclaim his love for Heather. The amethyst ring would be perfect. He glanced at the delicate ring in his fingers. An iridescent opal set in a halo design of diamonds. Perfect for Maggie.

"Well, gents, what do you think?" The clerk asked.

"I'd like this one," Ernest said.

"A wonderful choice." The clerk wiped the ring with a jewelers cloth. "I've had this ring for several months, but no one seemed to want it. Apparently it was waiting for the right person. You, sir."

"Do you have a small box?"

"Let me check." The clerk slipped through the curtain into the storeroom.

"Ernest, do you want to check out the Meinig Store? Friedrich Meinig purchased the first store in Sandy built by a man named Gerdes. He felt the Gerdes store need expanding so he constructed a larger building a few blocks east. The store has more square feet plus a dance hall and saloon. He may have more choices."

"No, Max. This is the one. A beautiful amethyst and four small diamonds. One diamond for each week I've known Heather." Ernest drew the ring close to his eyes. "And that one you are man-handling is perfect for Maggie. What do you say to a double wedding?"

Max left Ernest and reached a side window where he held the ring up to the light. The yellow band of gold matched the purity of Maggie's heart. A circle with no beginning or end reflected his eternal love for her. His mind fought with itself. Did he have the right to even ask her to marry him? With his life expectancy ebbing away, what could he possibly offer her? Yet, for even a few months, years, marriage would be worth it.

"Max," Ernest interrupted, "the clerk wants to know if you're going to buy that ring."

Max returned to the counter and replaced the ring in the narrow box. "Not today."

Chapter 26

The Fourth of July celebration started with a bang. Forty-four to be exact. The gun salute at sunrise awoke the town. The festivities had commenced.

After an agonizing night, Max rose. His head pounded. Marriage. Maggie. He needed an answer, yet no closer in the morning light. He tried not to disturb Ernest, yet his friend obviously tossed and turned for a different reason. They were like two ships passing in the night, each set his own course. Neither wished to distract the other.

A straight backed chair snuggled close to the side window became Max's prayer closet. He leaned forward, elbows on his knees, hands clasped and head bowed. Thoughts of Maggie consumed him. He strained to gain a right perspective and focus. The Lord's will must become his will. He struggled to relinquish all his emotional ties to Maggie and empty himself of sinful pride. Most of his life he'd lived his way. Now, with his spiritual blinders removed, he knew his way was not God's best. Sweat poured down his brow and mixed with tears. His body trembled. He cried out to the Lord through sobs. *Lord, I believe you have a purpose for my life. However long I have left, I want your best for me. I want to live for you, with or without Maggie. Show me your will. Cleanse me of my selfishness and grant me your peace.*

A quiet voice continued. "And Lord thank you for the miracle of faith you've given to Max. Help him to completely trust you in all things."

Ernest's hand rested on Max's shoulder. Max was overwhelmed with his dear friend's love.

"Thank you, Ernest. I didn't mean to disturb your quiet. Don't know why I trembled."

"You don't?" Ernest asked. "You entered into a deeper place with the Lord. The Holy Spirit convicted you of a self-centered attitude and made you aware that only in God's will can you be truly happy. Remember, when the Lord sets you free, you will be free indeed. Giving Maggie to the Lord was the best thing you could have done."

"I feel that load of burdens I've carried so long has vanished. I have peace, Ernest. Peace that the Lord knows what's best for my life and I will walk by faith, not by sight." Max straightened, wiped his face and glanced outside. "Whatever I face, I will cling to God's strong hand and trust Him completely. If Maggie remains, I will praise Him. If not, I believe it's the best for both of us."

Max removed his shirt and poured water into the wash basin. He lathered a wash cloth and wiped down his body. Ernest spread the curtains apart which allowed the morning light to brighten the room. The sun warmed Max's back. He inhaled deeply and stretched his arms toward the ceiling. The mirror behind the wash basin reflected the lump in Max's abdomen. He lowered his arms and covered his chest with a towel. Ernest's reflection assured Max that his friend had not seen it. Sick or not, the spiritual cleansing he'd received created a great start to a joy-filled celebration of his nation's birthday.

Max opened the window and glanced down the alley. Decorated wagons filled the street as the band tuned their instruments. Time to get the girls and join the throng.

Max and Ernest descended the stairs to find Maggie, Nellie and Heather on the porch.

"Good morning, ladies," Max said.

"Good morning to you as well," Maggie said.

Ernest offered Heather and Nellie an arm and escorted them to the white picket fence that enclosed the hotel's front yard.

"Max, are you all right? You look...I don't know...different." Maggie asked.

"I'm fine, Maggie." Max held her arm. "I talked to the Lord this morning and realize the importance of placing my life in His hands. All of my life. Every desire, hope and dream are now His. That also includes all the obstacles that rear their ugly heads."

"I'm glad, Max." Maggie's face beamed. "The same thing happened to me last night. I have been struggling with so much. Heather asked me why I kept everything to myself and I couldn't answer her. God is so gracious. I gave Him my worries and frustrations, and He gave me peace in exchange. I even prayed for Emeline." Maggie squeezed his arm. "Let's join the others. This will be a great day. God-planned."

They wove their way toward a platform where an official read the "Declaration of Independence." A prayer was offered and the Glee Club sang a patriotic song, followed by several numbers from the band. There were shouts back and forth of "Freedom," "America" and "Happy Birthday" from all sides of the street. The air was electric with excitement.

"Ladies, we have an hour before the parade forms for Meinig Park," Max said. "Anything you would like to do?"

"I wonder why we didn't buy ribbons to decorate our hats when we shopped yesterday," Heather said. "But, thanks to Ernest," Heather caressed his cheek, "we do have these small flags to carry."

Maggie removed her hat. "Don't know about you, but I'm going to tuck my flag into my new bonnet." She pushed the stick through the weave. "Which, by the way, neither of you gentlemen has commented on."

"Nor my new hairstyle." Heather plumped her hair mass. "Mrs. Moseley said it was the latest thing, She called it a pompadour. My flag will rest securely in my hair." She slid her flag through the mound of tresses piled on top of her head.

Even though the July heat simmered in the mountains, Max shivered. He had not been observant. Had not remembered the ladies shopped for new hats and hairdos. Women liked to be noticed, especially when something is new or different. He had forgotten that fine point.

"You ladies are lovely. Your beauty overtook my senses and I have been unable to speak." Max hung his head.

Maggie's eyebrows pushed together. "Are you serious, Max Sullivan? Thou speech is strange indeed and I am unaccustomed to the magnificent articulation."

They all laughed. Good friends, spending good times and sharing humor.

"Seriously, lassies, you're lovely. New hat, new hair style to celebrate another new year of birth for your nation," Ernest said. "And may I say, my adopted nation as well."

"Ernest," Heather squealed. "You mentioned you might move here and leave Scotland behind. Have you decided?"

"Yes, my sweet, Heather," Ernest said. "I have very few belongings in Scotland. I'll send a telegram to Mabel and George. What's left is now theirs. The few items I brought with me are the most meaningful."

Heather threw her arms around Ernest's neck, then immediately withdrew.

"I'm so sorry. I had no right to respond like that."

"I would have been disappointed if you hadn't," Ernest said. "I love you, Heather, and want to be close to you. Since that means living in America, then so be it."

Max glanced at Maggie. Tears formed in her eyes. Her smile said it all. Ernest and Heather were, indeed, perfect for each other.

"We forgot Nellie," Ernest said as he faced Nellie. "You are also a picture of loveliness. Your hat balances perfectly with your hair style and complements your dress."

Nellie scrunched her face. "Are you kidding, Ernest? If you're going to become an American, you best leave that highfaluting talk back on the British Isles. And, for your information, I've had this hat for five years now. In fact I wore it almost every day in Scotland and haven't changed my hairstyle since I turned twenty. Some things become comfortable through the years and if you changed it," Nellie paused. "Well, it just wouldn't feel right."

"You're so right," Heather said. "I feel as if I have a huge hay stack balanced on my head. You'll never know what a difficult night I had trying to protect this mass. In fact, I spent long hours propped in a chair to keep it looking good for you, Ernest McIntyre." Heather swatted at Ernest. "I imagine hundreds of tiny spiders are claiming their parcel of land up there and building nests." She scratched her head with the flag's stick. "In fact, Ernest, dear, this pompadour is coming down tonight. Only wanted something different for today." She blushed.

Ernest brushed his arm across his brow. "Whew, I'm sure glad to hear that."

Max offered Maggie his arm and led them back to the hotel lobby. He spaced five chairs around a table for the group then removed a flyer from his jacket pocket. Once unfolded, he flattened the paper on the table.

"Here's the events for the day," Max said. "Ernest, you and I may win enough contests to buy a fancy dinner tonight. First is the parade. It leaves town at one-o'clock with decorated horses in the lead, then the marching band, followed by the townsfolk."

"Think they would reverse that order. Put the horses last, if you get my drift," Ernest said.

"Yes, Ernest, I agree," Max chuckled. "Once everyone is at the park, lunch is served until two o'clock. The Sandy women are great cooks and bring enough for all the visitors."

"I brought a batch of my huckleberry muffins to share," Heather said.

Ernest gave her a hug. "That's my girl."

"Are there events for the ladies too, Max?" Maggie asked.

"Let me read the list. Then you decide." Max leaned forward as he read. "Three-legged race, foot race, hurdles, sack race, climbing a greased pole, catching a greased pig, and the sweepstakes running race. Of course there are three horse races, but without mounts we can't enter those. They also have something called "Go As You Please" race, one-half mile. Don't know what that means, but sure conjures many delightful images."

"Maggie, you and I can enter the three-legged race and maybe the foot race as well. Depends on how far we have to run," Nellie said.

"Both races are one-hundred-fifty yards. You can do it," Max said.

"I'd like to see one of you boys try the greased pole or the greased pig." Nellie added her preferences. "How tall is the pole?"

Max scanned the paper. "The pole is twelve feet and the pig weighs one-hundred and fifty pounds." He glanced at Ernest. "Not for me, my friend."

"I suggest we each enter at least one race and combine any winnings for that dinner Max mentioned," Heather suggested.

"A grand idea, my sweet. I second the motion," Ernest paused, "that is if we need to vote."

"No vote necessary," Max said. "I think we're all in agreement. This is starting out to be a wonderfully fun day. A day to remember with my four favorite people in all the world."

Noise from the street captured Max's attention. The band played, someone yelled directions for the wagon masters and mothers called their children to stay close. Max refolded the flyer and slid it into his pocket. He pulled Maggie and Nellie's chairs away from the table and offered each an arm.

"Wait a minute." Heather raised a hand. "My muffins. I'll be right back."

Ernest caught her arm. "No, my dear. I'll get them. Don't want to disturb your pompadot."

Ernest retrieved the room key from the desk clerk.

"Pompadour, dear," Heather called. "Pompadour."

Max led Maggie and Nellie to the street. Heather waited inside for Ernest.

"Now ladies," he said, "this will be the tricky part. Don't walk too close to the person in front. And while we do want to keep up, it will be more important to watch our footsteps."

Maggie and Nellie laughed and agreed with Max as the horses were directed to their place in line. Flowers were woven into their manes, some wore straw hats with holes cut out for their ears. Colored ribbons dangled from their bridles and swayed in the breeze.

"We'll admire the decorated wagons and horses at the park. For now let's listen to the band and pay attention to our feet," Nellie said.

Heather and Ernest joined them. Ernest carried a large twig woven basket. A red and white checkered cloth tucked around the muffins.

The bass drum boomed the downbeat. A snare drum joined with a marching riff and the brass instruments sounded the melody. Their music filled the streets with celebration.

"Nellie, they look so smart in their uniforms," Maggie said. "When did they get those, Max?"

"Don't know exactly how long they've had them. I came in '91 and they wore the same uniforms as today. The town donated money for several months. Collected enough, disputed the color and finally settled on royal blue with gold cords, buttons and epaulets. Most didn't want to wear ordinary hats, so a kind of helmet was ordered. Not sure I like the top piece. Looks like a small sword pointing to the sky, but once a special order is made it's difficult to return."

"Listen, Maggie, they're playing "Turkey in the Straw." Strange for the Fourth of July." Nellie leaned her ear toward the music.

"Could be a traditional marching song for these folks." Max high-stepped. "Get's the feet moving anyway."

The throng reached the park where another sign greeted them. Stretched between two cedar trees, above a make-shift platform, a large white sheet of fabric with the dates "1776 to 1900" emblazoned in red paint. The crowd scattered in several directions. Ladies organized their meal offerings on horizontal planks of wood that rested on four-foot stomps. Forty-foot cedars provided shade around the park. The horses and wagons occupied a far corner. Children played hide and seek while the men folk remeasured race tracks for accuracy. Pigs squealed in a pen as young children teased them with branches.

"Is this what organized chaos looks like?" Ernest asked.

"As soon as the women have the food ready all will be quiet again," Max said. "That is except for the pigs."

The fourteen band members gathered in front of the stage. As if orchestrated by an unseen force, everyone quieted and faced the group. A father called out to his son while a young mother comforted her crying baby. Even the wind stopped rustling the tree branches.

Trumpets and tubas raised. A roll on the snare drum brought the throng's right hands over their chest. Music started and voices joined. "Oh, say can you see..." Shivers traveled down Max's back. He loved his country, his state, his town and today, most importantly, his God. This was a great country of freedoms. He glanced toward Ernest. Moisture welled in Ernest's eyes, one arm wrapped around Heather, the other laid on his chest. A new American immigrant to this land of plenty and opportunity. Max was proud to be an American.

Eden Lake

Chapter 27

"Thank you, ladies of Sandy, for another delicious celebration dinner." A man wearing a skimmer with a white shirt, blue suit, and red tie waved an American flag in the air. He perched himself on a four foot high stump.

"While everyone is cleaning up," he glanced at the crowd, then pointed to several clusters of men. "You there, Harry, Bert, Joe, get a crew and move the planks and stumps back on the wagons." Then to the crowd, "The band will honor us with a couple of songs. Sing along, if you've a mind to."

"He didn't skip a beat, did he," Nellie said.

Max and Ernest assisted the crew as they lifted the make-shift tables and stump supports onto the wagons. The ladies placed their empty bowls and dishes into wooden apple crates, then the young men carried the crates to a buckboard for the ride back to town.

"Listen, Maggie." Nellie cupped one hand around her ear. "They're playing your song."

"Nellie, it's not my song. Let's sing along though." Maggie paused. "Heather, will you join us?"

The ladies sang in unison, locked arms and swayed to the music.

"Hello, my baby. Hello, my honey. Hello, my ragtime gal.
Send me a kiss by wire. Baby my heart's on fire.
If you refuse me, Honey, you'll lose me, Then you'll be all alone.
Oh, baby, telephone and tell me I'm your own."

Max locked arms with Maggie while Ernest hooked on to Heather's elbow. Before long more of the crowd joined them. A mass of humanity swayed as one while the band played on.

When the music stopped, the men threw their hats in the air. The children held hands and wove through the adults like a Western terrestrial garter snake skimming over Eden Lake.

"All right everyone, the big moment has arrived. It's time for the games."

More whooping and hollering followed. Women patted their men-folk on the back and the children grabbed their partners for the first event; the three-legged race.

"All you participants line up on the starting line and tie your inside legs together with that scarf around your neck or hankie in your pocket. If it's clean, that is." The crowd laughed and clapped their hands.

"Now remember, you must reach the finish line as a couple, still tied together. The winners will receive two-dollars. One-hundred-fifty yards isn't that far. Why I wouldn't be surprised if the old-timers beat out these young kids."

Max removed his neck scarf and tied it around his and Ernest's ankles. Ernest tied his scarf around their thighs.

"Our legs are now one. We can't lose." Ernest wiped his brow on his sleeve.

Max glanced down the row of competitors. Maggie and Nellie tucked their skirt fabric into the belts which shortened the length to just below their knees. Maggie held their skirts out of Nellie's way while she looped a scarf around their ankles and finished with a bow.

Heather called from the sidelines, "Max, Ernest, go boys, go. Maggie and Nellie I'm right there with you, all the way."

"Take your marks. Get set. Go."

The runners hobbled down the field. Max focused on the official who waited at the far end, a blue flag held high. With his arm around Ernest's waist and Ernest's arm on Max's shoulder they moved as one. The gap between them and the other teams widened. They were winning. Their first two-dollars for dinner was as good as in their pocket. The sidelines erupted in cheers. Some of the spectators ran along the edge to follow Max and Ernest to the finish line.

Max glanced at the smiling faces on the side-lines as they passed. He waved with his free arm. A bright face in the crowd seized his attention. Focus lost, his foot landed on a rock. The tumble threw Ernest off-kilter and the two men landed in a heap on the ground. The cheers grew louder as the winners crossed the finish line.

"Max, are you all right?" Ernest asked as he loosened the scarf knots.

"I'm fine, Ernest. How about you?"

"Nothing damaged but my pride. I thought sure we had that two-dollars. We were way ahead of the pack." Ernest gave Max a hand up and the men brushed off their trousers.

"What happened?"

"I became distracted, Ernest. My eyes focused elsewhere instead of on the goal. Must have stepped on something hard and down I went. Couldn't stop the fall once it started."

"What distracted you, Max?" Ernest asked.

"Emeline." Max wiped his brow with his scarf.

"Are you sure?" Ernest's smile disappeared.

"Pretty sure." Max scanned the crowd but found no sign of her.

Maggie and Nellie were panting when they reached the boys.

"Max, what happened?" Maggie asked. "I thought sure you were going to win."

"I must have stepped on a rock, or something. Lost my balance and down we went."

"We're fine, lassies. We'll win the next race." Ernest said. "Who won?"

Maggie held up two shiny dollar coins.

"Okay, the challenge is on," Max winked. "What's next on the bill?"

"Here's your favorite race, ladies and gentlemen," the announcer called out. "The Go as You Please one-half mile race. Remember now, anything goes, but you can't run. If you do, you will be disqualified by the judges."

"Let's sit this one out." Max limped with his first steps. "Need to regain my pride."

"How about a glass of home-made lemonade?" Maggie asked.

"You four go ahead. I want to walk off the kink in my knee." Max headed for the sidelines.

"Want company?" asked Ernest.

"No. I'd like to be alone for a few minutes." He paused. "I'll be back shortly."

Max wandered through the pack of horses and into the woods. He disappeared behind the platform, then hiked away from the deafening crowd noise. Once concealed by thick trees, he scanned the on-lookers of the race in progress. The men wore dark suits and the women donned small hats with a ribbon or feather. These sturdy pioneer women all had auburn or black hair. Not a single blonde in the group. And certainly not one who let her hair flow unkempt to her waist. Where was she?

This would be the ideal time to confront her. Emeline's attacks toward Maggie and Nellie needed to be dealt with. He was ready to meet the challenge. To protect his friends from her viciousness. He canvased the crowd but couldn't find Emeline anywhere. Maybe he fantasized her presence.

The race ended amid cheers and claps from the crowd. The sack race participants lined up, but Max had no interest climbing into a burlap bag. "May as well go back," he said to no one in particular. "Sure wish I'd brought Jed." A squirrel chattered and climbed to a branch above his head. "You see her, Mr. Squirrel? How I wish I was as agile as you."

Max returned the way he had come. The horses stomped their hooves and snorted as he elbowed his way between several. Something unsettled these steeds. The thousand pound creatures pressed in on him. He placed his hands on one and pushed hard. Then he repeated the action with another and another. Never seen horses act this way. Max quickly scanned the ground for any garter snakes that may have spooked the horses. He couldn't see anything that would cause this agitation. Two draft horses joined the mix and Max became swallowed up in the mass. He mustered all his strength to shove them apart. Through a small gap he glimpsed the back of a large black stallion galloping away. "Beelzebub." Max shivered. The horses quieted and resumed their usual stance.

Max inhaled deeply when he reached open air. He climbed into a buckboard to glimpse Emeline's black steed. The horse had gone. Max jumped to the ground and returned to his friends.

"What did I miss?"

"The sack race and the greased pig and pole competitions." Maggie said. "What fun to watch the men folk try and catch a slimy pig. They had smaller pigs for the children."

"I wonder if the pigs enjoyed it as much as the spectators?" Max smiled.

"They're setting up for the hurdle race, then the horse races in the next field. Why don't you ladies walk on ahead and find us a good spot?" Ernest directed Heather with his hat. "We'll be there shortly."

He sidled up to Max. "Any luck?"

"No. Only Beelzebub. He somehow forced the horses to fence me in. Felt like I was suffocating." Max brushed off his pants. "Then he ran into the woods and the horses reverted to their normal behavior."

Max removed his handkerchief from his back pocket and

wiped his hands. "It scared me, Ernest. I tried to keep my feet moving to avoid horse hooves. At the same time I felt my breath and life being squeezed right out of my body."

Ernest placed his arm around Max's shoulder. "I remember you confessed to me one day in Scotland when you missed an opportunity with Maggie. You said, "People always told me I was timid and shy." Max, I believe you haven't completely moved past that self-fulfilling prophecy. I've seen you face challenges directly."

Ernest grabbed a cup of water from a near-by table and offered it to Max. "But you slip back into what's comfortable. I want to share a passage from 2 Timothy. You know Timothy was timid and shy also. I believe he called on God's strength in tough situations. "For God has not given us a spirit of timidity, but of power and love and discipline." Memorize that verse, Max and proclaim it whenever you need to."

"Thank you, Ernest. That word was just what I needed today. She's a vixen, but with God's power I have the victory." Max shook Ernest's hand. "I'm so glad you're here. Now, let's find the girls. Don't want to miss the horse races."

Chapter 28

Only two races left. Dinner in the balance. Max mentally encouraged himself. He must win this one and the final race. If not, he would use the money from the sale of a story. But, deep down, he hoped it wouldn't come to that. He had reserved that money to purchase something special.

"Ready, Ernest?" Max asked.

"One hundred and fifty yards not tied to you? Should be easy," Ernest said.

The two men lined up, heard the caller's start, then bolted to the front of the pack. Max, determined to succeed this time, edged his way to the front. Soon he out-paced the other runners and crossed the finish line. Ahead of him, at the edge of the woods, someone waited with opened arms. Emeline. Max skidded to a halt before their bodies collided.

"What are you doing here?"

"I'm celebrating the Fourth the same as everyone else. You didn't think I would stay home and not join the festivities? I love games. Especially playing games with you." Her eyes twinkled.

Max placed his hands on his knees and bent over panting from the race. Once his breathing slowed he stood tall, planted his feet and glared at Emeline.

"I'm not playing games with you, Emeline. And I forbid you to bother Maggie or Nellie ever again. You've harassed them for the last time. The only one leaving Eden Lake is you, so I suggest you go back to that dismal home of yours, pack your bags, sell the cabin and move on."

"Oh, Max, whatever have I done for you to take such an attitude? I love you and want to spend the rest of my life with you. You can't force me to leave Eden Lake." Emeline stepped closer to Max and reached out to touch his face. "Can't you see how perfect we are for each other?"

Max grabbed her wrist before she touched him. Electricity riddled his body. He flung her arm down to her side and stepped backwards. A surge of courage raged through his being. He felt strong and in control.

"Emeline, there is no you and I." Max glared. "I've given my life to the Lord and He hasn't given any indication that you should become part of my future."

"The Lord? Ha." Emeline's face wrinkled. "What does He have to do with anything? You're in charge of your life. You and only you." Her voice deepened.

"Emeline, I've been praying for you. I hope you come to know the love of God as I do."

"There is no God of love, only hate. That is why I serve no celestial being. No one has power over me. No one's in charge, but me." Her eyes grew dark and her body jerked.

"I proclaim the power of Jesus Christ over you right now." Max raised his hand toward her. "You have no authority here. Leave me, Emeline and never return." Max closed his eyes and made the sign of the cross over his chest. A strong wind slammed into his face then dissipated as quickly as it came. He opened his eyes. She had vanished like the early morning vapor on Eden Lake.

Max thanked the Lord for the victory he'd received. Finally, a personal challenge confronted with strength and courage. No more timidity. Now to put his shyness to rest.

"Ernest, what race is next?" Max said as he joined his friend.

"Max, what on earth happened to you? You won the race, but since you didn't return the official couldn't award you the first place prize. So they gave it to the second place runner."

"Emeline waited. The power of the Lord overcame and I feel free of her and my timidity, Ernest. One more hurdle to conquer than I will be free indeed." Max's face glowed with success. "Who came in second?"

Ernest held up two coins. Max slapped his friend's back.

"One race left, Max. It's the Sweepstakes Running Race. A half-mile with eight-dollars to the winner." Ernest placed his hand on his chest. "I'm exhausted, so this one's yours."

Max's steps faltered as Maggie crashed into him.

"Where did you go?" Maggie asked out of breath. "You easily won the race but couldn't be found to award your prize."

"I needed to take care of something." Max brushed his pant legs.

"Was it the same thing you needed to be alone with last time you left us?" Maggie asked.

"Yes." Max's face squinted.

"It's Emeline, isn't it?" Maggie asked.

Max held Maggie's hand and led her to a quiet place away from the crowd.

"How did you know?"

"I saw her in the crowd, Max." Maggie swept a strand of loose hair off her face. "While you were lined up for the last race, I had a premonition something was wrong. Almost as if the Holy Spirit guided my eyes in her direction. As soon as I saw her I prayed for your protection." Maggie paused and surveyed the woods. "She smiled at me, Max. But not a sweet smile. An 'I'm-out-to-get-you' sort of smirk. The race started and my focus narrowed to you. After you crossed the finish line I glanced back to where she had stood, but she'd vanished." Maggie gulped. "I knew she waited in the woods for you."

"The Lord gave me the victory over her, Maggie. I don't believe she'll be bothering you or Nellie anymore." Max squeezed her hands. "I'm so glad you're here. Seems like only yesterday we were in Scotland. All those weeks together solidified my feelings for you. During these months apart since we returned home, my heart has ached to be with you again." Maggie's eyes filled with tears. "I'm thankful for Emeline." Max inhaled. "I know it sounds strange, but her attacks on you reinforced how precious you are to me."

"Your attention please." The official called over the crowd. "Your attention. Time for the final race. The Sweepstakes Running Race is taking all comers at the starting line. This is the big one folks. Eight dollars to the winner. Yes, that's right, eight United States dollars."

"That's you, Max," Maggie said, a gleam in her eye. "You've got to win this one. With my two dollars and Ernest's two, we'll have enough for a nice evening meal before the fireworks."

Max struggled with whether to stay and finish his conversation with Maggie or run the last race. How he longed to tell her of his love for her. Perhaps this was not the time or place. Too many people, too much noise and too many distractions. His focus lost, he hugged Maggie and the two met Ernest at the starting line.

"Ernest, are you going to run?" Max asked.

"No, Laddie, just saving your spot." Ernest chuckled and firmly gripped Max's hand. "Good luck to you."

"We ladies are forming a cheering section at the far end." Heather said. "We'll see you at the finish line." She, Maggie and Nellie hurried down the field.

"This is it, Max. Our fancy meal rests on the speed of those legs of yours." Ernest placed his hand in his pocket. "But don't worry none if you can't make it. I've brought extra money in case of an emergency. You just do your best."

Max surveyed the lineup. While he was not the youngest, he certainly wasn't the oldest either. Loggers are a strong lot, but he hoped more upper body strength than lower. Much of his energy had been sapped with the other races and his face-to-face with Emeline. He prayed his reserve tank remained full, or at least full enough to finish the race without too much embarrassment.

"Take your marks, runners."

Max waved to the girls who waved back from the far end of the field.

His heart pounded. Could he do this? Would there be enough stamina for a half mile? Sweat stained his shirt. He quickly removed his jacket and tie, flung them to Ernest and undid his shirt's top button.

"Get set."

He rolled his sleeves above his elbows.

"Go."

Max stayed with the pack. He kept his eyes focused on Maggie who jumped and waved her arms in the air. The cheering throng on both sides of the course deafened his ears. Some runners fell back. Max remained with the leaders. The horde thinned as the finish grew closer. Max sensed a runner on his left and right side, but kept his focus on Maggie. His legs weakened and his heart pounded. Max knew his body had had enough. *Please, Lord, don't let me collapse in front of Maggie. If you could give this sick body one more burst of energy, I sure would appreciate it.*

Peering to the sides, Max glimpsed only one runner stayed with him. All three ladies jumped and yelled, their voices rose above the din. *Well, Lord, this will probably be the last race of my life. You with me on this?* A sudden surge of energy burst through Max's body. His feet pounded the ground in rapid succession. Maggie's arms flung wide. Max headed straight for her.

The cheers rang through the trees. There were whoops and hollers. Hats were thrown, hankies tossed, hands clapped and a herd of feet headed straight for Max. All he wanted was to remain wrapped in Maggie's arms. Conscious of his sweat covered body, he tried to pull back. With each pull, Maggie's hug tightened.

A line judge moved toward Max. Maggie slowly released him. The judge raised Max's hand. "We have a winner." Max gazed into her eyes, then dutifully accompanied the judge to receive his reward.

"Here he is, ladies and gentlemen, the winner of the Sweepstakes Race. I believe I recognize this young man." The judge squinted. "Been here before?" He eyed Max up and down. "Over from Eden Lake. Is that right?" Max nodded. "Why, unless my eyes deceive me, this is Max Sullivan. Our famous mystery writer." The crowd applauded and cheered.

"Yes, sir. I'm flattered you remembered." Max gripped his hand in friendship. "I've been to Sandy's Fourth of July picnic several years. This year I have friends. One all the way from Scotland."

"Is that the one Miss Greene keeps spouting off about? Ernest this and Ernest that."

Max scanned the throng for Heather. Ernest was standing close beside her. Her cheeks reddened.

"That's me, your honor. And I don't mind a bit," Ernest said as he waved his arm. The crowd laughed. Some patted Ernest on his back.

"Well, Max Sullivan, it's my pleasure to hand you the prize money for a race well run. Don't know where you got that last burst of energy, but you sure left ol' Doug Olstrom in the dust."

"Thank you," Max said. "And thank you to the great town of Sandy, Oregon for hosting the best birthday party in these here United States of America."

Amid the shouts, Max descended from the platform.

"Okay, folks, time to clean up your messes, hitch up the horses and head back to town. Fireworks begin promptly at 9:45." He paused. "Oh, yes, don't forget to take the same children home that you came with." Laughter erupted.

Max reached his friends who remained out of the way of the wagons and horses. Ernest handed him his coat and tie. The band led the parade back to town playing "Maple Leaf Rag". Written a year ago, the tune remained a favorite in Sandy.

"You did it, Max. You won the Sweepstakes Race. I'm so proud of you." Maggie flung her arms around Max. This time he didn't try to pull away. He reciprocated her hug and pressed her close to him. How good she felt in his arms. If he released her, he feared she would be gone for good. No more mistakes. Scotland, New York, but not in Eden Lake.

Max pulled back enough to gaze into her beautiful hazel eyes. Eyes that glowed with mystery and longing. His desire to spend the rest of his life with her had never been so strong. Loose strands of

179

long red hair blew gently around her face. No words were necessary. She enticed him with her very being.

"Maggie, let's wait until the others are gone. A leisurely stroll back to town will give us time to talk."

He released her from his embrace and glanced around for Ernest, Heather and Nellie. Except for a few stragglers, the park had been emptied. Even the banner above the announcer's platform had been removed.

"I think we're alone now, Max." Maggie smiled.

Max clutched her hand and they ambled toward town.

"Since I was interrupted earlier with the announcement about the race starting, I'd like to begin again." Max put his jacket on and looped his tie around his neck. "Maggie, I made a mistake in Scotland and again in New York. I don't want to make the same mistake in Eden Lake."

"Mistake? Max, you were perfect in Scotland. You came to my rescue at the most critical time. You kept me focused to the discovery of the truth and not what I wanted to hear. You allowed me to be frivolous and carefree, yet gently pulled the reins back when necessary. No mistake that I'm aware of. I felt your support and encouragement at all times. The only mistake that may have been made, was on my part." Maggie hung her head. "I should have listened to you and Nellie more and followed your advice. I tend to be bull-headed at times. Or so my mother told me." Maggie inhaled.

"Maggie, my dear, I'm requesting you not say another word until I have finished."

"Max, I'm sorry. When I get nervous I rattle on. Sometimes about nothing at all."

"Like now?"

Maggie placed her hand over her mouth. "No more," she said in a muffled voice.

"Good." Max scratched his head. "Now, where was I?"

Maggie removed her hand from her mouth. Max responded in an instant.

"Don't say a word. I'll figure it out." Max paused. "Oh, yes."

Max came to a stop, faced Maggie and tenderly placed his hands on her shoulders.

"Maggie Richards," he inhaled deeply, "I love you."

Her eyes filled with tears and cascaded down her cheeks. Max removed his hankie and dabbed the trickles.

"Max," Maggie said in a quavering voice, "I love you, too."

Max enfolded her trembling body in his arms. This hug would be a forever-memory hug. Not one given in a rush. Not a good-bye hug with the prospect of never seeing each other again. Not a great-race-congratulations hug. This hug had permanence about it. This hug didn't stay on the surface, but seeped into bone marrow, sinew, brain cells and infiltrated every fiber of Max's being. This hug won the prize of all prizes. The memory of this hug would last forever.

Max backed up to gaze at this beautiful lady. The love in her eyes melted his heart. He did it. He had mustered enough courage and overcome his shyness. Freedom never felt so good.

"Wait a minute. You said you ramble on when you are nervous. Why would you be nervous with me?"

Maggie wiped her eyes on the back of her hand. "Max, I've been waiting since we met in Portland for you to fall in love with me. I fell in love with you when we sat together on that park bench. You were older and I assumed had a girlfriend, so I tried hard not to interfere." She paused. "When you were willing to come to Scotland and help me, I was filled with new hope. A hope that perhaps I had a chance. I fell in love with you all over again each time you rescued me from Lawrence. Parting in New York was the hardest thing I've had to do."

Max caressed her hair. "It was hard for me also, my dear. I have discovered that with the Lord all things are possible. In Scotland and on the ocean liner I still lived by my own wits. Sure is nicer with the Lord in charge." He kissed her forehead. "We better keep moving. Don't want to miss a well-deserved dinner before the fireworks."

Chapter 29

The proprietor of the Sandy Hotel deposited a stack of quilts in the lobby for guests to use. He also left several lanterns filled with oil and ready for the evening. Max carried three cozy quilts while Ernest toted two lanterns.

Spectators scurried onto the field securing their favorite viewpoint. They created a wreath of beautiful handmade blankets which encircled the open area. Max led his friends close to a grove of cedar trees. He and Ernest spread the quilts next to each other. An ice tea stand waited across the field for all comers. Max and Ernest strolled over and returned with glasses of lightly sweetened tea.

"Thank you, Max," Maggie said. "This is very refreshing after that scrumptious dinner."

Ernest assisted Heather to the ground. "I may not eat another meal." She paused. "Well, at least until breakfast." Ernest plunked down beside her on one quilt, Maggie and Max on another. Nellie had one to herself between these two love-struck couples.

"What kind of fireworks will we see tonight?" Nellie asked

"In the past they've purchased a large crate from a company back east," Max said. "It contains roman candles, sky rockets, pin wheels and lots of firecrackers. The children especially enjoy watching the tissue paper balloons rise in the evening sky."

"Tissue paper balloons? What are those, Max?" Ernest asked.

"They're four foot balloons made from tissue paper. Cross-wires are attached at the base to hold an oil soaked wick. The wick is lit and the colorful balloons ascend skyward. It marks the beginning of the firework show."

"Is there a balloon for each child?" Nellie asked.

"No, usually only ten or so," Max said. "But it's the privilege of all children entering first grade in the fall to hold the balloons while they're lit. Their favorite part is releasing them."

"What happens if there are more than ten students?" Ernest asked.

"Two or three children will hold one together. Their faces light up with excitement," Max said.

Four men carried a wooden crate to the center of the field. One man removed the roman candles from the crate. Another man gathered the pinwheels. The third man lifted out a smaller box filled with sky rockets. The firecrackers were last. Each man then placed their specific pyrotechnic in a predetermined location. The field resembled a giant pin cushion of fireworks, most of them aimed skyward.

The children pointed to the plethora of shapes and colors and eagerly awaited liftoff. A quiet murmur permeated the crowd. The children's voices mingled together as one.

"Balloons. Balloons. Balloons," they chanted. A man and woman draped with American flags carried two large baskets and halted center field.

"Yah!" the children shouted. The younger ones burst from the sidelines like a litter of puppies released from a cage. They surrounded the couple.

"How will two people help all those children light the wicks?" Maggie asked.

"Just watch. This may be the best part of the festivities." Max grinned. "At least, my favorite part."

As the balloons were given to the children, the father of each child approached. They assisted the children to create a large group circle. Fathers helped to carefully expand the flattened balloons and secure the oil soaked wicks. The balloons were set on the ground as children and fathers held hands. The band marched onto the field. They snapped to attention and played "The Battle Hymn of the Republic."

Max rose and assisted Maggie and Nellie to their feet. The mass of people became silent. Men removed their hats and many placed their right hands over their hearts. Some quietly sang.

An emotional time, Max held Maggie's hand, a lump in his throat. Her face glistened in the diminishing sunlight. Moisture pooled in her eyes.

"Are you all right, Maggie?" Max asked.

His heart warmed as she squeezed his hand. "I am now."

Max brushed away a trickle from her cheek. He glanced at Ernest and Heather. Their arms were wrapped around each other. Heather's face reflected her love for her Scottish man. Maybe tonight he would ask her.

The music ended and band members joined their families on

the sidelines. The children held their balloons while fathers lit the wicks. Beautiful red, blue, yellow, green and multi-colored balloons ascended in the night sky.

"This is magical," Maggie whispered. "I've never experienced anything like it." She gazed into Max's eyes. "Thank you for bringing us to Sandy for the Fourth."

He kissed Maggie's cheek and assisted her and Nellie onto the quilts. The balloons rose higher and higher blending with the stars. Some became dots of color. Others journeyed over the tops of near-by trees and disappeared.

"Max," Ernest called, "any chance of those balloons starting a fire?"

"Don't think so, Ernest. We've had enough rain the past few days to keep things moist," Max said. "But if you look beyond the beverage stand you'll see the water pump. They keep it close by in case a firework goes haywire."

Settled on their quilts, the crowd patiently waited while the officials lit their punks. They timed igniting the fuses perfectly so each explosion could be enjoyed. The pinwheels were saved for last. Ten spinning wheels changed color three times as they tossed sparks into the darkness. Townspeople stared into the sky in the hopes there would be more to come. Only a full moon and twinkling stars remained.

Families lit their lanterns, gathered their quilts, and left the open field. Fathers cradled sleepy toddlers and young mothers swaddled their babies from the night chill.

Max removed a box of matches from his coat pocket.

"Can we wait a few more minutes?" Maggie asked, her hand on this arm. "This was a magical night. I want to hang on to the excitement for another moment."

The full moon and star-filled sky broadcast light on Maggie's face. Max wrapped his arm around her shoulders.

"How about I take my quilt and follow the lantern light while you four enjoy the night sky?" Nellie asked.

"That won't be necessary, Nellie. We need to be leaving too." Max slid the lid off the box of matches, struck one and ignited the lanterns wicks. "These will light our path back to town."

Max assisted Maggie and Nellie to their feet. The ladies shook off the quilts and neatly folded them for the trip back to the hotel.

"Ernest, do you need some help with your quilt?" Maggie asked.

"That's very kind of you." Ernest rose to his feet. "Would you three mind coming this way for a minute?"

Ernest offered a hand to help Heather stand. The glow of the lantern brightened her face.

Max, Maggie and Nellie gathered around him. Max bent down to lift the quilt.

"Just a minute, please, Max. I have something to say before we head to the hotel." The glow from the lantern reflected off Ernest's face. He cleared his throat and inhaled deeply. Ernest tenderly clasped Heather's hands and gazed into her eyes.

"Heather, my dear, I've waited for just the right moment when our dear friends could be present to say these words. This is the first time I've watched fireworks. They were amazingly beautiful. They dazzle with motion, flashes of colored light and heart-stopping booms. But, Heather, their beauty could never compare to yours. Those fireworks were minuscule compared to the love in my heart exploding for you." Ernest released Heather's hands and removed a small box from his pocket. He knelt on one knee, eyes focused on his love.

"Heather Greene, I love you now and forever. I'm willing to leave Scotland to spend the rest of my life with you here in Eden Lake." Another deep breath and gulp. "Heather, will you do me the great honor of becoming my wife?"

Max's knees grew weak. A lump formed in his throat. Ernest's proposal said it all. To express a deep love in such a simple way amazed Max. Could his proposal be as beautiful? Should he propose? Max pondered Heather's face. Tears overflowed and moistened her cheeks.

Ernest held the ring toward Heather. Max's muscles tightened. Would she accept? The pregnant pause seemed to never end. Then Heather reached for the ring.

"Yes, Ernest. Oh, yes, I will marry you a thousand times over. You are the man of my dreams." She paused and chuckled. "And believe me, there have been a lot of dreams over the years."

Ernest rose and placed the ring on her finger. A perfect fit.

"Ernest, it's beautiful." Heather raised her hand to admire Ernest's choice. "I love it and I love you."

Max held back while Maggie and Nellie burst forth with hugs and congratulations. Women can be so giddy at times and this certainly hit the mark. Now his turn.

"Congratulations, Ernest." Max patted his friend on the back and grasped his hand. "Your proposal said it all. One to go down in the history books."

"Now it's your turn," Ernest whispered as he pulled Max toward him.

Max stepped back. "Don't know yet, Ernest."

"Max, how about a hug?" Heather opened her arms. "Sorry, young man, you lost your chance with me. Ernest beat you to it."

Max loved this jovial woman's sense of humor.

"I love you, Heather Greene!" Ernest yelled. "I love you. I want the whole world to know. I love you."

"Ernest, darling," Heather grabbed his arm. "There's no one here but our dear friends and the animals in the woods."

Max scanned the field. Except for the remains of the ice tea stand, it was completely empty. In the distance dots of flickering lantern lights escorted the crowd back to town.

"We better head back too. Doesn't take long for the night chill to replace the sun's warmth." Max picked up the last quilt and handed a lantern to Nellie. "Do you mind leading the way?"

"Not at all. I'll feel like a maid of honor in a wedding procession. Absolutely my pleasure." Nellie moved forward then halted. "Wait a minute. No one's leaving until this stupendous moment is sealed with a kiss."

Max's heart pounded as Ernest embraced Heather. The lantern light created a warm glow on the two figures who now became one. Their lips met. Max longed to kiss Maggie at the same moment. Restraint kept him in check. This was not his moment, it belonged to Ernest and Heather.

Chapter 30

July fifth started quietly. Not like the day before with all the street commotion. Max completed his morning stretches, dressed and packed before Ernest had opened his eyes. The rustling of sheets brought Max's attention back to Ernest.

"Good morning, soon-to-be married man. How do you feel today?" Max had brought up two cups of coffee from the lobby and offered one to Ernest.

Ernest leaned against the headboard and stretched his arms to the ceiling. "Ay, Laddie. I feel like Ol' Moses back home." Ernest sipped his coffee. "Springing out of Loch Morlich, glistening in the sun and singing to the world, "What a grand day to be alive.""

"Still no one catch that fish?"

"Nay, he's too sly." Ernest placed his cup on the side table and threw the blankets to one side. "I, on the other hand, caught the affections of the fairest lass in all the land. There's no feeling like what I feel right now. My heart could burst, Max."

"I'm so happy for you." Max beamed. "Did you and Heather make any wedding plans last night?"

"No. We were so immersed in the moment. Thought we'd do the planning when we return to Eden Lake." Ernest slid his feet into his slippers, scratched his ample belly and strode to the window.

"Another beautiful day, Laddie. What time does the coach leave for home?"

"Eleven o'clock is the first run. I'd like to make it if we can." Max buckled his luggage belt.

"Shouldn't be a problem. I'll get dressed and rouse the lassies." Ernest strode to the wardrobe.

Max placed his packed suitcase by the door.

"I forgot to check the gun supply at the stores. Maggie asked me last night if she could purchase one. She asked for shooting lessons as well." Max scanned the room for any items he may have left behind. "I think she's wise to carry a gun when she's alone. Never know if Emeline will return, and even though Molech showed kindness to her once, doesn't mean he will again." Max checked the wardrobe for missed items.

"I'll leave my case in the lobby, then I'm going to the store. Hopefully they'll have something." Max grabbed the doorknob and twisted the metal ball. "Let's meet in the lobby a few minutes before eleven."

Max listened at the girls' room. Still silent. They must have been extra tired or stayed up all night planning Heather's wedding. He quietly ambled down the hallway and then descended the staircase.

"Good morning, Mr. Sullivan," the desk clerk greeted Max. "I trust you and your friends enjoyed the celebration last night."

"Very pleasant evening indeed." Max opened his wallet and laid his money on the counter. "This should cover our stay plus extra for yourself and the cleaning lady."

"Thank you very much, sir." The clerk wrote a receipt. "You're leaving this morning, then?"

"Yes, on the eleven o'clock coach. I need to make a trip to the store. I'd like to leave my suitcase by the door, unless you object."

"No objection at all, sir. I'll keep an eye on it for you." The clerk placed Max's money in the cash register. "You have a pleasant trip home and come back again."

"Thank you. I may do that."

The sun peeked over the buildings and cast light on the empty street. Store keepers unlatched shutters, exposed "Open" signs and left front doors ajar to welcome customers. The crisp morning air filled Max's lungs as he inhaled the sweet smells of summer. He passed the Revenue and continued on to the Meinig store. The door, held open by a flatiron, appeared sun bleached and worn. The small sign on the wall read "Estab. 1880." Didn't seem old enough to have that much wear and tear.

"Good morning there," the proprietor greeted Max. "I see you're inspecting my front door. Anything wrong?"

"According to the sign this building is only twenty years old, yet the door looks almost worn out."

"That's the door from the old Gerdes store. He built the first store in town down the road in that vacant lot." He pointed south. "Gerdes was the progressive sort. He established the Sandy Post Office in 1873. When I bought him out, I saved the front door. Guess I'm a bit sentimental that way." The man stroked the door with his hand. "Needs work, or replacing. Maybe next summer." The gentleman wiped his hand on a rag then extended it to Max.

"I'm Joe. You here for the fireworks?"

"Glad to meet you, Joe. I'm Max and yes, I brought four friends over from Eden Lake for the celebration." Max clasped Joe's hand. "One of my friends asked his sweetheart to marry him last night."

"Who might that be?" Joe asked.

"Ernest McIntyre. I doubt you would have met him yesterday."

"Ernest, you say? The same man Miss Greene bragged about? Then you must be Max Sullivan." Joe's face brightened. "You ran a great race yesterday. And that means Miss Greene is engaged. About time someone lassoed that wonderful lady."

Max chuckled. Even though this small town swelled with visitors on the Fourth, thanks to the official, he and Ernest were famous. Wasn't sure if he should puff with pride or pull his hat brim lower.

"Now, what can I do for you?" Joe asked.

"Ernest and I were in the Revenue two days ago, but I didn't see any firearms. I'm interested in one for a lady friend."

Max followed the store owner to a side counter. Joe lifted a box from a shelf and set it in front of Max. Several Colts and Derringers were equally spaced. The black velvet cloth underneath contrasted with the shiny gun barrels.

"I have some rifles as well, but assumed a lady might want something she could slip in a pocket or carry in her bag." Joe picked up a derringer. "This is our most popular ladies gun. A .44 derringer only six inches long. Easy to conceal in a ladies handbag."

Max placed the gun in his palm to gage the heft. He pivoted the barrels and checked for fit precision.

"Do you mind if I point this at your white apron? Need to check the condition of the barrels. Looking for any rust or pitting," Max said.

"Not at all. I want my customers to be completely satisfied with the product they're buying." Joe stretched his apron tight.

Max scrutinized the inside of the barrels. He rematched the barrels and pulled the hammer back. Slowly he squeezed the trigger while at the same time he released the hammer. Max sighted down the barrel. Lastly he checked for bluing indicating whether the gun was new or used.

"I'm satisfied this is a new gun. Do you have some ammunition?"

"Absolutely."

Joe slid a step-stool in front of the shelves, climbed to the top step and reached for a small yellow box.

"The only women I know who carry weapons are saloon gals and ladies-of-the-evening." Joe winked at Max.

"Miss Richards is neither. She's a sweet, young lady who needs to protect herself when I'm not around." Max's face reddened with Joe's intimation. He had no business to make a judgement without meeting Maggie. Let alone an unfair judgement of Max.

Max laid the derringer on the counter. "I'll take this one and that box of bullets."

"Sorry, if I offended you. That's not my intention. It's just that I get no call for women's guns except for 'those' kind of women." Joe wiped his sweaty hands on his apron. "What were you and Ernest shopping for at the Revenue? If they didn't have it, I have a larger inventory of almost everything."

"He bought an engagement ring for Heather."

"May I ask you for a comparison? My customers are the best gage for my inventory."

"That's fine. I have a few minutes." Max eyed the gun one more time.

Joe removed his apron and picked a small key from his vest pocket. On a shelf opposite the cash register sat a wooden box. Joe slid the key into the lock, turned it and then pulled a drawer from the box and brought it to Max.

"I pride myself in stocking the best wedding rings outside of Portland. The best in quality, quantity, and brilliance of stone and settings." Joe beamed as he lifted a black velvet cloth off the rings.

"Do you see one similar to the ring Ernest purchased at the Revenue?"

Max calmly scanned the rings. No rush here and finding a similar ring would take time. Joe did indeed have a fine collection. A scintillating diamond grabbed Max's attention.

"I don't see one like Ernest's or even close to it. Your display is beyond anything I've ever seen." Max pointed to the dazzling diamond. "What can you tell me about that ring?"

Joe reached in his pocket and removed a jeweler's loupe. He handed the loupe and ring to Max.

"Here, look for yourself. This diamond is exquisite. One of a kind, you could say. Notice the many facets and how light ricochets in every direction. The halo of rubies cry out to the wearer that they are loved beyond measure, for now and all eternity. Any woman would be proud to boast of the man who gave her this ring." Joe winked again.

Max held the band tight as he examined the stone through the loupe. Joe spoke the truth even though he annoyed Max. In a small town shop owners do whatever they must to make a sale. Yet, his winks were totally unnecessary.

"What if it's not the right size?" Max asked.

"We have a wonderful blacksmith who is very capable. He can enlarge or reduce the size, whatever is needed. I aim to please my customer. A dissatisfied one will never return. Don't you agree?"

"Yes, I do." Max handed Joe the loupe and inspected the other rings.

"Do you perhaps need a wedding ring to go with the derringer?" Joe inquired.

"Perhaps. How long have you had this ring?"

"The one you are still holding? Oh, maybe a week."

"Now, Joe, deception does not suit you. If you hope to stay in business you need to be honest. I would venture to say you sell, maybe, one wedding ring a month. Most loggers come to Sandy already married and most eligible young ladies travel to other cities for the man of their dreams." Max stared at the clerk. "Care to revise your statement?"

"All right, I'm lucky if we sell a ring every two to three months. This beauty has been waiting for a year now. Sorry, Mr. Sullivan. I should have known you were not the typical yokel." Joe sighed. "If you are interested, I'll sell it to you for cost plus ten percent."

Max scratched his head. *Lord, this is too good to be true. You keep opening doors. I'm stepping through this one.*

"You've made a sale, Joe. The gun and the ring."

The streets were bustling with activity as Max wove his way back to the hotel. Maggie, Nellie and Heather waited on the porch. Ernest greeted him near the street.

"Beginning to get worried we would have to wait for the second coach. Did you find a gun for Maggie?" Ernest asked.

"Sorry, if I kept you waiting. The clerk was quite a conversationalist, but I found what I needed," Max tapped his coat pocket.

"The girls are ready. We better head to the station." Ernest leaned toward Max. "Did you purchase something besides the gun? Say a small bauble?"

"Ernest, what an inquisitive fellow you are." Max faced the street. "Yes, I did, but not a word to Heather." Max waved to the ladies.

"Good morning, Max. A glorious day, isn't it?" Heather asked. She slipped her arm in Ernest's and the two lovebirds kissed each others cheek.

"Yes, Heather, a glorious day to be sure."

"Good morning, Max. You seem like you're hiding a secret. Care to share?" Nellie asked.

"Nellie, take that detective hat off and just enjoy the day."

Max's heart thumped and pulse raced as Maggie drew near.

"Good morning, Max. Did you go for a hike this morning? Your cheeks are red." Maggie slipped her arm around his.

"No hike, Maggie. A short walk to the store. I purchased a gun for you. Perhaps we'll have time for a shooting lesson when we get home."

"That would be wonderful," Maggie said.

Max placed Maggie's suitcase on top of Nellie's then lifted the ladies suitcases, Heather's in his other hand. Ernest followed with his and Max's.

The horses stomped in anticipation of the journey. The driver assisted with the suitcases and Max helped the ladies inside the compartment.

"Max, do you think Emeline will be there when we get home?" Maggie's voice quivered.

"I pray not, but if she is, we're ready." *Please, Lord, no Molech either.* "I will feel better after you've had a few shooting lessons. Then you must promise me you will carry your gun at all times."

"I will." Maggie smiled.

Doors slammed shut. The coach rocked as the driver climbed aboard. Reins snapped, the horses lurched and the friends were headed home.

Max, Maggie and Nellie occupied one seat while Heather and Ernest were across from them. Heather snuggled up to Ernest like a baby kitten nudged into mom for warmth. Nellie soaked in the sights of Sandy one last time. Max tingled as Maggie slipped her hand inside his. An exclamation point to a glorious three days together.

Chapter 31

Max removed his jacket and wrapped it over Maggie's trembling shoulders. She crossed her arms over her chest and pulled the jacket tighter. She rounded her back and bent her head down.

"What's wrong, Maggie?"

"It's so much cooler here than in Sandy. I packed my shawl. Should have left it out."

"I believe Eden Lake is about two-thousand feet higher than Sandy. Always a bit cooler at this elevation."

Max climbed down from the wagon and lent a hand to Maggie, then Nellie. Ernest scrambled out the back. He stretched his arms to the sky and shook his legs. Jed leapt off the wagon and rushed to mark his territory.

"Ah, it's grand to be home again." Ernest inhaled the aromatic mountain air. "Wonder if I could build a sweet cabin like yours, Max, up here for Heather and me."

"I'd love to have you for neighbors. You need to talk with Heather first though. She has nice living quarters at the back of the store. Unless she's thinking about selling."

Max carried the girls' suitcases to the porch and unlatched the front door. Nothing ominous greeted him. Once inside he opened the shutters and windows.

"A bit stuffy in here," Nellie fanned her face. "Won't take long to air though."

"How about you and I catch us some trout for dinner?" Ernest asked Nellie. "You up to it, Lassie?"

"I'd love to get out on the lake and fish for dinner. It sounds divine. Let me change and I'll be right with you." Nellie disappeared into the bedroom. Ernest gathered fishing gear and placed it on the front porch.

"Maggie, this would be a good time for a shooting lesson. You game?" Max sat her gun and ammunition on the table.

"As soon as I get out of these frilly clothes and into something warmer. Won't take long."

The excitement in Maggie's voice warmed Max's heart. Even though she was a city gal, he delighted that she adjusted to mountain life so easily. Maybe she wouldn't mind living in the forest after all.

Max returned to the stables and settled Bess and Kate. He filled their troughs and water buckets. "Girls, you're the best." He stroked their necks. "You need a good brushing. I'll be back later." Max lugged a box of groceries from the wagon into the cabin.

"All ready, Max. Nellie and Ernest have left." Maggie bounced around like a school girl waiting for her first dance. "Anything I can do to help?"

"Not now. Maybe when we get back. You mentioned you'd like to curry Bess and Kate. Their manes and tails could use a thorough brushing as well."

"Oh, Max, I'd love to."

Max slid the box of cartridges into his jacket pocket and handed the derringer to Maggie.

"This is the same as Nellie's. Now we'll be gun-toting sisters." Maggie examined the pistol. "I may be a slow learner, Max, so please be patient. Never liked guns and never imagined I would own one. Guess because I always lived in a city and had no need."

"Well, I'll feel better you having protection when I'm not with you. Eden Lake is a peaceful place, but I've invaded wild animal territory. While your hand pistol won't do much, if any damage, it might scare a critter away." Max held the door open. "Sometimes we get human invaders that are not very hospitable. Better to be safe than sorry."

Max whistled. "Come on, Jed, time for some exercise."

Max led Maggie to a spot a ways from the cabin. Fir and small scrub trees encompassed the clearing. He unrolled a tube of paper, sauntered to the far side of the clearing and nailed the target to a large tree trunk.

"That's what you're aiming for. That target is about thirty feet away. Hard to shoot that far with accuracy since a derringer's major purpose was to be used in saloons and at poker tables. The closer you are to the target, the more damage you'll do. For now I want you to get the feel of the gun and become comfortable with it."

Max conducted a lesson in the pistol's mechanics then handed Maggie two bullets to insert in the chambers.

"Jed, you lay down over there. No wandering off." Jed coiled up under a bush.

"Now, Maggie, keep your arm straight. Don't bend your elbow. Hold the gun at eye level. Sight down the barrel to the target and pull the trigger."

Maggie followed Max's instructions, but her arm wobbled.

"Stiffen your arm, Maggie."

"Either the target's moving, or it's me."

Max chuckled. "Not the target, dear. It's you that moves all over. Let me help."

Max cozied up to Maggie's back and wrapped his left arm around her waist. He stretched his right arm beside her's and cushioned her gun-holding hand in his. With his stiff arm now supporting her's, Maggie aimed at the stationary target and pulled the trigger.

Maggie recoiled at the sound and screamed.

"I'm sorry, Max. Wasn't expecting it to be so loud. Small gun and all."

"Let's take your second shot, then we'll see how well you did."

They assumed the same pose. This time no scream and only a slight jump.

Neither bullet hit the mark, so Max suggested they move closer. With the chambers reloaded, Max encouraged Maggie to shoot without his support. The first bullet zinged off into the woods.

"Here, Maggie, support your right hand with your left. You may be steadier with both hands on the pistol."

Max faced Maggie and positioned her arms together. Their eyes met. Max's heart raced, his hands moistened. Tenderly he cupped her face in his hands and brought his lips to hers. A long passionate kiss. Max embraced Maggie. Another soft kiss brought tingling jolts throughout his body. Her sweet lavender smell enveloped his senses. Everything around them disappeared. Max knew only Maggie. Felt only her in his arms. Only her supple lips and enticing figure. Nothing could interrupt this moment of love.

Bang! The derringer exploded. The bullet landed inches from Max's foot.

Maggie's eyes widened. Her hand flew to her face. "Oh, Max, I could have shot you," she shrieked. "You swept me off my feet with that incredible kiss. I forgot I still held the gun. You're not hurt, are you?"

"I'm fine, Maggie. No harm done." Max placed the pistol in his pocket and held her hands. "Maggie Richards, I love you, but I don't think you'll learn to shoot a gun today. I'll be your constant protector instead of this derringer until you get the hang of it."

"I don't mind a bit. Maybe another day would be better."

"I agree." Max kissed her forehead. "You stay here. I'll get the target and we'll go home. It's getting late."

A pleasant stroll, hand-in-hand, back to the cabin, Max and Maggie hardly spoke. Jed chased after any brush movement. He brought a stick to Max, but Max didn't notice. Only Maggie filled his heart, thoughts and eyes. They stopped from time to time for another hug and kiss.

Nearing the cabin, Max noticed a heap on the porch. *Another gift from Molech?* Jed sprinted ahead, sniffed the heap and barked.

"What's Jed barking at?" Maggie asked.

Max came to a halt.

"Maggie, brace yourself. You may not like what I'm going to tell you."

Maggie's mouth dropped open when she heard about Molech's strange behavior.

"That can't be the same kind man I met in the woods."

"I know it's hard to believe, but it is. I'll take care of the dead animals. Why don't you curry Bess and Kate."

Maggie loved the smell of fresh oats and alfalfa. The light from the descending sun, low enough to touch Mt. Hood, peeked through the slat cracks. More than enough light to see. She found the horse combs and removed the burrs from Bess and Kate's manes and tails. The curry brush hung on the wall within easy reach. Maggie hummed while she brushed the horses.

"One of these days I'm going to ride one of you. Haven't ridden since Scotland and both of you are much wider than Peggy. But I'm willing to give it a try, if you are." Bess whinnied. "Okay. You'll have the honors."

A noise in the loft distracted Maggie.

"What was that, Bess? Kate, you hiding cats in the loft?"

A creaking sound above her head. Sounded like someone walked across the floor.

"Is someone up there? Hello?" Maggie remembered Max's story about Molech.

"Molech, is that you?" Maggie listened. The creaking grew louder. "Mr. Molech, it's me, Maggie."

Maggie set down the curry comb and carefully moved behind

the horses, keeping one hand on their rumps. She strained to see in the darkened loft. Something moved.

She opened the stable door for more light. Didn't help. A lantern hung by the door, a box of matches on a shelf. Maggie lit the lantern and held it high. The partially lit loft revealed nothing.

Maggie surmised the noise could be from raccoons. The movement she couldn't explain. Maggie lowered the flame. The creaking resumed.

Maggie raised the flame as high as it would go. A ladder leaned against the loft. She placed a foot on the bottom rung, then hesitated. Her hand searched her pocket for her derringer. *Max*. She'd have to go it alone. One foot followed another as she climbed the ladder. The lantern light reached the loft and filled the open spaces. Bags of alfalfa and oats were neatly stacked to one side. A thick rope hung from the ceiling. It swayed back and forth. Maggie placed the lantern on the loft floor and climbed to the top.

"You raccoons. Time to vacate the premises. Bess and Kate don't need extra lodgers eating their food."

Maggie circulated around the bales, but found no evidence of any varmint in the loft. She grabbed the rope to stop the swinging.

"Well, Bess, Kate, doesn't seem to be anything up here. I'm coming down now."

With the lantern safely on the loft floor, Maggie cautiously placed her feet on the top rung. As she lifted the lantern to begin her descent the rope oscillated in a circular motion. Maggie tried to feel a breeze through the slat openings, but none existed.

Chills ran up her spine as her heartbeats increased. Feeling each rung with her toe before applying weight, Maggie descended as quickly as she could. The floor boards creaked again. Her foot missed the bottom rung and she slipped to the stable floor. Grasping the lantern tightly she ran toward the cabin calling for Max.

"Something's in the stable." Maggie panted in Max's arms. "Or someone's in the loft. I heard noises and footsteps and boards creaking and that rope you have tied from the ceiling moved."

"Slow down, Maggie. Take a breath." Max tried to calm her. "Let's go back and you show me."

"I'm not going back in there, even if you paid me, Max Sullivan. Get the horses out. Find some other place for them tonight. Here," Maggie handed Max the lantern. "You go if you want, but you better be armed."

"You stay here. I'll be right back."

Maggie bent over, eyes closed, hands on her knees and practiced deep breathing.

"Maggie, darling, what on earth happened? Ernest and I heard you from inside the cabin." Nellie rested a hand on Maggie's back and rubbed.

"Nellie, there's something, or someone in the stable. I've never been so scared." Maggie hugged Nellie. "Thanks for coming."

"Max is coming now. Hopefully he'll have answers for you."

"Well, Max? Did you hear the creaking boards? Did you see the rope move?" Maggie asked.

Max glanced at Nellie. A glazed look in his eye.

"Maggie, I neither saw nor heard anything. No creaking, no moving rope and Bess and Kate were almost asleep. Let's go inside." Max wrapped his arm around Maggie's shoulders.

"I'll fix you some chamomile tea, dear. You've had three full days. Maybe just overly tired," Nellie hurried ahead.

The love of her two friends comforted Maggie, yet she knew what she saw and heard. No one could convince her otherwise.

Chapter 32

A fitful night for Maggie. Sleep came in spurts and chunks. Her pajamas soaked with moisture, she threw off the covers time and again. Each time she became chilled she would cover up then throw them off once more when drenched.

Poor Nellie. She slept soundly, or perhaps she was a good faker for Maggie's sake.

Maggie tiptoed into the living area, unlatched the front door and leaned against the porch railing. Her shoulders relaxed as she absorbed the crystal blue sky with brilliant moon and filled with sparkling stars. Their reflection on the lake was postcard perfect. The cool evening air refreshed her tired body. A push from Jed on her leg eased her pounding heart. She patted him. "You up too, boy?"

No light shone from Emeline's cabin. Maggie trembled at the thought the deranged woman could be hiding in the woods. Maggie always hated to be alone at night in the forest. The few times her family camped in the Larch Mountain Wilderness she clung to her stuffed dog during the night. Gradually the fluff wore off and he became a hairless mutt. She became petrified on those camping trips at the thought of needing to relieve herself.

An owl greeted Maggie and somewhere in the distance a wolf howled. She rubbed her arms, then scratched Jed's head. "Time to go in, boy. I sense animal eyes focused on me."

She glanced at Jed. His back hair remained smooth. "Even if you don't sense danger, I'm not comfortable out here."

Jed scurried down the steps to the side of the cabin. "Nature calling? Okay, but please hurry."

Maggie latched the door and dragged herself back to bed. Jed trudged alongside and lay beside her. "Always the protector, huh, boy?"

Oh, Lord, get the stable episode out of my mind. I need some sleep. Thank you.

"Hey, sleepy head. The morning's half over. You staying in bed all day?" Maggie rocked under Nellie's gentle hands.

The bright sunlight warmed the bedroom. Coffee aroma awakened her senses.

"My, that coffee smells good. I definitely need a caffeine jolt this morning."

Maggie dressed, brushed her hair securing it with U-shaped pins on the top of her head and entered the world of the living.

"I've got some breakfast for you in the warming oven," Nellie said. "You sit down and I'll bring it over. The boys are fishing."

A vase of freshly picked flowers graced the dining table. An open Bible lay beside it.

"What time is it, Nellie?"

"About ten. The boys should be back soon. They want to make a trip to town." Nellie chuckled. "I really think it's Ernest who wants to go to town to see Heather and talk wedding plans. We can go or stay here if you would prefer."

Nellie brought Maggie's breakfast to her. "How did you sleep last night?"

"Never worse. I tossed all night. Afraid I might waken you. Woke up drenched several times and finally Jed and I went out on the porch to cool off. So thankful we're sharing a room. If not, the boys would be sleeping on the porch. Then where would I go?" Maggie sipped her coffee. "Couldn't stop thinking about the stable noises and swinging rope."

Maggie bowed her head, thanked the Lord for the food and good friends. *And keeping me safe from whatever was in the stable.*

"I know none of you believe me, but I didn't make it up."

"We know you didn't." Nellie laid her hand on Maggie's. "You are as sound as the rest of us."

"What's that in your apron pocket?" Maggie asked.

"Oh, my. I almost forgot." Nellie pulled an envelope out. "This letter was in Max's mailbox. No one noticed the red flag was inside with everything that happened last night. Max found it this morning." Nellie laid the envelope on the table and returned to the stove.

Maggie filled her fork with another bite of flapjack and sipped more coffee. She glanced at the return address: Portland, Oregon.

"Nellie, do you think, maybe?" Maggie's hand trembled as she picked up the envelope and tore it opened. "Bring your coffee over here. I need moral support."

Maggie waited for Nellie to join her. She removed the folded paper from the envelope and used her speed reading skills, then clutched Nellie's hand.

"Nellie, they're offering me a graphic artist position. Remember the "Image is Everything" studio? The one I really wanted?" Maggie squeezed Nellie's hand. "They want me to begin the first of August."

Maggie scratched her head, wrote the day's date on the letter and calculated how long before August first. "That gives me twenty-five days to find an apartment, a church, figure out transportation, unless I find something within walking distance, furnish the apartment, settle in and find the closest grocery store."

"You're doing it again, Maggie."

"Doing what?"

"Letting your mind race without engaging your analytical sense."

"Huh?" Maggie scrunched her face. "Oh. You mean, should I accept the job, comes first. Moving details later." She refolded the paper, slipped it in the envelope and stuffed it in her skirt pocket. Spearing the last morsel of flapjack, she finished her breakfast.

"Come on. I'll soak your dishes then join me on the porch with your coffee." Nellie said.

Maggie glanced at the open Bible. A passage from 1 Peter had been underlined:"Be of sober spirit, be on the alert. Your adversary, the devil, prowls around like a roaring lion, seeking someone to devour."

The devil prowls around like a roaring lion? Maybe that wasn't a wolf I heard last night. Maggie refilled her coffee cup and joined Nellie on the porch.

"Nellie, what do you know about the devil?"

"The devil? Why do you ask?"

"The Bible lay open to 1 Peter and a passage underlined I hadn't read before. It frightened me."

"That's what Ernest read this morning. He's concerned you're being attacked by the devil. Thinks your experience in the stable was with a demon." Nellie sipped her coffee. "What I know is that as Christians the Holy Spirit lives within us, so the devil can't. He can harass us though and attempt to win us back, so Peter tells us to resist him and remain firm in our faith. Does that help?"

"Yes, Nellie. Thanks. Now the experience makes sense." Maggie glanced at the wondrous lake. "But why didn't Max hear the creaking and see the rope move?"

"It wasn't meant for Max. We agree that Emeline is demon-possessed and her intent is Max. You stand in her way. The only power she has at her disposal is evil. This morning the three of us concurred that we would intentionally pray for Emeline and her conversion. We're also praying the Lord will build a mighty wall of protection around you."

Maggie finished her coffee. "That's a lot to take in so early in the morning." She paused. "Okay, so late in the morning, but I appreciate the prayers. I'll pray for Emeline, too."

The sound of lapping water drew Maggie's attention. Max and Ernest rowed to the dock and secured the boat. Max carried the fishing supplies while Ernest hoisted a cluster of trout.

"Max and Ernest are coming, Nellie. What do I say about the job offer?"

"Tell the truth," Nellie said. "Max knows you applied for an artist position in Portland. Let's observe his reaction. If he understands the time constraint you're under....well, — who knows?"

Maggie's stomach churned as she anticipated telling Max she may move to Portland. Definitely closer to Eden Lake than Chicago. It would be nice to return to the Pacific Northwest. Yet, she longed to move to Eden Lake, not Portland.

"Good morning, boys," Maggie greeted Max and Ernest as they climbed the porch steps. "From that mess of fish, you had a good day."

"A perfect morning for fishing." Ernest held their catch in the air out of Jed's reach. "Not for you, boy."

"We were doing a bit more than fishing out there." Max nodded his head toward Emeline's cabin. "We hoped she would be home, or outside. We wanted to talk with her. But the cabin and premises were as dead as those animals Molech leaves behind." Max glanced at Maggie. "You are lovely this morning, but you appear to be tired. Not enough sleep last night?"

"Bits and pieces were all. I kept thinking about the stable incident. Nellie mentioned you all thought the devil was behind it. I saw the underlined passage in the Bible." Maggie turned to Ernest. "Do you really think Satan is after me?"

"Let me clean these fish and myself. I want to show you some scriptures that may shed light on Emeline's strange activity and your experience." Ernest placed the fish in a bucket and headed for the kitchen.

"We're taking the wagon into town later," Max said. "Do you

girls want to come?"

"I certainly don't want to stay here." Maggie squirmed in her chair. "Even though Nellie has her derringer, I feel safer with you men around. I'm praying for Emeline, but don't relish another episode like last night or my boating 'accident.'"

"Excuse me. I'll wash up now." Max left the girls on the porch.

"How about I make another pot of coffee while the boys clean up? Be right back." Nellie disappeared into the cabin.

All alone on the porch, Maggie removed the envelope from her pocket and placed it on her lap. With hands folded and eyes closed, she bowed her head and asked the Lord for wisdom. A sense of peace filled her with confidence that the Lord would give her the answer at the right time.

"May I join you?" Max carried two cups of coffee and offered one to Maggie.

"Thank you, Max. Yes, please, have a seat."

"I see Nellie gave you your mail. Apparently Joel brought the letter out while we were in Sandy. Is it important?"

"I've been offered a graphic artist position at a studio in Portland. They design magazine and book covers. It's a dream I've had for years. If I accept I would begin the first of August." Maggie paused to gage Max's reaction. "What do you think, Max?"

"I don't know, Maggie. Do you really want to move from Chicago?"

"Oh, yes, Max. I've wanted to move back to Oregon for quite some time. I miss the beautiful majestic landscape. They might allow me to live outside of Portland and mail my submissions to them. At least, I'm going to ask."

"That would be wonderful to have you closer. You can visit Jed and I anytime."

Maggie's heart ached. She didn't want to visit. She wanted to live here. Does Max really not understand how much she loved him? Had she not said it clearly enough?

"Perhaps you could illustrate my stories. My publisher is always looking for new talent."

Not the response she wanted, but for now it would have to suffice.

"It's getting late." Max clutched their coffee cups and headed inside the cabin. "I'll check on Ernest, then we need to go to town."

Maggie chilled. Max's shyness seemed to resurface. *Oh, Lord give him the boldness he needs.*

Chapter 33

During the ride to town, Max marveled at Ernest's Christian maturity. He listened carefully while Ernest shared his insights from scripture on combating Satan and demonic activity.

"All Christians, my dear friends, are targeted by demonic forces. We must be on guard and resist his evil attacks. Satan's purpose is to destroy our faith so that we deny Christ. The most important thing to remember is that Christ waged a battle for our souls, and won."

The wagon wheels bounced into ruts. Maggie and Nellie jostled then settled on the quilt covered straw. Max steered his horses to the right in the hopes to avoid future furrows.

Ernest continued, "I want you to memorize Matthew 28:18. "All authority in heaven and on earth has been given to me." Satan continues to assault us for his purpose, but remember that Christ lives within you and is greater than Satan and all his demons. You must be bold and courageous." Ernest's fist socked the air. "We're not fighting flesh and blood. We're fighting powers of darkness and only in Christ will we be victorious."

Max snapped the reins. Bess and Kate quickened their pace. He noticed Ernest's chest rise and fall in rapid succession while his friend's cheeks reddened and a pleasant smile bloomed.

"A little excited to see Heather, Ernest?" Max asked.

"Beyond a little excited. We're talking wedding plans today. She mentioned the pastor would be in town and hoped to make an appointment for this afternoon," Ernest said. "I get all tingly inside at the thought of being with my sweet lassie."

Max pulled back on the reins. Bess and Kate halted close to the Merc.

Joel hobbled out of the store to meet them. "Good afternoon, Mr. Sullivan, Miss Richards, Miss Cox and Mr. McIntyre. Sure is good news about Miss Greene. It's constantly Ernest this and Ernest that. I'm so happy for her." He paused. "And for you too,

Mr. McIntyre. You're a great couple."

"Thanks, Joel," Ernest said. "Is Miss Greene in the store?"

"No, she left me in charge. Went to meet Rev. Johansson about ten minutes ago." Joel offered a hand to help Maggie and Nellie out of the wagon bed. "You can wait inside if you wish."

Max looped the reins over the hitching post. He noticed Ernest meander to the side of the Merc under a grove of Douglas fir trees.

"Are you looking for something, Ernest?" Max asked.

"What do you think of having our wedding here? I'm not wild about the grange hall. I feel closer to God in the forest and there's enough cleared land for all Heather's friends. Do you think the pastor would object?"

"I don't think so. A lot of Eden Lake's weddings are outdoors. Heather may have other ideas, but if I know her, she'll love this setting. It's her favorite place to rest and dream."

Max left Ernest to imagine his wedding day. The setting was indeed perfect for them. Maybe Maggie would approve of this coppice as well. Yet, the lake inspired romance and on a sunny summer afternoon there was no place more appropriate for Maggie and he.

As Max rounded the corner of the Merc, Maggie, Nellie, Heather and Rev. Johansson greeted him. Rev. Johansson extended a hand.

"So good to see you again, Max. Heather thought we could meet in the fir grove to discuss wedding plans. Where's the groom?"

"He's in the grove, Pastor, but the planning should be for Heather and Ernest. We'll find something else to do," Max said.

"Oh, no you don't, Max," Heather grabbed his sleeve. "I want my best friends to be involved in the wedding from the planning day until we're married. Then you can all vamoose." Heather giggled.

No time at all before the ladies were huddled in conversation. Max observed the activity from the sidelines and chuckled as Ernest appeared in a fog. Rev. Johansson jotted notes and nodded his head in approval of Heather's brainstorms. A grand wedding was in the making.

Max relieved Joel of a tray with glasses of lemonade. "Thank you, Joel. That was very thoughtful."

"I'd do anything for Miss Greene. She's been so kind to me." Joel cast his eyes to the ground. "Not many people in this town are as nice. I want to do whatever I can to make her wedding special."

Max's heart broke for this young man who, because of a gimp leg, wouldn't have the same opportunities as other Eden Lake residents. The job at the Merc suited Joel. He had shared with Max that he would have liked to further his education, but a shortage of money stood in his way. Max conjectured money became the excuse when fear of ridicule terrified Joel.

"Well, I believe this wedding will be a joyous occasion, Heather," Rev. Johansson said. "Your friends' excitement shows on their faces."

Max held the tray of lemonade for everyone. "Joel made this for us."

"He's such a sweet boy," Heather reached for a glass, "always thinking of others. I'm so glad he's working for me. Makes my day brighter."

Rev. Johansson sipped the refreshing drink. "This lemonade is delicious. Now, is there anything else I can do?"

"This is off the subject," Max said, "but we're sure a demon-possessed person is threatening Maggie. How do we deal with it?"

Rev. Johansson removed his hat and wiped his brow. "I've dealt with two cases in my thirty years of ministry. One, we weren't able to help. He reminded me of Judas, who betrayed Jesus. He left our village one afternoon. When he didn't return we searched the near-by woods. Our concern was well-founded. We found him at sundown hanging from a tree." Rev. Johansson grew wobbly and dragged himself to a bench. "I'm sorry. Even though a long time ago, I replay the situation and wish there was something more we could have done."

"And the second?" Maggie asked.

"We prayed for the blood of Christ to cover the young lady. For the victory Christ won on the cross to fill her soul. For the demon to leave and never return. The change was dramatic. She later married, had three children and served the Lord with grateful enthusiasm." Rev. Johansson settled his hat back on his head.

"Thank you, Pastor. We'll trust the Lord to deliver this young woman, too," Ernest said.

Max drew near to the Rev. "I have another question. I know the greatest miracle is Christ's atoning death on the cross and the re-birth of sinners, but do you believe in miracles, like physical healing?"

"Absolutely, Max. And I believe if we're serious about imitating Jesus, we should be expecting miraculous healing through our prayers. We're admonished to call the elders if we're ill. They are directed to anoint the sick with oil and pray." Rev. Johansson inhaled. "That doesn't mean God will always answer our prayers in the affirmative. Sometimes He says, "No" and sometimes "Not now." But that doesn't diminish our faith or trust in Him. Remember Jesus' prayed, "Not my will, but Thine be done" before He was crucified. Nothing happens that God doesn't know about. He's in control and knows what's best for His children."

Rev. Johansson opened his tattered leather Bible. "Let me read this passage: "And we know that God causes all things to work together for good to those who love God, to those who are called according to His purpose. For those whom He foreknew, He also predestined to become conformed to the image of His Son."" Pastor closed the book. "That's Romans 8:28-29. Many people stop with verse 28 not understanding that according to verse 29 everything that God allows into our lives, including illness and suffering, is for the purpose of conforming us more closely to the image of our Savior."

"Thank you. That helped," Max placed his empty glass on the tray as Joel joined the group.

"Coming to get your empties. Still learning how to add the right amount of sugar to the squeezed lemons. Hope it was good," Joel said

"Very tasty indeed, Joel. Thank you for being so considerate." Nellie placed her glass on the tray.

"My pleasure, Miss Cox." Joel picked up the tray.

"Before you go, Joel, I have another question for Rev. Johansson." Max cleared his throat. "We're not elders of the church, but couldn't we anoint Joel with oil and pray for him. He witnesses silently for the Lord. I would like to pray for a spirit of courage for this young man."

"An excellent idea, Max, but why stop there? Why not ask our big God to heal the infirmity that holds him back? Why not ask for a lengthening of one leg?" Rev. Johansson smiled then turned to Joel. "May we pray for you, Joel?"

Joel wavered. Max caught the tipping tray of glasses.

"I've never been prayed for. Other than my mother when she said prayers before bed. I guess that would be okay." Joel rubbed his chin. "Yeah, that would definitely be okay."

Heather rushed into the Merc and brought back a bottle of olive oil.

"Joel, you sit down on that bench. The rest of you gather behind him and place your hands on his shoulders." Rev. Johansson knelt in front of Joel, raised both legs and placed Joel's heels in his palms. "I didn't realize the vast discrepancy in your legs. But that's not a problem for the One who created the universe. If He can do that, He can lengthen one leg."

Joel cleared his throat. "Ah, Pastor, I don't want to tell the Lord what to do, but do you think it would be all right to ask God to shorten one leg, instead of lengthen one?"

Chuckles arose realizing this young man believed that God had a sense of humor.

"Anything else you want?" The Rev. asked.

"No, I want God to be God and do what's best for me. Even if He says, "No," it's okay."

Silence filled the grove. Max closed his eyes as it didn't feel right praying with them opened.

Rev. Johansson prayed for a spirit of courage to enter Joel and the Holy Spirit's presence to reassure him he was loved dearly by the Lord.

"I feel the presence of the Holy Spirit with us. Please open your eyes and perhaps the Lord will grace us in watching a miracle."

Rev. Johansson poured a few drops of oil on Joel's head, then positioned Joel's legs side by side. He asked the Lord for a miracle. For one leg to shorten. For a young man to walk on level ground for the rest of his life.

The Lord honored that simple heartfelt prayer. Max shivered as he watched one of Joel's legs slowly shrink and match the other perfectly.

Hallelujahs and praise the Lord's were shouted for all of Eden Lake to hear. Max's mouth fell open. His God truly was God and had power over all things. He would never doubt again that the Lord didn't involve Himself in his everyday needs. A new sense of trust and awe filled Max.

Tears streamed down Joel's face. He jumped up and hopped around the grove. "Thank you. Thank you, all of you."

"Wait a minute, all we did was what the Lord asked us to do. Your thank-you's belong to the Lord," Rev. Johansson said.

"Oh my, I need something to calm my exploding heart. Joel, I'm so happy for you." Heather wrapped her arms around him.

"How about an ice cream sundae for all?" Heather asked. "Kind of a birthday party to celebrate Joel's future life."

Heather and Ernest led the way, hands clasped, their strides matched.

"You coming, Max?" Maggie asked.

"Not right now. You go ahead. I'll join you later."

Max waited until Maggie rounded the corner then laid a hand on his abdomen. The pain grew intense. He bent over and gagged. The sharp jabs lasted a few seconds, yet seemed like an eternity. Surgery stuck in his craw. He did not want to leave Eden Lake. Not with the wedding so close. If he did have the operation, followed by radiation, he could be gone a month or more. Loosing Maggie again was not an option. Another shooting pain brought tears to his eyes. In all the excitement the past few weeks, he had forgotten to refill his prescription for pain medication. *Lord, I need your help with this one. I don't want Maggie to see me in pain. Please, Lord, heal me.*

Max straightened and forced one foot in front of the other. He collapsed against the wagon. Bess whinnied and Kate swished her tail at some flies. "Won't be long, ladies and we'll head home."

The girls' voices escaped the Merc and floated in the air. What a delightful sound. Three giggling females planned the biggest event in Heather's life.

Heavy footsteps came his way, then a swooshing in the tall grass diverted his attention.

"Max. Max, where are you?" Ernest dashed through the grove, then saw Max by the wagon.

"There you are." Max's friend hurried to his side. "We've finished our sundaes. Don't you want one?"

Max turned toward Ernest, sweat dripping down his face. Max pulled a hankie from his back pocket and wiped the moisture off.

"You okay?" Ernest's brow wrinkled and eyes squinted.

"I'm fine. Must be hotter today. I probably didn't need to wear an extra shirt." Max's face paled.

"You're not fine, Max. Something is seriously wrong." Ernest clasped his arm and assisted Max into the back of the wagon. "It's your cancer, isn't it?"

Max nodded. "You can't tell anyone. Remember your promise?"

"So, we're going to gloss it over and call it heat stroke?" Ernest eyes scolded Max. "Max, this is serious. I'm going to buy two coach tickets and go with you to Portland."

Max grabbed Ernest's arm as he turned to leave. "You'll do no such thing. I'm not going to interrupt your wedding. I value our friendship and if you value mine you will honor my wishes. The pain is almost gone now." Max slid off the wagon and straightened.

"I forgot to reorder my pain medication. If I send a telegram today, it should be here in a few days. In the meantime, I'm praying for relief and request you do the same."

"I wish, just once, you'd think about yourself." Ernest stared at Max. "How many more opportunities are you going to miss with Maggie? Tell her about your cancer. Ask her to marry you or she'll accept that job offer in Portland, marry some other bloke and you'll never see her again. Women like her are rare. Don't lose her."

Max stared back. Tension mounted between these two men. Max extended a hand to Ernest. After some hesitation, Ernest clasped Max's hand.

"I won't say a word." Ernest paused. "Now. But when the time comes to tell the girls, whether you want me to or not, I will. They're not blind, Max. Nellie and Maggie, even Heather, recognize you've lost weight and your color is not good. Maggie's especially concerned. You've got to let her help you."

"I'll think about it, Ernest. For now, please let it remain our secret."

"Why don't we call the Rev. back and pray for you too?" Ernest asked.

"Not now."

The giggling girls exited the Merc. Max quickstepped to the front of the wagon.

"Max, you didn't come in for a chocolate sundae," Nellie said. "But we didn't wait for you either. They were delicious. Heather gave Jed a scoop of vanilla ice cream. He lapped it down in no time."

"I wasn't hungry, Nellie." Max slapped Bess on the rump. "Ready to go home, girl?"

Chapter 34

Maggie's favorite time of the day had arrived. The sun cast its final rays of light as dusk overtook Eden Lake. A rainbow of color dazzled the evening sky.

"Can we hurry to the lake? The evening sky should be beautiful tonight." Maggie accepted Max's assistance from the wagon, then sprinted down to the dock.

The evening sun dipped behind Mt. Hood reflecting a mirrored silhouette on the water. Slight ripples across the surface distorted the mountain's likeness. In the distance, birds sang their last tune of the day.

"What are you humming, Maggie?" Max asked when he reached her side.

"It's one of my mother's favorite hymns. She had a beautiful voice and accompanied herself on the piano Sunday afternoons. This hymn has become one of my favorites also. It's Charles Wesley's "Oh, for a Thousand Tongues to Sing". Do you know it, Max?" She asked.

"No, I don't. My folks attended church on Christmas and Easter, so I had little Christian training. Sing it for me."

Her sweet voice echoed across the lake. The words floated in the air and into Max's heart.

"Max, are those tears I see?" Maggie's forehead wrinkled.

"Those are such meaningful words." Max tossed a stick for Jed. "Wesley captured a wondrous image of God's grace. With Emeline's cabin in view, the line, 'The name of Jesus charms our fears' brings solace to my heart."

"Beautiful, Maggie," Ernest said. "Would you consider singing at our wedding?"

"That'll take a lot of prayer, Ernest. I've never sung publicly. Always thought my voice was a gift from God and I gave it back to Him with hymn praise. But only Him."

"Well, at least consider the idea," Ernest said.

"Have you all noticed there are no lights in Emeline's cabin?" Nellie asked. "No signs of life makes me uneasy. Maybe its time one, or all of us, trudge over there and have a heart-to-heart." Nellie glanced at her friends. "Would tomorrow be too early?"

"Nellie, we can't do that," Maggie frowned. "We can't saunter around the lake, and knock on her door." She brushed her hair off her face. "That doesn't seem right. What would be the point? She knows we've asked for no contact with her."

"But that's where you're wrong," Nellie said. "We do want contact with her. How else can we share Jesus' love and have the opportunity to cast Satan out? The more I commit her to the Lord in prayer the more I'm convinced that's exactly what we should do. We could take her something."

"Like what?" Max asked.

"Well," Nellie closed her eyes. "We have more than enough fish stew. And we can bake cookies in the morning. How about it?"

"The Lord has given you a gracious spirit of forgiveness and love for Emeline. I am humbled," Ernest said. "I suggest we all pray tonight, ask for a plan and formulate our idea in the morning."

All in agreement, they left the lake behind. Maggie's sweet voice accompanied their hike to the cabin.

"That tune sounds familiar," Max said. "Is that another hymn?"

Maggie chuckled. "No, it's one of the most popular songs this year. You might have heard it in Portland, "A Bird in a Gilded Cage"."

Maggie halted and faced Emeline's cabin. "I was thinking of two lines in particular which could apply to Emeline, 'You may think she's happy and free from care, she's not, though she seems to be.'"

"She's not in a gilded cage, Maggie," Nellie chided. "She lives in a run-down cabin."

"No, the song doesn't apply to her, but those lines tugged at my heart. You see, if we admit it, we're all unhappy deep down without the Lord. We may fool others with our cheerful demeanor, but inside, where it really matters, we're miserable. Something is missing. That's how I view Emeline. She's got to be one sorrowful lady." Maggie inhaled deeply. "Oh, if my mother could hear me say those words. What joy it would have brought her."

Maggie loved Max's arm wrapped around her. A sense of comfort and belonging overcame her. They walked in step up the narrow path to the cabin.

"Ernest, could you help me unhitch Bess and Kate?" Max asked.

"Be glad to."

The boys veered toward the stable.

"We'll have dinner ready when you're done." Nellie trekked up the dock and caught up with Maggie.

"Nellie, do you mind if I linger awhile?"

"Not at all. Dinner will be easy tonight. You relax and enjoy God's beauty."

Maggie loved Eden Lake. The freshness of the mountain air cleared her head. Too many concerns trapped her in a state of frustration. A response to the job offer pressed on her mind. Then Max's unspoken illness confounded her. Perhaps the time had come for her to challenge Max to tell the truth. She couldn't help if she didn't know the problem.

She fluffed a pillow and cozied into a porch chair, then noticed a small box on the table beside her. A cluster of partially wilted forget-me-nots graced the lid secured with a red ribbon. Under the box lay a cream colored paper with "To Maggie, Love Max" written in red ink. She loved romantic surprises.

Maggie glanced toward the stable. No sign of Max or Ernest. Her heart pounded at the thought this may be the gift she'd waited for. But, surely, Max would propose properly, not leave an engagement ring on the porch. Should she, or shouldn't she wait. Her heart skipped a beat with excitement and decided he meant it to be a surprise. She undid the ribbon and lay the tiny flowers to one side. A tingle of anticipation rushed through her body. Maggie lifted the lid and found a small hummingbird nest. So delicate and compact, she marveled at God's handiwork.

Gingerly Maggie placed her fingers around the nest and removed it from the box. She set the nest in her palm, brought it closer to her face and studied its' intricacies.

"Ouch." Maggie jumped from her chair and shook the nest off her palm. She grabbed her hand and squeezed tightly around her wrist. Instinctively she seized the note card, found a black spider crawling near the nest and smashed it with the paper.

"Max, Ernest, Nellie," she yelled. "Come quickly."

Max and Ernest bounded out of the stable and clamored up the steps. Nellie hurled the door wide and rushed to Maggie's side.

"What is it?" Nellie asked.

"What happened? Emeline again?" Max asked.

"Something bit me." She screamed and pointed. "Down there,

by the nest, I smashed it on the note card."

Maggie winced in pain. "I opened the gift you left me, Max. When I removed the nest from the box, I was bitten."

"Maggie, I didn't give you anything. What gave you that idea?" Max asked.

"Pick up the card, Max." Maggie pointed. "Carefully though in case the insect is still alive."

Max picked up the card,

"Flip it over, Max. Be careful." Maggie squeezed her wrist tighter.

"'To Maggie, Love Max.' That's pretty clear to me." Irritated, Maggie's voice quivered.

"This isn't my doing. Certainly not my handwriting." Max glanced across the lake. "Looks more like Emeline's."

"Can you identify the spider?" Ernest asked.

Max raised the card closer to his eyes and studied the spider.

"There's a red hour glass shape on its abdomen; a black widow."

Max glared across the lake. "We'll deal with her later. Your immediate need is a doctor."

"I'll saddle Kate and ride to town." Ernest rushed to the stable.

"Let me see your hand." Max easily found the source of penetration. Her hand had a bright red circle surrounding the bite. "Nellie, take a lantern to the ice cellar. There may be a chunk left. Bring some, quickly."

"Oh, Max, I feel awful. I wish now I had waited for you." Maggie's lips down-turned. "You would have told me it wasn't from you and this would never have happened."

"The doctor will know what to do. We need to get you to bed quickly though. Can you manage?"

"If you'll help with my shoes and blouse buttons, I can do the rest."

Maggie laid her head on Max's shoulder while he carried her into the bedroom and assisted as she needed. He raided his closet for an extra blanket and tore a dish cloth for rags. With a long strip of cloth he swathed a small ice chunk Nellie had brought. He tied the ice around Maggie's hand.

"This may help, but it might not. If nothing else it will cool the area."

Maggie began to sweat. Nellie brought a bowl of water into the room and placed it beside her bed.

"Put any ice you have left in the bowl, Nellie. We'll use it to wipe her forehead."

Maggie's pain increased. Confident Max would care for her, she closed her eyes and concentrated on managing her discomfort.

A chair being dragged across the floor meant Max came close to her side. It became the last sound she was totally conscious of.

Max noticed her forehead and face were profuse with sweat. He wrung out a water soaked cloth and wiped her brow.

"What can I do?" Nellie asked.

"Find a bucket. She'll become nauseated soon. In the kitchen you'll find a bottle marked aspirin on the top shelf to the right of the sink. Get two and a large glass of water."

Max found he needed to separate his emotions from the immediate circumstance. Soon Maggie would experience severe pain in her abdomen and back. He must be strong for her.

Maggie moaned and doubled over.

"The doc should be here soon, my love," Max said not knowing if she understood him. "Nellie's getting a couple of aspirin. It will relieve some of the muscle aches."

Max tried to reassure her, but wished he could reassure himself at the same time. He rubbed his wet hands on a rag, then mopped the sweat under his collar at the back of his neck. If Maggie dies he would accuse Emeline of murder. His head in a fog, Max realized he had no proof this 'gift' and spider were from Emeline. Yet, who else would do this dastardly thing? How would he prove it?

Max assisted Maggie to take the aspirin. He wished she would drink the entire glass of water, but was thankful the pills were in her system.

"I'm going to rub your back. Tell me if it's uncomfortable." Nellie warmed her hands.

Maggie moaned louder, grabbed her abdomen and pulled her knees to her chest.

Nellie secured Maggie's hair behind her head.

"Nellie, let's pray for Maggie's healing." Max closed his eyes, rested his hand on Maggie's shoulder and sought the Lord's healing power. Tears dripped down his face.

"I ache all over," Maggie said regaining awareness again. "And I'm going to be sick."

Max lifted the bucket to the side of the bed. He and Nellie hoisted Maggie into position. She heaved time and again. Then she flopped back on the pillow, her bedclothes drenched with sweat.

"Max, I'm scared. I've never felt this awful in my whole life." Maggie stammered.

"You're going to be fine. I'm sure Dr. Craig will know what to do." Max pulled the covers over her and wiped her brow with the cool water.

"Do you think the aspirins were in her system long enough before she regurgitated?" Nellie asked.

"I hope so. We can't give her more." Max straightened his back. "The doctor should be here any time. I've been praying he's not on a call. He leaves a slate board outside his door for messages if he's gone. Ernest might check with Heather as well. She may have some ideas."

"Max," Nellie whispered, "she'll be all right, won't she?" Puddles of tears filled her eyes.

Max's vacant expression answered her question. "We need to keep praying," he said.

Oh, Lord please heal Maggie. I love her so much, but You love her more. Please touch her with Your gentle hand and restore health to her body. Remembering Rev. Johansson's conversation, Max gulped, then added, *"Yet not my will, but Yours' be done.*

Chapter 35

Max hurried to the porch and carefully picked up the notecard with the smashed spider, the hummingbird's nest and the small box they came in. He placed them into another box for safe keeping. The sound of horse hooves and grinding wheels grew louder. Doc's buggy glistened in the moonlight. Ernest and Kate led the way.

"I'll take care of your buggy, Doc. You go on in," Ernest offered as he dismounted.

Max liked Dr. Craig the first time they met. The doctor was the same age as Maggie. Some residents looked askance at this young man who became their town's doctor. Most people felt wisdom came with age. Yet they also agreed that being fresh from medical school he would know the latest advances in medicine. "We can't have it both ways," said a member of the town council.

"Please, come in, Doctor. Thank you for coming." Max clasped his hand.

"I believe the Lord orchestrated my appointments today, Max, for this specific need." He placed his bag on the kitchen counter. "I'll wash my hands, then show me the patient. Ernest explained what happened while I hitched my buggy."

Max led Dr. Craig to Maggie's side. His stomach jittered as he grabbed another chair to take into the bedroom.

"Nellie, I presume." He nodded to Nellie. She sat close by Maggie rubbing her back.

"Yes."

"Do you know if Maggie reacts to bee stings? Swelling? Pain? Beyond the normal that is?"

"She mentioned as a kid she had to be careful. Her lips, tongue and throat would quickly swell. Difficulty swallowing or breathing followed. She said her mom applied a poultice of baking soda and vinegar on the sting site. If she didn't have any vinegar, Maggie sliced an onion and tied it with cloth where she was stung."

"Thank you. With that information, I expect her reaction to this spider bite may be more severe than normal as well." Dr. Craig tossed his jacket over a chair.

"Can you get me a cold glass of water and put on the tea kettle, please?"

Nellie scurried out of the room eager to do the doctor's bidding.

"Now, Max, tell me what you've done to help this sweet lady." While the doctor examined Maggie, Max gave an account of her symptoms and his care.

"Black widow spider bites cause all the symptoms you've mentioned plus paralysis of the diaphragm. Her breathing is not labored, so we may be in time."

Max met Nellie at the door and carried the glass of water to the doctor.

"Help me sit her up. She may drink once the glass touches her lips."

Maggie felt like a rag doll in Max's arms. He braced her while Doctor Craig placed one hand behind her head and brought the glass to her lips.

"Maggie, you need to drink this water," he said close to her ear. "Try one sip at a time to moisten your mouth and throat."

Max rejoiced when Maggie allowed the cool water to enter her mouth and swallowed.

"Lay her down again, Max. I'm going to give her an injection of cocaine. This drug has been used since '93 with good results. I'll monitor her closely. We'll ask for the Lord's protection."

The doctor cleansed an area on Maggie's arm, tied a band above her elbow and carefully slid the needle into a vein.

"I'll stay with her." The doctor slowly removed the needle. "You go get some rest or a cup of tea with that hot water I asked Nellie to boil."

"No, Doctor, I can't leave her side. I want her to see my face when she opens her eyes."

"You need rest. She doesn't need you now, but she will later. From the way you look, you're in no condition to help."

Max hesitated but realized the doctor knew best. He lugged himself into the kitchen, fell into a chair, doubled over and wept.

The comfort of Ernest's hand on his back slowed the sobs. He can't lose her now. He just can't.

"Here, Max, drink this tea. You need to stay well for Maggie." Nellie handed him a mug filled almost to the brim. "Ernest, I'll pour one for you also."

"The doctor will do his best. The Lord will do the rest." Ernest quipped. "This is difficult for all of us, but our faith tells us to trust. "Yea, though I walk through the valley of death, Thou art with me.""

"What if I lose her? She's not supposed to die. I'm the one with the lethal disease. Maggie needs to live. How can I face tomorrow without her?" Max blew his nose and wiped his eyes. Now bloodshot and swollen, he had a hard time focusing.

He stumbled out the door to the porch and glared at Emeline's cabin. If only a light glowed through her window he would ride over and...What would he do? Knock her out? Shoot her? Destroy her cabin in a rage?

Max rammed his fist into the railing. Jed nudged Max's leg. "I'm sorry, boy. I've completely neglected you." Max slumped to the porch floor, pulled Jed onto his lap and buried his face in his dog's fur. Sobs came in waves. Jed placed his nose on Max's shoulder and whimpered. Max's heaving body slowed. His face became covered with slobbery licks. "You're concerned for Maggie too." Max rubbed Jed's ears. "Thanks, boy."

"Max, Doctor Craig wants to talk with us." Nellie offered a hand to Max.

"I forgot to thank you for the tea, Nellie. I've been pretty ungrateful lately."

"You have other things on your mind besides thanking me for tea. Maggie is my dearest friend. I, too, can't bear to think of losing her. Let's listen to what the doctor has to say."

Dr. Craig sat beside Ernest at the dining table. Max and Nellie slide into chairs across from the two men.

"As you know the diaphragm is an essential component for breathing. Black widow spiders' bites cause paralysis of the diaphragm. Maggie's breathing may become labored. We'll monitor her all night. She's resting, albeit uncomfortably, but the cocaine has helped her muscles relax. I'll check in another half hour. If she's worse, I'll administer another dose. Her pain will continue for eight to twelve hours, while the nausea, sweating, and muscle aches could last for several days."

Nellie poured tea and offered banana bread. Everyone but Max ate a piece. He rose and paced. He wrung his hands together, then wiped the sweat off his brow with the back of his sleeve.

"Why didn't God heal Maggie when Nellie and I prayed for her? What did we do wrong?"

"You did nothing wrong, Max." Dr. Craig swallowed his tea. "You're expecting healing to come exclusively through prayer. I believe that God heals in more than one way. That's why I became a doctor. When Jesus came into my heart, He instilled a desire to help others through medicine. He's given me the ability to formulate medications." He reached for another piece of banana bread. "And to other physicians the skills to heal through surgery. We praise God however He chooses to heal. And we praise God when He chooses not to heal. Great saints were used to spread the gospel through their sufferings. The ultimate healing will be when we're received into our Savior's arms for all eternity. Besides, we're only camping out down here. We pitch our tents, but the Lord can pull up our stakes whenever He wants."

"I pray to have great faith like yours," Max said.

"Faith the size of a mustard seed is all you need. I believe your faith is blossoming into an entire mustard tree."

Doctor Craig removed his pocket watch and noted the time. "I know Maggie is special to all of you. I promise to use the skills God has given me to do all I can for her."

A scream from the bedroom shot the doctor out of his chair.

Max rose and rounded the table.

"No, sir." Docto Craig raised an arm to stop Max. "You stay here and rest. I'll call if I need more help."

The closed bedroom door shut Max out of Maggie's life. For better or worse, in sickness and in health, words he repeated day after day. The Lord confirmed in his spirit the time had come to ask Maggie to marry him. *Please Lord, heal her. I want to marry her and make this her home for as long as You give us.*

Minutes became hours as Max paced and waited for Dr. Craig to leave Maggie's room. Nellie kept the hot water at a low simmer.

"Nellie," Max woke from a short nap, "where did Ernest go?"

"He said he was fidgety waiting for word on Maggie's condition. He went outside, thought he may take a walk, or groom the horses. Anything to keep his mind active."

"Any word from the doctor?"

"None since he sequestered himself in her room." Nellie poured water into the tea pot. "Tea will be ready in five minutes. Can I pour you another cup, Max?"

Max tuned Nellie out. He left the cabin and ambled to the dock. The full moon and sparkling stars shone on the lake. His breathing, no longer labored, became an easy ebb and flow. Like the wave splash at the edge of the lake, his breaths were a reminder of how God's grace washes over him. One wave after another. One grace after another. A cleansing process to remove sin.

Max released the rope from the piling and climbed in his boat. He pushed away from the dock and placed the oars in the water. Jed whined and waged his tail.

"Not this time, Jed. You stay there. I won't be long."

Max lacked the energy to row. His meager efforts took him a few feet from shore. Lights from his cabin conveyed nothing out of the ordinary happened inside. Yet something extraordinary was happening. Maggie lay limp on a sweat soaked bed in excruciating pain and may not recover. The love of his life suffered, in danger of dying.

No hint of life from Emeline's cabin. If there were, what would he do? Too exhausted tonight. A new day may clear his mind and renew energy. For now, he needed to see Maggie. To hold her hand and stroke her brow. Time to return home.

Jed remained perched on the dock. His bark rang across the lake and through the woods.

"I'm coming, boy. You seem extra excited. Has something happened?"

His dog's excitement was contagious. Max gained new energy. He reached the dock, tied up and raced to the cabin, Jed at his heels.

"Max, there you are. We didn't know where you went." Nellie offered a cup of tea.

"Water, please. Cold water," Max said. "How's Maggie?"

"Doctor stuck his head out and said she seemed to be improving." Ernest handed Max the glass of water. "He said he'd be out again in a few minutes to talk with us."

Those 'few minutes' passed by as slow as a crawling snail. Max headed for the bedroom door. No more waiting.

"Max, you're back," said Doctor Craig as he exited her room. "I wanted to give all of you an update. Any more tea and bread, Nellie?"

Max tapped his fingers on the table. Ernest carried a tray with tea things and a plate of bread.

"Now that we're all here, I can tell you Maggie has shown signs of recovery. Her sweating has diminished as also her nausea. The muscle pain is better, but her breathing remains stilted."

"Doctor, why did Maggie scream?" Nellie asked.

"She thrashed about as I entered the room, moaning and groaning. I woke her as gently as I could. When I asked what was wrong she said she had a freakish dream. The cocaine may have contributed, but she said Satan attacked her. She saw herself in a bare room with only a chair to sit on. One door, across from where she sat, opened. A heavy sulphur smell filled the room followed by darkness. Satan appeared in the doorway and came for her." Doctor reached for a cup of tea. "I believe Satan plays havoc with us whether conscious or unconscious. I prayed for her and reassured her she was safe."

"That poor girl. She's been through so much this past week." Nellie dabbed her eyes.

"If you're in agreement, I would like to spend the night," Doctor Craig said. "Your davenport is fine, Max. I also request your assistance. Three hour shifts sound all right?"

"I'll cover anyone who needs more rest," Max said.

"No, you don't. You need sleep as well. It's either my way, or I'll stay up all night in her room." Doctor insisted his rules were the rules of the cabin. He gave instructions to keep her cool and warning signs to watch for.

"Anything that triggers concern, call me." The doctor lay down on the sofa, covered himself and snored before Ernest finished his tea.

"Max, you and Ernest get some rest. I'll take the first shift and call you, Max, in three hours." Nellie shoved them toward their bedroom, poured herself more tea and quietly entered Maggie's room.

Chapter 36

Dawn came to Eden Lake much as usual. The sun touched Mt. Hood, the birds sang and squirrels hopped from branch to branch in the tall trees. Everything seemed normal outside the little cabin in the woods.

Inside, however, things were not the same. Three friends nibbled their breakfast, shared small talk while their minds were occupied with thoughts of Maggie. With the night vigil over, they prayed this morning would bring hope for the life suspended in the stuffy depressing bedroom.

"How long has Doc been in there?" Max asked.

Ernest pulled his watch from his vest. "About fifteen minutes. I pray he'll have good news. Maggie must be pure done in."

Max paced until Jed pulled on a pant leg.

"Jed, what are you doing?" Max bent over and forced Jed's mouth open to remove his teeth from Max's trousers. "You go lay down."

He managed another few steps, then Jed sat down directly in front of Max, his food dish in his mouth.

Max patted Jed. "I did it again, huh, boy? I'll get your food and water. Thanks for the reminder."

The bedroom door opened. Dr. Craig crept from the bedroom and drew a cloth across his forehead. All eyes focused on him.

"Lady and gentlemen, time we opened the windows and let some fresh air and sunshine into this dingy cabin. I'm pleased to announce to you that our Miss Maggie is sleeping peacefully."

Relief and joy filled Max. The three shouted in unison, "Praise the Lord."

Max clasped Doctor's hand, hugged Nellie and Ernest, then collapsed in a heap. The load had been lifted from his shoulders. He wept tears of joy and thanksgiving.

"Nellie, if you have tea ready, and perhaps a piece of toast, our patient will need nourishment when she wakes." Doctor Craig washed his hands, splashed water on his face and packed his medical bag.

"Keep an eye on her for the next few days. Let her rest, sleep and eat as much as she wants. No hikes or wagon rides. Porch sits, book reading and soaking in the sun is my prescription. If you have any questions, or concerns, come get me." Doctor Craig picked up his coat and bag.

"I can't thank you enough, Dr. Craig for all you did for Maggie." Max firmly clasped his hand.

"You're very welcome. Bring me a couple of fresh lake trout sometime."

Dr. Craig said his good-byes and headed for the door.

"Can I help with your buggy, Doc?" Ernest asked.

"Thanks, Ernest. I can manage." Doctor left the cabin and closed the door behind him.

"Max, Maggie's toast and tea are ready. Would you like to take them in?"

"Thanks, Nellie. I would indeed." Max held the tray and entered Maggie's room.

His eyes adjusted to the dark, dank chamber. He placed the tray on the side table and reached for Maggie's hand. Clammy to the touch, he felt her forehead next. He detected no temperature, but still moist. Max carried the bowl of warm water to the kitchen.

"Nellie, would you be so kind as to dump this and bring in a bowl of cool water?"

"Be glad to, Max. How's she doing?"

"Still sleeping, and comfortably."

A knock at the door disrupted their conversation.

"Who could that be?" Nellie asked.

"I know one person it better not be," retorted Max. He observed Jed crawled under a chair. "This can't be good."

Max unlatched the door. He braced himself and opened the barrier between himself and the intruder.

"Molech. Good morning." Max took a gander at the porch. No dead animals. Bear lay down at the bottom of the steps. "Can I help you?" Max partially closed the door behind him concerned the sulphur smell might invade the cabin and nauseate Maggie.

"I wondered how Miss Maggie was doing. I heard she lay at death's door. Bitten by a spider, I was told." Molech crumpled his hat in his hands.

Max noticed a hint of sadness in this vagabond's eyes. Could this disgusting mountain man have compassion for another human being?

"Yes, she received a bite from a black widow yesterday. The doc came and…" Max squinted his eyes and shook his head. "Wait a minute. Who told you she was bitten by a spider and may be dying?"

"Why, the nice lady I met in the woods yesterday afternoon. Never seen her before. Sure is pretty though."

"How did you meet her?" Max asked. Nellie and Ernest leaned close to the door to hear every word.

"We sorta bumped into each other. I was bringing you some fish, since you said you liked them. I know you didn't care much for the other meat I brought. Caught more fish than I needed, so thought I'd share. Anyway, she appeared to be coming back from your cabin. Said a spider clung to a hummingbird's nest and poor Miss Maggie picked it up." Molech hung his head. "Didn't think I should intrude. Knew you'd be trying to cure her. So waited until this morning to check on her condition."

Shame shrouded Max. Those terrible judgements he made about this kind man were so wrong. He saw a little boy standing in front of him, not demanding anything but to please others. Not asking anything for himself, yet giving unselfishly to his neighbors.

"Would you like to come in?"

"Oh, no sir. I know I smell something awful. Don't want to infest your cabin. Someday I'll get me new duds, then I'll clean myself in the river. Just want to know if Miss Maggie is okay."

"She's over the worst of it, but doc says most symptoms may last several days. We're keeping her quiet and watching for changes."

"I'm so glad to hear that." Molech drew out a cluster of flowers from his overalls and handed them to Max. "I picked these paint brush and bear grass flowers a ways up the road. Thought they'd brighten her room. Well, I'll be going now." Molech's loose shoe sole caught between two porch boards. "Oops. Maybe someday, I'll get new shoes, too."

Molech and Bear headed up the road back into the woods. Nellie and Ernest opened the door farther and joined Max on the porch.

"Do you believe it? He really is a nice man as Maggie had said. She's a good judge of character. We should have believed her." Nellie bowed her head.

Max's mouth hung open from the shock. He tried to move but his shoes seemed glued to the porch. "I don't believe it. Ernest, would you say we have a gentle giant in our midst or a schizophrenic madman?"

"I don't know, Max. How about somewhere in between? Let's talk to Heather when we go to town." Ernest scratched his head.

"I'll find a container for these beautiful flowers, fill it with water and set them in Maggie's room." Nellie carefully clasped the bouquet in Max's hands. "Scrunched or not, Maggie will appreciate his thoughtfulness."

"Maggie? I need to get back to her." Max rushed to Maggie's bedroom.

He opened the curtain half way allowing the morning light to brighten this morose chamber. If she agreed, he would open it all the way and the window as well.

"Maggie. Maggie, how are you this morning?" Max leaned close to her ear.

Max assisted Maggie to roll onto her back. Her eyes opened.

"Max, is that you?"

"Yes, my darling. How do you feel today?"

"Like I've been dragged behind your wagon all the way from town. Every muscle aches, although not as bad as last night. Is it hot in here, or maybe I'm still sweating?"

"I'll open the window. It's a beautiful morning and a little breeze may clear your head." Max cracked the window for Maggie to breathe fresh clean air.

"That's wonderful, Max. Open it all the way." She inhaled deeply and exhaled through her mouth. "I feel like I'm on the mend. What a terrible night."

"Let me help you sit up. I have a cup of tea and toast for you. Both are probably cold. I can ask Nellie for fresh."

"No, I like cold tea, and toast sounds perfect."

Max folded the covers back and wrapped Maggie's arms around his neck.

"Hang on tight. I'll fluff your pillow and sit you up straighter."

"Oh, Max. I must stink worse than a skunk."

"Doesn't matter. I want to care for you in sickness and in health." He positioned her, then kissed her cheek. "Remember, I love you."

He placed the tray on her lap and tucked a napkin under the neckline of her nightclothes. Nellie entered with Molech's flowers nicely arranged.

"Maggie, you look so much better than last night. We all gave thanks to the Lord. Dr. Craig used his medical expertise and, here you are, still with us. What a gift from God." Nellie extended the container of flowers toward Maggie. "You had a visitor this morning. He brought you these flowers."

"A visitor? Who was it?"

"Molech." Nellie smiled and placed the bouquet on the side table. "Aren't they beautiful?"

"Molech? How did he know I was sick?" Maggie bit into the dry toast.

"Emeline." Max wiped crumbs off her mouth.

Max's eyes met Maggie's.

"Emeline?" She closed her eyes for a minute. "That cinches it, Nellie. No detective work here. So, it was her after all who left my 'gift'. Still want to take her your stew and cookies, Nellie?"

"Not this morning. As I watched you writhe in pain last night, my thoughts were not very Christ-like. I wanted to send her to hell personally. Then, that still small voice spoke, "She needs My love too." I had to agree, but forgiveness is not easy when your dearest friend is in torment."

With a tap on the door, Ernest peeked in.

"So good to see you sitting up, smiling and taking some nourishment." Ernest held his hand toward Maggie. "Heather will rejoice when she hears the news." Ernest paused. "Speaking of Heather, we are going to town today, aren't we, Max?"

"If Nellie is comfortable with our leaving, I don't see why we couldn't make a quick trip. There are a few things I need to pick up. And you, sweet recovering patient, your wish is our command. If there's anything you want from town, please let us know."

Max carried the tray to the kitchen and washed up. He made a list of groceries. First on the list: a treat for Maggie. He placed empty boxes by the door. Didn't want to forget to take them to the Merc to fill with food.

"Anything else you need, Nellie, before we leave?" Max asked.

"As a matter of fact, Maggie would like to sit on the porch. Would you mind carrying her out? I'll grab extra pillows for her back."

"Be glad to, if you promise to keep your gun close and stay within eyeshot. Emeline's a sneaky female who may try anything when she discovers Maggie's alive."

"I'm not going anywhere. My morning will be filled washing sheets and blankets. Thanks again for hanging that rope for a clothes line. It will be well used today."

Max laid his robe over Maggie's shoulders and scooped her up in his arms. A gentle wind crossed the porch.

"This breeze may cool and refresh your spirit, Maggie." Max gently positioned her in a chair.

"Max, I'm content today. I believe everything that happened drew me more into God's purpose. Even the nightmare awakened my spirit to accept the reality of Satan's power. After the doctor woke me up I felt afraid to go back to sleep. Scared the devil may return. Then the hymn "My Jesus, I Love Thee" filled my mind and I slumbered peacefully. Emeline can't hurt me. The Lord is on my side."

Max tucked a blanket around her and handed Maggie the latest edition of Blackwood's Magazine and a small volume of Robert Burns' poems. Jed nuzzled her hand.

"You stay with the girls, Jed. Be their protector." He scratched Jed's chest and turned to Maggie. "See you soon." Max kissed her cheek, then climbed in the wagon beside Ernest.

Chapter 37

"Good morning, my sweet bride." Ernest rushed to Heather's side and pecked her cheek. "You look lovely today."

"And a good morning to you and Max." Heather leaned toward Ernest for one more peck on her cheek and hugged Max. "How is dear Maggie this morning? I laid awake last night praying for her."

"She was as cozy as a caterpillar in a cocoon when we left," Ernest said.

"We moved her to the porch so Nellie could wash the bedding. She's much better. Thank you for your prayers."

Max picked out a juicy apple and crunched into the fruit. "Sweet apple, Heather. Add it to my bill."

"Have you found out where the spider came from?" Heather pulled a chair out from the table and plopped herself down.

"Well, that's an interesting story." Max scooted a chair beside Heather. "Molech came this morning. He was concerned about Maggie. Even brought flowers." Max placed his hat in his lap.

"Molech? You allowed that frightening filthy being into your cabin?"

"Hold on, dear. He may be dirty and reek of sulphur, but I believe he has a soft side. And no, not in the cabin. He stayed on the porch." Ernest found another chair, pulled it beside Heather and held her hand.

"A soft side, you say. Tell that to the Anderson's. He scared them to death." Heather slapped her hand to her chest. "My heart's racing with fear for you. Max, you get right back there, pack your belongings and all of you move to town. I don't want you disappearing like that nice young couple. If he's rigged up a way for Maggie to get bit, he probably has plans well thought out to get rid of all of you."

"Heather," Ernest interrupted her tirade. "Molech came out of concern for Maggie. He didn't leave the box. It was Emeline."

"Emeline? Not, Molech?" Heather inhaled deeply. "So your suspicions were true. She's not a sweet young thing as I thought."

She left the table. "Be right back."

Max tossed the apple core in the garbage and fished for his grocery list. "Ah, here it is. I'll fill the box with our groceries, then find something special for Maggie."

"You have something special already, Max." Ernest's face beamed.

"I do?" Max paused. "Oh, yes, the ring. Not with groceries, Ernest. The right moment will come, but not with flour and beans."

"Here you are, gentlemen." Heather emerged from the back room with cups of coffee. "Now you come and sit down, Max. I want to hear more about Molech's visit. And how Emeline fits in. Don't you leave one detail out." Heather wagged a finger at Max.

Max shared the details of the events of last night and this morning.

"I'm relieved Maggie's recovering. Dr. Craig has earned the respect of the town's residents. We're so glad he's here. And, number one, thanks to God for bringing the Doc to us." Heather sipped her coffee.

"However, I still suspect Molech of some underlying motive. I think he's a good actor. Then there's Emeline." Heather shivered. "She gives me the willies. I still say you should move to town."

Max arose from the table and ambled to a window.

"Move to town, Heather? What will that solve? Emeline needs to be held accountable for her actions." Max faced Heather. "And Molech? What to do with him? Maybe he is a harmless mountain man with no friends in the world. Yet, I agree, the Anderson's disappearance remains a mystery."

"Good morning to all of you. Am I interrupting something?" Rev. Johansson approached Heather. "Flowers for the bride. My yard is overgrown this summer."

"Thank you, Pastor. They're beautiful." Heather scurried to the kitchen.

"No, Pastor, you're not interrupting anything. In fact, you're right on time." Ernest said.

Max returned to the table bringing another chair.

"If you have a moment, we'd like to seek your wisdom and advice," Max said.

"My time is yours. The Holy Spirit nudged me this way for a reason. I love His leading. Always an adventure and most assuredly a blessing to me."

Heather placed a cup of tea on the table for Pastor. "Thank

you, Heather." He sipped the black tea. "Now, how can I help?"

Max cleared his throat. "Do you know a man named Molech?"

"Only by name. I understand there was some connection between he and the Anderson's several months back. How do you know him?"

"Like with the Anderson's, he's left sundry animals on my porch. Ernest and I followed his tracks and discovered what appeared to be his camp. Unexplained darkness and overpowering sulphur smell frightened us to the point that we left the area before he arrived." Max reached for a piece of zucchini bread Heather had brought to the table. "This morning he knocked on the door with a bouquet of flowers and concern for Maggie."

"I talked with Dr. Craig this morning. He told me of Maggie's recovery. Praise the Lord she's healing," Pastor paused. "Now you're confused as to whether Molech has a malevolent spirit or not."

"Exactly, Pastor," Max leaned on the table.

"Well, let me ask you. Has he ever been violent toward you, or threatened you in any way?"

Max recalled every instance of Molech's left-behinds and conversations.

"No, I can't say he's ever shown a violent side. Except when Ernest and I found his camp in the woods. The atmosphere drastically changed and we were frightened for our lives."

"But did you see him?"

"No, only a young buck. But we felt his presence." Max stroked the muscles on the back of his neck. His heart picked up its pace. That man was in the woods, he was sure of it.

"What did you find that indicated it was Molech's camp?" Pastor asked.

"Ernest, help me out if I miss something; a ragged blanket, pile of branches, old tobacco tin, rusted bowl, and tufts of animal hair."

"There were a few possum, rabbit and fox pelts also, but they were only scraps," Ernest added.

"Let me interject another hypothesis." Pastor tilted his cup for the final drops of tea. "You found what you assumed was Molech's camp, yet you didn't see him. You feared for your lives because of smells and darkness. Still you didn't see him. I suggest that while it may have been his camp, it may not have been either. Trappers roam through the Cascades all times of the year. Their campsites are temporary. They may have been scared off by a bear, thus leaving some pelts behind."

"But what about the strong sulphur smell and unexpected darkness?" Max asked.

Pastor bowed his head. "Lord give us wisdom to understand and defeat Satan." He raised his head and sighed. "Max, you mentioned a demon-possessed person threatening Maggie. Could not this same evil spirit create the confusion in the woods?"

"Even the sulphur odor?" Heather asked.

"Why not? Satan masquerades as an angel of light. It wouldn't be difficult to send darkness and smells your way. I don't think you truly understand the power that rests at his fingertips. The Lord admonishes His children to be on guard at all times."

"But Molech's stench reaches your nostrils before his form reaches your vision. And it lingers long after he leaves. I understand Satan smelling of sulphur, but why Molech if he's not from Satan?" Max asked.

"Before training for the ministry, I studied medicine, thinking I'd like to be a medical missionary. Remember Sodom and Gomorrah were destroyed by fire and brimstone, another name for sulphur. So man has known about this substance for a long time. In the '90's studies were conducted using sulphur to kill bacteria, fungi scabies and other parasites. Sicknesses in sheep were being attributed to fleas and ticks. When treated with sulphur, the ravage became controllable. Doc could fill you in completely if you want more information." Pastor raised his cup to Heather. "Any more tea?"

"I'll bring the tea pot out, but don't say another word until I return."

Max chuckled. Heather never wanted to be left out of any valuable information. Not a gossip, but wanted to be well-informed. She returned in a flash bearing a tray with tea pot and more bread.

"Okay, I'm ready," Heather panted as she sat down.

"Hopefully you've made the connection. If Molech lives in the woods, he's likely to encounter ticks and fleas for himself and his dog. I don't know where he acquired the stuff, but from your description, he uses it quite liberally."

"Would there be any side effects? Anything we might notice?" Max asked.

"Could be. That is, if he rolled up his sleeves or pant legs. Sulphur can irritate the skin leaving it dry, itching, and in some cases, peeling," Pastor explained.

Max leaned back in his chair. "So you're suggesting that I've got it all wrong. Molech isn't a menace. He's a filthy man, living in the woods with his dog, trying to survive. Does that sound about right?"

"I believe we all have a tendency to judge by appearance rather than by the heart." Pastor poured another cup of tea. "James illustrates that distinction clearly. He said that if a man came into worship with fine clothes and gold rings, he would receive a place of honor and special attention. Whereas, if a poor man entered, he would be directed to a lowly place. They made distinctions because of a person's appearance. God judges the heart, not the facade."

Max shook his head from side to side. "I've definitely made a royal mistake."

"And learned from this experience," Pastor added. "Here, let me show you something."

He reached in his pocket and pulled out a rock tied with a piece of string. He held it up for all to see.

"This rock is an aide to keep me humble. I found it traveling through eastern Oregon. It looked like any ordinary rock. Rough and somewhat ugly on the outside, yet it caught my attention. The Lord directed me to wash it and have it sliced open." Pastor undid the knot and separated the two halves.

Inside were incredible turquoise, creams, green and bronze colors. Max noticed the beautiful display of crystalline agate resembled the shape of the state of Oregon.

"This is called a thunder egg. Ugly to behold, but inside a gem. Native American legend tells us that these 'ugly' rocks were used as missiles thrown by angry gods, or "Thunder Spirits". The gods dwelt on Mt. Jefferson, south of here, and Mt. Hood. When thunder storms occurred, the angry, jealous gods would hurl these rocks at each other. The Lord taught me a mighty lesson through this rock. It changed my perception of the people I serve."

Max held half of the rock while Heather and Ernest examined the other half. Their blunder magnified by a simple piece of God's creation. Molech was part of God's creation too. They had misjudged and condemned him.

"But what about the Anderson's? He scared Mrs. Anderson to death. They disappeared and Joel found Jed cowering in their shed. Obviously animals have a good sense of danger. Max said Jed still cowers when Molech shows up." Heather rested her arms on the table eager for Pastor's explanation.

"Heather, did Mrs. Anderson say he threatened her, or that he brought dead animals with the intent of leaving them, as with Max?"

"I'm a bit dense here, Pastor. You're right. All she said was he stunk and brought dead things. She probably was scared by his size and dirty clothes, plus the smell. Jed might have been frightened by him or his dog. Oh, Lord, forgive me." Heather bowed her head. "I see this poor man in a whole new light. What can we do for him?"

"What does he need?" Pastor asked.

Heather rattled off a list of ideas. "Clothes, shoes, decent food, a place to stay..."

Ernest interrupted, "Dog food, a fishing pole, a new knife, gun..."

Max added, "Medical supplies, friends... and the Lord."

"Don't forget his first need: a bath," Heather pinched her nose tight.

Max's fear of this man evaporated. Molech had been sharing with him, but Max shared nothing in return. Molech offered a portion of his food supply, while Max didn't even offer him a cup of coffee.

"Heather, do you have extra-extra-large shirts and coveralls? Ernest, what size shoes do you think he wears? We also need socks, new hat and a real hankie." Max's excitement spilled over to Heather and Ernest.

Heather grabbed a box and handed it to Max. "Put what you find in here. I'll get a towel and bar of soap."

"I believe my work is done. Thanks for the tea and bread, Heather," Pastor said.

Max grabbed Rev. Johansson's hand. "Thank you very much for following the Holy Spirit's prompting. Those spiritual blinders have fallen off my eyes and I see much clearer now, at least Molech."

"How about the demon-possessed person, Max? Need my help?"

"Not yet, Pastor. The Lord is prodding me to confront her. Please pray for me."

"I will, Max. The Lord be with you."

Chapter 38

Max packed the box of groceries in the cabin's side door while Ernest cared for the horses. A gentle breeze blew through the opened windows. Any residual sulphur smell from Molech's earlier visit had gone. Sheets hung over a line stretched behind the wood stove. Max touched them. They were dry. He glanced out a window and noticed two blankets draped over the clothes line.

"Nellie? Maggie? We're home." Max called with nary an answer. He set the grocery box on the counter and searched for the girls. "Nellie? Maggie?"

"Max, we're on the porch." Nellie called.

Max hid Maggie's treat behind his back. The chocolate softened in his hand. Should have had Heather wrap the cookies in paper.

"Did you have a profitable day at the Merc? How's Heather? In a dither over wedding plans? Has she set the date?" Maggie fired questions. Max stopped beside her chair, relieved she was her old self again.

"All is well at the Merc. You can drill Ernest about the wedding. Now, close your eyes, Miss Richards, and open your hands," Max requested.

Maggie squinted her eyes shut and stretched out her arms. Max laid one of Heather's famous oatmeal-chocolate-raisin cookies in her palms.

"A special treat, for my special girl." He turned to Nellie. "There's one for you too, in the cabin."

Nellie disappeared in a flash.

Max slumped into a chair beside Maggie. He noticed the notebook of Portland's unsolved cases on the table. "Has Nellie solved any of these yet?"

"Her mind is amazing, Max. She made notes on several pages and anticipates a conclusion to one case when she returns to Portland." Maggie caught a cookie crumb in her hand.

"And what have you been doing?"

"I've been reading stories in the Blackwood Magazine." Maggie flipped through the periodical. "I liked your story, but disliked the illustration. I don't think the artist captured the essence at all. Here's my idea." She handed Max her drawing.

"Maggie, this is perfect. Exactly what I hoped for, but the publisher hires their own artists and I had no say in the matter. We need to collaborate." Max paused. "Let's discuss this when you are fully recovered."

The afternoon sun doused the wild flowers with light. Their sweet scent drifted to the porch. Max heard the buzzing of bees as they hurried from one bloom to another. Close to the end of honey making season.

"I'm content living here, Maggie. I tell myself that it's enough to enjoy the beauty of the lake and surrounding forest. Fragrant flowers, glistening sun on the water and a majestic mountain view. Yet, I've lacked something. Since you've come, I've discover the missing piece." Max held Maggie's hand and gazed into her eyes. "It's you, Maggie. You complete it."

"I love it here, too. The beauty of the Cascades, your cozy cabin, but most importantly, I love being with you."

Max dropped his head. "I have an important question to ask you. But not now."

Max scooted back in his chair and glared across the lake. "This entire picture has one spoiler: Emeline. She needs to be decisively dealt with before Eden Lake becomes our Eden on earth. Has she bothered you today?"

"Not even a whisper of her presence. That cabin across the lake never seems to change. I haven't seen smoke rise from the chimney, a door or window open, her horse or any movement to suggest someone lived there." Maggie bit into her cookie. "This is delicious. Thank you, Max."

Max wandered to the railing. His fingers clenched the timber. His knuckles turned white. "I'll not rest until I've confronted Emeline. She needs to be held accountable for her actions. Rev. Johansson cleared up misgivings I had about Molech. One down, one to go. I'm compelled to face Emeline and put an end to her harassment."

"Molech? What did Pastor say?" Maggie asked.

"I'll have Ernest share our conversation with you and Nellie. I'm on my way to meet that devious female. Pray for me, Maggie."

Max entered the cabin. He opened the sideboard drawer and

removed his gun.

"Max, what are you doing?" Nellie asked.

He loaded his firearm, placed extra cartridges in the belt, then strapped it on.

"I'm going to Emeline's cabin and have it out with her."

"You need a gun to do that?"

Max positioned his hat on his head. "Never know about bears and cougars around here." He faced Nellie. "And other evil beings." He closed the drawer. "My faith is growing but I believe the Lord asks us to be prepared at all times. I pray that includes weapons of choice."

"I fear for you, Max. Maybe Ernest should go along."

"No. This is something I need to do by myself."

"What about Jed?"

Max glanced at his trusted dog. Jed had protected Max from mama bear and a certain death fall from a cliff, but this was something he needed to do alone.

"You take care of him, Nellie."

"I need to ask you something before you leave. It may not be the best time, but it's been weighing on my mind since the day we arrived." Nellie closed the door, then gripped Max's hand. She escorted him to the far side of the cabin.

"Maggie and I know you're sick. It's painfully obvious. When Maggie lay in bed last night, you confessed to Ernest and I that you had a 'lethal' disease. I understand Ernest has known for some time, but you kept me in the dark. And Maggie, too. She loves you, Max, with an incredibly unconditional love. You need to tell her. If you're worried how she'll react, why not leave that up to her. If you want to marry her, ask her. I believe with every fiber of my being, she'll say yes."

Max fell against the wall. His legs trembled, yet they held him fast.

"Nellie, I've wanted to tell her, but I've believed for a long time, asking her to marry me would be unfair knowing my time on earth is short."

"How do you know that? The Lord's the only one who knows. He may heal you." Nellie inhaled and forced out the air. "If you don't ask her, she's ready to accept the job in Portland. I tell you straightaway, this is the last chance you'll get. You should let her make the decision not to marry you, not be so presumptuous and make it for her."

If steam rising from under a collar could be seen, Max knew

he'd see it rising from Nellie's. So totally right, Nellie gave him the verbal lashing he deserved. He had been wrong to not tell Maggie about the cancer. He had been wrong to not ask her to marry him in Scotland. He couldn't afford to be wrong again and not ask her. For better for worse, in sickness and in health.

"You're right, Nellie. I needed to hear those words. I love her with all my heart." Max sighed. "First, Emeline. Then, Maggie. Pray for me."

Max kissed Nellie's cheek and squeezed her shoulders. "Thank you."

Out the door, he stopped by Maggie's chair and leaned close.

"I love you, Maggie." One last gaze into her beautiful hazel eyes and Max left the porch, then headed toward Emeline's cabin.

"What if she's not home, Max?" Maggie called after him.

"Don't worry. She'll find me. She always does." He blew her a kiss.

Chapter 39

Squirrels scampered through the underbrush and clung to tree trunks as they followed Max. At another time, they would be fun to watch. This wasn't the time. Max focused on what to say when he met Emeline. Like an actor rehearsing his lines, Max repeated key phrases he wanted to remember. His holstered firearm swung by his leg and reassured him with each step. He laid his hand on the gun.

Max proceeded, one heavy foot in front of the other. How he prayed he could be instantly transported into tomorrow and the impending conversation would be over. The outcome? Emeline released from demonic possession and a new child added to the family of God. His heart pounded as he realized he'd passed the half-way mark. With each step he was farther from his cabin and closer to Emeline's. Sweat dripped down his back.

His hand slid to his sidearm again. Max stopped. Convicted by the Holy Spirit it was time to fully trust the Lord, he undid the buckle and rolled the belt around the holster. Carefully he laid his gun on a rotting log at the side of the path. Time to move again.

Emeline's cabin came into view. Max's pace slowed. Then halted. He closed his eyes, inhaled deeply and listened to the air as it left his body. A final prayer escaped his lips. "Father, help me remember I am Your child and in Your care. Lord Jesus, let my words be Your words. Holy Spirit grant me Your strength."

As Max slowly raised his eyelids, a fuzzy image came into view. Emeline. Not twenty feet away she had planted herself directly in his path. Her presence filled him with foreboding. Beside her, Beelzebub pawed in the dirt and flared his nostrils.

"So, Max, you've finally decided to venture my way. I've been wondering when you would come." Emeline removed her straw hat. Her hair caressed her shoulders. Strands blew around her face. "I baked more fudge this morning for an occasion such as this." She motioned toward his cabin. "I've had my eye on your sweet

Maggie all day. Looks like you have a loafer on your hands. I would
be more exciting." She moved toward him. "Why doesn't she do
something? She'll lose her girlish figure if all she does is sit and eat.
I bet she doesn't even know how to ride a horse. Not meant for the
woods, that one."

"Stop right there." Max stretched out his arm. "You and I need
to have a serious conversation. No more of your tricks and sweet
talk. You had me fooled. I thought you were simply a young
woman seeking friendship until Ernest suggested there was more
to you than meets the eye. After you tried to drown Maggie, I knew
for sure something was wrong. Nellie commanded you to stay away,
yet you continued to harass us."

"Something wrong? With me? Aw, Max, how can you say such
things?"

"You didn't succeed in drowning Maggie, so you tried again
with a black widow spider."

"What? She was bitten by a black widow?"

"Emeline, don't play coy with me. We know you left the box
with her name on it. You placed a black widow on a hummingbird's
nest."

"I did no such thing. Where's your proof?" She stepped closer.

"We have a witness. Molech met you in the woods and you told
him Maggie had been bitten."

"Molech? That vile disgusting excuse for a man who roams the
forest? You can't take his word for anything. He's insane, you
know." A twinkle escaped from her eye.

"What do you mean insane?" Max's brow wrinkled.

"You don't know?" Emeline responded in a singsong. "Well,
you will soon enough."

She inched her way closer.

"Don't take another step." Max pointed. "I believe Molech.
When Judge Baker arrives I'll speak to him about filing attempted
murder charges against you. Nellie, Maggie, Ernest and Molech will
be my witnesses. I emphatically told you in Sandy to get out of my
life and stay away from Maggie. Obviously you don't listen. Or,
perhaps, you have no control over your actions."

"Oh, Max, you're taking everything too seriously." Emeline
stretched her hands in front of her with an admiring glance. "It's
true, I meant to scare Maggie so she would leave. Never thought
she had enough gumption to hang around. But to murder her?"
Emeline stroked Beelzebub's neck.

"Let's play a game." She tilted her head. Her eyes darkened. "If

I promise to bake fudge every day, then you'll send Maggie packing."

"No, Emeline."

"If I promise to love you greater than that woman on your porch," she pouted. "Then you'll tell Maggie to be gone."

"No, Emeline." Max's heartbeat quickened.

"If I promise to make you the king of your castle," Emeline threw her arms in the air. "And live with me forever."

"Enough! You sound like Satan tempting Jesus. He offered Christ three 'if-then's' and each time was countered with scripture."

Drops of sweat covered Max's face. "Emeline, all you have to do is believe on the Lord Jesus Christ and you will be saved. My friends and I have been praying for your demon to leave. Our desire, and the Lord's, is that you come to the light and receive Jesus Christ as your Lord and Savior."

Max wiped his face with his sleeve. "Here's my 'if-then.' If you will come back with me, then the four of us will fervently pray for your release from the demons that control you. The Lord desires you to become a child of God. He loves you, Emeline, and died for you. Please let us help."

"The Lord? I don't want to hear anymore 'God-stuff.' I told you before there is no god. You're all a bunch of weaklings. Can't stand on your own two feet, so you invent a "someone greater." I've been on my own since I was ten years old. I never needed anyone and never will." Emeline said in a raspy voice.

Dark clouds billowed and swirled around Emeline and Beelzebub. Violent winds erupted. A dirt devil wind whipped debris and dust in the air. Ominous signs for Max.

Emeline's hair entwined her body. Her beauty faded. Her perfect skin wilted. A strong sulphur odor permeated the air. With arms outstretched she moved toward Max. A screeching sound bellowed from her gaping mouth.

"You'll never get me to turn to your god." Beelzebub reared up and pawed at the sky. "And you will never convict me of attempted murder." Emeline snarled. "Max, you've lost."

"Lord, in Your mighty name, protect me from the evil that surrounds me. I pray for Emeline that You would be victorious in this place. That she would experience Your power over Satan. That the evil spirit indwelling her would be cast out."

Dust blew in Max's eyes. The trees swayed violently causing branches to crash to the ground.

Max's heart burned as Emeline's fiery eyes stabbed him. A battle waged for her soul. She twirled, her hair and skirt spinning out of control. Eerie shrieks pierced the air. Max prayed and commanded God's power to overcome the evil and cast it back to the abyss. Beelzebub pranced in a dither, frothing at the mouth.

Max wrapped his arms around his chest as Emeline plunged toward him. He shut his eyes and waited for contact. Almost as quickly as the wind began, it stopped.

Quiet pervaded the woods. Max opened his eyes. Emeline lay in a heap at his feet. He stooped down and lifted her up. Her eyes were vacant. The blue color had turned to gray. Her pale moist face had a death-like quality.

"Emeline," Max whispered. "Are you all right? Call on the Lord Jesus. He will save you."

Beelzebub trotted to Emeline's side. Emeline's feeble attempt to grab a hunk of mane failed. Her eyes pleaded. With laced fingers making a foot-hold Max boosted her to the horse's back.

"Emeline, you're taking your first step toward a brand-new life." Max said as he walked alongside Beelzebub. "Maggie, Nellie and Ernest will join me in prayer for you."

Max glanced up at Emeline. Her face was drawn and haggard. The twinkle no longer shined in her eyes. She pulled Beelzebub's mane to the right. Max stood motionless as she nudged the stallion's side and headed toward her cabin. Her body slumped as the horse plodded away from Max.

"Emeline," Max called. "What are you doing? Please, come with me."

Drained of energy, his breathing slowed. Pulling a cloth from his back pocket, Max wiped his face and neck.

"Oh, Lord, what should I do now? I believe my words were Your words." Max removed his hat and wiped the sweat from his forehead. "I'll let her rest tonight. Holy Spirit, invade her cabin and her heart."

Max forced his feet to take him home. He fastened his firearm around his waist. Maggie waited. Beautiful, spirit-filled, Maggie. What a contrast. "Send Emeline our way, Lord."

Chapter 40

Three days passed since Max's confrontation with Emeline. She never came to the cabin. His disappointment seeped into Maggie, Nellie and Ernest.

"I'm off to town," Ernest said. "Anyone want to come or need anything?"

"I'd like to come along," Nellie responded. "I need to send a telegram to Portland's police chief. My vacation is coming to a close. These unsolved cases intrigue me. I'm eager to get started. Maggie, I'll ask Heather if she has more drawing paper. I noticed you're about out."

"Thank you, Nellie. I appreciate your thoughtfulness." Maggie bowed her head. "My vacation is ending soon also. Ernest, please ask Heather if she's settled on a wedding date. I'm hoping Nellie and I can still be here."

"Couldn't imagine you sweet lassies being gone. If she hasn't chosen a date, I'll insist she does." Ernest grinned.

Before Max closed the door behind Ernest and Nellie he glanced at Emeline's cabin. Dark and dreary as usual. He continued to pray for her and hoped for a conversion before he met with Judge Baker. A trial and verdict would be so much easier if she confessed to her actions, repented and sought forgiveness.

"Maggie, you seem to have regained your strength. Are you up for a hike to Lost Lake?" Max asked. "We'll pack a sack lunch. You should bring your small sketch pad. Lots of visual stimulation up there."

"Do you think we'll be safe?" Maggie's voice shook.

"Safe? From what?"

"Safe from Emeline?"

"I don't think she'll bother us ever again. I'll take my sidearm through. This is prime time for huckleberries, a favorite delicacy of Cascade bears. Jed will be our lookout."

Max loved hiking around Mt. Hood. The vibrant high-elevation flowers dotted the landscape. He stopped from time to time to

243

point out beargrass, monkey flower and paintbrush. An osprey circled overhead.

"What's that incredible magenta flower?" Maggie pointed.

"That's called shooting star." Max stepped off the path and pinched several stems of the bright blooms.

"Maybe you'd like to press them in your sketchbook. You could capture their details later."

"A wonderful idea, Max. Would you mind picking some monkey flower as well?"

Max delighted as the little girl in Maggie emerged once again. Her wonder and amazement over God's creation was a joy to behold. He placed his hand in his jacket pocket and fingered the little box.

The hike to Lost Lake remained uneventful. If any deer, cougar or bear were in the area, they were invisible. Max smiled at his mutt's unabashed excitement. Jed leapt at any underbrush noise or movement. His nostrils worked overtime from the forest smells. Max retrieved walking sticks for Maggie and himself, cutting off part of the bark for a smooth handle.

"There it is, Maggie. Look through the stand of trees straight ahead." Max held her shoulders from behind and faced her toward the lake. "Do you see it?"

"Oh, Max, it's beautiful. Come on, let's run." Maggie grabbed his hand.

Max peeked over Maggie's shoulders when they reached the lake. His moist face and heavy breathing were tell-tale signs of fatigue. He hoped Maggie didn't notice.

"There, Max. That old log close to the water." She pointed toward the bank. "Let's sit there. A perfect place for drawing." Maggie rushed to the log and brushed off fir needles. She surveyed the view for the best angle. Max joined her and spread lunch on the downed trunk.

"Lost Lake is approximately three times the size of Eden Lake. Since it is so far from civilization, the only people we may meet would be trappers and hikers like ourselves." Max handed a cheese sandwich to Maggie. "I often come here to clear my head from writing." He tossed a chunk of dried venison jerky to Jed.

Max laid his jacket beside him and found a perfect dog stick. He threw it in the water. Jed bounded from Maggie's side and leapt into the crystal blue lake. Maggie's laughter ignited Max's emotions. He leaned over and kissed her. Sweet Maggie. Max's heartbeat raced. His knees quaked.

Water splashed on his and Maggie's face. A distinctive wet-dog smell filled their nostrils.

"Oh, Jed, do you have to shake off right here?" Max said.

Maggie laughed, then Max joined her. It felt good to be free from the heavy load Molech and Emeline had placed on both of them. This would be a good day.

"You know, Maggie, I haven't thought much about Molech or Emeline these past three days. Do you remember when we were in Scotland and someone told you, 'Worry is an old man with a bent head carrying a load of feathers'?" Max asked.

"Yes," Maggie giggled. "And the rest goes, '...carrying a load of feathers he thinks is lead.'" Maggie laughed harder. "I remember it well. Sweet, patient Dr. Shane shared that with me. Once I exchanged the lead for feathers in my mind, my shoulders were as light as a — feather." She chuckled. "I released a load of worry that day."

"I love your laugh, Maggie. I've got to admit laughter is a good stress-reliever after the week we've had."

Max arose and clasped the stick to throw it again for Jed.

"Go, Jed. Way down by the lake now." His dog followed Max's direction.

Max lifted his arm and extended the stick behind his head. Maggie gasped as he released it into the air.

"What, Maggie? What's wrong? Did you hear or see something?" Max scanned the woods.

"You, Max." Her brow wrinkled and moisture filled her eyes. "I saw you."

"Me? What do you mean?"

Tenderly, Maggie reached to Max and laid her hand on the protrusion at the edge of his belt. Max placed his hand over hers, then cuddled next to her on the log.

"I've been waiting for the right moment. Our days have been so full, that moment never seemed to come." Max held both of her hands and gazed into her eyes. "Maggie, there's no easy way to say this. I have cancer."

Max's heart broke as he watched Maggie's expression change. One minute a little girl giggling, amazed at God's creation. The next, stunned. Fear, desperation and sadness rolled across her face. Jed dropped the stick at Max's feet and gave them another shower.

"No more, Jed. You go exploring or lay down."

Max found a cloth napkin in their lunch pack and wiped Maggie's face and hands, then his own.

"Thank you for telling me. I've known something was wrong, but to hear the words. What a difference there is between knowing and hearing." Maggie wiped a tear from her cheek. "As long as you didn't verbalize your illness, I thought it might go away. But to see and feel the lump creates a whole new reality."

Max hugged her. "I'm sorry it's taken me so long. I've been weighing the options: surgery, medication, radiation, long periods in Portland. I believe God gives a person trials to make them stronger. This is mine."

"But Max, He also gave people, like Dr. Craig, gifts and skills in medicine. If your doctor suggested treatment, why don't you accept it?" Her tears burned and streamed down her cheeks.

Max held her hands. "It's too late for treatment now. My doctor in Portland said that once the lump noticeably grew, it would probably have spread to other parts of my body."

Maggie crumbled into Max's arms. He held her close. Tears filled his eyes as well.

"Maggie, I'm so sorry for the hurt this has caused you. I love you so much. You mean everything to me." Max held her face in his hands and kissed her. "Can we let this subject go and enjoy the rest of our time here? I want this day to be joyful. Any day with you is a gift."

Max swept her tears away from her cheeks with his thumbs, then tenderly kissed her.

"I promise not to mention it again today, if you promise to let us pray for you tonight." Maggie's eyes glistened. Her gaze pleaded with Max.

"I promise." Max wanted to snatch the hurt in Maggie's eyes and toss it into the depths of Lost Lake.

"Maggie, I need to ask for your forgiveness. I should have told you when you arrived from Portland. I didn't want your time at Eden Lake clouded with concerns for me." Max paused and studied her eyes. "Please, forgive me."

"Of course, I forgive you. I love you so much." Maggie wrapped her arms around Max's shoulders. "Hold me."

Max slowly got to his feet and helped Maggie off the log. He embraced her. Their bodies pressed together. The moment was only a moment, yet for Max it seemed hours. He wanted to stay in this position the rest of the day. Feeling her warmth, hearing her heart beat and reveling in the sweetness that was Maggie. Life couldn't get better than this.

Max gazed into Maggie's eyes. He brought his lips to hers. Her sweet lavender fragrance evoked a feeling of calm and tranquility. Max pulled her closer melding their bodies into one. The smoothness of her lips cried out for more. This euphoric moment became the capstone of the day. Max clung even tighter as he nuzzled her neck. Maggie reciprocated his advances. The two lovers became lost in the moment.

A wolf's cry pierced the quiet. Max released Maggie with eyes still locked on hers. This kiss would echo in his memory for all time to come.

"Oh, Max, I love you." Her eyes filled with tears.

Max's heart thumped. "I love you, too."

A tug on his pants, then two paws on his hips. Jed. "Okay, boy. I haven't forgotten you." Max reached for another piece of jerky. "Here you are. And if I'm not mistaken, that was a wolf's cry we heard. Almost time to leave."

Max gathered lunch papers, rolled them into a ball and shoved them into his coat pocket.

"We'll leave the bread scraps for the squirrels. Or, Jed, whichever comes first." Max spread the scraps along the log in hopes that more than one animal would get some. "Let's hike along the lake edge for a while."

Max led the way stomping down overgrown brush. Maggie tucked two edges of her skirt under her belt to avoid snags. When downed tree trunks were in their way, Max helped Maggie navigate them.

"Max, look at that bird. It's diving into the lake." Maggie's mouth hung open. "What is it?"

"An osprey. They build their nests high in the trees. A great vantage point to spy the shimmering trout near the surface." Max pointed in another direction. "There's a group of pintail ducks. Their food is on the bottom of the lake, so they stay close to the bank at meal times."

"Oh, Max, I know it's not right, but I envy you. This is a writer's and artist's paradise. I would love to live here and create my illustrations. So much inspiration all around."

"Have you decided about the job offer in Portland?" A lump formed in Max's throat.

"It's the only offer I have and I don't want to go back to Chicago. I believe it will be a good job. Portland is close to the mountains and the ocean, so it is like having the best of both worlds." Maggie hung her head. "But I don't feel totally settled with the decision. I believe the Lord has something else in mind. I need to be patient."

"May I be so bold to make you another offer?"

"Another offer?" Maggie's face scrunched.

"A few days ago we discussed the possibility of you illustrating my stories. I'm sure my publisher would be in agreement. He's usually open to explore new talent and you're very talented." Max reached in his pocket. Still there.

"I would be honored, Max. But commuting from Portland is not something I would enjoy, especially in the winter months."

"I wasn't thinking about either of us commuting." Max cleared his throat. He swung Maggie off her feet into his arms and held her close. "Maggie Richards, would you do me the great honor of becoming Mrs. Sullivan? Will you marry me?"

Max waited. His heart raced. Perspiration dripped down the back of his neck. Maggie's eyes glistened. Still no response.

"I don't know how long I have," Max said, "but if you're willing, for better for worse, in sickness and in health, I want to live the rest of my life with you by my side. There will be hard times ahead, but together, with the Lord in our marriage, I believe we'll be just fine." Max waited. Maggie blushed and the tears ran down her cheeks.

"Maggie, dear, you said you wanted to be swept off your feet with a proposal. This is the best I can do." Max paused. "I need to set you down." He swung her back to the ground and reached in his pocket. Then he bent one knee and gazed up at Maggie. Max held the tiny box toward her. "I love you with all my heart. Will you marry me?"

Maggie lifted the lid. Her mouth gaped as she glimpsed the dazzling ring. The diamond sparkled as the sun's rays bounced off each facet.

"Max Sullivan, I love you with my whole heart and would be honored to be your wife. Yes, I will marry you. For better, for worse, in sickness and in health. I promise to be with you always and forever." Maggie sighed, then offered a hand to Max and motioned for him to rise. She gazed in his eyes. "And I'll even illustrate your stories."

Max tenderly slid the diamond band on Maggie's finger.

"A perfect fit, my dear," Max said and stared into her eyes. "A perfect fit, like you."

Max grabbed Maggie around her waist and raised her as high as he could. She hollered and sent the ducks and osprey flying. Their squawks rang through the air. Max laughed. Jed ran circles around the couple, his barks echoed across the lake. What a glorious day indeed.

"You swept me off my feet. I will never forget this day, Max." Maggie regained her footing and caressed Max's face. "So this is what the Lord had in mind. Sure didn't need to be patient very long."

"One more kiss to seal our engagement." Max enfolded Maggie in his arms. "Now we need to go home."

"Home." Maggie clutched Max's hand. "Oh, Max that sounds wonderful. Our home."

Chapter 41

"What's going on?" Ernest asked Max and Maggie as they entered the cabin. "You both crack your funny bones at the same time?"

Max smiled at Maggie.

"We've had a glorious day at Lost Lake. A perfect hike with the perfect gal." Max staggered as Jed pushed his leg. "Oh, yes. Jed had a great time too, dousing us with lake water."

"There's more on your faces than a perfect hike and some lake water." Nellie said. "Looks like you two are ready to burst."

Max held Maggie's left hand and extended it toward Nellie and Ernest.

"She said, "Yes,"" Max beamed.

Nellie squealed as she rushed to Maggie and embraced her. The two women giggled and danced together. Max received a hug from Ernest, but no dance moves for these two.

"Congratulations, Laddie. You couldn't have found a better mate." Ernest hugged Maggie. "What a bonnie pair you two make. Your face is beaming, Lassie. Wait until Heather hears the good news." Ernest paused. "You better be well grounded for her hug."

"This calls for a celebration." Nellie hurried to the kitchen and flung cupboard doors wide. "Let's see what we have." She pushed boxes and sacks aside. "Got it. I'm in charge of dinner tonight. You three can go to the porch. The master chef needs quiet and lots of room."

Max hung his coat on a hook and slid his revolver in the drawer.

"Maggie, can I pour a glass of water for you?" he asked.

"Thank you. I'm parched." Maggie headed toward her bedroom. "I'll put my things away and be right with you."

"Meet you on the porch." Max elbowed the front door and pushed it open. "Here, Ernest, I brought a water for you also."

"Thank you, Max." Ernest gripped two glasses and placed Maggie's on the table. "Did you sweep her off her feet as she requested?"

"I did indeed. Well, at least as best I could standing in the brush." Max guzzled his water. "How refreshing after that long hike. And you and Heather, did you make any decisions?" Max heard Maggie's hums and positioned a chair close to his.

"Here's your water, Lassie." Ernest handed her a glass. "Now I can fill you in on my visit with Heather." He wet his throat, then continued. "She's set the date for one week from today. The Pastor is available and Nellie agreed to wait until then. What about you Maggie? Wedding plans? Do you need to go back to Chicago?"

"We've haven't discussed any wedding plans," Maggie winked at Max. "But I wouldn't miss your wedding. As far as Chicago, yes, I'll have to return to pack my apartment and take care of some personal matters. It won't take long. I'll give my furniture to friends or the mission. Only personal items will come back to Eden Lake."

She turned to Max. "I've got an idea, Honey. Why don't we have the wedding here with all your friends, then our honeymoon in Chicago? I'd love to introduce you to my friends and it will only take me a day to clean out my apartment. What do you think?" Maggie's excitement calmed. "That is, if you think you'll be up to it."

Max stared at the lake. "I think it would be a wonderful idea. We could extend our return trip and stop in several cities." He caressed her arm. "Then board the train at our leisure. A wonderful honeymoon. I'm sure Joel will take care of Jed."

"Max," Ernest spoke in secretive tones. "Have you told her?"

"Yes, Ernest. Maggie knows about my cancer." Max hung his head.

"And, he's agreed to let us pray for him tonight. We're going to ask the Lord to heal him. To remove the web of disease that threatens to devour his life." Maggie's loving gaze touched Max's heart.

"Dinner will be ready in one hour." Nellie found a chair in a flash and joined the others.

"Now, did I miss anything?"

"Only that Max and I are going to marry here then take the train to Chicago to disperse my meager earthly possessions. We'll make it our honeymoon." Maggie gasped as she caught her breath. "I thought of something else. Nellie, we can empty your place at the same time."

"Maggie, you amaze me. You became engaged this afternoon and still thinking about me." Nellie raised her water glass. "A toast, if you please, to my dear friend, Maggie Richards, the future Mrs.

Max Sullivan."

The clinking of glasses became lost in the sound of horse hooves and squeaking wheels. Their attention turned toward the road. Max arose and descended the steps. He grabbed the harness and guided the buggy to a stop.

"Heather, my love." Ernest hurried down the steps and ran to assist her. "What a wonderful surprise." Ernest hugged Heather then escorted her to the porch.

"I'll get another glass of water." Nellie arose. "Need to check on the dinner anyway."

Max moved a table back, widening the area for Heather's chair.

"Heather, what a treat to have you here." Maggie hugged her, then slowly passed her left hand in front of Heather's face. She remembered Ernest's comment and secured her feet in place.

"What? Max, you did it. Well, I'll be." Heather grabbed Max and crushed him in her arms. He stepped back to regain his balance. "And you, sweet Maggie, what a beautiful bride you'll be." She held Maggie's hands in hers and spread their arms wide. Heather regarded Maggie. "Yes, indeed, a beautiful bride." She released Maggie's hands. "Now, I'll take a hug."

Max and Maggie sat close to each other, while Ernest and Heather plopped down in chairs across from them.

"What did I miss this time?" Nellie handed a glass of water to Heather.

"Nothing, Nellie. Heather congratulated us and that's about it." Max said.

"Now, my love, why did you come to see us?" Ernest asked. "Not that I'm complaining, but I thought we covered everything earlier."

Heather's nose sniffed the air. "Something smells wonderful. Who's cooking?"

"I'm cooking a celebration dinner for the newly engaged couple. Won't you join us, Heather?" Nellie asked.

"If you're sure you have enough I'd love to." Heather licked her lips. "Hmmm, smells delicious."

"Heather, will you please tell us why you're here." Ernest implored her.

"Honestly, I'm not sure. I was stacking the shelves for tomorrow, getting ready to close the store, when I had a sudden urge to hitch up my buggy. Thought I'd take a spin around town, you know, give Sadie a bit of exercise." Heather sipped her water. "We were reaching the edge of town, when I had the strangest feeling.

Like someone was behind the wagon pushing it this direction."

"Did you turn around? Was there someone shoving you?" Ernest asked.

"Not a soul. Yet the prompting continued. I asked the Lord to give me a sign this was His doing. Sadie entered the woods as I pulled on the reins to redirect her back to my stable. She wouldn't budge. I pulled harder and she tossed her head up and down and whinnied. She still refused to turn back." Heather finished her water. "So here we are. There must be a purpose." She sniffed the air again. "Besides dinner that is. Are you four doing something tonight?"

"We're going to pray for the Lord to heal Max of his cancer." Maggie said. "We'd love to have you join us."

"Max, another 'finally.' It took this young sprite of a gal to get you off your duff about marriage and now healing. I figured it was cancer. Thank you, Lord for a stubborn horse." Heather blew Sadie a kiss.

The friends enjoyed light-hearted conversation throughout Nellie's delicious dinner. The cabin filled with laughter, something amiss for several weeks. Max couldn't take his eyes off Maggie. She was, indeed, beautiful.

"Ladies and gentlemen," Nellie said as she carried dessert to the table. "I give you the piece-de-résistance, dark chocolate cake."

Max led the clapping. "A most impressive dinner, Nellie, with such limited supplies."

"I'm curious," Heather said, "how did you make the chocolate cake?"

"The usual ingredients," Nellie winked. "I'll tell you the secret after you've tried a piece."

Max lifted the coffee pot from the stove and filled everyone's cups. Each person forked a bite and placed it in their mouths at the same time. A chorus of oohs and awes filled the air.

"Truly, delicious," Maggie said. All agreed. "Now tell us the secret."

Nellie grinned with that, 'I know something you don't' look.

"It's sauerkraut."

"Sauerkraut?" Max dropped his fork. "Can't be that awful fermented cabbage. I never buy it."

"I know," Nellie said. "I bought it today when we were in town. I had a premonition tonight would be special."

With tummies satisfied and table cleared, the group reconvened on the porch. The circle of chairs were brought close together. Each one stationed themselves close enough to hold hands.

"Ernest," Nellie said. "Would you lead us in prayer for Max? I've thought of you as our spiritual father. You were so strong for us in Scotland and without your example, we may never have come to the Lord."

"I'd be honored." Ernest cleared his throat. "I will begin and leave time for each of you. Then close."

All heads bowed as they joined hands. Their prayers were simple and straightforward. No one needed to tell the Lord what they hoped for. They prayed out of obedience and were confident His will would be done. The prayers were as humble children, acknowledging His power to heal and His love for Max. The sense of the Holy Spirit's presence pervaded the atmosphere.

"We pray this in Jesus' name," Ernest said after a time of silence.

Max placed his hand on his abdomen.

"The lump remains." Disappointment in his voice, Max glanced at Maggie. "Maybe the Lord has another plan for me. I want His will, no matter what."

A squeeze from Maggie's hand reassured Max.

"I do too," Maggie said, tears trickled down her cheek.

"Someone's coming," Nellie faced the road. "It's Molech."

Max's grip on Maggie's hand tightened. *No more dead animals, please. Not tonight.*

"Good evening," Molech said. "I came to see if Miss Richards was better. Haven't been around lately, not feeling well." He patted Bear. "Lay down, boy."

"Hello, Molech," Max's voice lacked enthusiasm. "That's very thoughtful. Maggie is here. Won't you join us?"

Max turned to Heather. Her hand covered her nose and her eyes were as big as a wagon wheel.

"Don't believe you've met Miss Greene," Max said.

"Howdy, Miss Greene," Molech hesitated. "You run the store in town?"

"Yes, I do." She uncovered her nose and practiced shallow breathing. "Nice to meet you."

"Looks like something's going on here. I don't mean to intrude." Molech scratched his head. "Haven't seen that lady across the lake in a while to learn about Miss Richards. So figured I'd come right to the source."

"I'm very well, Molech," Maggie said. "I want to thank you for the lovely flowers you brought. They brightened my day."

"You're very welcome." Molech glanced at the group. "I better go. Don't want to be a pest."

"You're not a pest," Ernest said. "We were praying for Max's healing."

"Healing?" Molech's brow lowered. "Healing from what?"

"Cancer." Ernest responded.

"Well, if there is anything one needs to be healed from, its cancer." Molech removed his hat exposing a bald spot. "Max is my good friend. Can I join you?"

"Molech, I appreciate your concern for me. You are my friend as well. The others have finished praying, but I would welcome your prayers," Max said. "I must ask you though if you're a Christian. Do you believe in Jesus Christ as your Lord and Savior?"

Molech reached into his pocket. He extended his hand to the group. A small cross lay in his palm.

"I got this from a pastor. I had no-good upbringing. But he taught me about God and Jesus." He held the cross toward Max. "Will you hold this while I pray?"

Max released Maggie's hand. Molech lay the cross in Max's palm as if it were a special gem worth thousands of dollars. One smooth spot in particular had been rubbed to an indentation.

"Do—do you mind if I—I put my hands on—your shoulders?" Molech stammered.

"Not at all." Max noticed Heather had difficulty breathing. *Please Lord, send a breeze to clear the air.*

Large, warm hands covered Max's shoulders. He sensed a spirit of peacefulness in this mountain-man he had wrongly judged. Repulsive or not, Max vowed to learn more about Molech. Emeline had said he was insane. Max wondered if she spoke of herself instead.

So quiet at first, Max barely made out that Molech was speaking English. Then words emerged, child-like and heartfelt. "God, this is my one true friend in the whole world. He needs more time with Miss Richards. I know You love him and he loves You. Please, Lord, heal my friend, Max. Thank You. Amen."

At the word 'amen' a warm and tingling feeling filled Max's abdomen. He opened his eyes. Molech had backed away from the group and stood in the path of a light breeze.

"Ernest, Maggie, something's happening." Max pulled his shirt away from the lump. "There is a strange sensation pulsing through my body. It started at the lump, but has spread to my feet and hands."

Max's friends stared in amazement as increment by increment the lump lessened. What started as a cantaloupe size bump shrunk before their eyes. The mass continued to diminish until Max's abdomen appeared normal.

"Molech, I believe God said, "Yes" to your prayer." Max glanced at Molech who grinned exposing blackened and missing teeth.

"Thank you, God," Molech said, his face raised to the sky.

"Your color," Maggie exclaimed. "Max, you're not pale anymore. You look healthy." Tears flooded her eyes. She rose and offered her hand to Molech. "I believe the Lord directed you here tonight and I want to thank you for following His leading."

Molech's face twitched. He hid his hands behind his back.

"Oh no, Miss Richards. You don't want to be touching me. Besides it weren't me who did the healing, it was God." Molech sluggishly navigated the steps and rubbed Bear.

"We gotta go now. Interrupted too much of your evening." Molech replaced his hat. "I'll be seeing you."

"Mr. Molech," Heather's voice quivered. "Will you stop by the store tomorrow? I have something for you."

"I never go to town, Miss Greene." Molech eyed Heather.

"You could come to the back door." Heather said.

"Maybe. Just before you close okay?"

"That would be fine."

"Wait a minute," Max hurried to the edge of the porch. "Here's your cross."

"No, Max. You keep it. It's the only thing I've got to give you." Molech's eyes filled with moisture.

Max gazed at this lonely man. As quietly as he had come, he was gone.

"Praise the Lord for healing Max," Ernest said.

"And praise the Lord for Molech," Max added.

Chapter 42

Max's health continued to improve. He grew stronger each day and relieved Ernest of the chores that had once been too strenuous. Chopping kindling became a joy and strengthened his weakened muscles.

"Max, do you think we should take the boat across the lake? Emeline hasn't made herself known for four days now." Ernest said. "I'm concerned. I remember reading in Matthew that if a person is cleansed from possession of an evil spirit and remains empty, more evil spirits will take up occupancy."

"I, too, am concerned," Max said. "We need to make every effort to share the Lord with Emeline before she falls into greater depravity."

"Let's speak with the girls and pray for direction." Ernest rose to find Nellie and Maggie.

Max rubbed Jed's belly. The dog's favorite spot lately was at Max's feet. Wherever his master went, Jed followed and stayed close. Max reminisced about the day Joel found the forlorn mutt in the Anderson's shed. Another unsolved mystery awaited answers.

"Here they are, Max." Ernest led the girls to the porch.

"Ernest tells us you feel we need to search for Emeline." Maggie sat close to Max.

"I do. We're concerned for her spiritual and physical well-being." Max held Maggie's hand. "Do you ladies have any ideas?"

The girls studied each other's faces, then simultaneously stared across the lake.

"Such a beautiful pristine lake." Maggie's face scrunched. "It's hard to believe something so evil lay on the other side."

"And if you reverse the perspective," Nellie added, "it becomes a great spiritual lesson. We are all like Emeline's cabin, filthy inside, wrapped up in our own goodness which will never do with God. His word for it is sin. Yet, the Lord, in His grace, washed us from the inside out. In His eyes we are like that lake—spotless."

"What a great image of our transformation," Max paused. "Now to the situation with Emeline. Any thoughts?"

"It seems like whenever one of us hikes in the woods, she's there," Maggie said. "Maybe we all need to take a walk." Maggie glanced at Jed. "I've got dibs on the dog."

"How do we know she's gone, never to bother us again? Or if she is still in her cabin, more demons may have established residency?" Ernest painted a real-possibility picture. "I stepped on a hornet's nest once. It wasn't very pretty. Confronting Emeline may stir up her hornet's nest."

"There's only one way to find out. I, for one, am ready for battle." Nellie neared the porch steps and pivoted. "My weapon of choice is the armor of God. You can wander, or wait here for Emeline. The only way we'll know for sure if she's still there, is to go into her cabin. I ask for your prayers."

"Nellie, are you sure?" Maggie's forehead wrinkled. "She's not to be taken lightly."

"Maggie, dear, I've faced her before. This time I feel more spiritually equipped."

Nellie descended the steps, moved to the road, then turned back to her friends. "However, like any investigator, I'd like a sentry on lookout duty. If she comes down the road, I need to be warned."

"I'll do it," Ernest responded. "What do you want me to do?"

"Take one of Max's revolvers and stand at the fork in the road. If you see her coming, fire a shot in the air. If she stops and asks what you're doing, make something up. You're good at that. You might also have a talk with her and I'll get away as quickly as possible."

"Sounds like an undercover caper," Max said. "You've obviously had more experience than us. Maggie and I will wait here, in case she comes this way."

"And pray." Maggie put her palms together. "Be careful. Please."

—✳—

Nellie waited for Ernest. With a revolver tucked in his belt, they left Max and Maggie behind in the relative safety of the cabin. The forest rang with the calls of warblers. Woodpeckers tap, tap, taps echoed through the trees. These sounds spoke to Nellie of "business as usual," but fear and trepidations birthed her own churning stomach noises.

"Here's the fork in the road. Are you sure you're up to this?" Ernest asked.

"I've had experience sneaking into homes and businesses. But I knew what to expect if an intruder entered the premises," Nellie said. "I have no idea what to expect when I face Emeline. I've been praying she's not home. I'd welcome the opportunity to search for any clues as to her next move." She touched Ernest's arm. "Thank you for being my guard. Remember, one shot if you see her coming."

"One shot." Ernest checked the chambers. "Unless I'm attacked by a wild beast. Two legged or four legged." Ernest held Nellie's hand. Seriousness in his eyes, "You be careful now, Lassie, you hear?"

"I will, Ernest. Be back before you can count to one-hundred in French." Nellie hurried down the road.

"Wait, that's not fair. I don't know French," Ernest called.

Nellie barely heard Ernest. Her mind focused on Emeline. She recalled the armor of God and mentally dressed for spiritual battle. Nellie's investigative prowess would be put to the test.

Emeline's cabin came into view. Dark, dreary and uncared for. Oregon grape invaded the entire ground around the cabin. The front yard was suffocated by bramble berry vines while wilted wild honeysuckle clung to the porch railings. Spider webs covered the two front windows. An uninviting dwelling to be sure.

"Emeline. Emeline. Are you home?" Nellie called. With no response, she explored the unkept yard. No firewood in the lean-to, only a few pieces of kindling. She found what remained of a stable for Beelzebub with moldy straw, now home to a family of mice. Bramble berry thorns caught her skirt. She ripped the vine free scratching her leg.

Nellie lifted the cistern lid. Empty. She carefully reached the porch steps. Many were worn and decayed with sections rotted away. Carpenter ants scurried across the boards and disappeared into crevices. Once on the porch, she chose her steps cautiously. A few creaks from the floorboards rattled Nellie's nerves.

"Emeline. Emeline. It's me, Nellie. I want to talk with you." Nellie pressed her ear to the wooden door, but heard nothing. She glanced at Max's cabin. A lovely view, indeed. Max and Maggie were close to the railing. Nellie waved to them not knowing if they would see her minuscule arm raised in the air. A slight movement like a blade of grass blowing in the wind emanated from her friends' bodies.

Nellie knocked on the door and held her breath, hoping beyond hope that Emeline was not home. There were no woodpecker or warbler rhythms to interrupt the silence. She wiped the moisture off her forehead, then used the hem of her skirt to rub a clean spot on one window. She peeked in. Too dark inside to distinguish forms of any kind.

With her hand on the doorknob, the time had come to venture inside. Nellie quieted her breath. She shut her eyes and prayed. *Lord, protect me with Your armor. Holy Spirit grant me wisdom in my search. Nudge me to not remain a moment longer than needed.*

The knob grated. Unlocked, the latch gave way for Nellie to enter. An odious smell filled her nostrils. Nellie faced the lake, coughed and inhaled clean, fresh air. She cracked the door further. No escaping the odor and no mistaking it either — sulphur. Nellie tied her handkerchief over her nose. Not a lot of protection, but better than none.

"Emeline. Are you here?" Nellie knocked again on the door. Still no response. She stood erect and mentally weighted one leg on the threshold. Her heartbeat raced. *One, two, three.* In one swift movement, Nellie flung the door toward the inside wall, lunged forward on one foot and bent as far to the floor as possible. No scream from behind the door. In an instant she hurled the door closed and made ready for the attack. Emeline wasn't there. Nellie's heart slowed.

She lost her footing from the crouched position and fell to the floor.

"Yuck! What have I put my hand in? And what's that nauseating smell?"

With the sun fully on the back side of the cabin, very little light shone through the only two front porch windows. Nellie retrieved the candle and matches she had placed in her skirt pocket and lit the wick. A glimmer of light brightened her area of the cabin. She held her goo-covered hand to the flame. "Smashed poo of some kind. Double yuck!" With the light close to the floor, it exposed dozens of droppings and urine splatters. She raised herself from the floor and held the candle high above her head. A flutter of wings sent small black bodies hurling toward her. Frantic, Nellie brandished her arms helter-skelter shielding her face as best she could. Candle wax sprayed on her blouse. With flame extinguished the screeching sound diminished.

"Bats. Why did there have to be bats? I hate bats." With her only handkerchief tied over her face, she wiped her bat-dropping covered hand on her skirt. Nellie relit her candle. She spied a kerosene lamp on the floor not far from where she stood. *Please Lord, give me oil in the lamp.*

A sloshing sound from the lamp's base gave her hope. With the minimal light through the windows and now the kerosene lantern, she blew out the candle. She waited for her eyes to adjust. Nellie held the lantern high, but saw no one. "Anyone there?" The only sound was the flutter of bat wings from the rays of light that disturbed their sleep. She lowered the lamp and faced the unknown. Dark recesses and rooms to explore ignited shivers through Nellie's body.

Step-by-step, Nellie moved toward the fireplace. Cobwebs veiled her face. Thoughts of the black widow spider alarmed Nellie. She dropped the lamp on the floor and briskly ripped the cobwebs from her face and blouse. Nellie's fingers combed through her hair, brushed her shoulders and beat her skirt. The light extinguished. In her haste, the lamp tipped and spilled any remaining oil on the floor. *Thank You, Lord the flame was out and the chimney didn't break. Could have been a disaster.*

"Oh, Lord, I blew that one. Literally, blew it." Nellie relit the candle and continued to the fireplace. She bent down to feel the cinders. No warmth remained. Sifting through the ash, she found no evidence of a recent fire. No wood chunks, only fine ash.

She moved toward the kitchen. Each step brought another creak. Nellie stumbled into a small kitchen table and one chair. The table had three legs, the fourth side propped up with a piece of log. The chair lay on its side, the legs displayed signs of gnawing creatures.

Nellie reached the cupboards. Nothing sat on the counters but dust and debris. From what, Nellie couldn't tell. No knobs on these cupboards, so she placed her hand underneath the door to pull each open. The first and second cupboards were bare. "Old Nellie Hubbard went to her cupboard to get her poor dog a bone." Nellie stopped reciting. Two cupboards left.

One door hung precariously from a hinge. Her mind conjured an image of what she might find in the final cupboard. It wasn't pretty. Her pulse raced as she pulled the door open with the candle close to the edge.

"Eek!" Nellie jumped as four mice scurried back and forth. Three disappeared into a hole in a back corner while the fourth one leaped toward Nellie. Her hands protected her face. The candle fell to the counter. She groped in the darkness and found the wax cylinder. It had broken in two. Nellie shoved one half into her pocket and lit the longer section.

"Oh, Lord, give me Your peace."

One room left. Would Emeline be stretched out on her bed? Dead from some horrible manner. *Nellie, get ahold of yourself. Where's this great, strong detective you always thought yourself to be?* Amazed how she could get used to sulphur smell, she removed the handkerchief from her face and wiped the sweat from her brow. New determination coursed through her veins. For Max, Maggie and Ernest, she would be strong. The armor of God was meant for the defensive battle except for the sword of the spirit, which is the Word of God. Nellie quoted victory scriptures to herself. She sang Martin Luther's "A Mighty Fortress is Our God." Verse one out loud, anyway.

She inhaled deeply, sulphur or not, and made her way to the bedroom. Nellie held the candle high in case of more cobwebs. There was no door to the bedroom, so she boldly entered. Her foot caught on something and she dove headlong into the bed frame. She managed to hang onto the candle. The flame remained lit.

Her head throbbed. She realigned herself, brushed her hair from her face and expected to see Emeline's body on the floor. The light revealed a rolled up blanket tied with twine. Perhaps Emeline planned to take this with her, but forgot. Or, out of necessity, left it behind. Relieved she hadn't tripped over Emeline, Nellie examined the bed. The rope frame was frayed and torn in places. A small pillow, stuffing everywhere, lay near the head.

A harsh scrapping sound caught Nellie's attention. She faced the doorway. The sound came from the main room. Nellie stepped over the blanket, arm outstretched as she held the wax taper.

She stopped by the table and listened. The sound, louder this time, came from a far dark corner. "Emeline, is that you? It's me, Nellie. I came to find out if you were all right." No response. Her steps shortened yet remained deliberate. Her heart raced and her blouse moistened. A few more steps. She blinked her eyes to clear the moisture dripping down her forehead. Light from the candle flame shone in the dark corner. Nothing was there but a pile of rags and two fireplace sized logs. Nellie froze and waited, puzzled how noise could emanate from this mess.

Maybe an imagined noise instead of real. The mind plays tricks like that sometimes. Then the rags moved. Nellie held her position. How she wished she had brought her derringer. Two piercing eyes stared at her from the rags. Little by little the rags moved aside to release a raccoon. He stared at Nellie as if nothing had changed and shoved a log across the floor which made a harsh scrapping sound.

"Oh, mister raccoon, how glad I am to see you." Nellie placed her hand on her chest.

Creaking on the porch announced someone had arrived. Nellie shivered and blew out the candle. She tiptoed across the cabin floor and hid by the side of the front door. The footsteps halted. Nellie glanced out the dirty window. She sensed a large form by the door. The doorknob creaked as it turned. Then the door opened exposing a human silhouette. Nellie held her breath and prayed. Time for the defensive armor. She closed her eyes and waited in the deathly silence.

"Nellie? Are you here?"

Nellie jerked and screamed, "Ernest. Ernest, am I glad it's you." She hugged Ernest with all her strength.

"And I'm glad to see you, Lassie. I got worried waiting so long. I counted to one-hundred in Gaelic, then English and with the sun dipping lower, figured it was time to fetch you." Ernest coughed. "It stinks in here. Come on, let's go home. You can share your investigation when we reach Max and Maggie. They must be worried."

Nellie closed the front door behind them.

"Oh, Ernest. I've so much to tell you all." Nellie pushed her fingers through her messed locks. "I feel like hundreds of spiders are crawling in here. I must look a-fright. Cob webs, mice, raccoons, bats and my head is splitting. But, no Emeline. I'm sure she's gone."

Ernest turned Nellie toward the fading sunlight. "You've got blood running down your face. What on earth did you do?"

Nellie handed Ernest her handkerchief. "I thought my eyes were stinging from sweat. Didn't think it might be blood. Emeline's bed and I had an unexpected meeting." She waited while Ernest tied the cloth around her forehead.

"Now, let's get back before the night critters come out. If you don't mind I'll hold your hand. Don't want you falling down."

"Thank you, Ernest. Your hand gives me extra security and I sure need it right now. You're a true friend."

"I have never met a man I could despair of after discerning what lies in me apart from the grace of God."

—*Oswald Chambers*—

Chapter 43

"How's it look?" Nellie asked Maggie as she removed the cloth bandage from her forehead.

"It's healing nicely. The lump's not quite as large, but you're still pretty green and purple." Maggie applied a clean cloth. "Maybe you should leave the bandage off and let the air get to it. There's no sign of infection."

Nellie leaned her head against the back of the chair.

"You're probably right. Let's leave it off tonight." She glanced across the lake. "My heart breaks for that young lady. Wherever she is, I pray the Lord will protect her."

"Maggie, Nellie, you ladies ready?" Nellie heard Max call from the porch steps. "Bess and Kate are hitched up and eager to go to town."

The girls grabbed their bonnets and handbags. Nellie checked the wood and cook stove, then followed Maggie to the wagon. Nellie waited for Maggie to climb in front with Max, then allowed Ernest to assist her into the back of the wagon. She fluffed up the oversized pillows Heather helped her sew and created a comfy spot for her and Ernest.

"Ernest, do you think we did the right thing by leaving Emeline alone?" Nellie's frown softened some pre-mature lip creases. "I mean, should we have gone back the day after Max confronted her?"

"We may never know, Lassie. Many times the Lord calls us to service and we aren't privileged to witness the end result."

Ernest gazed at Emeline's cabin as they rode deeper into the woods. "After my mum passed, I found my grandmother's tattered Bible. She had stuck a scrap of paper at the third chapter of John and underlined verse sixteen. On the paper Grandma Effie had written "For God so loved Ernest, that He gave His only begotten Son, that if Ernest would believe on Him, he will not perish, but have everlasting life."" Ernest dabbed his eyes. "My grandma knew me as a ruffian. She often called me a scalawag. But she prayed for me every day."

"Did she ever know you became a Christian?"

"That's the sad part. She passed twenty years before I gave my heart to the Lord."

"But your mother knew."

"No. My mum went to her eternal home a short six months before I came to faith." Ernest blew his nose. "But here's the amazing Holy Spirit at work. Under my grandma's written verse, my mum had scrawled "I'm trusting God for Ernest, too.""

"Ernest, that's so touching." Nellie wiped her eyes.

"One generation prays for present and future generations, trusting God to bring family members to faith. We need to trust the Lord that any seeds we may have planted in Emeline, someone else will water."

Nellie considered Ernest's words as the wagon bumped along the road to Eden Lake. *Who, in my family, would have prayed for me? Who am I praying for?*

Raised in an orphanage, Nellie never knew her parents. She assumed they could still be alive and she may have an opportunity to find them. She reviewed her prayer life and discovered her petitions were devoid of any requests to find her family. Prayers for friends, yes. Co-workers? Not much. This would have to change. Nellie fully understood that each believer had a role. One planted, one watered, one nourished and another harvested. *Lord, as I begin this new job, show me what my part is in growing Your kingdom.*

"Whoa, Bess, Kate. We're here." Nellie braced herself as Max pulled the reins directing the horses to the side of the Merc.

Nellie held Ernest's hand as he assisted her off the wagon. She brushed her skirt and stomped her boots. Stalks of straw fell to the ground, their earthy scent filled her nostrils.

"Well, am I glad to see you four." Heather greeted the group with a smile. "Here's my latest cookie creation."

She lifted the glass lid from the container. "You help yourself and I'll put on the teakettle." Heather stopped and squarely faced Nellie. "My dear, what happened to you?"

"I'll fill you in while I help with the tea things, dear." Ernest tenderly held Heather's arm as they entered the Merc.

The corner table sat empty with a vase of beargrass on a crocheted doily. Nellie wandered to the dress rack. Heather stocked a small supply, but most women shopped in Sandy for new frocks.

"Can I help you, Miss Nellie?" Joel hobbled from the back room, his ankle wrapped in cloth.

"Just looking, Joel. Thank you." Nellie said nonchalantly, then glanced at the young man. "Joel, what on earth did you do?"

"Oh, Miss Nellie," Joel tilted his head. "I got so excited about having two legs the same length I went for a run. Well, I wasn't watching and my foot went into a mountain beaver hole. Doc said it's only twisted and to stay off it as much as possible." He chuckled. "He don't know what it's like to have a short leg all your life, and then not. But Miss Nellie, looks like you found a mountain beaver hole too. Looks sore."

"I'm fine, Joel. Thank you for your concern."

"Here's your tea." Heather carried the tray to the table and poured tea for everyone. "Nellie, can I help you?"

Nellie returned to the table. "Thanks, Heather, just looking."

"Heather, do you have your wedding dress yet?" Maggie asked.

"No, I don't. I've been looking in catalogues to order one, but it takes so long to ship things. It certainly won't get here before Saturday. And I don't think Ernest will wait." She winked at him. "I've got an idea. Why don't we three girls go to Sandy and look over their merchandise? Joel can watch the store."

"I, for one, would welcome the outing," Nellie said. "In truth, I'm looking for some new clothes before I go to Portland. Most of my old skirts and blouses are — well, old."

"Oh," Heather cried. "I've got the best brainwave yet." She glanced at Maggie with a gleam in her eye. "Why don't we make it a double wedding? We'll never forget each other's anniversary that way."

"That's a marvelous idea, Honey," Ernest agreed. "Max, Maggie, what do you think?"

"I'm all for it, if Maggie is."

"Yes. Let's do it." Maggie's face sparkled. "Nellie can be bridesmaid for both of us."

"In that case, our trip to Sandy is officially scheduled for to-morrow morning," Heather said.

"Did Molech pick up his clothes box?" Nellie asked.

"He must have. I set it on the back steps before closing last night and it was gone this morning." Heather smiled. "Hope he finds warm water for a bath."

No one noticed two men enter the Merc except Nellie. They were dandies, not from around Eden Lake. Definitely not loggers. Black three piece suits, stiff collars and plain ties signaled Nellie they were detectives. She'd seen their kind before. Expressionless, all-business, probably spoke in a monotone. They had the usual tell-tale bulge under their jackets.

Nellie tuned out the conversation around the table. She'd trained her ears and eyes to eavesdrop. Joel met them at the counter. Nellie pushed her chair back enough to be in full view of their lips. What she observed unnerved her. Moisture on her hands and forehead were followed by a quickening in her chest. Joel pointed to their table.

"Good afternoon," the taller man removed his hat. "I'm sorry to interrupt your conversation. My name is Bishop and my partner is Crawford. We're detectives searching for a missing person."

Nellie wiped her hands on her skirt and waited for Max to introduce them. She noticed Maggie and Heather staring at her and suspected they presumed she would take the lead.

"This is Miss Nellie Cox." Max didn't stop there, however. "She's a detective from Portland."

Definitely front and center now. The two men faced Nellie.

"Miss Cox," Bishop continued. "We've been hunting a man for five months and have reason to believe he may be in this area."

"He's a tall man, over 6 foot, and heavy. Maybe 240 lb. or more," Crawford joined the conversation. "Probably dirty, with worn out clothes and may have a dog with him."

"No, it can't be," Maggie gasped.

"What 'can't be' ma'am?" Bishop asked as he jerked his head toward her.

"Do you have a name for this man?" Nellie intervened.

"Frank Savage, but sometimes goes by Frank Molech." Bishop studied Maggie's reaction. "Miss Richards, is it? If you have any information you must tell us."

"Before we tell you anything, I would like to see some identification." Nellie leaned forward.

Both men flashed their badges and identification cards. Bishop flipped his wallet closed in record time and slid it back in his jacket pocket. "Now, Miss Richards, what do you know?"

"I defer all questions to Miss Cox." Maggie rubbed her arms.

"We have met a man that meets your description." Nellie coughed and drank her tea. "Could you tell us why you're looking for him?"

"He may be dangerous, Miss Cox," Bishop said. "He escaped from the Oregon State Insane Asylum in Salem. We've been instructed to take him back to finish his sentence."

267

Nellie heard Maggie gulp and whisper to Max. "Remember what Emeline said? That he was crazy?"

"What's that, Miss Richards? You've talked with this man?" Bishop asked.

Nellie waylaid the question. "We've had conversations with Molech. He seems of sound mind to us." She paused. "Why was he judged insane?"

"He killed two homesteaders over by Veneta," Crawford said. "A young couple. Just settled in and making friends. We found him holed up in their horse shed several weeks later. A grisly crime so I've been told."

Heather eyes bulged and she grabbed Ernest's hand. "The Anderson's," she exclaimed.

"What's that?" Bishop asked. "You folks seem to know more than you're letting on. One of you better talk."

"Max, you fill them in," Nellie said.

Max leaned on the table, fingers locked and cleared his throat. He cocked his head and stared at Bishop.

"I can tell you about the few times Molech has come to my cabin." He shifted in his chair and scooted to the backrest.

In no hurry to be the informant, Max ran his fingers through his hair, then he summarized his meetings with Molech. He didn't mention the hunt in the woods for Molech's camp. He had resigned himself that Emeline had caused that scare. Then he explained Molech's gentle side. Flowers and concern for Maggie and praying for Max's healing.

"I don't believe any of us would deem him dangerous," Max said.

"I didn't say he was dangerous. I said he may be dangerous," Crawford corrected Max. "It's not our job to judge, only to capture and return."

"How did he escape the hospital?" Ernest asked.

"The hospital is composed of several detached buildings, each connected by tunnels," Bishop said. "Kept the patients from seeing the public and vice versa. Laundry and food deliveries were also dispensed through the tunnels. Savage managed to conceal himself in a delivery cart and exited the building."

"Perhaps he's changed. Does the State take behavior into consideration?" Max asked.

"We were told a local pastor visited Savage and saw a change in him over the years. Whether he got religion, we don't know." Crawford pulled up another chair. "Do you mind?"

The group moved their chairs to make extra room.

"Here's the story we were told." Bishop leaned forward, his elbows on his knees. "During the trial, Savage admitted his guilt and seemed proud he had eluded detectives. He changed his name from Savage to Molech when he discovered Molech in the Old Testament. He decided the crime he'd committed was as evil as the Canaanite deity. The last few years, he had been a model inmate. But something set him off. No one knows what, and he escaped."

"Our job is to return him to Salem, where he can receive counseling and finish his sentence," Crawford added. "If, as you say, he has changed, that's in his favor. He will be reevaluated before released. He has no family for support. May be a tough road ahead."

Max glanced at the group. All displayed expressions of sadness. Maggie's eyes were moist. Nellie held her head in her hands. Heather clung to Ernest and dabbed her face.

"I hate myself for even thinking this." Max closed his eyes, then gazed at Bishop. "We have a missing couple. They've been gone for a few months now. Their dog became my dog and he's scared to death whenever Molech comes around."

"Oh, Max," Maggie cried. "It couldn't be. It just couldn't be."

"These men are here to do a job whether we like it or not." Max rubbed her arm. "I totally agree with you and feel like a snitch, but what else can we do?"

Max pushed his chair away from the table. He hung his head. "I'll take you to the Anderson's place."

Chapter 44

Max trudged up the path to the Anderson's homestead, Jed close on his heels. The two detectives followed. One grumbled about the wear on his boots.

"Hope this is it, Crawford." Bishop grunted. "I want to get back to a good home cooked meal. Most of these backwoods people don't know how to cook."

Max ignored them. He had little patience with grumbling or ill-speech about anyone. Maybe "backwoods people" didn't know how to cook like city-folk, but they were mighty thankful to have food when many did without.

A fallen log by the side of the path provided an excuse to stop. Max plopped down and removed a boot.

"Feels like I've got a rock." He shook his boot upside down, then repeated the process for the other. Max had no desire to hurry to the Anderson's cabin. Secretly, he hoped Molech would hear them coming and run deep into the woods. Prayed these sourpusses would never find him. That Bishop's boots would wear clean through and he'd have to walk on bare feet. That a pack of wolves would attack. Or a cougar. He was open to any suggestion to slow the inevitable.

Max shoved his foot into his boot. *Lord, forgive me. They're only doing their job.*

"Wait a minute." A noise in the forest startled Bishop. "Let me check my firearm. You too, Crawford. Need to be ready for anything."

"You're not planning to shoot him, are you?" Max scowled at the men.

"Only if we have to, Mr. Sullivan. Only if we have to." Bishop holstered his weapon.

Max rubbed Jed. "It's okay, boy. If I were a dog, I'd be whining too."

Mr. Anderson had chosen a beautiful setting for he and his

bride to call home and raise a family. The folks from town had lent a hand to erect the small two bedroom dwelling made with hand hewn logs. They had also built a shed large enough for one horse — all Anderson could afford. As they drew closer Jed became agitated.

"You remember this, huh, boy." Max pet his dog. "Yep, your old home. Haven't been here in quite some time." Max raised his voice. "But don't run on ahead now, ya hear, boy?"

"What are you yelling for? Your mutt is right beside you." Bishop grew irritated. "How much farther?"

Max didn't feel like answering. Besides the path to the cabin lay within eyesight.

"Look through the trees, the cabin's right there. The shed is behind." Max pointed.

"Here," Bishop grabbed Max's arm and pulled. "You get behind us. If Savage attacks we don't want you between him and us."

Not many people could rile Max, but Bishop hit the top of his list. If this man represented the mannerisms of detectives, he felt sorry for Nellie. Maybe she would bring some sensibility to the force in Portland.

The early afternoon sun pierced through the trees and shone directly on the cabin roof. Vegetation smothered the yard. Bramble berry vines covered the porch. Neglected this long made the dwelling easy prey for trappers, hikers and four legged animals hunting for refuge.

"You check the cabin. I'll go round to the shed." Bishop gave orders like a drill sergeant.

"If you're done with me, Jed and I will go back to town," Max said.

"No sir. You stay right there. We may still need you," Bishop barked.

Max found a good resting spot and placed an arm around Jed. "I pray he's not here, Jed."

He watched Crawford wipe dirt from the front windows with a rag from his back pocket. Crawford peeked inside, then tried the front door. It opened. Max wanted to shout, "You can't invade someone else's home. Stay out of their cabin." Privacy vanished with these two. They were worn out from hunting their missing man. Max knew they would scrutinize every corner of the cabin and shed for any clue Molech had been here.

"You. Sullivan. Get in here," Bishop billowed from the shed.

"Jed, it's all right with me if you bite him," Max muttered under his breath. He forced himself to his feet and trudged to the shed.

"It reeks of sulphur in here. There's been some kind of fire and a pile of animal bones over there," Bishop pointed. "When you saw Savage, did he smell of sulphur?"

Max recognized the markings that were distinctively Molech's. Two indentations in the straw were sure signs of sleeping spots. A pile of animal pelts filled a back corner. In another corner a heap of old tattered clothes laid slapdash in a cardboard box. Max drew closer. They were Molech's old clothes. He had picked up the box from the Merc. Max grinned.

"Sullivan! I asked you if the crazy smelled of sulphur." Bishop seemed on the verge of a nervous breakdown.

"Yes." Max didn't feel like divulging any more information than necessary.

"And the bones, the pelts and that box over there. Are these the markings of the man you know as Molech?" Anticipation grew in Bishop's eyes.

"Yes." Max hated being there. Bishop seemed to jump with glee at the prospect they had found their man.

"Nothing in the cabin out of the ordinary. Very homey setting." Crawford joined them. "From the wedding photo on the mantle, they were very young when they married." Crawford faced Max. "How long had they lived here?"

"Mr. Anderson brought his bride here." Max scratched his head. "To answer your question, less than a year. No children yet."

"This is a mighty sweet set-up. Too bad Savage destroyed their plans." Bishop chimed in.

"How do you know Molech had anything to do with their disappearance?" Max's anger rose.

"Once a killer, always a killer is my motto. Especially if you're nuts." Bishop studied the pelts. "Just like a wild beast. Get a taste of blood and can't stop."

"If you don't need me anymore, Jed and I are going back to town," Max fumed.

"You're of no use now. Leave whenever you want." Bishop brushed him off. "Crawford and I will stay and wait for this deranged brut to return."

"Remember, you work for the State and your job is to take him back," Max scolded. "I'm sure they expect him to be unharmed when returned. He's my friend. If I hear you caused him any trauma, I will personally make a trip to Salem. Then I will do everything in my power to bring charges against you."

"Get off your high horse, Sullivan. No one is going to hurt him unless it's in self-defense," Bishop said.

"We promise to do our best and take him back peacefully," Crawford assured Max.

"Come on, Jed. Let's go." Max slapped his leg. With head bowed, he turned his back on the Anderson's home. *Oh, Lord, let all be well. Please take care of Molech.*

Helpless to protect Molech, Max dragged himself down the path to Eden Lake. Jed stayed close beside him. Even his dog lost any spring in his step. The two bedraggled companions hung their heads. No game of fetch or chase the squirrel ensued on the lonely trip back. Maggie, Nellie, Ernest and Heather would be waiting for them. What would Max tell them? He'd like to say, someone has been sleeping in the shed and nothing more. But the pelts, bones and sulphur smell provided strong evidence Molech and Bear had been there. Maggie would be heartbroken. Max understood the camaraderie she felt toward him. Molech had proven himself a gentle, compassionate friend. Then Bishop and Crawford showed up.

Max prayed the Anderson's would miraculously be at the Merc when he got back. That they had gone on an unexpected extended trip and neglected to contact anyone. Perhaps to San Francisco for a second honeymoon. But that didn't make sense. They wouldn't neglect Jed and their horse. Maybe an emergency and they knew the good people of Eden Lake would fill the gap until they returned. Wishful thinking quickened Max's step, yet he cautioned himself to keep his optimism in check.

Passing through the Merc's front door, Max's friends stared at him with expectant eyes. He found his chair and slumped down. "Sorry," was all he could say.

"Oh, Max." Maggie grabbed his hand. Wells of tears were released. Max reached for his handkerchief and dabbed her cheeks.

"I know, Darling. The evidence clearly showed Molech and Bear were staying in the shed." Max glanced at Ernest. "Now we need to pray the Anderson's show up or we discover what happened. I won't believe Molech had anything to do with their disappearance." Max paused. "On a bright note, Molech's old clothes were heaped in a box in the shed."

"Well, that's something to rejoice in," Heather said.

Silence filled the Merc. No customers entered. Max's heart grew heavy with concern for Molech. He saw the same concern in his friends' eyes.

"Nothing more we can do here," Max said. "If you girls want to get an early start for Sandy tomorrow, we best be on our way."

"Oh, my," Heather said. "I didn't realize how late it was. Time to lock up."

Max, Maggie and Nellie waited on the porch for Ernest to say his "good-bye" to Heather. A commotion down the street caught their attention. Ernest and Heather hurried outside.

"Look," Nellie said. "It's those uncouth detectives with Molech."

Max moved a few steps toward the three men. His and Molech's eyes connected. Molech said something to Bishop, then trudged toward Max.

"I don't want you thinking I'm a bad man," Molech frowned. "I repented of what I'd done in Veneta. If I could give those two their lives back, I would. Now I go to face whatever punishment I deserve. I will accept it and wait until I'm released."

"What will you do then?" Max asked.

"I don't know. Ain't got no family." Molech hung his head. "You're the closest friend I got, Max. I know I want to live in the mountains. But also need to earn my keep."

"Molech, I must ask you a question. Do you know what happened to the Anderson's?"

"No, Max. I don't. They were gone when Bear and I started camping in their shed. That was after Joel took their horse and your dog."

"I believe you. And if you want to come back to Eden Lake after you're released, I'll see what I can do about declaring Emeline's cabin uninhabited." Max put his hand on Molech's shoulder. "Perhaps you can live across the lake from Maggie and I. The logging companies are always looking for strong workers. I'll put in a good word for you. Would you like that?"

"Oh, yes. Oh, Max that would be wonderful." Molech's eyes sparkled. "A job. Can't remember the last time I had a real job. And I would be a good neighbor. I promise not to bring you anything but fresh caught fish." Molech gulped. "I'll be on my best behavior at the hospital. I know I shouldn't have broken out, but that's between me and the doc." He glanced at Bear beside his feet. "Don't know what to do with Bear while I'm gone. He's a good hunter and probably could fend for himself."

"Don't you worry about Bear. I'll take him with me." Max glanced at Jed. "Bear seems much calmer than the first time we met. Jed will get used to him."

Max extended Molech a hand. An extra strong handshake indeed. Max patted Bear. "You stay with me, boy."

Bear stared at Molech, confusion in his eyes.

Molech bent down. "Yes, Bear. You stay with Max and Jed. I'll be back as soon as I can." Molech buried his face in his dog's fur and hugged him.

Molech returned to the detectives. He mounted his horse, and galloped to Max. "It's time I changed my name back to Frank Savage. Sounds better, don't you think. And thanks for the new clothes. First I've had in years."

"You're welcome." Max pulled the horse's reins to face the detectives and swatted its rump. "Good-bye, my friend."

"God had strewn our paths with wonders and we certainly should not go through life with our eyes shut."
—Alexander Graham Bell—

Chapter 45

"I've never clerked before," Max said restocking dry goods. "Heather may return and have to redo all I've done."

"Don't you worry, Laddie." Ernest wiped down the counter. "She's a very forgiving woman. Maybe she'll like your new system better and change everything around."

Barks outside distracted Max. He replaced the lid on the coffee can and headed outside.

"Joel, what's happening?"

"Nothing much, Mr. Sullivan. Bear and Jed were chasing a squirrel up that tree. The varmint disappeared so they took to chasing each other." Joel laughed. "They're entertaining me."

Dust rose from the road as the mules pulled the coach the final leg from Sandy to Eden Lake. Max checked his pocket watch. Right on time.

"Ernest," Max called through the Merc door. "Better come and help the ladies with their purchases. Send three ladies off for the day and they're sure to return laden with parcels." He glanced at Joel. "Mind the Merc for a while, okay? We'll be right back."

"Will do, Mr. Sullivan."

The two grooms-to-be hurried to the coach stop. Max opened the door while Ernest offered his assistance. The ladies were glowing.

"Hello, you three. Have an eventful day?" Max asked, then realized the ladies hadn't heard him. Maggie, Nellie and Heather surrounded Max like a brood of hens and gabbed away as if he were invisible. Max moved aside as they trotted behind the coach to claim their goods.

"Do you ladies need a hand? Ernest and I are ready to help." Max offered.

The coachman piled boxes on the wooden platform.

"That one's mine. And that one." Nellie pointed.

"I'll take the large one over there and that smaller one beside it." Maggie directed.

"And you, ma'am? All the ones left?" The coachman asked Heather.

"Yes. Everything else is mine."

Max moved closer. "Do you ladies need any help?"

"Oh, Max, I missed you." Maggie put her hand on his arm and touched his cheek with hers.

"That would be very nice," Heather responded.

Before Max and Ernest knew it, all the packages were piled in their arms. They followed the shoppers back to the Merc.

"Where should we set these?" Max asked. Once the packages were out of Max's arms, he turned to Maggie. "Did you leave anything in the store?"

He loved her laugh. It lightened the load and brightened the room. How Max looked forward to their married life. He planned extended hikes, long days on Eden Lake and trips to Portland to visit Nellie.

"If you ladies will excuse us, Ernest and I are going to talk with Rev. Johansson." Max smiled at Ernest, eyebrows raised. The ladies were so enraptured with their trip and purchases, they hardly noticed the men. "Ready, Ernest?"

"Ready as I'll ever be." Ernest glanced at Heather. "Sure hope she's as excited about me as she is with what's in those boxes."

As Max and Ernest reached the doorway they were met by two men. They appeared to be in their thirties, with long, scraggly beards, sweat-stained brimmed hats, and scarves double wrapped around their necks. Their pants were tucked in stained and scratched knee-high boots with a leather satchel slung across their chests.

"Good afternoon," the taller and thinner man said. "Wondered if you could tell us if you have any law officers in this town."

"None here. We've never had the need." Max responded. "There's one in Sandy though. Stage coach office is down the street four, or so, blocks."

"Well, who would have the authority if you needed one?" The shorter man said in a husky voice.

"Any one of us residents, I would imagine." Max stretched forth his hand. "My name's Max Sullivan. What can I do for you?"

"Nice to meet you, Mr. Sullivan." The taller man clasped Max's hand. "I'm Harrison, and this is Perry. A group of us are hiking the Cascades. We started at Mt. Shasta with Mt. Rainier as our destination. The others went on to Sandy earlier."

"How about some water?" Ernest asked.

"That sounds wonderful," Harrison said.

Max invited them to a table and gathered four chairs. By now the girls had finished organizing their purchases and joined them.

"Now that we're all here," Max said, "what can we do for you?"

"We were hiking the trail east of here and came across, what looked like, remains of two people." Perry reached in his satchel. "Not much left, however. With all the wild animals living in these parts, only some bones and pieces of clothing remained. We did uncover a satchel that was water damaged and torn in places, but found this journal intact." Perry handed the small book to Max.

Max carefully opened the journal. He read the inscription inside the front cover. "These are the events in the lives of Robert and Sarah Anderson: married May 1899."

Max's jaw dropped. He glanced at his friends. Their eyes expressed their emotions.

"Did you know them?" Perry asked.

"Yes. We helped build their cabin not far from here," Max said. "They've been gone several months. We had no idea what happened to them."

"I think if you read the last few entries," Harrison said, "it will clear things up."

Max flipped through the journal to the last pages with writing on them.

"Sarah and I delight in the woods around our cabin. We decided to walk toward Mt. Hood today. Jed didn't seem to feel well, so he stayed home." Max rubbed Jed's ears who lay beside his chair.

"The late winter snows still cling to the tall tree branches and patches of white, cover the ground where the sun doesn't reach." Max flipped to the next entry.

"Robert loves living here in the wilderness. I pray I will become accustomed to the cold. He tells me winter will soon end and the crocus will stick their heads through the ground. It is indeed God's country. I trust Robert completely although it seems he's becoming disoriented at present."

Max glanced at Heather. Her eyes glistened. He read the next entry.

"Robert says everything is fine, but I sense uncertainty and maybe fear in his voice. We are too far from Eden Lake and darkness is closing in. How I wish I was better at directions and reading the sun. I'm writing this while Robert walks in several directions trying to get his bearings. Wolves howl from far away and the coldness has seeped through my clothes. We aren't prepared to spend the night in the woods."

"I don't know if I can read anymore," Max said. "I'm sure it's very difficult for you ladies."

"No, please, Max," Heather laid her hand on his arm. "I need to know what happened. The Anderson mystery needs to be put to rest."

Max turned another page. "This appears to be the final entry."

"Robert found a stream we can follow. Perhaps it empties into Eden Lake. Whatever our outcome, if someone finds this please tell the people of Eden Lake we love them. All our relatives have lives of their own, so give our cabin to someone who needs it. Take care of our horse and Jed. They've served us well. Robert and I promised before God we would love each other for better or worse and stay with each other until death do us part. Looks like we may leave this earth together. A bit earlier than expected. God be with you all, Sarah Anderson. March 14, 1900."

Max gently closed the journal. He was grateful to Ernest who wrapped an arm around Heather's shoulders. Max felt the need to be comforted as well.

"Thank you for bringing this to us," Max said to the hikers.

"I see we brought it to the right people," Harrison said. "We buried their remains and marked the grave with a cross made from tree branches. I drew a rough map where we found them if anyone needs to know." Max folded the paper map and placed it inside the journal.

"We better be going. Still a long ways to Mt. Rainier." Perry and Harrison rose.

Max clasped their hands and accompanied them to the Merc's front door. Nothing more needed to be said. The mystery of the Anderson's was solved. Max vowed to do his best to get this information to the proper authorities. Molech could no longer be held a suspect or charged with the their disappearance.

Max held Heather's hands and helped her out of the chair. He wrapped her in his arms. If anyone knew the Anderson's better than Max, it was Heather. She needed extra support and he needed a hug too.

The weddings were postponed an additional week. Max had talked with Rev. Johansson and they agreed the town needed time to mourn the Anderson's loss. But Saturday, August 4, 1900, arrived with a flourish. The sun shone precisely on the spot where the two wedding couples would recite their vows in less than one hour. The guests poured in. Some brought chairs, others blankets while many preferred to stand. Fragrant flower bouquets were placed on the ground opposite each other and created a make-shift aisle. The music group, who played for worship at the grange hall, filled the air with Heather and Maggie's favorite hymns.

Inside the Merc, the floors had been scrubbed, counters emptied and pushed aside. The wedding cake, three tiers high, graced the counter where the cash register once sat. A large punch bowl with cherry-apple juice waited to be served from the opposite end along with coffee and tea.

The Merc clock struck eleven. Max and Ernest stood on each side of Rev. Johansson. Both were as antsy as a five year old before his turn to recite in the church's Christmas program. The brides' entrance music played.

"Well, Ernest," Max said. "This is it. I'm glad you're staying in Eden Lake."

"Me, too, Laddie. While I miss Scotland, this is my home now. Heather and I, you and Maggie." Ernest gazed skyward. "Can't wait to find out what the Lord has in store for all of us."

Max glanced toward the Merc. Two young girls skipped down the aisle as they tossed rose petals in the air. Joel followed them with the wedding rings tied to a pillow. Jed pranced beside him, a white scarf around his neck. Nellie followed Joel and Jed leading the brides toward their grooms.

The moment Max had anticipated since first meeting Maggie at the Meier & Frank lunch counter had arrived. All those years in between, while he worked, wrote, added rooms to his cabin, travelled to Scotland, met Ernest, fell in love with Maggie again and back to the States. Max felt confident for the first time. No more timid and shy. No more wondering about his purpose in life. No more cancer and no more living alone.

The butterflies that had infiltrated Maggie's stomach in Scotland now invaded his. *Was this really happening, Lord? How can I ever thank you enough for your grace and opening my eyes to the truth of life with you? I love you, Lord and praise you for Maggie. Help me to love her as you do, and to be worthy of her.*

The music stopped. Max gazed into Maggie's eyes. "You're so

beautiful."

He offered her his arm, then faced Rev. Johansson. Max listened intently to the message. *I will love her, Lord, as you loved your church, sacrificially, and I will gladly give my life for her.*

Max held Maggie's hands as they faced each other. He repeated the pastor's words verbatim. Then it was time for the "I do's."

"Max, will you take Maggie Richards to be your lawful wedded wife, for richer or poorer, in sickness and in health, for better for worse, until death parts you?"

Max cleared his throat and gulped. "I did eight years ago. I did in Scotland. I did in New York and I most certainly do now in Eden Lake. You are, and forever will be, the love of my life. Yes, I do."

A few more ceremonial words, then Rev. Johansson said, "I now pronounce you, Ernest and Heather, and you, Max and Maggie, husband and wife. You may kiss your bride."

Max's legs wobbled and his palms moistened. Those were magical words.

"Kiss your bride." His bride. This forever moment, sealed with a kiss.

Max caressed Maggie's face, then brought his lips to hers. There it was. That sweet lavender fragrance that will always be Maggie. Their lips, tender and moist, joined as one.

"It gives me great pleasure to present, Mr. and Mrs. Ernest McIntyre and Mr. and Mrs. Max Sullivan," Rev. Johansson raised his hands behind each couple.

Amid the cheers and claps, Max embraced his wife. "I love you Maggie Sullivan and I promise to honor, cherish and respect you for as long as the Lord gives us." Max brushed a loose curl from her face. "Let our journey begin."

"For not even the Father judges any one, but He has given all judgment to the Son, in order that all may honor the Son, even as they honor the Father. He who does not honor the Son does not honor the Father who sent Him."

John 5:22-23

A note to my readers,

I am honored that you read this, my second book, in the MNM Mystery Series. I hope you have enjoyed Max's story, and also gained some insight into your walk with the Lord. Each of us travel the path God has set for us and in that journey, we face obstacles that can either shake or strengthen our faith. As with Max, Nellie, and Maggie, I pray your faith grows stronger in the Lord daily. May He direct you in the way you are to go to achieve his purpose for your life and be a blessing to others.

As a thank you, I'm including an excerpt from the third, and last book in this series. Here are two comments from fellow writers:

I like the way it has gone from being an action-packed mystery thriller to delving into the past of this very interesting character. —Holli, Oregon Christian Writers

I have to say what stands out to me… has been the seamless, natural way you weave the truths of the Gospel into narrative and dialogue. Very impressive! It draws the reader alongside the characters and lets them see the effect those truths have in daily life. — Gwendolyn, Oregon Christian Writers

Solving this case might resurrect her past...
or she just may end up dead!

Prologue

February 26, 1910 Goble, Oregon

Jesse sank several inches into the soggy ground. Water seeped over the top of his leather shoes, soaking his socks. Even though he shivered in the cold, beads of sweat peppered his brow.

He knew he was sick.

No. He knew he was dying.

Nausea increased. The pain from the embedded bullet permeated every inch of his being. Not long now and he'd be dead. His final wish: to see his mother, hug her and tell her he loved her. Goble was a long way from Chicago, but Jesse would rather die close to his mom than the menacing Black Hand gang.

Jesse stumbled to a clearing in the forest and lit his pipe. He labored to stand tall, sucked the flame into the pipe bowl, igniting the dried leaves, and released puffs of smoke. The habit calmed him.

He gripped the pipe's stem between his teeth and withdrew a small leather bag from his trouser pocket. Inside, a gold brooch nestled in a bit of fabric. Jesse unwrapped the pin and cradled it in his hands like it was a newborn pup. He rubbed his fingers over the smooth amethyst at the center of the delicate gold filigree work. Images of his beautiful, overworked mother flooded his mind.

His mother had prized this brooch. A keepsake from her mother, she wore it on special occasions. While she was at work, Jesse had snatched it from her dresser and left the apartment. But deep down, he knew that when she found it missing, her heart would break.

The time had arrived to return this treasure and place it in her hand. Then, he would ask her forgiveness for all he had done to hurt her. Tomorrow would be a good day...

The pipe slipped from his mouth and fell to the ground.

The brooch tumbled from his hand and disappeared into a pile of leaves.

Jesse grabbed his belly and reeled from the pain.

"Lord, forgive me. I'm yours. Please take care of Mama."

One last excruciating stab through his torso and Jesse plummeted to the earth.

Chapter 1

February 28, 1910, Gobel, Oregon

"You must be Detective Cox." A middle-aged man walked toward her. "I'm Chief Kinnard." He removed his hat and knocked it against his pant leg. "Mrs. Mitchell, at the boarding house, said you'd already left. Why didn't you wait for me?"

Nellie Cox, flinched at the sound of irritation in his voice, then faced the disheveled man. "I wanted to get here as soon as possible. A Mr. Hanson dropped off a gallon of milk and offered me a ride. I've only been here a few minutes searching for anything unusual on the path from the road to this clearing."

Kinnard clutched a smoldering cigar between his teeth, his gravelly voice slurring out the side of his mouth. "The body lay over here." He stepped forward. "Let's make this quick and get back to town. Don't want to be here all day. That sky's preparing to dump a blanket of snow. When it does, we'll lose the body's imprint and the possibility of finding more evidence."

A thin layer of snow already stuck to Detective Nellie Cox's skirt hem and boots as she trudged across the soggy ground. A plethora of footprints cut into the area surrounding the investigation scene. The snow had melted in a clearing where branches encircled the impression site. Fewer boot prints in this area, raised her hopes that evidence hadn't been completely obscured.

Kinnard brushed his walrus mustache out of the way and scraped a smattering of tobacco stuck to his tongue. "How long have you been working for Chief Frank?"

"Eight years." Enough time to hone her skills as an investigative consultant. At the top of Portland Police Chief Daniel Frank's out- standing detectives list, Nellie loved her work.

"I'm surprised you didn't take a job like secretary or store clerk. Those positions are better suited for women. Indoor jobs and better wages too, I would suspect."

Nellie sighed. "I believe it's time women apply for jobs that meet their qualifications. And while I realize my wages amount to half a man's salary, it's a far sight better than the measly nine dollars a week I'd earn as a salesclerk and much more engaging too." She scooted around a puddle. "An added bonus is I get to venture out in the wild open woods and meet interesting people like you." A fake smile crossed her face.

Kinnard cleared his throat. "And you cut your hair. Why'd you do that?"

"I have more important things to accomplish in the morning than pile long tresses on top of my head and pray they stay in place throughout a busy day."

The sun's rays struggled to reach the ground as the dense fog cloaked the treetops. Nellie tugged her knit hat lower over her bobbed hair. She secured her coat button under her chin and shivered. Two cups of coffee had raised her eyelids and provided temporary warmth, but irritated her stomach; a reminder of the necessity for food in the morning.

February's nippy wind cut through her four layers of clothing. If she'd shimmied into a corset, the extra layer might have created added warmth, but Nellie refused to wear the constrictive piece of clothing. She had one exception to the rule—being invited to a fancy ball— which had never happened. Nellie wrapped her scarf tighter.

"I expected Chief Frank to send me a man who could withstand the elements. You seem unsuited for our winter weather."

"I'll be fine." If she were in Portland, she'd cozy up to a crackling fire in her tiny apartment. No fire tonight. Chief Frank had assigned her to solve the mysterious death in the jerkwater town of Goble. He'd enticed her with, "You can work on your next crime novel at the same time." Nellie could have said "No," but hoped to advance the possibilities for women in the workforce, not maintain the status quo. The Goble Boarding House had a room available. "Yes," had seemed the logical answer, so she'd packed a few belongings, a stack of paper, and boarded the train. Now she was ankle-deep in both snow and an unsolved death.

"How did you find the body?"

"Hikers on their way to Astoria stumbled over the corpse and notified us. The remains were lying face down." Chief Kinnard pointed at the ground. "Doc Watson estimated the body had laid here two to three days. Deteriorated little because of the cold."

Ashes flicked from the cigar drifted in the air while the smoke stung Nellie's eyes. She dabbed the resulting moisture with a hankie.

"My men scouted for a backpack or anything he may have dropped, but they came up empty-handed."

"What about the contents of the victim's pockets? Anything that would identify him?" Nellie coughed and moved upwind to avoid the annoying smoke.

"His personals are back at the office. When you're done here, you can go through the box." Kinnard pulled a handkerchief from his pocket and wiped the brown cigar slobber that dripped to his chin. Nellie closed her eyes, eyebrows scrunched. She'd seldom encountered such a disgusting man.

"So, what can you tell me?" Nellie tried to move her toes, but they wouldn't budge. If her feet froze, the rest of her body may soon follow. "So far all we have is a male who laid on the ground a few days. It's hard to unravel with so few details."

"Doc Watson estimated the man about forty years old. Probably shot, but said he'd have a detailed report on my desk when we returned." Kinnard lit another match and touched the flame to the end of his cigar. "For now, Cox, just do your thing, so we can get back to the station."

No dilly-dallying around with this man. No wedding ring on his left hand, but that didn't mean he wasn't married. Seems like the wife of the town's police chief would make sure her husband went to work in something less shabby than a shirt with a frayed collar and cuffs.

"How many officers did you bring for the investigation?" Nellie side-stepped around Kinnard and focused on the imprint of the dead man's body. Kinnard, occupied with his cigar, didn't immediately answer.

She knelt next to the faint impression from his torso and used a scrap of bark to push aside a pile of embedded leaves. A closer examination revealed an angular object. Nellie undid the top two buttons of her coat, retrieved a hatpin laced through the inside jacket lapel, and picked at the object while Kinnard busied himself kicking snow a few feet away. The exposed part formed a cylinder into which she threaded her pin and pried it from the ground. Nellie grasped the wooden smoking pipe with a clean hankie and held it close to her eyes. She found no damage and prayed there would be a smidgen of tobacco left in the bowl. With the hankie wrapped around the pipe, she nestled it deep in a pocket for safekeeping.

"In a small town like Goble, there's one part-time officer and me." Kinnard finally said. "Lots of curiosity seekers, so I threw the branches down to mark the area. The residents came out on their own. In all my years as chief, we haven't found a dead man." He brushed ash from the stogie and shoved the mushy rolled leaves back between his lips.

Nellie inspected the larger trees surrounding the area. Inch by inch, she scrutinized sections of bark, hoping to find a mark or rub from a gun barrel. Kinnard's cigar smoke tickled her nostrils again and triggered a thought to check for cigarette or cigar butts on the ground.

Nothing but boot tracks.

"I'd like to sit on this dead tree trunk and think awhile. Don't suppose you'd have a thermos of hot chocolate in your car?" When her question produced no answer, she looked up to find Kinnard had meandered to the other side of the clearing, out of earshot. In all her previous investigations, the chief had engineered the operation. Not this time. Kinnard not only showed an unwillingness to lead the investigation, but he also seemed to care even less about assisting her.

"Well, Lord, it's you and me on this one."

Nellie reached into her satchel for a notepad and pencil, along with a seamstress measuring tape. She glanced at the last place she'd seen the chief, but there was no sign of him.

Branches broke in the distance. Nellie stiffened. If a cougar or other wild animal scouted these woods, she could be easy prey. As the crunch of dried limbs intensified, she scanned the forest. Her body shuddered when an ominous shadow came into view. Stories of Sasquatch circulated among mountain people, but she didn't believe the creature existed. Still, her heart rate increased.

"Oh, Lord, I need your protection now."

Nellie focused on the emerging creature.

"Well, Cox, are you done?" Kinnard's gruff voice reached her before he pushed his way through the foliage.

Nellie released her breath and closed her eyes. *Thank you, Lord.*

"You frightened me, Chief. It's easy for the mind to play tricks left all alone in a strange place."

"You? Frightened?"

"Yes, I'm sitting here imagining what lurks in the woods. There could be a potential murderer on the loose as well as wild animals." Nellie stood and brushed off her coat. "I'm concentrating on the matter at hand, and you abandoned me."

"Nature called. I didn't think I needed to inform you."

Nellie pulled her coat tighter, repositioned her hat over her ears, and prayed for patience.

"You ready to go now?"

"Not yet. Would you assist me for a moment?" Nellie asked.

"Depends. What do I have to do?"

"Hold this measuring tape where I ask. I'm curious about something." Nellie handed Chief a seamstress tape.

Chief Kinnard placed his hat on his head, followed Nellie's directions and called out the numbers for every measurement. She jotted down the values, and when finished, placed her supplies back in her satchel.

"Thank you for your help. There's nothing else here. Hopefully, I'll find something in the man's belongings. This case intrigues me. Why, and how, did a dead body come to be way out here?"

Kinnard plodded toward his car. "You coming or need more time?" He removed the cigar stub from his mouth and flung it into the woods.

"Yes, I'm finished here. I think my toes are frozen." Nellie limped behind Kinnard.

"Sorry, you'll have to bear the mile or so back to the station. There's no heat in this '06 Buick, but at least we've go a roof over our heads."

Great. Once in the passenger seat, she prayed he wouldn't light another cigar. She rubbed her legs and heard the distinct sound of a match being lit.

Made in United States
Troutdale, OR
06/03/2023